DEATH IN A LIGHTHOUSE

"…a wildly unusual story, heavy on action, questionable motives, and dubious twists… The pace is frenetic, the murky characters are well-defined, and the story builds to an exhilarating conclusion.
—Nicholas Litchfield from his introduction

"…never boring, never dull…" —*Paperback Warrior*

"…his prose was propulsive and machine tooled and this is an absorbing quick read for devotees of the pacy thriller." —F. J. Harvey

"…Aarons manages to sustain the fast pace right up to the final paragraph." —John Pringle

"Aarons was consistently entertaining, even in his lesser books." —James Reasoner

MURDER MONEY

"*Murder Money* offers a fascinating mystery that explores layers of deception, treachery, and lurking threats… every character has something to hide, creating a thrilling atmosphere filled with suspense and unexpected twists."
—Nicholas Litchfield from his introduction

Death in a Lighthouse
Murder Money
EDWARD S. AARONS

Introduction by Nicholas Litchfield

Stark House Press • Eureka California

DEATH IN A LIGHTHOUSE / MURDER MONEY

Published by Stark House Press
1315 H Street
Eureka, CA 95501, USA
griffinskye3@sbcglobal.net
www.starkhousepress.com

DEATH IN A LIGHTHOUSE
Originally published and copyright © 1938 by Phoenix Press, New York, as by Edward Ronns. Reprinted in a paperback edition by Parsee Publications, New York, 1945 as *The Cowl of Doom*.

MURDER MONEY
Originally published and copyright © 1938 by Phoenix Press, New York, as by Edward Ronns. Reprinted in an abridged paperback edition by Select Publications, New York, 1942 as *$1,000,000 in Corpses*.

All rights reserved under International and Pan-American Copyright Conventions. Copyright © 2025 by Stark House Press

"The Elusive Gangster and the Money Tree"
© 2025 by Nicholas Litchfield

ISBN: 979-8-88601-145-6

Text design by Mark Shepard, shepgraphics.com
Cover design by Jeff Vorzimmer, ¡caliente!design, Austin, Texas
Cover art by Rafael deSoto from New Detective, January 1948

PUBLISHER'S NOTE:
This is a work of fiction. Names, characters, places and incidents are either the products of the author's imagination or used fictionally, and any resemblance to actual persons, living or dead, events or locales, is entirely coincidental.
Without limiting the rights under copyright reserved above, no part of this publication may be reproduced, stored, or introduced into a retrieval system or transmitted in any form or by any means (electronic, mechanical, photocopying, recording or otherwise) without the prior written permission of both the copyright owner and the above publisher of the book.

First Stark House Press Edition: June 2025

7
The Elusive Gangster
and the Money Tree
by Nicholas Litchfield

13
Death in a Lighthouse
by Edward S. Aarons

139
Murder Money
by Edward S. Aarons

266
Edward S. Aarons
Bibliography

THE ELUSIVE GANGSTER AND THE MONEY TREE

by Nicholas Litchfield

Bestselling American novelist Edward Sidney Aarons (1916-1975) was born in Philadelphia, Pennsylvania, and began writing at a young age. As a student, he won a collegiate short story contest in 1933, which foreshadowed his future success as an author. Before fully dedicating himself to writing fiction, Aarons held various jobs, including newspaper reporter, mill hand, salesman, and fisherman.

He is best known for his long-running "Assignment" series, which features tough CIA operative Sam Durell, code named Cajun due to his Louisiana upbringing. This series, consisting of 42 books, garnered widespread recognition and achieved remarkable commercial success, selling over 23 million copies and being translated into 17 languages by the time of his passing. Critics responded favorably to his work, with renowned book reviewer Anthony Boucher of the *New York Times* praising the series as "among the best modern adventure stories of espionage and international intrigue" (Boucher, 1960a). Boucher frequently drew attention to the "unusually good" story ideas, the "reasonably complex and unhackneyed" characters, and the "happy balance between large-scale melodrama and intimate emotions," which gave the series "more substance" than other espionage books (Boucher, 1961). He noted that Durell's missions were "fascinating" and plausible and admired the "relentless pace and crisp prose" (Boucher, 1955).

In contrast, Boucher was not a fan of Ian Fleming's Secret Service agent James Bond, criticizing the author's "basic weakness as a storyteller" due to a lack of story; he felt that the protagonist's triumphs were "too simple" and lacked the necessary "intricate suspense" that readers expected from this genre (Boucher, 1960b). Boucher cited Stephen Marlowe and Edward S. Aarons as examples of superior storytellers in tales of international intrigue, referring to them as "more flamboyant and colorful" than their peers (Boucher, 1964).

In addition to his success in espionage fiction, Aarons established a notable presence in detective fiction during the 1940s and early 1950s.

Reports suggest he published his first mystery novel at the age of 22, fully committing to writing as his true vocation (Marchino, 2023). According to the *New York Times*, Aarons "sold his first story when he was 18 and his first novel at 19," and prior to focusing solely on novel writing, he produced an impressive repertoire of 200 magazine stories and novellas (New York Times, 1975). Aarons experimented with various fiction genres but primarily concentrated on mystery and suspense. Under the pen name Edward Ronns, he published many stories in prominent publications such as Street & Smith's *Detective Story Magazine*, *Thrilling Detective*, *Detective Short Stories*, and *Clues Detective Stories*.

Using his pseudonym Edward Ronns, Aarons published over two dozen crime novels with various paperback publishers, including Fawcett, Avon, Pyramid, and Graphic. His earliest copyrighted work, *Death in a Lighthouse*, was released by New York publisher Phoenix Press on January 2, 1938. The novel was later reissued as *The Cowl of Doom* by Hangman's House in 1946.

It is a wildly unusual story, heavy on action, questionable motives, and dubious twists, where Aarons seems to deliberately push the boundaries of credibility with each chapter. In the opening pages, the hero, Peter Willard, a respectable reporter for the *New York Morning Star*, wakes up with a bandaged head in a woman's apartment in Gramercy Park, unable to recall the events of the past three years. Much has happened, and none of it is good.

Peter is revealed to be a hunted public enemy—possibly a notorious gangster and murderer known as "the Deuce." He is part of the criminal outfit of Sicilian racketeer Aces Spinelli, and the previous night, a patrolman's bullet grazed his head during a robbery, accounting for his injury.

Despite his wound, Peter begins to see things more clearly and wishes to make amends for his criminal activities. However, his attempts to escape Spinelli's gang and turn himself in land him in deeper trouble. Gang members Aces Spinelli, Shifty Dalton, Trigger Malone, and Gold-Teeth refuse to let him confess to the police. His ex-fiancée, Diana Woodward, who is now engaged to Peter's brother, Ralph, wants nothing to do with him and actively seeks to have him incarcerated. The police also do not want to hear his defense; they only wish for his admission of guilt so they can send him to the execution chamber at Sing Sing Correctional Facility.

Special investigator Arthur Chase, a man determined to get handcuffs on Peter, may be the only person willing to listen to his excuses.

While reviewing *The Net*, a quality mystery from 1953, *Paperback*

Warrior noted Aarons' vivid and immersive descriptions, highlighting how he skillfully evokes a rich soundscape that captures the essence of the environment (Paperback Warrior, 2020). Although Aarons' writing improved greatly over time, *Death in a Lighthouse* exhibits a similar degree of excellence, creating captivating coastal backdrops and striking chase sequences among the sand dunes of Lighthouse Island and the icy waters of Litte Swamp Creek. The pace is frenetic, the murky characters are well-defined, and the story builds to an exhilarating conclusion.

Arguably, the alternative title, *The Cowl of Doom*, more accurately reflects the essence of the story, as it pertains to the mysterious underworld lord known as the Cowl, who is depicted with a vulture's face. This character embodies a far more intriguing aspect of the narrative than the lighthouse or the referenced death, which ultimately holds less significance within the overarching plot. This is a minor complaint, of course, and does little to detract from the overall enjoyment of a captivating crime novel that masterfully weaves suspense and deception throughout its pages.

Aarons' subsequent book, *Murder Money*, also released by Phoenix Press, was published on June 1, 1938. It was later reprinted as *$1,000,000 in Corpses* by Best Detective Selections in 1943, although the original title is the better choice. Isaac Anderson of the *New York Times* called the story "wildly improbable" but relished the fact it had "speed, action and gore enough to satisfy the most bloodthirsty fan" (Anderson, 1938). Like *Death in a Lighthouse*, the story unfolds rapidly, immersing the reader in action from the very first pages.

The protagonist, Leo Storm, is a man of leisure who has recently moved to the affluent resort town of Kennicut, Maine, where he has purchased a cottage at nearby Devil's Mount. As an amateur detective with some experience in the field, Storm's curiosity and passion for solving crimes lead him into a series of dangerous situations.

During a nature hike with his personal assistant, Xerxes Byron Nikopopolis—nicknamed "Poppo"—Storm decides to take a stroll through the woods alone. There, he discovers a briefcase lodged in the fork of a tree, containing a substantial sum of money—specifically, a quarter of a million dollars in clean bills.

Aarons' story takes an enthralling turn with the arrival of Toogy, who works for Wheels Burton, the owner of the upscale Shady Grove Club across the bay. Toogy demands the briefcase, brandishing a gun as a form of persuasion, but his plans are thwarted by the sudden appearance of the Sheriff, a Native American who is in the pocket of wealthy resident Myron Coulter.

Soon after, Storm and the Sheriff encounter the Coulter family while walking along the road to town. A tire blowout halts Coulter's Cadillac, and while the Sheriff replaces the tire, Myron Coulter's new secretary, Valerie Feather, ventures into the woods, presumably in search of the briefcase. Before Storm can reach town, he is robbed at gunpoint by a stranger who takes the bag of money from him.

From this point onward, several interesting narrative threads are introduced, including the murder of spiritualist Dikran Nakesian, who is killed during a séance intended to expose a conspiracy threatening significant donations to the Spiritualist Foundation. As Storm investigates Nakesian's death, he receives a frantic call from singer Dawn Detras, uncovering deeper connections to the crime involving her jealous boyfriend, Lucky Lamonte, and illegal dealings with Wheels Burton.

Storm navigates a treacherous landscape filled with law enforcement scrutiny and shifting allegiances. As he confronts suspects and unearths dark truths, the distinction between ally and adversary starts to fade. The stakes rise when counterfeit money and hidden motives come to light, leading to explosive confrontations that threaten everyone involved.

Murder Money offers a fascinating mystery that explores layers of deception, treachery, and lurking threats. Every choice carries weight, and every character has something to hide, creating a thrilling atmosphere filled with suspense and unexpected twists. Aarons' descriptive flair brings the vibrant and quirky characters to life, while the blend of natural beauty and the region's opulence provides a contrasting backdrop that enhances the evolving blood-soaked drama.

A *New York Times* book critic once remarked about another of Aarons' novels, "There are enough tough characters in this story to people a five-foot shelf of tales of murder and mayhem" (I.A., 1947). The same could be said of *Murder Money*. Each protagonist and antagonist is vividly drawn, showcasing Aarons' commitment to giving even the minor characters distinctive quirks and personas. The characters' names alone are a delight to behold: Aces Spinelli, Shifty Dalton, Trigger Malone, The Cowl. Just as in *Death in a Lighthouse*, *Murder Money* presents a formidable cast of hip, larger-than-life figures. With names like Lucky Lamonte, Wheels Burton, Dawn Detras, Romwell Taite, Hunk Hubert, Myron Coulter, Leo Storm, and Valerie Feather, these colorful and wry monikers linger in the mind long after the last page is turned. Yet, while these characters may entertain, their motives intertwine in a web of treachery that raises questions about morality and trust, leaving readers on edge long after the story concludes.

—April 2025
Rochester, NY

Nicholas Litchfield is the founder of the literary magazine *Lowestoft Chronicle* and editor of twelve literary anthologies. His stories, essays, and book reviews appear in *BULL, Colorado Review, Daily Press, The MacGuffin, The Virginian-Pilot, Washington Square Review*, and elsewhere. He has authored three novels: *Swampjack Virus, When The Actor Inspired Chaos and Bloodshed*, and *Hessman's Necklace*. He has also written introductions to numerous books, including twenty-four Stark House Press reprints of long-forgotten noir and mystery novels. Formerly a book critic for the *Lancashire Post*, syndicated to twenty-five newspapers across the U.K., he now writes for *Publishers Weekly*. You can find him online at NicholasLitchfield.com or Twitter: @NLitchfield.

Works cited:
Anderson, I., (1938). 'New Mystery Stories.' *New York Times*, 12 June, p. 98.
Boucher, A., (1955). 'Criminals At Large.' *New York Times*, 10 July, p. BR20.
Boucher, A., (1960). 'Criminals at Large.' *New York Times*, 22 May, p. BR33.
Boucher, A., (1960). 'Criminals at Large.' *New York Times*, 5 June, p. BR24.
Boucher, A., (1961). 'Criminals at Large.' *New York Times*, 26 March, p. BR28.
Boucher, A., (1964). 'There's a Spy Between the Covers.' *New York Times*, 7 June, p. BR7.
I.A., (1947). 'Reports on Criminals at Large.' *New York Times*, 28 December, p. BR10.
Marchino, L. A., (2023). *'Edward S. Aarons.'* [Online]
Available at: https://www.ebsco.com/research-starters/history/edward-s-aarons
[Accessed April 2025].
New York Times, (1975). 'EDWARD AARONS, NOVELIST, 58, DIES,' *New York Times*, 20 June, p. 38.
Paperback Warrior, (2020). *'The Net.'* [Online]
Available at: https://www.paperbackwarrior.com/2020/09/the-net.html
[Accessed 9 April 2025].

Death in a Lighthouse
EDWARD S. AARONS

Writing as Edward Ronns

Chapter One
ALL FOOLS' DAY

Peter Willard opened his eyes, glanced at the calendar on the wall beside him, and hastily screwed them shut again.

"Hell!" he murmured. "It's impossible. Nobody makes calendars three years in advance."

He kept his eyes closed, not caring to stare any longer at the ugly little red imp that marked the date as April 1st—All Fools' Day. For some moments he was aware only of the low drone of distant motor traffic, like the sound of a swarm of bees or the monotone of the ocean's surf. Tenderly he touched the aching, throbbing part of him that was his head.

It was bandaged.

Peter Willard struggled to return to wakeful consciousness. His gray eyes blinked many times before they consented to remain open. The expression that dawned in them and the grim mold of his youthful features spoke of alertness, swiftness, and a keen, agile brain, such as could belong only to that type of adventurer who is born squalling for excitement. The length of his lean, lithe frame and the ripple of muscles beneath his clear skin indicated that Peter Willard had the physique to follow the calls of his nature.

He groaned a weak greeting to the crisp spring breeze that whisked into the room. A clouded look crept into his eyes, accented by two deep creases that led avenues of determination to the corners of his firm, tight-lipped mouth. Several perplexing questions chased themselves around in his mind like beetles trapped in a jar.

He wondered, above all, where he was. This strange, sunny room couldn't be his cozy West-Side apartment. Delicate engravings adorned the cream-colored walls, above a low, modernistic bookshelf crammed with gaudy-jacketed novels. There were two doors leading from this room, one of which was slightly ajar and opened into the typically tiny Manhattan foyer. There was a desk, but it was a fragile affair, not at all the sturdy, battered relic on which he was wont to ply the implements of his journalistic profession.

And the room had a definite feminine touch. He distinctly traced the scent of jasmine perfume in the air. Peter grinned wryly and considered the original question.

All Fools' Day ... That was wrong. The calendar was three years in advance. He dismissed that problem for the moment.

DEATH IN A LIGHTHOUSE

The third question, which completely overshadowed the other two, was the bandaged, aching head he so unwillingly possessed. He could explain everything, by an effort of the imagination—except the pistol.

Peter found it under his pillow, pressing into the tender rawness of his scalp. He picked it up, examining the blue-black snubbiness of it and appreciating its murderous, lethal appearance. He broke it open and sniffed. His wan features went even whiter.

He sprang out of bed, alarm sending quick thrills up and down his spine. Quickly he strode to the window, and glanced out and far down to the neat tracery of walks in the little park below. His eyes swept the skyscraper horizon as he struggled to orient himself. At last, with a satisfied click of his tongue, he placed his locality. He was in an apartment overlooking Gramercy Park.

"So far, so good," he thought. "Someone is playing the Good Samaritan to Peter."

Names flashed into his mind. He thought of the New York *Morning Star* and his reportorial job on it, his covering the strange and unlawful doings of one Aces Spinelli. Spinelli had no brains of his own, yet he very cleverly baffled the forces of metropolitan law and order. Peter was sure that Spinelli had fired the shot that cut a swath through his scalp. What he wanted to know was what he had done in return, and what it all had to do with a .45 Smith & Wesson with three empty chambers, and a woman's apartment in Gramercy Park, of which he was the solitary occupant.

The last event that he could remember was cornering Spinelli with a list of highly embarrassing questions on one of those twisted, narrow streets of the East Side. Spinelli had acted with his famous Sicilian impatience, and hot flame had split the night, to put a temporary end to Peter's activities. He remembered no more.

But didn't he?

Peter ran his fingers jerkily through his dark, rumpled hair. The apartment was strangely familiar. The tiny cluttered desk seemed intimate, filled with belongings that he vaguely knew to be his. The weapon—the pistol with the empty, powder-stained chambers—was his, he was sure, although he had never before owned a revolver. It was just yesterday, too, that he had pulled off the sheet on the calendar, uncovering the leering, satanic imp....

Ah, but that was impossible. The date was three years ahead....

Peter pulled himself together with a snap. He needed a drink. From a sideboard he selected a glass and a bottle of cognac. Beads of perspiration stood out on his forehead, and his black hair felt suddenly damp.

He drained half of the liquor glass and wiped his palms on his legs. They were bare. He found he was only semi-clad.

"Hell!" he repeated. "It *is* impossible. No one makes calendars three years in advance."

He bounced on his toes and finished the cognac. He shivered. Something unpleasant was about to come to light in this strange room.

"The date is true," he blurted suddenly.

He did not recognize the rasping sound as his own voice. He examined the calendar more closely, and the imp grimaced back at him.

"It might be a practical joke," he observed. Perhaps it was Larry Rorke's work. But the calendar was absolutely orthodox. Peter muttered slowly, "Either it's a fake, or I've been running a marathon with Rip Van Winkle!"

His eyes fell upon a newspaper slipped under the door, and he snatched it up to study the date. It corresponded to the wall calendar. Peter suddenly felt very weak. He took a second glass of cognac, spilling most of the contents of the tumbler before the liquid touched his lips. He sank into a chair and read slowly, feeling his insides turn over in nauseating fashion.

His picture—a bad one, but recognizable—stared insolently at him from the front page, under the caption:

NOTORIOUS GUNMAN WOUNDED IN FRAY
Clue Sought in Devrie-Carton Jewel Robbery

Police threw a dragnet out for the gunman known as Deuce, of increasing criminal activity for the past three years in association with the Aces Spinelli gang.

In the shooting that occurred when Devrie-Carton's was looted last night, Patrolman I. Schmidt identified one of the gang as the Deuce and insisted he hit him at least once while firing after the fleeing criminals....

The snub-nosed pistol dropped from Peter Willard's limp hand and thudded dully on the carpet. He touched his bandaged head and stood for a moment like one who sees a bottomless chasm crack open beneath his feet. Then he whipped toward the desk, searching frantically. His trembling fingers encountered hard, glinting objects. He brought them to light for a brief instant, and as quickly threw them back, slamming down the top of the tiny writing desk. The objects were ruby rings, sapphire pendants, and diamonds of all shapes and sizes.

Peter laughed weakly.

"I think I've gone crazy..."

He sat down on the bed with a suddenness that was almost a collapse, and rested his throbbing head in his hands. Three years of blankness! A mad, hazy series of tangled pictures, punctuated by sounds of staccato guns and screaming sirens, followed by unpleasant deaths. Woven into the pattern of insanity was a pair of eyes—narrow eyes, bright with fierce power, bird-like, vulture's eyes over a hooked, predatory nose.

He was a hunted public enemy, a notorious gangster, perhaps a murderer.

Peter's years of journalistic training came to his aid in preserving his reeling mind. He did not give way to the shrieking suspicions that threatened to unbalance him.

He simply asked himself, "Why?"

Like a rocket bursting in a night sky came the illuminating answer. He'd suffered from amnesia for three years. Of course. A different man, a Mr. Hyde, with his conscious, moral mind cloaked in abysmal darkness.

"How? When? Where?"

How the answers came swiftly. The shot Spinelli had fired, creasing his scalp, had been followed by total loss of memory of who he was, what he was, and where he belonged. The pieces clicked together in his mind like the conclusion of a jig-saw puzzle. He knew so much; the rest would follow.

Walking to the window, he threw it wide open. A soft breeze sighed into the room, ruffling his curly dark hair, playing on his wan, drawn features. Far down on the sidewalk a blue-coated figure—tiny and apparently impotent from this height—glanced upward. Peter ducked in quickly and slammed down the window. His lips were ashen, and a hunted look clouded his cold gray eyes.

The breeze had knocked over a picture that stood on the desk, together with a bulky envelope. Absently he stooped to pick up the articles, while his agile brain raced quickly, dodging and twisting in a desperate effort to find a loophole in the wall of circumstances that hemmed him in. He glanced curiously for a moment at the picture. An attractive girl. She explained the faint scent of feminine perfume in the air of the apartment. He replaced the photograph with an expression of distaste, wondered to what he had descended during the three unknown years. Hopefully he tore open the envelope, seeking some clue, only to find a thick pad of currency. Four hundred dollars in small notes. He replaced that, too.

He became aware of pounding somewhere in the next room, a curiously imperative knock. He crossed the apartment to the foyer and opened the hall door.

"Hello, Shifty," he said without hesitation.

Shifty Dalton was a short, squat man with sandy hair that was slicked down with some compound until it shone and parted exactly in the middle. His lips were permanently twisted into a cunning grin, and he wore a dubonnet-colored shirt with a flashy blue suit. A scoop felt was pulled low over his eyes, which were slightly crossed.

Outwardly, Shifty Dalton might have been taken for a hard-boiled, rather sad-looking specimen of the genus a man who lived by his wits and whose primary interests in life were clothes and the daily racing sheets. Shifty Dalton did not look particularly vicious, and yet Peter knew that the bulge in his breast pocket was not due to the presence of strong cigars or a racing form, but something that could spurt instant death from a recking muzzle. Peter had no doubt—indeed, he knew, from some corner of his numbed mind—that this same short, squat man who entered the room and flung himself in a square, modernistic chair was a killer more than twice over.

The police knew Shifty's record. They knew, as well as they knew the numbers on their respective badges, that Dalton was guilty of several outrageous crimes. Three times they had pulled him in and attempted to send the sandy-haired man up the Hudson. And three limes, with the help of some great power behind the scenes, Shifty Dalton had been set free. Third degree did little to break his stubborn denials of criminal activity. Relentless, battering questions for hours on end brought nothing from the man's twisted lips but a stream of violent curses. So three times the police had had to sigh and turn him loose, knowing full well the path that Dalton would take.

Shifty Dalton was a dangerous customer, Peter decided, to encounter so soon after his awakening. Dalton was no fool. Peter would have to be careful of what he said. He must show no sign of any change in himself.

Shifty began, "The Cowl wants you to see Aces—quick."

"Cowl?" Peter sparred indifferently, reaching for his necktie. "And who is the Cowl?"

He wracked his mind in an effort to penetrate the blank that hung like a dark curtain over a corner of his brain. Behind him, Dalton pushed his felt hat back over his sparse growth of hair and unerringly directed a stream of tobacco juice into the wastebasket.

"Shaky, aren't you, Deuce?" he asked sympathetically. "You look kind of funny to me—but you didn't get creased enough to forget the boss—not quite, I'll bet. Spinelli had a message from him today."

"He used me enough yesterday!" Peter snapped sullenly, and indicated the newspaper. He held his breath, studying the other's manner closely.

If it should be his picture, then—

"Yeah," Shifty sighed. "That was a pretty good job, I heard the Cowl say. But we got another, a final one, before the Cowl moves his headquarters. Boy, I can smell the sea breezes already! Now come on. Aces wants you snappy, and snappy it is!"

"You'll have to wait until I get dressed."

Peter discovered some clothing neatly arranged in a closet, and wondered who could have taken such care of it. He thought uneasily of the girl.

Dalton hit the wastebasket once again, impatiently, and gazed crookedly at him.

"Aren't you taking the jewels with you?"

"Why should I? They're safe enough here."

"Spinelli wants 'em—for the Cowl."

Peter offered his visitor a drink and took one for himself. When he set down the glass, he had made his decision. It was a startling idea, one that appealed to his inborn sense of gallantry and romance. It pleased him, and it was the best plan that had yet offered itself. He hesitated, picked up the snubby .45 he had dropped on the floor, and weighed it tentatively in his hand. The man referred to as the Cowl was the man with the vulture's face—but the Cowl could wait. There was a more pressing wrong to be righted; there were the stolen jewels to consider.

Peter said carelessly, while knotting his tie, "The jewels are in the desk. Get them out, apple-blossom."

As Shifty put his glass down and reached into the desk, Peter walked behind him on his bare feet. He drew his arm back and brought the butt of the revolver down with crushing force on Dalton's head.

The man collapsed without a sound and slipped to the floor.

A sense of satisfaction filled Peter Willard, and he paused for a moment to enjoy the sensation. He felt as though he had won the first skirmish in a long-drawn-out campaign. He pocketed the weapon and scooped up the jewels. Then he found a felt hat, and slipped his feet into soft patent-leather shoes. Before he closed the door, he adjusted the hat so that it concealed the bandage on his head.

Chapter Two
"I AM THE DEUCE"

The air in the street tingled in his nostrils. A reckless smile fought to curl about Peter's lips, and his eyes sparkled with the joyous prospect of interesting events to come. As yet he could not appreciate the depth of the situation he was in.

"Hello, Deuce," came a voice. "Where you going, all alone?"

Peter whipped around, all cold inside. A heavy-faced man with a broken nose edged up to him on the pavement outside the apartment house.

"Trigger—"

"Where's Shifty?"

"Upstairs—checking the stuff."

"And where you going?" Trigger Malone repeated.

"I," Peter said, "have business to transact."

He grinned and punched the gangster lightly in the abdomen. His knuckles encountered something hard and metallic, and the grin faded slightly. Trigger's heady eyes were bleak.

"Funny—Shifty didn't say anything."

"There are telephones, aren't there?"

"Don't you think you'd better wait?" Trigger insisted.

"Can't. It's too important. I'm acting on the Cowl's orders," Peter said crisply, and strode off down the pavement.

Trigger rubbed his blue chin and entered the apartment house. Peter hailed a taxi and tumbled inside, barking an order.

"Carton's."

Devrie-Carton's was not very crowded at that late hour in the morning. Indeed, it was never very crowded. Devrie-Carton's catered exclusively to those who could afford to pay for the excellent gems they handled. As a result, their glittering store was usually impressive with its emptiness.

On this occasion, however, as Peter jostled through the Fifth Avenue crowds and entered the establishment, he saw a little knot of men standing in the shadowy interior, close to the massive safe that had been looted the night before. He glanced quickly at the group. Their conversation came to him as a low, monotonous hum, often broken by exasperated remarks from the silver-haired M. Carton. (M. Devrie had nothing to say, M. Devrie having died some years before, leaving only his name immortalized on the store window.)

Peter approached the first clerk who condescended to look at him, and from his coat pocket took a plain brown paper bag. The contents clicked as he tossed it on the glass counter top.

"Good morning," he said. "I have some things for M. Carton. I believe they belong to him."

The clerk's eyebrows went up a fraction of an inch, and he delicately picked up the paper bag in well-manicured hands.

"From whom do they come?"

The tall, lean man grinned.

"From a chap named Peter Willard, with his compliments."

The clerk stared doubtfully at the bag, then nodded a greeting to someone standing silently behind Peter. He turned to find a short, rotund little man with a bald head and pale blue eyes gazing, as though hypnotized, at the paper bag.

"Mr. Chase?" asked the clerk politely.

"Dear me!" The little man started, tearing his glance from the bag and addressing Peter. He was supremely unconscious of the salesman's presence.

"Did you say your name was Peter Willard?"

"It was Willard who prompted me to this act," Peter replied evasively. He saw the newcomer's pale blue eyes twinkle, as though they were laughing at something he did not understand. Mr. Chase had in his hand a folded copy of that morning's paper, with his picture facing outward.

"May I ask," Chase sighed, "what the contents of that bag are?"

"I don't see what authority you have to ask, but if the clerk will bring it to M. Carton, I am sure you will discover the contents for yourself."

Pulling down the brim of his soft felt hat, Peter walked slowly to the entrance. The bald little man accompanied him.

"My name is Arthur Chase. You haven't heard of me, but I happen to be interested in a family of Willards, from Jersey. Head of the family is named Jed. Is your Peter Willard connected with them, by any chance?"

"Yes," Peter murmured. "He's Jed Willard's nephew."

"Ah—thank you."

Peter plunged into the Fifth Avenue crowd, glad to shake loose the inquisitive little man.

Back in the store, a sudden hubbub of excitement arose as Monsieur Carton turned the paper bag upside down and emptied its contents on the plate glass counter top. A shower of sparkling gems rolled before the curious eyes of the metropolitan detectives.

"But these are—*mon Dieu!*—but these are the gems stolen from me last night! Who brought them? How did they get here?"

The clerk lost his superior air and turned pale.

"That man who gave them to me! The man who just went out! A tall, broad fellow—I couldn't see his face very well because of his hat, but I'd swear he looked like one of yesterday's gunmen!"

"You are a little late in thinking that, aren't you?" Arthur Chase's voice was mildly reproachful.

"But you—you stood and spoke to him—walked him to the door!"

"Because he interested me."

"And he wasn't—ah, what's his name?—the Deuce?"

"I don't think so," was the strange reply.

It was a little park, nestling green and strangely alien in the shadows of the towering steel and stone buildings. The early afternoon sun dappled the bright green of new grass and budding leaves with a warm, golden tint. It was yet early in the afternoon as Peter made his way wearily into this haven of refuge.

A bench beside a rippling, chuckling fountain beckoned him, and he sat down. He threw back his head and let the warm sun play on his features. His light gray suit, neatly cut and once fitting his lithe, athletic form, was now sadly rumpled; his shoes were spattered with mud, and his tie was awry. But Peter Willard didn't care. He was trying to adjust himself to the incredible fact that he had engaged in criminal activity for three years. The glow that had filled him after returning the Devrie-Carton jewels had lasted only a short time. He realized only the futility of trying to right all the wrongs he must have committed while his mind had been empty of all recollection of his former life.

Thoughts of his home at Little Swamp Island, the stately house on the knoll overlooking the marshes and the sea, thoughts of his uncle, his aunt, his brother Ralph and his sister Jane, sent a shiver of sickness through him. Then he remembered Diana Woodward. He had been engaged to marry Diana, who was so lovely and so cool. He longed suddenly, with a dull aching inside him, to see her once more.

He rummaged experimentally in his coat pockets and found a battered pack of cigarettes. Thoughtfully he lit one and inhaled deeply and gratefully of the cool, trickling smoke. His head still throbbed with the wound from the crime he did not recall, and he cursed softly under his breath.

Gun battle—

He put his hand in his pocket and found the weapon there, the one he had automatically put in his coat on leaving the Gramercy Park apartment. With another soft curse, he took a quick stride across the gravel path and hurled the blue-steel thing into the waters of the fountain. It gave him a sense of relief and satisfaction—

A hand was on his shoulder, tapping roughly. A policeman.

Peter's first thought was that he had been identified as the notorious Deuce. Coolly, his lean face wearing a mask of surprised innocence, he faced the red-faced, irate officer.

"And what d'ye think it is, throwing things into a public fountain?" came the bluecoat's thick, outraged voice. Then, suspiciously: "What was it?"

Peter felt a sudden desire to laugh aloud. His tone was carelessly indifferent as he said, "It was a gun. I threw away a gun."

"Gun?"

"That's right."

"Oh yeah?" The officer surveyed him doubtfully.

"Yes." Peter replied again, calmly.

"You aren't crazy, are you?"

Little lines appeared about Peter's eyes as he smiled.

"No, not now. I have been quite insane, though, for a number of years."

As Peter had expected, his jest made the officer snort his disbelief.

"That will be enough monkeyshines out of you, young feller! Move along now, and don't violate any more park ordinances, or you'll find yourself in trouble."

"Any rules against my resuming my seat here?" Peter asked pleasantly.

The officer grunted in non-committal manner and trod heavily away. The smile on Peter's face faded.

He found himself trembling slightly. He tossed away the cigarette and lit a fresh one.

His mind raced along a new avenue of thought. He said to himself: "I'm innocent of these crimes I may have committed! Morally, I am free from guilt. But my hands, my fingers—they pulled triggers that must have spurted death and destruction of unknown quantity and violence. These things my body did, without the consent or knowledge of my mind. Satan himself displaced my conscience and rode my body for three years through the dark pathways of crime. The problem is: would a jury judge me guilty?"

The prospect of living his life in startled, trembling fear was not one that appealed to Peter. Gazing at the broad back of the policeman, he knew he could never go on living as a cowering fugitive from justice. Nor could he forever hope to evade the vengeful clutches of the mysterious underworld lord, the Cowl. He had to decide one way or the other.

To think with Peter was to act, and for him there was only one solution. Flipping away the cigarette, he walked with purposeful steps across the little park.

"I'll give myself up," he said, and felt better for the words. "I'll take my chances with a jury. Then, if I get a break, I can start over again."

Absorbed as he was with his decision, he did not see the smart roadster until it was almost on him. Only the swiftness of his reflexes saved him from injury or possible death. Even before he recovered his balance from the startled leap, he turned to stare at the long, green roadster that had missed him by an eyelash. A startled white face, under a smart and saucy green hat, was turned toward him, eyes wide with fright and astonishment.

The picture on that desk! The girl of the photo!

Peter was willing to swear that it was she. But before he could be sure of his identification, the girl turned about and the roadster swept out of sight. Peter brushed the dust from his trouser legs and kicked thoughtfully at a pebble.

For some reason, he could not recall the girl. Yet he knew he was acquainted with her. But who she was and how her picture came to be in the apartment, he did not know. Obviously she was connected with the unknown Cowl, the man with the vulture's eyes. That being the case, if she had recognized him, it would be a matter of minutes before Spinelli and Shifty Dalton were put on his trail, anxious to catch up with him and wring an explanation for his morning's activities. He wracked his tortured, injured brain for a vague hint, some incident that would give him a clue. Then, maddened by the blank veil across his mind, he gave it up.

"We've forgotten much," Peter told himself. "We can forget this girl, too."

He halted before the swinging doors of a little police station. Adjusting his hat at a more conventional angle, he took a look at the warm sun above, listened to the hum in the air, breathed the tang of the open. Then, with shoulders squared, he pushed into the gloomy, yellow-lighted interior of the station house.

There were few officers in evidence. Those that were in sight lounged on the benches that lined the wall. The house sergeant glanced up at Peter's approach and surveyed him over the top of his spectacles.

He said in a thick brogue: "Well, and what is it you want?"

"I'm giving myself up," Peter replied quietly.

The house sergeant sighed, and examined the tall, broad-shouldered man before him. Putting aside his pen, he leaned back in his swivel chair with the attitude of a martyr.

"And what heinous crime have you been about committing?" he asked with thick sarcasm.

"I am Peter Willard."

"Ah! Indeed!" A glint of humor appeared in the officer's blue eyes. "And do ye know what, acushla machree? I'm Pat Murphy!"

Peter's opinion of the metropolitan police force sank lower than he would have believed possible. It was incredible that twice in the period of an hour he should speak to members of the force and still be unrecognized, with his picture sprawled over the front page of every paper in town.

He asked patiently: "Do you have any newspapers here?"

The sergeant had resumed his laborious scratching with the pen. With a curt nod, he indicated a rumpled pile of papers. Peter, striding toward them, reflected that three more steps would make him a free man again. He choked down the passing temptation, found the front page of a journal, and thrust it under the sergeant's nose, his blurred picture uppermost.

"Look at the picture," Peter suggested quietly.

The sergeant looked.

"I," said Peter, "am the Deuce."

At the house sergeant's wide-eyed surprise and sudden gesture toward his pistol holster, Peter smiled and raised his arms ceilingward.

"You needn't be alarmed. I am giving myself up quite voluntarily—macushla!"

Chapter Three
OUT OF THE FRYING PAN—

Sergeant Murphy reached for the telephone, never taking his glance from the tall man before him. His blue Irish eyes presented a paradox of cold harshness and hot distaste.

"I don't know what your game is, thug, but I know the answer—and that's the hot seat for you!"

A voice rattled from the receiver, and Murphy grunted into the telephone: "Tell Arty Chase to get in touch with me at once!"

Then began the little chain of incidents that reversed Peter's optimistic hopes of eventual release. Unceremoniously thrust into a cell, pending orders from headquarters in Spring Street, he was shocked by the utter finality of the clanging bars behind him. He sat down slowly on the uncomfortable cot and fought down the rapier thrusts of many imps of doubt that pricked his mind with disconcerting questions.

Abruptly he came to the conclusion that he needed a lawyer.

He searched In his unfamiliar clothing, and brought to light a wallet containing twenty-two dollars and some small change.

"Not so good," was his comment to the scrawled walls.

There was his family, of course, but he could not appeal to them. The past he determined to forget, all of it, as completely as he had forgotten the years that resulted in his present dilemma.

By parting with half his precious capital, he managed to persuade the guards to procure for him a lawyer—any kind of a lawyer—to hear his case and present his comments.

The lawyer turned out to be a Mr. Goldner. At his first appearance, Peter wondered whether his heart was as ugly as his face. It was a face that looked as though it had been molded of rubber and then squeezed together from top and bottom. The features were crunched together in a manner that made them all tend to converge toward his nose: his eyes were slightly oblique, slanting downward to his misshapen, fleshy nasal organ, under which drooped a full-lipped, down-curving mouth.

The comments Goldner made were as distasteful to Peter's suddenly sensitive ears as his features were unpleasant to his eyes.

"Your story is ridiculous," the man said, as Peter concluded a rapid sketch of his predicament. "*I* don't believe it, let alone a muckle-headed jury. You, with your reputation, will be lucky to get a life sentence; and me, with *my* reputation, would be the laughing stock of my profession if I presented such an argument for you. Criminal lawyer I am, Deuce—or Willard, if you prefer—but your doings go against even the low morality such a lawyer is supposed to have. I wouldn't defend you, and neither would any other man in New York. Not with your record!"

"Is it as bad as all that?" Peter protested, while little muscles twitched in his lean face. "I don't even know what I've done! Have I committed murder?"

"No-o. At least, that would have to be proved."

"Listen here, I've been suffering from amnesia. I had no knowledge of who I was or what I was doing. In a manner of speaking, I was insane. You could make a case of that, couldn't you? Couldn't you?"

"So what would happen? Instead of the chair, you'd be sent to a lunatic asylum—and I assure you, friend, a penitentiary is much healthier than a criminal nuthouse."

Peter blanched.

"There is no hope of my being entirely acquitted?"

Goldner laughed mirthlessly. He shrugged his sloping shoulders, spread his pudgy hands and pulled at his nose—which habit might explain its misshapen size.

"Not a chance. I could make out a case for you, sure I could. But you know how it is—it's becoming a popular fad to plead temporary insanity. And you're saying it lasted three years! The people wouldn't have it, Deuce—Mr. Willard. The people would protest and rise in wrath—"

"Oh, don't orate!" Peter sighed.

"Furthermore, you say you haven't the money or the possibility of raising the money for an adequate defense. Such a trial as yours would require the testimony of experts, psychiatrists, what-nots. I couldn't do it, and you can't, so who will? Then you say the head of the Aces Spinelli gang is a big man, someone you called—what was it?—the Cowl. Well, who is he?"

"I don't know."

You see?" Goldner asked in gloomy triumph. "It would be good psychology, maybe, to drag a big man's name into this. But you don't even know who this leader is! I'm sorry, Willard, but I must turn your case down."

The cheerless Mr. Goldner departed, taking with him Peter's ten dollars.

Peter blew smoke viciously at the wall and wished he could have a drink. He felt more and more uneasy, completely trapped in the meshes of an altogether unpleasant predicament. Hunted, on the one hand, by the Cowl, who would soon become fearful of what Peter might say or do; on the other hand, in the clutches of a not-so-merciful Justice. Young, vibrant with life, he definitely arrived at the point where he no longer fought down his regret at having given himself up to the hands of the law.

His mind raced in circles, as surely imprisoned as his physical self in the walls he himself had so carelessly erected. He regretted now the impetuous decision that put his head in a noose. If he were free, he reflected, he would take his chances avoiding the law and the Cowl—but no, he would not avoid the underworld leader. Rather, he would seek in his own way to redeem the wrongs he had done society by wiping out the evil blot that hovered over the metropolis like some darkly lowering, menacing cloud—the Cowl.

But he was not free—

The door clanged. Another prisoner, wretched and drunk, was cast in the cell with him. A thrill like the barely perceptible touch of a feather rippled up his spine and ended in a tingling, prickling sensation at the back of his scalp.

Shifty Dalton—

Peter stretched his long legs to the floor and stood up, his hair almost brushing the rough concrete of the ceiling. He felt a sudden light bursting upon him; a new buoyancy entered his spirits.

"And what," he asked softly, "are you doing here, my little white gardenia?"

Aloud, for the benefit of the guard who might be lurking in the corridor, he called: "Can't a man have privacy here? Must I stay in the same cell with this bum?"

The answer came back to him from the far end of the corridor, where the guard stirred in his chair.

"Quiet, you! What d'you think this is—a hotel?"

Shifty Dalton grinned and winked in exaggerated fashion. The effect of that wink on his crossed eyes were grotesque.

"'At's right, Deuce. Don't let on you know me. Not yet. I'm arrested for being drunk, that's all."

Peter stared coldly at the squat, cross-eyed gunman. His blood flowed in streams of ice through his pulsing veins. The Cowl had evidently caught up with him. It was due to the girl of the photograph, of course.

She had spread the alarm.

Peter asked: "Well, what's the game?"

Shifty glared crookedly for a moment, then assumed a confidential air.

"Listen, Deuce. The chief knows why you're here. He knows about the sparklers, too. He thinks you're nuts, but he says he knows why you did it, too—"

Petet thrust a hand deep into his trousers pocket and leaned against the rough stone wall, rubbing his shoulder soothingly against the cold concrete.

'Well, I'll bite. Why am I here?" he demanded.

"I don't know! The boss don't tell me everything, But he says you won't stand a chance, not with the coppers. He'll frame you into the seat, sure, whether you turn stool pigeon or not."

"And what gave him the idea I was turning squealer?"

"You ain't got any other business with the law, have you?"

"Perhaps I have. Personal business."

"You," said Dalton, thrusting his coarse features close to Peter's, "ain't got no personal business. Nothing is personal to the Cowl, and you know it."

Peter grimaced wryly as he received the full benefit of Dalton's alcoholic breath, and he stepped aside from the gunman.

"You still haven't answered the pertinent question, my withered stinkweed. What is the idea of you being here?"

"Ah, cut the wisecracks, Deuce! Be yourself! I'm here to get you out of all this!"

Peter drew back his head and laughed softly.

"And how does your giant intellect propose to accomplish that impossible task? Provided I want to get out?"

"You'll come out whether you want to or not!" Shifty snapped, his friendly air dropping momentarily from him like an ill-fitting mask. "Like this—"

Dalton rolled up his wide trouser leg and swiftly unstrapped a gun that had eluded the officer's routine search.

"Now you'll do as I say," he rasped, levelling the weapon at the tall, smiling man, "and no more flowery language out of you, either."

Peter laughed. The sound was like the brittle clinking of ice in a glass.

"I never thought you could be so witty and clever, my sweet little nasturtium."

Shifty glared uncertainly, then went tense. The sound of a guard's footsteps reached their cell. Quickly he flattened his squat form against the wall, waiting, gun levelled warningly at Peter.

Had Peter chosen, he could have prevented the incident that followed. But he did not choose. The memory of Goldner's words still burned painfully in his mind. He leaned indolently against the wall. The impossible had happened: his predicament was dissolving into shreds like a fog before a gale of wind. Peter had no doubt that the thug could carry out what he planned.

Two men were coming down the corridor, and Shifty grinned as he heard:

"Just one good picture of him for this afternoon's front page, buddy. That's all I want."

The guard and a newspaper photographer, equipped with camera and plates, halted before the door. The guard turned his back to the cell and stood close to the iron bars. Dalton struck swiftly, brought the butt down with a cracking thud on the jailer's head. The man sagged, and the pseudo-newspaperman caught him, lowering the sagging body softly to the ground.

Nimble fingers dipped into the guard's pockets and extracted the keys. A moment later the man who had accompanied the guard opened the cell door and dropped the guard's body unceremoniously on the floor.

"Hya, Shifty. And fancy meetin' the Deuce here!"

The fake cameraman grinned, displaying a solid row of gold teeth. Thrusting his hands deep in his pocket, he waved a revolver at Peter. "Now, Deuce—let's go!"

Peter followed between the crouching forms of the gunmen, every faculty alert to seize the first opportunity. He hardly trusted the sandy-haired Dalton after the attack on him that morning in the apartment. Peter thought it significant that no mention had been made of the affair. Once out on the street, he planned to outwit Shifty and Gold-Teeth, but until that time his best course was to follow and ally himself with two gunmen.

Only the house sergeant and two patrolmen were in the hearing room of the station house. One was asleep and the other deeply engrossed in a newspaper. It was Sergeant Patrick Murphy who glanced up from his pen and ink duties at the desk and saw the three shadowy figures in the cell row corridor. With a choked exclamation, he sprang to his feet, upsetting his chair, his fingers struggling to release his heavy gun from its holster.

He never touched it. Shifty fired, apparently without taking aim. Murphy staggered, clutched at his gold buttons, and crashed to the floor. The sound of the report echoed through the building.

"That breaks it!" Shifty cried.

The two other policemen sprang up, their white faces drawn and tense. From the doorway came a sudden fusillade of fire. Peter, as surprised as the patrolmen, whirled to discover three darkly dressed men in the doorway, dully gleaming weapons in their white hands.

The first patrolman fell without a chance to defend himself. The other threw himself desperately behind the desk, gaining time to draw his weapon and fire into the gangsters. Reports crashed heavily through the yellow-painted halls. One of the gunmen cursed and dropped his weapon, clutching at his shattered hand.

"Come on, Deuce! Run for it!"

Urged on by the smoking muzzle of Dalton's gun, Peter knew that the slightest sign of disobedience would mean his death warrant. With Peter closely guarded between them, the five men poured through the doorway and spilled out on the deserted street. A black sedan was parked in front of the precinct station. The men tumbled into it, one or two returning the increasing fire from the stunned police.

The motor hummed and the machine lurched.

"Just a minute— Where're we going?" Peter shouted above the blast of fire and screaming of tires, as the heavy car swept around the first corner.

His reply was an impatient exclamation from Shifty:

"You're going to hell, rat!"

Something hard crashed down on Peter's tender, wounded scalp. A sudden explosion of lights danced before his eyes, and an agonizing pain shot through his head before he tumbled forward on the floor of the car.

Chapter Four
THE GIRL OF THE PHOTO

Inside a back room of a hotel on lower Broadway, four men sat and stared at a body on the floor. Yellow light filtered through drawn blinds. The four men shuffled their feet uneasily, smoked endless chains of cigarettes, and started whenever footsteps sounded in the corridor beyond the door. They were waiting for the Cowl.

Occasionally one of them cursed and expressed a desire for a drink. It was uncomfortably close in the room, with the sun beating down on the drawn blinds and the windows shut tightly.

Shifty Dalton broke the strained silence by recounting for the fifth or sixth time the events of that morning.

"I thought he looked kind of funny when I first saw him. I even told him so. He had a queer look in his eyes, like—hell, like he didn't know me at first. I thought it was the lead he got in his hair, then. But when I turn around to get the jewels, wham!—he smacked me down and out like a light! I can't understand it, unless that bullet turned his head. The stool! Going to the police, giving back the sparklers— What the hell is his idea?"

The sandy-haired gunman glared at the unconscious man on the floor and added: "You know what I think, you guys? I think—"

"But it's not your business to think, Dalton!" came a suave, well modulated voice, in striking contrast to Shifty's harsh tones.

A fifth man had entered the room by a side door leading from an adjoining suite. More than one of the startled gangsters shivered, wondering what was behind the hood-like black mask that concealed the newcomer's face.

"Wondering what got into the Deuce," the Cowl observed, "won't get you anywhere. I happen to know just what is troubling him."

"What is it?" Dalton demanded with extraordinary lack of caution.

"None of your damned business," was the calm reply, almost as if the speaker were very bored or very tired.

"Well—he ought to be knocked off."

"Perhaps he will be," murmured the Cowl, and began to prod Peter Willard with the point of his shining black shoes.

Pain of a different sort from that which throbbed in his battered head revived Peter and brought him struggling back through murky darkness to the lights of the hotel room.

Looking up into seemingly incredible heights, he saw a grinning, dark-skinned man in dinner clothes, whose white teeth gleamed in the electric lights as brilliantly as the impeccably valeted shirt front. But there was something odd about the man's face. The upper part, the eyes and nose, was absent. As Peter's vision cleared, he saw that the man wore a black mask, a strange sort of mask that fitted tightly over his head and came to a harp point at the rear of his skull. At last—the Cowl!

Peter struggled up to a sitting position on the carpet.

"Awake at last?" came the deep, curiously vibrant tones of the man in the mask. "Awake, *Willard?*"

Peter nodded and rubbed his throbbing head. He staggered to his feet, giddiness forcing him to clutch at the wall.

"So you do know my name?" he muttered.

'The Cowl laughed at Peter's question, and lit a cigarette. Peter took in his surroundings, noting that the sunshine behind the Venetian blinds indicated that the day had not yet died. In the room, besides the masked man, were Shifty Dalton, the pasty-faced Spinelli, broken-nosed Trigger Malone and Gold-Teeth, the fake cameraman. Quite a collection of society's prize parasites, Peter thought.

"Willard, I always knew your name," the Cowl finally replied. "There is no need to pretend ignorance now. I knew it shortly after I stopped our friend Spinelli here from putting an end to your intriguing questions, three years ago. You were in a daze; you did not know who you were. When you asked for a connection with me, I very kindly employed you—on probation, of course, until I unearthed your real identity. I must know the antecedents of all the men who do—ah—work for me."

His emotionless voice irritated Peter.

"Dirty devil! So that's how it all came about! And you wouldn't see to it that I received proper medical attention?"

The masked man laughed with obviously genuine amusement, his perfect teeth flashing as his lips parted in a smile.

"But why should I? You were useful, highly useful to me, my boy! After a while, I came to depend on you. You were quite valuable to me, and that is what is so distressing—this use of the past tense. You *were—*"

"Emphatically correct the first time," Peter returned. "I was. But no longer. I'm through, I know who I am, and I can recognize your work as dealing in dirty, murderous affairs—which is something you can't see and ought to visit the police optometrist about."

Their glances clashed, slithered by each other like the foil blades of fencers. Peter stood erect now, tall, broad-shouldered, lean and rakish, his gray eyes cool and narrowed to alert, icy slits. They never faltered in meeting the giant's partly concealed, deeply lustrous pools of fierce light.

The masked man in dinner clothes grinned pleasantly.

"And so you do the story-book thing, take the noble path and give yourself up, eh?"

"That was a mistake. I want nothing more to do with the police."

"Quite sensible and correct. It was a mistake. One of several you made today, which, strangely enough, is fortunate for me. Had you kept your head, you could have been highly dangerous. As it is, you are now my guest. Or should I be frank and say prisoner? But now what will you do, Peter?"

If the man aimed to string him with his sardonic attitude, Peter was equally bent on disappointing him. No trace of emotion was reflected on his hard face. He was rapidly recovering his air of careless indifference, behind which lurked the dynamic power, the strength and alertness which were such an integral part of him.

"If you are sensible, Peter, you will do what your brother Ralph and your ex-fiancée are doing—working for me! I say ex-fiancée, because Diana Woodward is now engaged to your brother!"

The news came to Peter with the stunning anti-climax of a brutal uppercut to the jaw of an already sagging man. It was impossible. The whole day had been a hideous nightmare, and now this—

"You're lying," Peter said quietly, conquering the fury that swept through him as he stared at the smiling, giant devil before him. The Cowl shook his head and continued from behind his strange, silken mask.

"I'm not," he sighed. "It is most unfortunate that your memory had to return at this precise time. In a month or so I should not have cared, being in a position beyond all harm. Now, however, I must take you into consideration, especially with your splendid moral discernment between right and wrong."

"I won't work any longer with you," Peter stated icily. "I want nothing more to do with you. Haven't you made enough of a mess of my affairs?"

"Ah, but you see, you might create havoc now with mine! That, I consider, would be most unfortunate. I see you no longer understand me. I am the complete egoist. I put my comfort, my security and my safety before any other consideration, as is natural. But as far as having nothing more to do with me—do not fret yourself over it, Peter. I am most sorry, truly sorry, but you most certainly won't."

Turning abruptly to Shifty, the Cowl continued, with a swift change of manner: "All right, tie him up tight and throw him on the bed. We'll come back for him after dinner tonight."

Peter knew at last, and was strangely calm about it, the fate planned for him. The Cowl had just pronounced his personal death sentence on Peter Willard. They would come back, these men, sheltered by the dark of night. Together with Shifty, Trigger and Spinelli, he would be taken to some dark, isolated spot—

It was now or never.

Silently gathering his muscles, Peter sprang across the room like a long, lithe cat, full on the retreating man's back.

The masked man grunted and staggered. Peter whipped an arm about the gang leader's throat and wrenched, struggling to twist the huge man about so that his body would protect him from the fire of the others. Out of the corner of his eye, he saw Dalton jump to his feet in alarm, his hand darting to a bulging pocket. A gun appeared miraculously in his grip. Spinelli and Malone were scant seconds behind him in following his example.

"Don't shoot him here, you fools!" the Cowl gasped.

With the first fury of the assault spent, Peter slowly came to realize that the massive strength of this giant was too much for him, weakened as he was by the wound on his head and the subsequent slugging he had received. Slowly Peter felt his grip weakening, slipping, while his muscles stretched and cracked under the torture of his will to conquer.

Suddenly it was all over. With a quick movement the giant outwitted him, threw him off balance, and was free. Instantly Peter found himself covered by three relentless-looking muzzles.

"Don't shoot him now, Shifty," the Cowl said easily, straightening his rumpled coat and tie. His shirt front was crumpled beyond repair. "Tie him up, and make it tight. Tight, I said!"

With these words and a mocking bow, the Cowl was gone. Peter realized, despairingly, that he had failed even to dislodge the mask and catch a glimpse of the face of the man who had condemned him to death.

A few minutes later he was alone, trussed and gagged on the bed, watching the yellow light from the setting sun behind the Venetian blinds. His body throbbed and ached. He choked back a groan.

"So the whole insane thing ends like this," he thought.

Bitterness twisted his lips beneath the gag. He couldn't even die like a man, but had to go out as the Cowl's morons were disposed of—in the dark, in the night, without a chance. Throughout the whole day he had moved about at the will of the Cowl. If he ever got out of this scrape, he vowed there would be some fireworks on his own account.

Darkness choked the silent hotel room. At intervals Peter dozed, to awake with a start every time innocent footsteps sounded beyond the door. His legs and arms went numb with the tightness of the cords that bound him and no amount of struggle made any impression on Shifty's efficient work.

It happened on one of the occasions when he awoke, every nerve tingling, at the sound of feet moving nearby. Peter wrinkled his nostrils. There was a subtle trace of vaguely familiar perfume in the air. His mind snapped to attention. The picture in the Gramercy Park apartment, the girl of the photograph—again!

He was sure it was she. She was here in the dark room, cautiously moving toward him. For one long moment he held his breath, then expelled it through the gag in a long sigh of relief. Something was going to happen.

"Deuce!"

The whisper came out of the air nearby, and a soft scent came to his nostrils. A tingling of his body, from some sixth sense, told him that the girl was standing beside the bed, bending over him.

"Deuce, darling! Are you all right?"

Soft, cool fingers ran quickly over his face, found the taped gag over Peter's mouth and tenderly removed it.

"This is Phyllis, darling. Are you all right?"

"To date, yes," Peter said, gratefully wetting his lips. With the mention of the girl's first name, he found he knew her last. "You're Phyllis Gale?"

He regretted the utter blackness that made her invisible to him. A choked sob came out of the darkness. He felt the girl draw away from him.

She whispered: "Then it's true? You don't know or remember? You are really someone else? The Cowl said so, but I didn't believe—"

"Phyllis," he interrupted abruptly, "do you know who this masked man is?"

The answer was hesitant.

"Yes. So should you."

"Unfortunately, I can't remember. Who is he?"

"I—I'd better not tell you."

Peter sighed and decided not to press the question.

"It's quite true," he said, suddenly assuming an attitude of gay carelessness that he was far from feeling, "about my name. I am really Peter Willard, all right. Our little friend, the Cowl, knew it all along, and kept it a secret with which to tickle his fancy when alone with his villainous thoughts. But that is beside the point. The major question before the house is that of my immediate future—whether there is to be any or not."

Phyllis shuddered in the darkness.

"I know. I heard the Cowl say they were going to—to—"

"Bump off little Peter."

"They want to kill you, because you remember who you are! They mustn't! Oh, Deuce, they mustn't! That's why I'm here." Her sentences came in quick gasps. "I daren't set you free now—they would know. It must appear natural, as though you did it yourself. And I have a plan."

Peter's spirits soared, then dropped suddenly as on the melted wings of Icarus.

"You're in danger here, at this moment?"

"That doesn't matter, but I must hurry. Now listen carefully. They will take you through the lobby— This is the Gladmoore Hotel, on lower Broadway. Your only chance is to make a break for it while still in the hotel. Shifty will give you a gun."

"Dalton?" Peter's voice was frankly incredulous.

In the darkness the girl bit her lip. Peter could not see the tears in her eyes. She went on with a rush.

"Yes, Dalton. You've forgotten everything, haven't you, poor Deuce? The man is in love with me—in a way. Of course, I never—but anyway, he will do anything I ask of him."

"For a price?"

"Perhaps."

"Then tell him to keep his gun. Don't do it. From what I hear of you," he jested grimly in the darkness to the shadowy figure of the girl, "you're a pretty swell kid. But I'm not worth much just now, not two pins in a tailor's shop. Shifty is a hybrid, a cross between a gorilla and something lower, such as you crush underfoot. I couldn't accept your help under these conditions."

The girl's voice rose in pitch under the intensity of her emotion.

"But you must! This is ridiculous—I can keep Dalton at arm's length. Now listen and do what I say. I must leave you soon. Shortly after cutting your bonds, Shifty will hand you a gun, and you must pretend to use him as a shield to make your escape."

Peter surrendered to the girl's resolute insistence.

"Don't worry—I'll use him for more than a shield," he said tersely. "And I sincerely hope they have little respect for his carcass and plug him."

"Then you'll do it. At ten o'clock. It's nine-thirty now."

There came a breath of air as the girl got up to leave.

Peter called: "Phyllis, wait. You've forgotten several little items. First, I must see you tonight, after I get away. I only know what you look like from your photograph, you know. I may have known you for years—but I can't remember, of course."

Silence in the utter darkness. Phyllis pushed away an insistent memory of arms and an identical voice whispering softly to her. Then Peter felt the edge of the bed go down again as she seated herself.

"Very well. Be at the Gramercy Park apartment at midnight. Take a ride on the subway—anything—but steer clear of the Cowl's men, if you get away."

"I'll get away."

"And Peter—"

"Yes?"

A soft, cool hand brushed over his brow. The fingers trembled slightly as they touched his lips. He felt her bend over and kiss him. Soft, moist lips pressed fleetingly on his own.

"If I got along for three years without my mind," Peter said quietly, in answer to her silent wish, "I shall certainly be all right now. Don't worry about me. Now, blessed infant, be good and stick this mouth bandage on again, and we'll await the opening ceremonies."

There was a lilt to his pulse as the door closed noiselessly, and despite the inconvenience of the gag, his mouth curled into a twisted little smile as he composed himself to wait for thirty minutes to pass.

Chapter Five
DIANA AND ACTAEON

The ceremonies to which Peter referred were not long in coming. Again footsteps sounded in the corridor, halting outside the door. One by one, four men slipped into the room. The yellow electric bulb in the ceiling sprang into life.

Shifty Dalton glanced at Peter with apparent satisfaction and ripped the taped gag cruelly from his mouth.

"Still here, eh?" he asked, his lips twisting into a grin.

"Quite," Peter sighed. The ropes were slashed away from him, bringing quick pain in his ankles and wrists as circulation was restored. He examined the three other men, recognizing Trigger Malone as the man he would have most difficulty in overcoming. The remaining two were of a miscellaneous breed of gunmen; Trigger lacked both heart and brain.

Peter's face was calm as he examined his captors. Inside him was a tension of steel springs. Every muscle was a flame crying to burst into blazing action. Yet his hand, as he accepted a cigarette from Dalton, was as steady as if carved from a chunk of granite. He dared not consider the possibility of Dalton's failing to do his part.

"Now listen, mug," Dalton grunted. "We're taking you through the lobby, and we don't want any monkey business or you'll get it right there, right in the crowd. Unless you want some innocent people to get hurt, act naturally and walk ahead with me. Trigger, Batty and Jake will follow—covering you, see?"

"Very clever," Peter yawned in the gangster's face. "But I make no promises, wallflower."

Shifty's illy-proportioned features were stony and without expression under Peter's gray glance. They started down the corridor after Batty—with the gigantic ears—had placed a hat on Peter's head and concealed the ragged bandage on his scalp.

If the elevator operator thought it curious that five men should proceed in such dour silence, he thought better than to remark on it. They found the lobby only sparsely occupied, with small groups of guests scattered about the deeply carpeted floor. Feathery chills tingled up Peter's spine as he walked beside Shifty, chills springing from the knowledge that three relentless trigger fingers on as many weapons were pointed at him.

Quickly the four men and Peter marched across the open expanse. His heart sank. The door was but a dozen paces away, and Dalton had made no effort to hand him a weapon of any kind. Then—

"I hate to do this, mug," Shifty muttered.

Peter breathed a silent prayer of relief as Dalton lurched against him and something cold touched his palm. He did not need to glance down to see what it was. His finger curled about the trigger, and the little lines about the corners of his mouth grew deeper.

He glanced cautiously at Shifty, who had grown somewhat pale. Suddenly, with a deft movement, he gripped Dalton by the forearm and whirled the gunman off balance, thrusting him between his own body and the trio following.

"Hey! Hey, what—"

Trigger leaped forward, a pace ahead of his confederates, only to have Shifty's body catapulted into him. The two men staggered backward, obstructing the other pair of gunmen.

A woman screamed shrilly as she observed the blue-nosed automatic in Peter's hand. Several grim-looking men started from their deep lounge chairs, only to subside at a wave of Peter's gun. Trigger was quick to take advantage of Peter's momentary distraction. He whipped about, keeping his revolver in his pocket.

"Get that guy! He's the Deuce! Wanted by the police!"

Peter grinned and leaped for the door. A stranger loomed before him, scowling, and the full weight of Peter's body—from the knuckles of his hard fist through his muscular arm, shoulder, hip and thigh—landed on the deluded gentleman's jaw. He crashed down like a felled ox, and in a moment Peter was in the revolving door.

Crack!

Trigger fired blindly, and bullets starred the heavy plate glass. Then Peter was on the street, a cool night wind bringing him refreshing strength. He raced madly for the corner.

From somewhere came the shrill blast of a whistle. Another shot rang out, the heavy report of a bluecoat's pistol. Beneath the marquee of the hotel the baffled gunmen hesitated, staring after the vanishing figure of their escaped captive.

On the corner Peter halted abruptly as a patrolman pounded toward him. It would not do to be pulled in as a possible witness and then be recognized as the Deuce. The patrolman hailed him. Peter glanced quickly about and ducked across the street. A taxi cruised leisurely along the curb; with a desperate leap, Peter reached the running board.

"Central Park West!" he gasped to the phlegmatic cabby. "Westview Apartments—and step on it!"

It was the Cowl who, all unwittingly, had given him the idea. He had an hour and a half before meeting Phyllis Gale in the Gramercy Park apartment. In that time, he planned to do much. First to locate Diana Woodward. With her he would be safe, he could hide out until the first hue and cry was over.

He felt a sense of reckless power, now that he was free. A carefree smile touched his lips. In his eyes shone a light of coming battle, a glad anticipation of coming to grips with the enemy at last on equal terms. He was free now, free both from the unsympathetic forces of the law and the vengeful dangers of the Cowl.

Aside from his practical motives, he longed to see Diana, the girl whom he had intended to marry three years ago. Peter preferred not to believe the Cowl's bitter words. Diana couldn't be engaged to Ralph—unless, Peter thought with a shock, she believed him dead; or, worse still, knew his identity as the Deuce.

If the latter were true, he would soon straighten it out. Diana would believe and be eager to understand.

The elevator whined to a stop, and Peter stepped into the hushed luxuriousness of the corridor. He smiled as he thought of the numerous times he had trod this way to the door he had so often haunted. It seemed as though only a day had passed since he had last seen her.

A musical tinkle came from behind the ivory-colored door in answer to his pressure on the bell. A smile of anticipation was on his lean features as the door opened a trifle and a colored maid peeped out.

Peter laughed.

"Hello, there, Pauline! Is Di in?"

Pauline looked and gasped, her eyes wide with fright.

"Mister Peter! I—I thought you was—"

"Not quite," he said, and stepped into the familiar apartment. "Very much alive—but lucky to be so. I haven't much time, though, and I must see Diana. Is she in?"

"Yes, I am in."

Peter whirled, breathless, to drink in with thirsty eyes the vision of Diana Woodward. Yes, she had grown lovelier, even more beautiful. She stood staring at him, with shocked surprise in her dark, emerald eyes. She was dressed in a sheer evening gown and a light fur wrap, evidently prepared to go out. Her fingers trembled and touched her lips with a nervous gesture as she regarded her strange visitor.

With one stride the tall man was before her, his arms about her. He lifted her cameo-like face to his and drank in the fragrance of her raven hair. He pressed his lips tightly on hers.

Those red lips, so maddeningly attractive, were cold and unresponsive. Peter released her suddenly, feeling an intangible chill. He said, in a suddenly hoarse voice:

"Diana—it's I—Peter!"

Like a knife blade came the brittle response:

"Or the Deuce?"

Cold congealed within him. He searched deep in her wide eyes, but in their emerald depths he found no hint of the warm light that used to greet him so long ago. The atmosphere was charged with electricity. His lithe frame was suddenly straight and formal.

"Yes, I was the Deuce. But no longer! Darling Di, I am Peter Willard once more! You will listen, and you'll understand—"

"But I understand everything, Deuce."

Assailed with a sudden suspicion, he asked: "Have you seen me for the past three years?"

"No."

"Ah, then you don't understand! You don't know anything! I've been known as the Deuce, but I can explain. Please—you are going to listen to me!"

"Not necessarily."

Diana walked to a Chinese red stand and extracted a cigarette from a box.

"You see, I do understand, Peter. I was afraid you would come here; I should have expected it and made preparations."

"Preparations? Why? I don't know what you mean."

"I should have informed the police," she explained coldly.

Peter laughed uncertainly.

"I've been through hell today, Diana. I've been foolish, I suppose, imagining anyone could have faith in me. It's too much to ask point-blank. But if you'll let me tell you the circumstances—"

"I know all about it," she said impatiently. "Even your silly excuse. Amnesia, or something, wasn't it? You look perfectly normal to me."

Pins and needles rippled up Peter's spine. His eyes were bright with excitement as he gripped the girl's arm, not realizing he was hurting her.

"Of course I look normal! But how did you know about the amnesia? How could you possibly know? I awoke, in a manner of speaking, only this morning!"

"Please—you're hurting me!"

Peter released her. Waited.

"Ralph telephoned an hour ago and told me," she breathed.

"Ralph?" even more incredulously.

"We are engaged."

So the Cowl had spoken the truth! The tall man stood motionless in the center of the room, staring at the beautiful, cold girl before him.

"How could Ralph have told you? How could he know anything about me, that I came to my senses, when it was just this morning?"

"A friend told him of your silly story."

"Friend? You mean the Cowl? What is this man's name?"

"The Cowl's?"

"The greatest crook of them all!" Peter laughed harshly.

"I wouldn't tell you if I knew it—which I don't."

Again the refusal to divulge the masked man's identity!

"And you think my story's silly?" Peter went on. "You won't believe me? You won't listen to what I have to say in my own defense, Diana?"

"No." The tone was flat with finality.

"But I hoped—well, you know how I've always been mad about you, Di. I thought—"

"That's all over, long ago; I could not love the Deuce. I will not be mixed up in your affairs. Why did you come here?"

"I wanted to explain everything," he protested, bitterness making his voice harsh. "I thought that you, of all the people in this horrible, upside-down world, would believe me and trust me. I hoped to find a place of security from my enemies—"

"The police?" Diana inquired scornfully.

"And others."

"You'll find no hideout here, Peter! I've been too patient in speaking to you so long. I never thought you'd have the nerve to come and see me, after your notorious work. You've been associated with all manner of crimes; your alias has been a headline feature in the newspapers! I want nothing more to do with you. You must leave, and leave at once."

Peter shook his head and rested on the settee, making no move to get up. Diana—an utterly indifferent, cold and hostile Diana—walked to the telephone.

"I'll give you five minutes before I call the police and tell them the Deuce has appeared! You had better go at once."

Still Peter sat, stunned and unbelieving. Diana and Ralph! And Ralph must be mixed up with the Cowl. Yet Peter knew his brother as shallow and vapid, empty of all purpose and strength. How could it be? Was it possible for the Cowl to dupe Ralph into being his willing accomplice? And how much would Diana really know about it all? That explanation of her amazing knowledge concerning his amnesia sounded thin. Had she known who he was all these years, had she lent her assistance to making him the blind automaton, the Cowl's tool? And who and what was this Cowl, who had such long tentacles that he could ensnare in his underworld traps people of all walks of life, taint the very city air with his unseen, mysterious presence?

The dark-haired girl sat by the telephone, coldly watching him, while the frozen iciness inside him paralyzed him. As their eyes met, there was a desperate clash of wills, he striving to make her believe, she to be rid of him.

The doorbell rang.

The sound was like the smashing of a thousand glasses in that utterly silent, tense chamber. Pauline thrust her frightened face into the living room.

"A Mr. Arthur Chase, Miss Diana."

Diana Woodward straightened, and a curious, twisted smile touched her red lips.

"Will you go now, Peter?"

But he failed to connect the name with the little man who had spoken to him in Devrie-Carton's. He shook his head negatively. Diana shrugged and turned to the little colored maid.

"Show him in, at once."

To Peter's perplexity, her eyes reflected the triumphant smile on her ivory features. They narrowed suspiciously at the sight of Peter's apparent calmness, then—

"Mr. Chase! I was never so glad to see you! I've never been more terrified in my life!"

Peter stood up, suddenly startled by the artificiality of her tone. He towered over the short, pudgy investigator, whom he recognized, too late, as the man with whom he had conversed in Devrie-Carton's. Mr. Arthur Chase passed a plump white hand with tapering fingers over his bald head in a characteristic gesture, as though he were running his fingers through a shock of non-existent hair. He stared in astonishment at Peter.

"Dear me!" he said mildly. "The man all New York is looking for! The Deuce!"

Peter halted his spring for the door in mid-leap. Diana leaned against the ivory-colored panel, covering him with a tiny, pearl-handled revolver that, at pointblank range, was suicide to challenge. Turning, he saw to his dismay that the detective, too, had in his hand a much heavier, dull black repeater.

Peter shrugged and put up his hands.

Chapter Six
ENTER THE PRESS

The odor of anesthetics hung stickily in the overheated atmosphere of the room. The presence of tense waiting, of dread and anger permeated the thick velvet curtains and the dark, oak-panelled walls.

A swinging door opened suddenly to reveal the masked Cowl. The dark giant pealed surgical gloves from his bony, talon-like hands and tossed them with his white smock into a corner. The articles were smeared slightly with red.

The Cowl glanced carelessly at the waiting group that watched him. Tension in the air snapped as he said softly:

"Jake will live. That policeman's bullet hit nothing vital. But this is another score we must settle with the Deuce."

Shifty Dalton sighed audibly with relief, avoiding the grateful glance Phyllis Gale cast him from the lounge. Trigger Malone burst into voluble excuses, assisted by Batty, only to be cut short by a shrug from their leader.

"The reason he got away is obvious. He is far more clever and luckier than any of you!" The Cowl turned with fear-inspiring suddenness to Shifty. "Dalton, I wonder where Deuce got that gun?"

The monkey-like visage of the gangster was masklike. "I don't know, boss! He didn't have it on him when I searched. You were there—you saw for yourself."

"Then someone visited him while you were away," the Cowl mused aloud. "Very odd! If someone saw him alone, why didn't they release him then and there?"

A strained silence cloaked the room. Amusement tinged the Cowl's lips, and he glanced slowly from one to the other. He looked last at Phyllis.

"Peter Willard," he began, "is a menace to our safety. I think you all know and appreciate that. Twice he has gotten away from us today, and has already contacted the police. And all this happened while he was in a befogged condition, overwhelmed and bewildered by his sudden awakening. He grows infinitely more dangerous with each passing moment, as he comes to accept the situation he is in. How much of our plans he knows—how much he remembers— none of us can tell. But we must get rid of him! Trigger and Batty will stay here in New York and see that the job is done—right."

Phyllis plucked moodily at her glove.

"Is it necessary? I mean, that we get rid of him? I don't believe he would talk or remember your—"

"My what?"

"Your—our—plans."

The Cowl grunted and glanced at his watch. His eyes were invisible behind the strange black hood he wore to conceal his identity. "He may and he may not," he said. "But too much is at stake to risk the slightest chance of interference."

At that moment Spinelli came in, and the masked man turned to the slender, sallow gang leader—the nominal head of the crew.

"Did you get the tickets?"

"Sure."

The Cowl rubbed his long-fingered hands together with a dry, rasping sound. He shrugged into a light topcoat and reached for the door. Paused.

"Good!" His lean, saturnine smile took in the assembly. He continued abruptly: "Phyllis, you will go down to Little Swamp Island on Saturday. Trigger and Batty will stay here to get the Deuce. If Jake recovers sufficiently, he may follow you to Willard House. Close up the two apartments; we won't need them. Tomorrow wind up all affairs here and pack whatever you need. I, myself, am going tonight. That's all."

In another building, across the width of the city, three men were closeted in close conference. The room reflected the careless, haphazard character of its tenant, Larry Rorke. Cigarette stubs were scattered about with a let-them-fall-where-they-may attitude. A battered typewriter stood on an equally battered desk. It was essentially a man's room, one very much lived in.

Larry Rorke, crime reporter for the *Morning Star*, nervously walked the length of the smoke-hazed room and back. Tall, heavy, ruddy-faced, with red-gold hair, he reflected anxiety and perplexity in every movement. The second man, Arras Gordon, was shorter and somewhat stockier, with pale brown eyes that were almost yellow. Steel-rimmed spectacles perched primly on his narrow nose, and a scar disfigured the left side of his otherwise handsome features. He sat and stared into the fire that burned low on the hearth. The last member of the trio, in a hack driver's outfit, watched his two companions with bewilderment in his watery eyes.

Rorke said: "The Deuce is Peter Willard. There isn't any doubt about it. I'm as positive of that fact as I am that I stand here."

The other studied the glossy tips of his shoes.

"It is incredible."

"But true! Peter Willard was our friend, Arras. We know he is no criminal—the one I must picture for my sheet. There's no reason for it! He was comfortably fixed; newspaper work was more of a hobby with him than anything else. But something's horribly wrong somewhere, and it's up to us to find out what it is. That's why I 'phoned you to drop around."

"Yes?"

"You were with Peter the day he disappeared three years ago. He told you he was after Aces Spinelli for a story. Did he say anything else? It's damned curious, because Spinelli's gang is the one the Deuce stars in."

Gordon shrugged. "No, he said nothing. All this was gone over before! The police got nowhere in searching for Peter, and I confess that I, personally, had come to believe that Peter is dead. This identification of the, er—Deuce, was it?—is most disturbing. What makes you think Peter said any more to me about Spinelli?"

Larry Rorke thrust his hands deep in his pockets.

"You know Aces Spinelli?"

"I knew him before I stopped working."

Rorke laughed.

"Yes, you did come into money. I always forget you're a bloated plutocrat now, Arras. You never told me, by the way, your source of income. If it's a good racket, I'm curious to know about it, as an old friend."

"I blush to confess it's inherited," Gordon said snappishly. "But see here, Larry, you won't get anywhere questioning me, of all people. I—"

Rorke was no longer listening. He stood with his back to the fire and whistled an off-key tune. When he spoke, he had apparently gone off on a tangent.

"You know Baron von Tolz, don't you, Arras?"

"Rather well."

"He's angling to buy the old Willard House, isn't he, from Jed Willard?"

"I heard something about it. Why? I can't see what it has—"

"You can't see anything, Arras; you're astigmatic. Dollars to doughnuts—" He broke off suddenly. "Suspicion assails me! We all know someone with brains is behind Spinelli. Could Aces be tied up with Von Tolz?"

Gordon protested mildly: "You are growing fantastic, Rorke. Where is there the slightest connection between the baron and this Sicilian racketeer?"

"The Willards might prove a connecting link."

"The baron is above—"

"I know, I know," Rorke groaned. "My flights of imagination are on the wings of a bat! Still, Tolz is a well-known financier, isn't he? One of the biggest this side of Mars."

In the glow of the fire, Gordon's steel-rimmed spectacles gave off splinters of light. He said in his cold, precise, studied manner: "All this is not helping us locate Peter Willard. Have you had any practical ideas?"

Rorke, awaking to the presence of the taxi-driver, paid him off. The hack driver departed readily.

"All I've done," Rorke admitted, "is to tip off my cabby friends to be on the lookout for him. I can't make heads or tails out of the rotten business. The Deuce is Peter, and yet he isn't. He isn't true to character. What do you think of Peter—or the Deuce—voluntarily giving himself up to the police, and then having his friends shoot their way to free him again?"

"Did he do that?" Gordon asked in surprise.

"Early this afternoon."

"Perhaps those who got him out weren't his friends."

"Nonsense! They were members of Spinelli's gang."

"Perhaps," Gordon repeated, sighing heavily and adjusting his glasses, "perhaps Peter has broken away from Spinelli."

Larry stared, snapped his fingers exultantly.

"That'd explain it! But why? Why the sudden change? If only I could once find him! The fellow is as elusive as a greased pig!"

DEATH IN A LIGHTHOUSE 47

Gordon got out of the chair, some of Rorke's excitement at last communicating itself to his own stoic self.

"Did you try Diana Woodward's?" he asked.

"Not yet," said Larry, and reached for his hat. "I haven't seen that crooning lady for many a moon—but we're going to make up for it, right now!"

Back in the apartment of the radio singer, Arthur Chase said quietly: "You may put down your hands."

His deft fingers coursed rapidly over Peter's body and extracted the heavy weapon in his coat pocket—Dalton's gun.

"This is most fortunate, Mr. Willard," said the pink-faced little man. "You *are* Peter Willard, I presume?"

"He is," Diana interposed quickly.

Peter nodded, his eyes narrowed to glittering slits, sunk deep in his wan features. "You're from the police?" he asked.

"You may put it that way. Yes. Dear me, but this is a most astonishing piece of luck! Unprecedented! You are quite an elusive character, young man."

Chase beamed benignly, his pale blue eyes twinkling, as always, with hidden amusement. He turned to Diana.

"And you are Miss Woodward, I take it?"

Diana nodded.

"I intended to question you on the possible whereabouts of this man, in view of your former connection with him. However, that won't be necessary now. Luck! It's too good to be true!"

Keeping Peter covered, he fished in his bulging pockets and withdrew a dangling pair of handcuffs. "Sorry, young man, but I can't exactly trust you. You have a great many things to explain, including your incredible actions this morning in Carton's. These will have to go on."

Chase stepped closer to the tall, rakish man and extended the glittering steel chain. Peter's eyes became gray-blue chips of ice in an impassive face. His mind was a coolly clicking, analytical machine, weighing his chances. Then he struck out desperately.

With one arm he knocked up the weapon in the detective's hand, and with the other he seized Chase's shoulder. Spinning the detective around, as he had done with Shifty, he reached for and found the weapon in the investigator's hand.

It went off with a thunderous crash in the apartment, punctuated by a smaller bark as Diana, leaning against the door, fired blindly at Peter.

Something hit his shoulder like the flat side of board wielded with inhuman strength, and he went spinning to the floor, his grip on Chase partly broken. Instantly the detective crashed on top of him, pinning him to the carpet with unsuspected strength. But not again would Peter be overwhelmed as the Cowl had conquered him. The determination to remain free of both the law and the underworld made Peter forget the numbing pain of his shoulder and his weakened condition. He fought with desperate strength against the heavy weight of his opponent.

His hand was still on the gun, with Chase covering it. With a heave, Peter drew up his knees and planted them firmly in the detective's stomach. He kicked out powerfully. Chase grunted and fell sprawling backward. Instantly Peter was on his feet and lunging after him.

Chase recovered and swung expertly, but Peter took the blow, allowing it to glance off his cheek bone. He replied with a deliberate, smashing uppercut that left the outcome no longer in doubt. His bunched knuckles contacted the detective's jaw with a crisp, sharp crack. Chase fell over backward, crashed off the lounge, and lay still.

Peter breathed heavily. Picking up the revolver from the floor, he turned to face Diana, momentarily expecting another smashing, heartless shot.

None came.

He swore softly as he saw the inert figure of the radio singer on the floor by the door. Diana Woodward, after firing the shot that hit him, had fainted. He continued to swear, finding some relief in it. His eyes, in his battered, bloody features, were narrowed to thin, glittering slits. There were many things he wanted to tell Diana Woodward.

A groan from the lounge warned him that Chase might yet return to the picture. Quickly he gathered the slender woman in his arms and removed her to a chair. Then, without a backward glance at the shambles of that ivory-colored room, he flung open the door and raced like a fleeting shadow down the corridor.

He ignored the elevator, choosing the safe obscurity of the stairway.

A moment later he ran across the broad avenue. He leaped across a rickety trolley-car just as a window high up in the face of the towering apartment house shot up, and a faint, shrill whistle sounded in the night air.

Chapter Seven
THE GRAMERCY PARK APARTMENT

"It's no use," Arthur Chase said wearily, turning back into the apartment. "He's gone. Either lost himself in the park or boarded that trolley. Of all the fool chances to take!"

His eyes danced with little lights as he took in Diana's dishevelled appearance. "Dear me, what happened to you?"

"I fainted. After I shot him," she replied coldly. She reached for the small closet that sheltered variously shaped bottles. Glasses clinked. "Have a drink?"

"Thank you—I certainly need one. Not as young as I once was." Chase sipped appreciatively, his eyes never leaving Diana's. Finally he said: "I beg your pardon, but did I hear correctly? Did you say you shot at Peter Willard?"

"And hit him." Diana's short, nervous laugh was far from melodious. "Not too seriously, I'm afraid."

"But why shoot him?"

"Foolish question! He's a criminal, isn't he?"

"Ah—is he?"

Diana looked up, startled. Her rouge and lipstick stood out as scarlet blotches on her white skin. "You mean—Peter is *not* the Deuce?" she asked, and her husky voice that charmed millions of radio listeners trembled as she spoke.

Chase carefully punctured the end of a cigar.

"Oh, Peter is the Deuce, well enough. I simply asked if he is a criminal."

"Certainly you know the answer to that!"

"I wish I did," Chase said regretfully. "I should, but I don't." He leaned forward, tapping the girl unceremoniously on her knee. "It seems that I have my original task to do. I thought it was too easy. Luck! I never have any! But in any event, you are still here, and you can clear up several questions for me."

"Ask all you want. I'm quite willing to help you."

His voice was mildly reproachful. "You don't care much for Peter Willard, I gather."

"No."

"Well, why this change? You were engaged to him once—right?"

"Years ago," Diana murmured, shrugging her shapely shoulders. Her lowered emerald eyes reflected cynical distrust. "Times do change, you know."

"So they do," Chase agreed. He leaned back in his chair and thoughtfully examined the glass of amber liquid, turning it in his tapering fingers. "But you were engaged to be married, so you must have known Peter Willard quite well—I mean, his character, his temperament, personal habits—such things."

"I suppose I knew him better than anyone else."

"That's what I hoped, Miss Woodward. By the way," he changed the subject abruptly, "have you read this evening's papers?"

Diana shook her head negatively.

"Then tell me: is Peter the sort to become frightened just before a critical, decisive moment? Turn coward, we shall say, before a crisis?"

"No, decidedly not. He's quite stubborn and actually pig-headed at times. He possesses a great amount of determination, and if he once sets out upon a track, Peter will not turn back until the end is reached."

Mr. Arthur Chase leaned forward again. "Then do you believe that Peter, assuming that he is a criminal, became frightened just before a great and final coup and gave himself up to the police?"

"Peter wouldn't do such a thing. He'd see it through. I know he would."

"Ah!" Chase passed the palm of his plump hand over his bald pate. "But that is exactly what he didn't do! Today he walked into a precinct station and gave himself up as Peter Willard, alias the Deuce! Of course, if you read the newspapers, you would have known about it."

Diana sank back, biting her lip.

Chase sighed. "I wish I knew why he did it. Was it voluntary, was it against Spinelli's wishes? I wish I knew what happened after he got out, from the time he escaped to the time he came here. Did he finally break with Aces? Is his story true?"

"Are you asking me?" Diana asked, sarcasm curling her lips.

"No." Chase was abruptly curt. He emptied the glass and set it with meticulous care in the center of the tray. Reaching for his hat, he asked, "What was Peter talking about before I came?"

"He wanted me to hide him. He told me some impossible story of having just awakened—having suffered from loss of memory for three years. It was too ridiculous for words."

"He told the story to the attorney, too, who didn't believe him, either."

"Of course not. It's too fantastic!"

"Not so fantastic as some of the things that have happened lately. Not entirely, Miss Woodward. I believe it, myself."

In the silence that followed, Diana poured herself a second drink, then stood up.

"Do you think Peter will return?" Chase asked.

"No— At least, I hope not."

"I may find it necessary to question you again during the next week. Can I find you here again?"

"I'm afraid not. My fiancé—Ralph Willard, you know—invited me to Willard House in Jersey for the fortnight. I'm leaving tomorrow."

"How inconvenient," Arthur Chase murmured.

He shrugged, elaborately bowed himself out. On the stone steps leading to the pavement, he teetered for a moment, undecided. The night was unusually warm and pleasant. He decided on a walk through the park. His words, as they came on the night air, addressed to no one in particular, were:

"Perhaps it would do no harm to discover the railroad fare to Little Swamp Island...."

Five minutes later, the battered Ford roadster belonging to Larry Rorke pulled up, and as soon left. Its occupants remained as much at a loss as ever. No one answered the bell in Diana Woodward's apartment.

A crowded trolley-car was no place for a fugitive from justice, Peter soon decided. Curious glances, cast his way because of his desperate leap aboard, continued to linger in his direction. His haggard, wan face and disheveled clothing were to blame.

Apart from his appearance, there was his wounded shoulder to consider. He felt a warm trickle soaking into his shirt and, glancing down, saw the head of a tiny scarlet rivulet working down the palm of his hand.

Peter swung off at the next stop. Dodging his way through the stream of traffic, he engaged a vacant cab. Not until he was safely seated in the security of the rear cushions did he realize the extent of his weakness. The nervous energy that had kept him going throughout the day vanished like tense springs suddenly gone dead. He reflected that he had eaten nothing save a scanty breakfast many hours before. It was eleven-thirty now.

"Gramercy Park," he ordered the driver.

Silently Peter slipped into the apartment, shutting the door behind him with an imperceptible click. He froze in the darkness and listened. There was no sound. There was in the hushed air just the faintest trace of Phyllis' perfume, far weaker than it had been that morning—which seemed so long ago.

He whispered softly into the darkness: "Phyllis?"

There was no answer.

He held Chase's gun in readiness. Proceeding on cautious feet, he crossed into the dark bedroom. The apartment was unoccupied. Puzzled, he switched on the lights, tense and ready for the blaze of guns. Nothing happened.

Peter expelled a long breath. Picking up the girl's photo from the desk he stared at it for a long moment, but, try as he would, he could remember nothing. The picture tantalized him, with its whimsical smile playing about the soft little mouth. The flimsy frame came apart easily in his hands, and a moment later he put the picture away in his pocket.

His glance next fell upon a familiar envelope. He grinned as he opened it and found the roll of money he had discovered and left that morning. Four hundred dollars in tens and twenties. Peter removed the bills and put them in his wallet. They would be useful. He needed everything on which he could lay hands in his war against the Cowl.

Acting upon this drought, he made a further search, discovering a powerful flashlight. From the table near the bed he picked up an envelope. Before he could open it, the telephone shattered the silence with its shrill buzz. He stuffed the letter in his pocket. Cautiously he lifted the receiver and muffled his voice with a handkerchief.

"Peter?"

"Yes. Phyllis?"

"I can't make it, Peter. The Cowl—"

"Was there any trouble over my escape?"

"Not too much. But the Cowl is cleverer than he pretends to be."

"I know, Phyllis."

"Peter, there is some money on the desk. You'll need it. It's mine—"

"Yours?"

"Use it. I have plenty more."

"Thanks," Peter grinned. "I've already appropriated it."

"Peter—" There was a thoughtful pause, then: "I think something is going to happen which will vitally concern you. The Cowl made a few remarks that set me thinking. Listen—I may be out of the city for several days. If anything turns up, is there any place I can call you? You must not stay in the apartment—it's too dangerous."

Peter hesitated and glanced about the room. His gaze fell upon a newspaper, and he made a sudden decision.

"Call me at Larry Rorke's apartment," he said crisply. "He's a reporter on the *Morning Star.*"

"Can you trust him?"

"I must. But I want to see you. Where and when can I?"

"At the Grand Central—" There came a sudden silence. Then: "Tonight—"

The telephone was dead. Peter jiggled the hook, then gave up. Phyllis had been forced to cut the conversation short. But he had learned what he wanted to know.

His brow knit in puzzlement. Clearly the girl was hand in glove with the Cowl, yet her sympathy was with him, for she had helped him escape the Cowl's murderous hirelings.

Walking to the window, he stared moodily into the light-studded night. His glance fell downward to the street in time to observe a second taxi pull up behind his own waiting cab. He watched, almost expecting to see Phyllis, but was startled to see two men leap to the sidewalk.

One of them glanced up and waved wildly. Peter sprang back from the window and leaped for the light button, plunging the apartment into abrupt darkness.

Trigger Malone and Batty....

The elevator whined in the corridor. Peter was too late. Desperately he whipped back into the apartment, locked the door, and ran immediately to the bedroom window.

The room overlooked a narrow alley-way between the apartment house and the next building. A fire escape, perhaps ten feet from the window, was his avenue to safety. But first he had to reach it. Opening the window wide, he crawled out upon the sill, his feet reaching carefully for support. There was a decorative ledge about six inches wide running the length of the building. Peter stepped out on this, holding desperately to the window with one hand, and reaching for the next with the other.

Inside the apartment came battering at the door, then shouts. Silence, and the faint click of a key. Peter reached the fire escape and was down one flight before the open window was discovered. Batty's large-eared head was thrust into the night. Peter froze into the shadows.

"No one here. He didn't use the elevator, either. He must have taken the stairs," Peter heard the gangster say.

"I told you to stay down there and watch them!" Trigger snarled.

The head withdrew, and Peter was halfway down the second flight before he heard a triumphant shout above him. Batty had returned for a second look.

"There he is!"

There was nothing to do but run for it. Peter went down the treacherous steps three at a time, his long legs trembling and aching with the desire for rash speed. He wondered why they held their fire, and every muscle of his tired body was tensed for a stunning shock. The gangsters withdrew, however, after murmuring for a moment together. Peter reached the sidewalk. Here he found the explanation of Trigger's desire to take him without the use of firearms. The broad backs of two patrolmen loomed down the pavement, only a few yards from the alley entrance.

He dug a cigarette from his pocket and struck a match before the patrolmen saw him. To the unsuspecting observer, Peter was an ordinary pedestrian who had stepped into the shelter between the two buildings to keep his match aflame. The bluecoats were not suspicious.

Peter walked slowly across the sidewalk, inhaling deeply. Pausing by his taxi, he murmured to the waiting driver:

"Grand Central—and get around that corner before stepping on it!"

Chapter Eight
THE TERMINAL TRAP

The cab lurched, whined, and went roaring around the corner with utter disregard for safety and the New York traffic laws.

Peter settled back in his seat, sighed with relief, then sat bolt upright and stared back through the rear window at the ribbon of asphalt spinning out behind him. Pulling away from the curb was the second taxi, occupied by Trigger Malone and Batty. Peter swore softly and opened the slide behind the driver's seat.

"We're being followed," he said, annoyed. "You know what to do?"

The driver nodded and tucked the gum he chewed between his teeth. The taxi rocketed down a side street, missing a bus by a miracle. They roared down another street, then doubled back on their trail. At the intersection opposite City College, a red light forced them to halt.

Peter glanced back again. The pursuing taxi was drawing up beside them, its occupants leaning tensely forward.

"Never mind the lights!" Peter shouted. "Keep going!"

The driver, fortunately, was in his element. The taxi lurched again, careened across the thoroughfare and turned east. They screamed around another corner, then darted up a tiny street.

The lights snapped out.

Peter, watching in the rear, had the satisfaction of seeing his pursuers roar unsuspectingly past. "All clear," he said. "Now get to the terminal."

The motor raced, but the taxi did not move.

"Ain't it time," the driver said, without turning his head, "that you and me had a little talk? I'd like to know what all this skylarking is about. Who are those gorillas? They'd have given their eyeteeth for a popshot at you back in Gramercy."

Peter took several twenties from his wallet and asked quietly: "Does this answer your questions?"

The driver shook his head.

"Nope. I ain't risking my life and job for any dough, fella! Y'see, I know who you are, Deuce!"

A cold muzzle chilled the nape of the driver's neck. Turning his head cautiously, he stared into cold gray eyes in a grim, drawn face, supported by capably broad shoulders.

"You don't have to do that, fella!" he protested. "I'm with you, see? Only I got to know what I'm doing before I do it!"

"What do you mean—you're with me?"

"What I said. You're all right. I got the inside dope, but you're just an amateur at this stuff. Why do you want to go to the terminal? You'll never get out of town tonight. Every rodman and copper is keeping his eyes peeled for you!"

Peter lowered his gun. "I know it. I don't intend to leave town. I'm meeting somebody in the terminal. The money's yours, anyhow."

"Okay. I only wanted to see you don't get hurt."

Peter grinned at the strange cabby. The taxi was put quickly into reverse and backed into the main street. Despite the man's words, Peter took no chances of betrayal. He kept the gun pointed at the cabby's head and informed him of that fact.

A block away from the station, however, Peter's new-found ally paused in his gum chewing to say, without turning his head:

"Our little friends are playing follow-the-leader again. And they got reinforcements."

Peter turned and saw to his dismay not one, but two cabs following hard on his trail, maneuvering in a manner that left no doubt as to their purpose. A red light flashed against them, and this time it would have been utter folly to buck the heavy stream of cross-town traffic. Peter opened the door as the warning yellow light blinked.

"I'm getting out here. You drive around to the front of the station and wait for me there. I'll be back in fifteen minutes."

Few of the hurrying travelers paused to notice the tall man who entered the terminal with long strides and took up a position where he could see most of the main entrance. Leaning against a marble column, Peter examined the swiftly moving crowd. There was no sign of his pursuers—but neither could he find Phyllis.

He leaned against the smooth, cold marble for support, realizing how tired and exhausted he really was. His eyes smarted under the glare of lights, and his head throbbed with the roar of the station. He was uncomfortably close to the moment when he would have to stop his activities and rest—if he could.

The crush of humanity swirled about him unconcerned, not realizing that they passed within a few feet of the most notorious man of the day. Suddenly Peter straightened his lithe figure. To his nostrils came the familiar scent of perfume that was inescapably associated with Phyllis.

He turned, then shrank back, paler than before. Phyllis had passed close behind his back. But with her was another man, a stranger whose face he could not see. What was more important, three grim bodyguards trailed behind at a respectful distance!

Peter had not been discovered. Had they passed in front of him, Peter had little doubt but that he would not, at that moment, be left standing on his feet.

His brow knit in a frown. Why had Phyllis told him to come to the terminal if she was to be with Spinelli's hoods? And who was her escort, the tall, well-dressed man whose back was turned to him? Was he the Cowl?

A sudden commotion in the opposite direction attracted his attention. Through the jostling stream of people, Peter made out the broken-nosed Trigger Malone and Batty, waving frantically to catch the attention of the bodyguards. They caught sight of Peter and surged forward with a shout.

Then began a drama in that vast building, a desperate game of life and death with innocent travelers, ignorant of the vital play about them, as pawns.

The man with Phyllis turned and saw the two gunmen. Peter caught a vague glimpse of a darkly handsome, middle-aged face. He backed against the base of the column, his narrowed gray eyes darting in all directions. On one side were the two gunmen, rapidly threading through the crowd; on the opposite side was the stranger, with Phyllis and the three bodyguards, now all aware of his presence.

He caught sight of the girl's white, startled face and their glances met; reproving gray and frightened blue eyes clashed. Then Peter turned and moved toward the street doors. Before he had taken three steps, he doubled back. A score or more of plainclothesmen, recognized as such because they clustered about a bald, pink-faced little man, Arthur Chase, formed a cordon before the various street entrances. With Arthur Chase on the scene, Peter was trapped.

The only way out was toward the trains. With long strides Peter moved toward the gates. A small clearing gaped momentarily on the marble floor, and Trigger and Batty, not daring to open fire, broke into a run toward him.

The line of detectives drove forward, without arousing undue commotion but efficiently sifting through the unsuspecting crowd for the Deuce. Then one or two detectives caught sight of Trigger Malone and Batty, and surged toward them. Peter's racing thoughts grasped the fact that it was turning into a three-cornered struggle, and his only chance was to slip out between the two forces.

To his dismay, the gates were all closed by the alert station master. Peter ducked behind a column and took stock of the situation. Trigger and Batty had momentarily lost him, pausing on a low flight of steps and glancing anxiously about for him.

The crowd that streamed along the booths by the walls offered Peter his chance to escape. Gathering himself, he raced across the floor. Above the roar that filled the terminal he heard Phyllis scream, and he threw himself flat just in time to escape a singing bullet as Trigger, callously indifferent to the crowd, drew his weapon and fired.

The thugs were now uncertain, hesitating between him and the cordon of detectives. Peter got up, and this time reached a newspaper booth surrounded by perhaps a score of people.

They stared at him with frank curiosity.

"That was a nasty spill you took," an elderly gentleman observed. Peter realized that Trigger's shot had gone unnoticed in the multitude of sounds that bubbled in the terminal as in a giant cauldron.

He nodded absently to the old man and felt his wounded shoulder. The shock of hurling himself to the hard floor had started the wound bleeding again. He would have to get out of the station, quickly. He glanced about to find Phyllis, but she was gone, with the man who had been at her side.

The police had surrounded the embattled gangsters now, and Peter realized that Trigger and Batty would pay little attention to him from then on. It was his chance to slip off unobserved.

Peter, moving swiftly, clattered down the steps of a subway entrance. Carefully protecting his flaming shoulder, he made his way across the platform through the jostling crowd, and a moment later he was on the street, breathing the cool night air with gratitude and relief.

Now that the crisis was over, he suspected that the affair had been a well-laid trap for him. Although his heart struggled against the conviction of his suddenly crystal-clear mind, he reasoned that he had been tricked by the mysterious girl of the photo. In a flash of light, he believed that Phyllis might be acting for the police, for Arthur Chase, as a spy in the Cowl's camp.

So Phyllis, as a prospective ally in Peter's single-handed battle, proved an empty hope. For all practical purposes, Peter stood once again alone against the world....

His lungs suddenly ached for tobacco. He walked into a cigar store, conscious of a curious veil that was dropping like a curtain over his mind. Gratefully he lit a cigarette and stood on the pavement, inhaling deeply.

One against the world....

One against crime, with the law snapping at his heels....

"Hey, fella!"

Peter shook his head like a swimmer coming out of water. Someone was hailing him from across the street. The hack driver. Peter smiled wanly as he crossed the avenue. He had been wrong. The unknown cabby was his ally....

The driver helped him into the cab. For some reason, Peter's head felt curiously light and he swayed awkwardly on his feet, as though drunk. The street, he noticed, insisted upon a slow, exasperating revolution.

"Looks like little Peter comes to the fade-out," he whispered.

His last conscious picture was the face of the driver, staring at him with fright and alarm on his freckled features. Then the ground rushed up at an angle and, in spite of the vague feeling of two arms gripping and supporting him, Peter tumbled into darkness.

Chapter Nine
THE DEUCE COMES BACK

Rain beat a slashing tattoo against the window. Tobacco smoke hung fragrantly in the room. Peter sniffed, opened his eyes, and found himself in bed, clad in a crisp, cool pair of pyjamas.

There are some rooms in which the visitor is instantly made to feel at home, as though the cozy walls and furnishings themselves smiled a welcome. This was such a room. A vast sense of peace and security lapped about him in soothing waves.

After some minutes he sat up carefully, conquering a spasm of dizziness. He found his way to the bath, where he washed, shaved, and examined his appearance in the mirror. He was shocked at his pallor, but a careful removal of the stubble on his chin did much to improve his appearance.

Good old Larry Rorke ... The ragged bandage about his scalp was removed and replaced by a small, neat piece of surgical tape. His wounded shoulder, too, had received medical attention.

Vaguely Peter remembered the cabby helping him up the stairs. He smiled as he recalled Larry Rorke's open-mouthed amazement, the yelps of delight from the reporter. Rorke had guaranteed him safety, after Peter had babbled out the amazing story of the day's events. And with the help of Rorke's cab-driving friend, Peter had been put to bed, his wounds dressed, and Larry had gone out, saying: "God help my conscience—and my job, too, if the boss ever finds out I'm hiding the biggest story that's broken in the last ten moons! But since I can't turn traitor and refuse to bring in information, I'm going *out* to find what new clues there are in the terminal shooting!"

Peter shrugged into a gaudy dressing-gown as the door slammed and Rorke entered the flat, carrying in his arms a great paper bag full of food. His glance fell on Peter's hand, resting on the table within instant reach of his gun.

"Awake, Sleeping Beauty?" Larry grinned. He jerked his ruddy head toward the snubby automatic. "There's no need for concern, Peter. You're quite safe here, my prodigal friend."

"I may be an unmannerly guest," Peter returned, "but I can't help entertaining the sneaking suspicion that I'm the fatted calf, the great news scoop the *Star* is slavering for."

Larry Rorke clucked his tongue in despair.

"How cautious you've grown of late!" He poured scalding hot coffee. "You'll discover about seventy dollars missing from your little wad of cash. I used it to buy clothes for you, in the latest styles, which are something to cheer about, let me tell you."

"I can't help wondering why you're bothering about me."

Larry waved a disparaging hand and bit experimentally into a doughnut. Peter continued earnestly:

"You know I'm branded as a criminal. I'm the Deuce—there's no getting away from that! You know my situation better, perhaps, than myself, for you've been writing up my exploits for three years!"

"Criminal—my aunt Tillie, may the saints preserve her!" Rorke denied. He ate the doughnut and found it good. "But we'll save all that until Arras arrives."

"Gordon?"

The red-haired man nodded.

"None other. He helped me find you, with the aid of our good Thomas, the taxi-driving fiend. In payment for certain doctor bills and hush money to the landlady—she's certain you're a dissipated rummy—you're going to be guest of honor, speechmaker and toastmaster all in one at a grand powwow between just Arras, you and myself."

A new voice entered the conversation; crisp and methodical.

"Talking about me?"

Arras Gordon entered, shook hands with Peter. Taking off his raincoat, he seated himself carefully, so that the scarred side of his face was in the shadow.

"We both believe your story, Peter," he began. "You were more or less delirious when you told it to us last night, so it must be, all things being equal, more or less true."

"Sure!" Rorke added heartily.

Peter was not fully convinced. "Where's the girl's picture?" he demanded of Rorke. "It was in my coat pocket."

Rorke glanced at Peter's hard, lined face and handed Phyllis' photograph over without a word.

"She must be kept out of this," Peter insisted.

"Why? What else do you know about her that you haven't told us?" came from Gordon.

"Not a thing."

Larry interrupted dryly, stretching his legs: "I know a thing or three about the young lady. Show Arras the photo, Peter."

Gordon scanned the girl's picture thoughtfully. Larry asked casually: "Know her, Arras?"

"No."

Rorke's face betrayed his surprise. "Sure you don't? You're an intimate associate of her uncle."

Muscles twitched in Gordon's sharp features. He adjusted his glasses and moved uncomfortably.

"To whom are you referring?"

"I refer to your very good friend, Baron von Tolz."

Gordon laughed, a short, high-pitched bark. "I see what you mean. The picture does bear a resemblance, of course, but I would never identify this strange girl mixed up in Peter's affairs as the baron's niece."

Larry shrugged and tossed the photo back to Peter, who replaced it in his pocket.

"There's one other little item in your possession, Peter," the reporter drawled. "That's a letter, which I didn't open, out of respect for your beauty nap. Suppose you open it here, will you?"

Peter swore softly and got out the envelope he had picked up in the Gramercy Park apartment. With a disgusted exclamation at his own forgetfulness, he tore it open.

In the fading light, he saw it was a legal form for the transfer of the title of a house. It was not yet signed. The present owner was named Jed Willard; the prospective buyer of Willard house was written as Baron von Tolz!

"I think," Rorke grinned, "that proves our little female friend is connected with our Prussian nobleman."

Peter leaned back in the easy chair. In his mind the clues lay like a tangled skein, baffling his clumsy efforts to unravel the intricate knots. Gordon was gone, leaving only Larry staring into the dusk, chewing thoughtfully on a battered pipe.

"It's a cinch you daren't poke your nose out of this door," he muttered. "The town is alive with agents gunning for you—both the law's and the Cowl's. You wouldn't have lasted many more hours if Thomas hadn't picked you up."

Cursing softly, Rorke began pacing the room.

"The sum total of our knowledge is far from nil," he began hopefully. "We know a great many things, little things—but they don't make a coherent picture. I suspect many more things, but they must be proved. I *feel* still other clues, but they're no more than uneasy shadows, which even I can't crystallize into tangible suspicions. We know, however, that Gordon lied. He did recognize Phyllis as Baron von Tolz' niece. Why didn't he admit it?"

"Does it have any connection?" Peter wondered.

"I don't know. There isn't a particle of evidence connecting the baron with Spinelli's gang, except that letter you found. It was known that the baron is angling for your uncle to sell Willard house. But how did that title come to be in the Gramercy Park apartment? Phyllis Gale said it was her apartment, hence its presence can be traced to her, again leaving our nobleman with clean skirts—but implicating her as deeply as before. Can it be that her activities are unknown to her uncle?"

"That's hardly logical."

"Then we have the Cowl. Let's examine him, apart from the girl. Who the devil is he? You say he is tall, wears dinner clothes easily, has strong white teeth and a nasty grin. His voice changes—we cannot go by that. He must be one of those people who speak in a baritone one minute and reach lyric tenor the next. His eyes are dark, you say, yet that could be only the effect of the mask throwing them into deep shadow. Beyond this physical description we know nothing. We can guess he's accustomed to moving in society by his dinner clothes. Undoubtedly he's the brains behind Spinelli. The police know someone guides Aces along yet they can't put their finger on the masked man. He's far too clever for them."

Rorke sighed with regret. "It's too bad you broke with him immediately. You could have turned the trick by remaining in good standing in the Cowl's camp."

Peter shrugged.

"That morning I knew nothing. I didn't foresee all this—I didn't have time. And I can't go back now."

"No, the Cowl is out for your scalp. So are the police. They have a special cell in the Tombs quivering with the anticipation of receiving your carcass—"

The buzz of the telephone interrupted Rorke. He answered it and Peter heard the mechanical sound of a high-pitched, excited voice in the receiver. Larry straightened abruptly and glanced curiously at Peter.

"Who is it?" Peter asked.

Larry nodded to the photograph of Phyllis Gale. At once Peter was on his feet, moving to the telephone, but Rorke waved him back.

"Where are you?" he asked.

Peter strained his ears to catch the faint reply. "That makes no difference. I want to speak to Peter Willard."

"I'm Larry Rorke. It's quite all right to talk to me."

"Is Peter there?"

"No," Rorke answered curiously.

Peter heard the girl's voice ask anxiously: "Is he all right?"

"He's safe. Everything is all right."

"And he left word with you to receive my message?"

"Sure."

"Then tell him," the voice came, "that Jed Willard is going to be murdered!"

Several days after All Fools' Day, fate again chose to play with human souls—three people who were in the train that rumbled over the North Jersey flatlands. Three people who stared into the warm, sunny April morning and thought about each other, each unaware of the other's presence.

There was Phyllis Gale, with her small, piquant face, her challenging blue eyes and her halo of auburn, flame-like hair. Her thoughts ran a wild gamut of hope and despair. The necessity for action created a tension within her that transformed her nerves into white hot, vibrating wires. She was thinking of Peter Willard, the tall, crisp-spoken, slender young man with the figure and face of a reckless corsair—the Deuce. She was torn between hope and fear for him. She had seen him face his enemies with a cool, mocking smile on his lips, and she had seen him, head sunk on his shoulders, weary and staggering, a blind light of despair and defeat in his dazed, sightless eyes....

In the next coach was a little man with a bald head, a man who continually passed startlingly white hands over his hairless scalp: Arthur Chase. He did not know what he expected to find at the end of this journey. He only felt that the trail of the Spinelli gang, of Aces and the Deuce, topped by the genius known as the Cowl, led to lonely Willard House. His knowledge was incomplete, even sketchy, but he had in his grasp the ominous, sinister thread of hidden purpose woven into the amazing events of the past few days. And that thread-like maze led to Willard House.

If any of the somnolent travellers in the last car had cared to lift their respectable noses from their copies of the *Times,* they wouldn't have seen anything very startling; merely a man attired in a light gray suit, a man who stared somewhat sullenly at the green plush of the chair in front of him. The slouch felt hat that was pushed back on the man's dark hair revealed a brilliant piece of white that could only be a strip of court plaster on the man's scalp.

The Deuce (a title Aces Spinelli granted him after putting two holes in his body) could not be called handsome. Beneath the furrowed brows, deep-lined with the rakings of bitter thought, were two gray eyes, deep in luster, with the light of quick intelligence behind them. His mouth was firm, with little lines of humor about the corners—humor that now was rarely exercised. The lips were distorted almost into ugliness by the twisted, down-turned grimness that changed what might have been a pleasant mouth into a bitter, tight-lipped gash above a determined chin.

Whatever Peter Willard was thinking, it was not reflected on his lean features, unless it could be said that his thoughts were far from pleasant. His gray eyes were troubled, occasionally sparkling with intense anger while the lips were tucked in yet more tightly. There was about him now an aura of sheer despair and grim ruthlessness, a desperate determination that revealed the emotional tidal waves surging behind diose keen gray eyes.

Faces and names floated before his eyes: a dark face crowned with raven hair, red lips that curled in mockery behind a wisp of smoke that floated as a curtain between them. That was Diana. Another face, oval, piquant, with fright in the deep blue eyes—that was Phyllis. Most intense, however, was the face of a man whose nose was sharp and hooked, whose teeth were white and even, whose features were those of a bird of prey, vulturine, lusting, cruel and mocking. And that was the Cowl.

Peter drought soberly: "I am Peter Willard. I am also the Deuce. I have one job to do—and that is to get the Cowl."

With every revolution of clicking, rattling train wheels, the Deuce was going back....

Chapter Ten
MURDER IN PLAIN SIGHT

Sunlight smoldered down on the little fishing village of Rapahawney. Wavelets lapped about the barnacled piles of the dock and flickered incessantly, casting their glittering spears of light into the wind. A low drone of distant surf filled the heavy air, carried by a lazy shore breeze that was just enough to offset the unprecedented heat of the April sun. Sea gulls wheeled over the calm inlet, dipping every so often into the sea or skimming just over the crests of the swells. A heavy odor of fish hung in the atmosphere, mingling and battling with the invigorating smell of the sea.

The only human visible on the rickety wooden wharf was an aged negro, sitting slumped over, his bare feet dangling in the water and a battered straw hat protecting his woolly gray head. The negro watched a tall figure, minus coat and with rolled-up sleeves, who was engaged in untying the rope that held a trim white yawl to the pier.

The tall, broad-shouldered man leaped nimbly ashore and surveyed the craft with satisfaction.

"That should do it," murmured Peter Willard. "We'll take off for the house."

The negro blinked sleepy eyes at Peter.

"I still cain't believe I ain't dreamin' about you, Petey, boy. You come just like you was dropped from heaven, which is where I thought you was, an' no mistake!"

Peter laughed. His grimness left him, and his lean features became younger, pleasanter. He breathed deeply of the pungent air as his glance rested on his colored companion.

"It's I, all right. In the flesh, Joe."

He stared avidly across the vista of low marshland to the north, beyond the inlet. The only visible traces of human work were the slender, gossamer towers of a coast guard radio station, hazy in the distance.

"How's everything up there, Joe? All right?"

Joe Lemons opened his yellow eyes wide in amazement.

"H'ain't you been home yet, Petey?" He still clung to the name as though the man before him were a boy of twelve. Peter shook his head, and Joe Lemons made a clucking sound, pushing back his misshapen straw hat to scratch his woolly thatch of hair. "You sure oughta visit. You ain't been home for three years, boy! You oughta—"

Peter's features clouded.

"Joe, do you know where I've been?" he asked.

The negro stared at the glinting water and shrugged.

"I heard tales, Petey, boy. You know I don't believe 'em."

"Who told you these stories? Who was talking about me?"

"Nobody told me—but I couldn't help hearing old Jed and your good-for-nothing brother, Ralph."

The lines on Peter's face deepened, and his lips curved downward in a grim expression. So they knew what he had been and what he had done! But old Joe Lemons did not believe, and that was a ray of consolation.

"How's everybody at home?" he repeated.

"Reckon everybody's in good health, Petey, boy. Got a flock of guests up there now. I brought supplies over only yesterday evenin'."

"Who's there?"

"Your old girl friend, for one—Diana Woodward. Then they's the whole family—baby Jane came home from college for Easter, you know. Then a man with glasses and a scar on his face. Got yellowish eyes. Gordon's his name."

"Arras Gordon?" Peter asked, surprised.

"He's the friend of the foreigner—the man with the yacht. A baron, or something."

"That would be Baron von Tolz."

"Something like that, Petey, boy. Carries hisself like he was made of wood. All stiff-like," Joe Lemons confirmed.

The idea of many guests at Willard House was not startling to Peter. It increased the danger, he reflected, but it made the prospect of his sudden surprising appearance all the more enjoyable.

"Anybody else?" he asked.

"Doc Whitney and his wife. A bankin' man, or lawyer—a Mr. John Hark. That's all I know of, Petey."

Peter's gray eyes grew troubled as he reviewed the names. He thought: "Out of all that crowd, someone intends to murder Jed Willard—"

Aloud, he said: "Let's get going."

There was a few moments' delay while old Joe Lemons glanced shoreward and called Peter's attention to several low banks of clouds that massed over the horizon. Distant lightning flickered. An April thunderstorm, a shower.

"I'm going anyhow. It's only six miles."

The aged negro chuckled.

"Yassuh, Petey." He stepped into the stern of the vessel with amazing agility. "An' I'm a-goin' with you."

"And so am I," came another voice, new to the conversation.

Peter whirled and stared, angry, amazed and suddenly—for a brief moment—very happy. It was Phyllis.

She was dressed in white, her auburn hair glinting in the late morning sun, her deep blue eyes twinkling with her frank admiration of the man's appearance. At the sight of his startled face, she laughed.

"So this is how you look when you've had time to shave!"

Peter grinned. "You came down on the same train?"

"We do meet at the oddest places, don't we?" she nodded. "And yet I expected to see you here. You and trouble are synonymous."

Peter's face grew harsh in the brilliant sunlight.

"You couldn't very well expect me to stay away after your telephone call, could you? Not that I understand much of what this new affair's all about."

"You got enough out of it to be here, I see," she retorted. Biting her lip, she went on, "And before you drown me in questions, let me tell you all I know—and that is that Jed Willard is in great danger."

"From whom? And why? And how do you know about it?"

"I don't know anything for certain," she said with a pretty shrug of hopelessness. "I thought I knew who threatened your uncle, but something's turned up since then that's made me change my mind."

He remarked abruptly: "I'm not sure that this isn't another trap, like the Grand Central."

The girl was startled. Then she laughed again, and Peter had an uncomfortable feeling that her laughter was directed at him.

"You're too suspicious, Peter. You know, I'm getting quite used to calling you Peter! It's a much nicer name than the Deuce."

"I'm a much nicer person, too," he admitted with a trace of a smile.

"I'm sure you are. But you don't seriously imagine I deliberately led you to the station?"

"What else? What else is there for me to think?"

"I can explain it, and I will. But first let's get started for Willard House. I couldn't imagine how I was to get there."

She seemed poised, possessed, and completely sure of her position. Standing there on the dock, the girl appeared so fresh, so wholesome and radiant, that it was hard to connect her with the life of the Deuce. Peter suddenly wished that the girl were not mixed up in his affairs.

"I might have known," he said bitterly, "that, when there is going to be trouble, you would appear."

"And vice versa," she returned lightly.

She stepped carefully into the yawl and deposited a small black case in the cubby hole. She followed Peter's inquiring glance.

"It's a typewriter—a real one," she hastened to explain. "My uncle sent for me to do some stenographic work."

"Baron von Tolz, the Prussian?"

"Yes. You found out?"

Peter nodded, but his puzzled air remained in spite of her explanation. He was not surprised to find Larry Rorke's theory confirmed. Yet all the questions raised by the girl's identity remained. She mystified him completely. Why did she accept her duties with her nobleman uncle if Von Tolz was, as Rorke believed, the man in the mask—the Cowl? Or was the Prussian financier completely ignorant of the activities in which his American niece engaged?

"Better shove off, Peter," came from Joe Lemons. "Storm's comin' up fast."

Phyllis suddenly gasped and tugged at Peter's sleeve.

"Yes, hurry! I forgot—I was really so glad to see that you're all right, Peter—" her glance softened unaccountably—"that I quite forgot our train had another passenger for Rapahawney. A Mr. Arthur Chase. Perhaps you know him. If you do, it would be best to leave immediately."

Peter started, turned about to see a small, stout figure running in the distance, arms gesticulating wildly. He wasted no further time. Spinning the auxiliary motor, he nosed the yawl out slowly into the channel. Old Joe Lemons heaved on the rope and the sail rattled slowly up the mainmast, the breeze bellying out the canvas. The slender craft heeled over. Peter took his place at the tiller and navigated the craft expertly between the two sand bars that flanked the channel.

Thirty yards or more of rippling water was between them and Chase when the latter reached the spot where they had been standing. He shouted desperately to them, and when Peter's reply was a carefree, undignified thumbing of his nose, he drew a revolver from his pocket and waved it threateningly.

"Come back or I'll fire!"

"Keep the motor going, Joe," Peter said quietly to the wide-eyed negro. He indicated that Phyllis should take cover, at the same time crouching to make his body as small a target as possible.

The man on the dock, however, did not follow up his threat with action. Throwing up his hands in disgust, the detective wheeled and trotted out of sight.

Masses of clouds overhead continued to blot out the blue April sky. A low rumble of thunder echoed over the mainland. Lightning flickered. With a throbbing motor, a coast guard cutter, long and lean and gray, swept through the Rapahawney Channel and headed north, heeling after a tiny white sail far out to sea.

Rain spattered the deck suddenly with April's huge tears. Peter frowned at the lowering clouds and ordered Joe Lemons to haul in the sail and proceed under motor power.

Visibility was suddenly very poor, blotted out by driving curtains of rain, which swept the crests of the restless green sea. Despite Peter's objections, Joe Lemons took the wheel and Peter, with the girl, sat in the shelter of the cubby hole, comfortably protected by a heavy tarpaulin that they shared.

He examined Phyllis in curious silence for several long minutes, noting the character of her chin and the dreamy expression of her eyes as she stared out over tire rain-swept vista of the sea.

"Comfortable?" he murmured.

"Yes. Very."

"Then suppose you explain that little incident in the railroad station," he asked abruptly.

Phyllis laughed, her voice tinkling over the patter of the rain.

"It's really quite simple. You can't imagine, Peter, how horrified I was when I saw you there. When I telephoned, I intended to tell you that we should meet at the station on Saturday—today. Then I began to tell you that my uncle was leaving that night! I had to hang up suddenly because I suspected someone was listening."

The man nodded. He felt suddenly like a small boy who is being chided for unworthy thoughts.

"So you see," the girl concluded, "it wasn't entirely my fault. And when I saw you there, with Trigger and Batty coming for you, I—I—"

Tears were suddenly in her eyes as she turned a wan little smile toward him. There came a slapping of water as the yawl lurched dangerously, and Phyllis was thrown into his arms. He tightened them about her, and pressed his lips for a fleet moment on hers. In their eyes, for that brief space of time, there glowed a mutual happy understanding.

Willard House was a landmark of some note on the Jersey coast. It was situated in that barren stretch of marshland between the lusty, sprawling bathing resorts of the South Jersey shore and the thickly populated beaches frequented by the overheated populace of the New York metropolitan area. In this desolate section, stretching for miles on end, an empty, mournful waste of wind-rustled marsh grass and deep, silently flowing salt water creeks, stood the rambling stone mansion of the Willard family.

It was seven miles from the mainland. They were seven impassable miles of large and small flat islands, all covered with the coarse reeds that grew on land and in shallow water alike, so that, to the uninformed observer, it appeared as a vast, flat meadow or plain. To build a road over that area, or to have telephone wires strung up, was beyond even the purse of old Jed Willard—in the far-fetched event that he did wish to break the precious, aloof isolation of his house. The only means of communication with the outside world was by boat to Rapahawney, six miles south, or by means of a radio transmitter that had recently been installed.

As a landmark, Willard House was visible for miles because of the way it towered above the surrounding marshes and the heaving plain of ocean waters. Originally, more than half a century ago, there had been a lighthouse standing guard over the treacherous sea. Jetties had been built, sand artificially induced to pile up from the ocean bed, and there appeared out of the waste of dunes a sizable island, rising in safe security above the worst northeasterly storms the Atlantic could bring to bear upon it. The place was labelled with the rather unimaginative title of Little Swamp Island.

Old Jed Willard was a man with definitely fixed ideas of his own. He caused Willard House to be built on Little Swamp Island. He raised bulwarks against the sea, and then transported trees—not without great difficulty—and nourishing red earth from Pennsylvania. Out of the mournful, foam-lashed waste of swamp land he formed a sizable, tree-dotted lawn about the massive stone mansion. He invested money in engineers, who built a private beach on the seaward side of the island and equipped Willard House with a dock. They saw to it that Jed Willard got full value for his money when he bought two motor launches and installed the latest, most modern power plant for his isolated house. When it was completed, Jed Willard literally possessed a private world of his own, outfitted with the cleverest conveniences modern science could offer and—this was Jed Willard's primary object— far removed and free from the hubbub and more nerve-wracking aspects of civilized metropolitan centers.

By some wizardry all his own, the powerful, sixty-year old retired financier persuaded the government to allow the semi-demolished lighthouse nearby to stand. It was useless now as a guide to navigation, and was no more than a crumbling, moldy base perhaps seventy yards out to sea. Its sole use was as a picturesque object of scenery and a frequently used goal for the Willard swimming parties.

Shortly after noon, the last gray cloud rolled by overhead to expose the blue of the sky once more. The sun reappeared and shone down hotter than ever. The climb of the mercury was unprecedented, and threatened to break all temperature records for that date. It was an ideal day, as blonde-haired Jane Willard thought, for swimming. The sea sparkled, and the appearance of a white sail beating toward shore and the jagged light tower presented an altogether attractive picture.

Jane suggested the swimming race to the lighthouse and back. The party on the veranda of Willard House eagerly agreed, and it did not take long for the entire company to change into suits and race down the smooth, whitely glistening beach.

Mrs. Phoebe Willard, of course, mindful of her years and her figure, made her annual excuse of fear of rheumatism and remained on the veranda with the empty glasses of liquor that the party had put aside. She watched with twinkling eyes the smooth-limbed, slender figure of Jane with the dark, short Arras Gordon; she took in the tall physiques of the men, from Dr. Whitney with his handsome wife, Miriam, to gray-haired John Hark and the imposing, square-shouldered, ramrod posture of Baron von Tolz.

In a brief moment, all that could be seen of the group were their dark heads and flashing white arms as they beat their way to the somber lighthouse that pointed like a gaunt, jagged finger to the sky.

There were some who did not take the race seriously and lingered on the tiny beach surrounding the lighthouse to rest and regain their wind. Eventually, however, they came straggling out of the surf, laughing and exhausted and dripping wet, eager for the warmth contained in the Willard's well-stocked cabinets.

It was then that Jed Willard came out of the house, clad in his bathing suit. He was a man of sixty, with the physical build of a man only half his age. His face was lean and weather-beaten, his hair a snow white crest of dignity. He sported a closely trimmed white mustache over the tight-lipped, deep gash that was his mouth.

He glanced indulgently at the stragglers coming out of the sea, and his features relaxed as he waved in response to their gay gestures.

"Going swimming, Unks?" Jane bubbled, sprinkling cold water at him mischievously. "If you are, hurry and join us. We're having drinks, and the way we feel, there won't be a drop left for you unless you hurry!"

"Time me, baby Jane. I can still swim circles around you youngsters," Jed Willard said.

His lips smiled, but there was no corresponding light of humor in his eyes. Paradoxically, Jed's eyes remained utterly bleak.

He trotted down to the shore and plunged without hesitation into the cold ocean waters. The party stared after him for a moment, then turned to the warming drinks Jane handed out. Only Phoebe Willard kept her eyes on her husband. They were kindly, understanding eyes, but now there was added to their gentle expression a tired, troubled look....

She saw Jed Willard climb out upon the small lighthouse beach and make his way up the crumbling ruins. She remarked on it, and those on the veranda turned to observe their host. Jed Willard climbed to the topmost, jagged rocks and stood so for a moment. Facing the shore, he waved in a vague, jerky fashion to the party.

It happened, then....

Jed Willard toppled over, with a suddenness that was paralyzing. His body twisted and fell to the beach below.

"Oh!"

Phoebe Willard started from her chair, then collapsed and covered her face with her aged, veined hands.

"It's happened!" she moaned.

There was a brief moment of startled exclamations, then, following the fleet-footed, golden-limbed Jane, they streamed down the beach to begin a mad dash through the surf to the lighthouse.

Baron von Tolz kept his head.

"Someone go for a boat—not you, Dr. Whitney!" he called gutturally. "He's probably had a stroke of some sort!"

Arras Gordon swerved and ran toward the docks and the launches.

The occupants of the yawl evidently observed the incident, also. The craft changed its course and beat into the wind toward the tiny lighthouse beach. The swimmers reached their objective many minutes in advance, however, while Phoebe Willard stood in the surf, unmindful of the water swirling about her feet. Her face was white and suddenly very old.

Ralph Willard was in advance, with Jane and Dr. Whitney close behind. He stumbled over the jagged rocks toward the spot where Jed Willard lay. At the same moment, the yawl tacked about and a lithe, clean-cut figure dived into the water....

Those who thought Jed Willard had succumbed to an unexpected heart attack, due to the sudden strain of swimming, felt chilling tingles of apprehension as they caught sight of the body. It sprawled awkwardly, the arms outflung and one leg curiously bent under the other, as though broken.

When they lifted the heavy body, they saw the sands were stained a deep red. Doctor Whitney, with sure, deft fingers, stripped off the jersey and uncovered Jed Willard's chest.

Close to the heart was a deep, ugly-looking bullet hole.

Chapter Eleven
QUESTIONS AT WILLARD HOUSE

Dr. Whitney did not examine the body for more than a moment before he got to his feet, mechanically dusting the sand from his soaked flannels. His face was yellow in the sunlight.

"Jed Willard is dead," he announced briefly. His voice rasped.

There came a chorus of horrified gasps. Young Jane swayed forward and asked, unbelieving: "How could he be? How could it happen?"

"Not from any natural causes," Whitney replied grimly. "He has—been shot."

There on the jagged island, with the lighthouse pointing a desolate, accusing finger at the sky, the little party shrank together and stared in stupefied wonder. Again it was Jane who dared to voice the unspoken question that burned in everyone's mind.

"You mean—Unks committed suicide?"

The tall doctor was startled; his pale, sunken eyes were sullen as he replied to the girl's question.

"I couldn't say. Perhaps— At least I hope it was suicide."

"You hope—?"

"I mean your uncle may have been murdered!" Whitney snapped brutally.

Diana Woodward sighed and collapsed with a slight moan, and Ralph Willard clumsily tried to revive her. Dr. Whitney, avoiding Jane's stunned glance, stared at the white sands, a baffled, angry light in his pale eyes. John Hark turned his back quickly to the group, struggling to stifle an insane desire to laugh in the face of tragedy. The dark baron took Jane in his arms and rapidly whispered unheard words to her. Mrs. Whitney sobbed loudly, the mascara from her eyes—which she had made up on returning from the first swim—forming unsightly dark rivulets down her rouged cheeks.

"Who did it?" Jane whispered. "Somebody must have done it. Somebody had to do it. Unks had no reason, he hadn't any at all, to kill himself."

Baron von Tolz turned to the shore, where the swimmer from the yawl plunged through the shallow waters toward them. The entire party turned to stare with varied expressions of fear, or awe, or dull interest at the lithe, broad-shouldered man coming toward them.

"Perhaps this newcomer can explain," the baron suggested, with a hint of strange savagery in his voice.

The swimmer was Peter Willard. Had it been any one else, the emotions of the group would have gone their original way. As it was, this second shock served to counteract the horror of the body on the beach. It was Jane who first recognized the muscular figure and grim face as belonging to her brother.

"It's—it's Peter!" she whispered hoarsely, and there was awe and fright in her voice. "Oh, it's not true! I'm going mad!"

"It's I, Jane," Peter said quietly. Turning to the stiff baron, he said deliberately: "I seem to have come back too late."

"But I don't understand— If you mean about your uncle, yes. I was just telling Miss Jane that perhaps you had something to do with this ghastly affair!"

"You recognized me?" Peter asked sharply.

The nobleman smiled.

"Not I. How could I, my dear man? I've never seen you before. It was Jane who recognized you."

The girl flew suddenly to Peter and clung, trembling, to his dripping frame.

"You! Peter, I thought—we all thought— Where have you been, Peter? Where? Three years, and now you return—"

"I've come back at a strange moment."

"Indeed you have," said Dr. Whitney. "Your uncle Jed has just been murdered."

"Where have you been, Peter?" Jane insisted. "What have you been doing? Why didn't you write, or communicate? We thought—"

Peter shook his sister gently.

"It's not for me to answer those questions. Some time, I hope, they will be answered. But not now ..." he concluded, and stared with bitter gray eyes at the white-haired man on the sand.

It was fantastic, unreal, a fragment torn from the wildly fluttering pages of a nightmare. The party stood petrified, staring at each other, their senses unable to react to the swift turn of events. Only Diana and Ralph seemed oblivious to the prodigal's strange return at such a tragic moment. Mrs. Whitney, however, her cosmetic complexion hopelessly ruined, took a step forward as though in a trance and pointed a trembling, accusing finger at Peter.

"And this is what you came back for?" she shrilled, moving her head jerkily toward the recumbent body on the sand.

They followed her nod mechanically. A little sheet of water spread over the beach and lapped toward the corpse, with nature's total indifference to the death that possessed it. The party turned to see the launch ground slowly on the sands. Short, dark-haired Arras Gordon leaped out, hastily adjusting his steel-rimmed spectacles.

"What was the matter?" Then, seeing the body, "He's not dead, is he?"

Dr. Whitney nodded.

"Murdered," he amplified grimly.

His omission of the possibility of Jed Willard being a suicide echoed louder in the hushed air than his spoken word. Gordon stood still for a moment, then observed Peter Willard. He shook hands with him after an exclamation of surprise, being the only man there to acknowledge the nephew's presence in such a manner.

"The prodigal returns," he murmured in his New England accent. "What brings you here?"

"I'd rather not say anything just now."

Mrs. Whitney interrupted shrilly.

"No, you'd rather not talk now—you might give yourself away!"

Her husband was annoyed. "Will you stop being insane, Miriam? You're speaking very wildly."

"But he's guilty! Why should he return now, if not to kill his uncle, especially when we all know what he's been—"

Dr. Whitney slapped his wife cruelly across the mouth.

"Now will you be quiet!"

Miriam collapsed, stepping backward a few paces. She stared dumbly at the giant figure of the medical man. Her hand was across her swelling lips. A trickle of blood welled between her ringed fingers.

Whitney's face was even more sallow than before. He muttered: "I think we'd better get the body ashore."

Arras Gordon went off in search of John Hark, who had wandered off in the ruins of the lighthouse. Hark returned first, closely followed by his searcher. As though in a sun drenched nightmare, the men approached the body and lifted it—not without difficulty, for Jed Willard was a heavy man. Von Tolz stood near Peter and touched his shoulder.

"You'd better come with us."

Peter noticed that the man spoke with a guttural accent in these moments of excitement. He felt curiously disappointed. There were three men present, the baron, Hark, and Whitney, who possessed the towering height and build of the Cowl! But the baron's voice did not in the slightest resemble the cultivated, suave tones of the masked man, the object of Peter's vow of destruction.

There was something in the man's dark eyes as he stood beside him that irritated Peter.

Angrily he said: "You pretend to accuse me? You want to keep an eye on me?"

The Prussian was embarrassed. "I don't know, really, Mr. Willard.

Your return is at such a strange time, is it not?"

"So is your niece's—Miss Gale's," Peter snapped. "She was in the yawl with me."

The baron's stiffness dropped for a moment, and a startled expression of disappointment was clearly visible on his face.

"Phyllis?"

"And an old colored man," Peter continued. "Two people were with me at the time Jed Willard was killed. This is one crime that isn't going to be pinned on the Deuce, Baron von Tolz!"

The body was carefully brought ashore and transported to the rambling, tree-shaded mansion. Phoebe Willard accepted the news with strange resignation, and extended a casual greeting to Peter, as though he had been away three hours, not three years.

"The Lord giveth and the Lord taketh away," she murmured, and the quotation was startling, because Phoebe Willard pretended to be a modern woman, keeping abreast with an era that had little recourse to the consolation of religion.

Dr. Whitney vanished to concoct several prescriptions for Diana and Mrs. Willard. Jane bravely refused anything. The men raided the liquor cabinet and downed various ryes and brandies neat. Arras Gordon, alone, took nothing. He meticulously explained, adjusting his steel-rimmed spectacles, that he was a total abstainer.

"I think the first thing to do," he suggested, "is to get in touch with the proper authorities. We are alone here, and I need not emphasize the suspicion that secretly bothers us all. One of us here may be a murderer—"

"Nonsense!" Ralph exclaimed, fingering his mustache nervously. "Old Jed shot himself."

"Face the facts, man!" Gordon insisted. "There was no gun on the island, and your uncle wasn't shot from the sky! Someone on shore did it, and we're the only people for miles around. For the solution of this crime and the protection of all of us, we should waste no time in communication with the police."

"That immediate problem is taken away from us, I think," said Peter quietly, putting down his brandy.

He pointed out to sea. Everyone turned to observe the lean gray shape that plowed swiftly along the shore. It was a coast guard cutter. The vessel came in close to the beach and launched a boat. Its occupants consisted of a white-clad, pudgy person and two sailors. The tiny boat bobbed in the surf and skimmed the breakers to the beach. Strangely enough, the cutter moved off almost at once, swinging in a wide arc and disappearing toward the south from whence it came.

"You will find that the man in white is quite capable of handling any criminal activity he encounters," Peter said mirthlessly. "His name is Arthur Chase."

"Peter!" Phyllis began warningly. She plucked nervously at his sleeve, and he smiled reassuringly.

"I think that Mr. Chase will find our situation here much more interesting than me."

Jane drew Peter aside now. Her voice was low, almost a whisper. "Peter," she said with lowered eyes, "we haven't had a chance to verify certain things we heard of you, but even before you reply, I want you to know I believe you. If this man coming here is on your trail— He's a detective, isn't he?"

"He is."

"Then you're the man the newspapers call—the Deuce?"

"Incredible as it seems—I was."

A hurt, puzzled light entered his sister's blue eyes. Somehow she had hoped against hope that he would not answer that way. The man felt acutely miserable, feeling through all his bitterness that he had deserted her.

"I can explain it all, Jane, kid," he said quietly, squeezing her hand. "Meanwhile trust me, despite what's going to be said soon."

His sister nodded. They watched Mr. Chase's slow ascent of the sloping beach and tree-studded lawn, and at the last moment Peter stepped forward from the veranda and advanced to meet him.

There was a curious twinkle in Chase's pale blue eyes as he saw the tall man approach him. He cast a warning glance at the two sailors, who tensed visibly. Then he halted as Peter confronted him.

"You've come for me?"

Chase put his tongue in his cheek.

"No-o. Not exactly. But as long as you're here, I must—"

He dug in his pockets and extracted handcuffs. "You got away from these once, Deuce. This time, however—"

"One moment, Chase," Peter said earnestly. "Do you have any idea of what's happened here, not fifteen minutes ago?"

"It rained," said Chase dryly, and for once he was fated to be discomfited.

"Yes, it rained," Peter snapped bitterly, "rained death!"

Mr. Chase did not betray his startled surprise. Only his pale blue eyes became stony and wintry as he examined Peter.

"What have *you* done?"

Peter shrugged.

"I did nothing. I came too late."

"For what?"

"To prevent the murder of Jed Willard!"

For once Mr. Chase was capable only of, "Eh?"

"Jed Willard, my uncle, was murdered a few minutes before I landed on Little Swamp Island. I saw him die— So did everyone else."

"You mean he was murdered in plain sight? Before everybody? Where did this take place?"

Peter indicated the jagged finger of the lighthouse.

"Out there. Everybody saw him fall. When we got there, he was dead."

"How did he die?" The question came with explosive force.

"It looked to me like a rifle bullet."

Mr. Chase appeared suddenly to put on the brakes. A bland little smile spread across his features, and he spread white hands.

"You realize this fantastic story will take only a moment to check?"

"Of course! And I was about to suggest to you that you devote your time and effort to finding the murderer. I say murder, because the question of suicide is out. I happen to know that an attempt on my uncle's life was planned."

"Oh, you did? And where did you get that information?"

Peter shrugged and did not answer the question.

"The killer is someone in that group," he said quietly, indicating the curious people on the veranda.

Chase stepped quickly on the porch, followed by the two sailors. Dr. Whitney led him into the house, where he examined the body of Jed Willard. Chase stood motionless for a moment, lost in thought, and then turned to Peter. The handcuffs dangled from his fingers.

"It'll be several hours, young man, before the cutter returns. Unfortunately, it was called to aid a small vessel struck by lightning in the recent storm. If you give me your word, I'll not put on these awkward things, but will detail Randall here to watch you, and stay beside you in the meantime."

"Fair enough," Peter admitted. "I'm only interested in catching the murderer. My own fortunes depend a great deal on your success. You'd learn a great deal about other matters, and who is behind them."

Chase stared curiously at him. "You're quite right." He chewed his lower lip thoughtfully. "You'd better stay with me for the next few hours."

Peter grinned at what he thought was the detective's lack of trust in him. "I'm not running away, Chase," he said quietly.

"No, no—it's not that. But I imagine someone here is very much afraid of the Deuce—namely, you. Afraid of what that man knows—

and does not know," Chase said cryptically. "Having committed one murder, this person may not hesitate to commit another."

"I wish he would try," Peter smiled grimly. He laughed, a short barking laugh that boded no good for someone. "You're a strange man to be a detective."

Arthur Chase shrugged.

"There's more in this affair than meets the human eye," he misquoted.

More there was, indeed.

A strangely disquieting aspect soon disclosed itself to the twinkling eyes of the detective. He summoned all the inhabitants of Willard House, including Henry and Janet, the butler and maid. The only person absent was the hysterical wife of Dr. Whitney.

"We are faced with an unwelcome, unpleasant situation here," he addressed the assembled group. "It is by coincidence that I am present to take charge. I think no one will dispute my authority in this case. I'd like to suggest, first, that no one make any attempt to leave the island. The first thing to do, of course, is to communicate with the local authorities in Rapahawney, and through them to the county seat. I notice there is no telephone, but I do see radio antennae. Will you, Peter, please accompany me?"

Peter moved off, with Randall pacing sullenly at his side. He wondered about the conversation that would burst forth as soon as he was out of earshot. He had an unpleasant suspicion that it would center about himself.

The radio shack was in the rear of Willard House, and it was toward this that the three men made their way. The second sailor who had accompanied Chase remained on the lawn, leaning against a giant elm that still dripped with the rain from the recent downpour.

Within the interior of the wooden cabin, a single light burned, creating a dull yellow fog in the interior. The room was furnished with a single desk, the transmitting instruments, and several broken down chairs taken from the attic of Willard House. Chase glanced thoughtfully at the lighted electric bulb.

"Is this usually left burning during the day?" he inquired sharply.

"As far as I can remember, no," Peter replied. "It may be a new custom, however—I haven't been here for three years."

"It may be—but I doubt it. About the light, I mean."

The detective approached the transmitter and threw the switch. Nothing happened. Annoyed, he examined the mechanism.

"You make your own power here, don't you?" Chase asked.

"Yes, the motors are down in the basement. Why? Is anything out of order?"

"It doesn't seem to work," Chase replied, his voice curiously muffled. "It's very curious."

"What is?"

Chase straightened and dusted his hands. His eyes had lost the twinkle that habitually sparkled there.

"Isn't the radio usually kept in first-class order?"

"It was always kept in tiptop shape."

"Then it's doubly curious. There are two tubes recently taken from their places. Without them the transmitter is useless."

The two men, avowed enemies, stared at each other in the yellow light of the cabin, and shared a common apprehension.

"You mean they were deliberately taken out?" Peter asked.

"Just that— Perhaps by someone who wants to isolate Little Swamp Island for a time!"

"So much the better," Peter murmured, and smiled curiously.

Chapter Twelve
THE METHOD OF MURDER

Many things were whispered about Dr. Virgil James Whitney. In social circles, these things were told in strictest confidence, told almost invariably to shocked listeners and, as invariably, followed by glances of dismay and—rarely—pity in Miriam Whitney's direction. These same facts were known in other than social circles, where they were stated in a most matter-of-fact manner. They were written down for posterity in the neat reports in police headquarters, Spring Street, Manhattan.

This is not to say that the good doctor was a notorious criminal. But he had been a guest of the state for five years, and thus it was only natural that records should exist, and that gossip-mongers should exaggerate the stray tales they heard.

It was said that Dr. Whitney was a monster, a human fiend, in his treatment of his wife, Miriam; but there were no reports to that effect in Spring Street. It was whispered that he had never really received his medical diploma from Johns Hopkins University, that he practiced without a license; on these rumors, too, there were no reports in Spring Street. On the contrary, they had there a copy certifying Virgil James Whitney as a registered practitioner. He had his license, which had not been revoked by the police—merely suspended.

Nevertheless, the man had done penal service, and it came about in this manner: Dr. Whitney had been accused by a tragic-eyed husband of criminal medical practices, been found guilty, and sentenced to ten years, later reduced to five.

After leaving the gray institution on the Hudson, he lived an exemplary life. One of poverty, it is true, but he refrained from straying from the path of virtue. The desire for earthly comforts was strong within him, however, and when he met Miriam Bond, daughter of the Massachusetts Bonds, he saw and he conquered.

There were other reasons whispered why Miriam had married Dr. Whitney after a whirlwind courtship, but they need not be mentioned here—thus delivering a return slap to the gossip-mongers. It is acceptable that the daughter of the Massachusetts Bonds fell head over heels in love with the handsome, masterful doctor who was almost twice her age. For Dr. Whitney, although of humble origin, had acquired charm and polish and cultivation and, with his indomitable strength of mind, had easily made the flighty Miriam Bond his willing captive.

Having gained a firm foothold in the upper strata of society—for Miriam Whitney brought to her husband not only her heart but a goodish amount of money to boot—Dr. Virgil James Whitney gave up his medical practice, announcing to a relieved world (at least the police were relieved) that he was henceforth to be considered as retired, practicing only when emergency demanded his services.

Arthur Chase, with his remarkable memory for odd facts, had the whole of Dr. Whitney's record at his mental fingertips.

Clouds once again spread an ominous canopy over the island. Huge, warm raindrops came down in sheets out of leaden skies, to the accompanying cacophony of darkly muttering, crashing thunder, lurid lightning and pattering rain, mingling with the dull monotone of the storm-lashed surf.

Thunder pealed over the veranda, and the lightly clad party shivered. The screen door slammed, and Dr. Whitney appeared with his wife. Miriam had recovered from her hysterics sufficiently to use with skill the contents of many little boxes, so that now she looked her original, youthful, pale blonde self again.

"Fully recovered, I see," the dark Baron von Tolz commented, and carefully adjusted a monocle, the better to survey the doctor's wife. He held in his fingers a long Russian cigarette.

Dr. Whitney nodded his handsome head and glanced quickly at the hazy white faces on the dim porch.

"Where's the detective and Peter Willard?"

"I do hope he's taken him away," Miriam commented.

"Who?" asked the newly-arrived, auburn-haired Phyllis.

"Peter—the detective," Miriam said, not very clearly. She showed not a sign of embarrassment. "After all, he is dangerous; we must all know that. Isn't it obvious that he returned simply to—"

Phoebe Willard caught the woman's eye, and Miriam abruptly stopped talking.

"Why? Why should Peter want to kill Jed?" Ralph wanted to know, displaying an utter lack of tact.

"The will, you know!" Miriam rushed on, gaining confidence by avoiding Phoebe's eye. "When poor Jed learned of Peter's gangster life—we all know he's the man the papers call the Deuce—Jed became furious, which was the first time I knew the poor man to get into a temper. He immediately wished to change his will. That's why Mr. Hark is here, isn't that so?" She turned to the lawyer for confirmation. "To give him legal advice?"

Hark shrugged uncomfortably and twiddled the slender stem of a cocktail glass.

"Yes, that's it, he wished to speak to me about it. But I doubt if he'd cut Peter off, once his anger simmered down."

"Well, it's a motive, anyhow," Miriam Whitney said triumphantly. If she looked for applause from the weary, white faces about her, she was doomed to disappointment.

Phyllis spoke again, her voice brittle with antagonism.

"If you're trying to pin the guilt for this affair on Peter Willard, you're looking in the wrong direction. You forget, Mrs. Whitney, or perhaps you didn't know, that I and Joe Lemons were in the boat with him. We all saw Jed Willard fall from the tower and hit the beach."

"Of course! Of course!" Dr. Whitney hastened to say. He glanced venomously at his wife. "We know Peter couldn't have done it. And despite what that pudgy detective says, there isn't one of us who disliked Jed. Quite the contrary. Not one of us had the slightest shred of motive, and if we did, how was he killed, in plain sight of all of us? I confess that's what puzzles me more than all the other questions."

"That is what I now propose to find out," said Arthur Chase.

The detective sloshed up the veranda steps, with Peter and the sailor Randall close behind him. His white suit was soggy and dripping. He patted his round face with a damp handkerchief, staring into the hissing curtain of rain beyond the porch. Thunder cracked and lightning whipped in blinding, molten streams across the curtained background of scudding clouds.

"Dear me," he commented, "it's rained twice today, and at the most inconvenient times."

"These cyclonic storms," Whitney put in pedantically. "We get one side first and then the other. It may rain twice again today if the wind shifts and the thunderstorm returns. Fortunately, it isn't too raw for comfort."

Arthur Chase suddenly lost interest in the weather. He turned to the assembled group who sat about the veranda. John Hark's eyes blazed with a greenish light in the midday gloom. Dr. Whitney anxiously watched his wife, while Diana and Ralph whispered together in a corner. Phoebe Willard broke the awkward silence.

"Well, young man," she said abruptly—she called everyone young, although Chase was the oldest man present—"suppose we get on with all this foolery. What are you going to do?"

"Do? Dear me, I shall find your husband's murderer."

"But we do not know for certain that he was murdered."

"Perhaps not. But if he was, I repeat, I shall find his murderer."

"That you will not do," Phoebe Willard said firmly. "Not among us, at any rate. Not one of us could have had the slightest desire to murder Jed."

"It remains to be seen. Be that as it may," Chase said quaintly, his blue eyes dancing faster than ever, "here I am and here I start. Inasmuch as I am the only person present who is capable of dealing with this matter, I really think no one will object if I ask a few questions."

"In that case"—young Jane stepped forward—"I think you'd better have one of us speak for all. At the important times, we were all together."

"Indeed? That is going to make it more difficult— for me, I mean. You, Miss Jane, might as well be that spokesman. Do you think you could name these times you think were important?"

"Of course. First of all, we were all together, every single one of us, here on the porch—before Unks came downstairs. Either he slept late or he was working in his study on a real estate deal—" she glanced at the monocled baron—"but he came out here on the veranda too late to join us in our swim."

Chase nodded with interest.

"You all went for a swim?"

"Yes, we raced to the lighthouse and back."

"And what time was this?"

"Shortly after twelve. Perhaps twenty minutes after."

"Did Mrs. Willard accompany you?"

Phoebe Willard shook her head and Chase, with a little smile, returned to Jane.

"I want you to think carefully, Jane. Did anyone land on the lighthouse beach and fail to return for some time?"

"We all stopped breath, of course. And the men were left behind."

"Which men?"

"Baron von Tolz, Mr. Hark, Doc and Arras."

"Arras?"

"Mr. Gordon."

"Thank you. These men remained on the lighthouse while you and Miriam Whitney and Diana Woodward swam back?"

"Yes."

"What about Mr. Ralph Willard?"

"Oh, he came back with us—with Diana, rather. Oblivious to everything."

Ralph smiled nervously and smoothed his black mustache. His brother, the Deuce, remained inscrutable, sitting on the rail of the veranda.

"Now about these men," Arthur Chase pursued. "Why did all of you remain on the lighthouse?"

Von Tolz sighed with quick impatience and brushed Jane aside.

"Please let me tell this, Miss Willard. At this rate, it will take all day to unearth a few simple facts. The fact is, Mr. Chase, that we laughingly gave the girls several yards start, while we remained on the little beach. You forget that it was a race."

"Ah—that was it. But then what happened? Did everyone return to shore before Jed Willard appeared on the veranda?"

"Yes, we all returned before our host appeared."

"Who was the last to leave the lighthouse?"

Von Tolz hesitated.

"Why—I don't know. I didn't particularly notice. We all jumped in the surf at the same time, I imagine."

"Nonsense!" Dr. Whitney interrupted, and Chase smiled. "I started off several minutes after Gordon, and Hark was close behind me. You were the last person on the island, baron!"

Von Tolz appeared surprised.

"Was I?"

Arthur Chase passed his hand over his bald pate and pursed his lips. Miriam Whitney squirmed uncomfortably in her wicker chair.

"Aren't we wasting time, Mr. Detective?" she inquired, with a characteristic about-face of her opinions. "The murderer might have been an outsider, you know—if it was murder."

"It was murder, I'm sure. And no outsider did it. One of the persons present is the murderer."

Chase glanced at Peter, who nodded imperceptibly.

He went on: "I haven't really begun to—ah—waste time, as you describe it. If we aren't progressing by leaps and bounds, you must be patient. These things aren't exactly cross-word puzzles, and at least we've gotten off to a good start, whether that's apparent to you or not. But let me try another angle of the case. Someone said that Jed Willard was killed in plain sight. You all saw him fall. Is that true?"

"Yes," said John Hark quickly.

Von Tolz stared curiously at the attorney.

"I did not see you anywhere about after the swim," he said with careful emphasis. "Nor was Dr. Whitney on the veranda at the time Jed Willard fell."

Chase turned to Hark. The latter's eyes snapped with a green blaze of anger. His face was suddenly grayish-blue in the momentary glare of lightning.

"Evidently you are mistaken, Mr. Hark. It seems that you and Dr. Whitney were absent from the veranda at the time of the killing. Can you recall where you were?"

"I'm not sure where I went—probably in the house for a drink."

"Drink?" sneered the baron, and his dark features were twisted in an odd grin. He seemed to take delight in retaliating for his embarrassment regarding his lengthy stay on the lighthouse. "There was plenty to drink right here within reach of your arm!"

Hark's tongue flicked between his lips.

"But I didn't shoot him!" he said in a strange voice.

"Why not?" Chase asked naively.

"Why not?" the lawyer echoed. "Why should I? We were old friends. I don't recall what it was I went in the house for. Perhaps an aspirin."

"Did you hear the shot?"

"No, but Phoebe cried out, and I came outside at once. But I was too late to see Jed fall."

Chase sighed and turned to Whitney.

"And you? Where did you go, when you said you were standing on the porch and saw Jed Willard die?"

"Pardon me, but I said nothing of the kind. Neither did I authorize anyone to speak for me," was the curt reply. "I was in my room, changing from my bathing suit into my slacks, as you can plainly see. I came down in time to join the dash for the lighthouse."

Dr. Whitney spoke the truth, for he was clad in wet flannels and a yellow polo shirt, through which the muscles of his large frame bulged and rippled.

Henry, the butler, appeared on the veranda to announce that luncheon was ready. Phoebe Willard impatiently waved him away. Chase, searching for a cigar, was quickly offered one by Von Tolz—from Jed Willard's humidor.

"We have three alternative directions from which Jed Willard may have been shot," Chase summarized between violent puffs on the cigar. "He may have been shot from Peter's yawl, but the three people on her alibi one another. He may have been shot from land, in which case the only logical suspects are Whitney, Hark, and Henry—or someone as yet unknown. The third direction—"

He paused.

"Yes?" asked the baron.

"The third direction is from the lighthouse itself."

"Ah—but it was deserted!" Ralph Willard protested.

"Yes, so it would seem. But Dr. Whitney, from your examination of the bullet wound, what is it that suggests itself to your mind?"

"I've found the bullet. It entered the left side and pierced the aorta, causing internal hemorrhage and instant death. The bullet appears to have travelled with terrific force. It was from a light rifle, a .32- calibre, I should say, although I am no authority on ballistics. I know little about such things."

"Enough to be very helpful, doctor. You say the bullet appears to have had a great deal of force. That would suggest a rifle nearby, the bullet having been fired at close range."

Baron von Tolz twirled his monocle carelessly.

"Are you trying to say that Willard was killed by someone on the lighthouse?"

Arthur Chase smiled.

"Not necessarily. But by a rifle fired *from* the lighthouse. Suppose we go out there and take a look around. The ladies need not accompany us."

The launch nosed through driving curtains of rain into the channel of Little Swamp Creek and passed the white-hulled yacht of Baron von Tolz. Heads appeared over the rail of the pleasure vessel, startling Peter. Arthur Chase, too, noticed the yacht's crew.

He said, turning to the baron: "You neglected to tell us of your men aboard the *Junker*. Why didn't you tell us of them?"

Von Tolz was surprised.

"I never gave it a thought. These men have never been here before. There are five of them, and they could have no connection with Jed Willard. I insisted they remain aboard when I realized that Willard House could not comfortably accommodate them all."

"Of course," Chase nodded. He glanced up at the low-flying shreds of torn clouds and said: "Rain's going to stop soon."

Then his gaze dropped to the radio antennae of the *Junker* as they slipped past.

"You have a radio, baron?"

"It's out of order," Von Tolz replied laconically. "And I have no radio man to repair it. I had to hug the coast coming down here."

Presently the lighthouse loomed over the glistening mahogany prow of the launch. The metal-edged bow ran softly into the thick sand, and the party of men leaped onto the wet beach, their slickers and raincoats shining in the rain. Above them towered the round base of the antiquated, semi-demolished building that thrust up into the gray mists.

"Be careful," Peter warned. "Concrete's slippery now."

Chase led the way in clambering over the rocks, and stood at last on the ledge where Jed Willard had died not two hours before. The detective turned to the baron, rain streaming into his face.

"You saw Jed Willard fall?" he inquired, his voice high above the rush of the storm.

"Yes. I was on the veranda with the ladies."

"Show me, as nearly as you can ascertain, the way he stood and the direction he fell."

The baron hesitated, then shrugged his shoulders, massive and square in his trench coat.

"No, I can't be sure. I would rather not show you; I might be wrong. I don't want to mislead you."

"I saw it," Ralph interrupted quickly. "I saw it very clearly."

As Ralph took his place on the ledge, Peter glanced with calculating eyes at Hark, Whitney, and the suave baron. In his narrowed gray eyes was a cold light that boded no good for the murderer of Jed Willard.

Ralph decided on his position on the ledge and turned toward the shore. Willard House was only a vague blur through the driving sheets of rain.

"He turned and waved, like this. Then he—"

"He faced the shore?"

"Yes. He waved, and the next moment fell to the right and over the ledge—on to the sand down there."

Chase walked to the edge of the shattered section of cement and stared moodily at the tiny beach ten feet down. Then he turned to his left and examined the round brick wall of the lighthouse. A little window was in direct line with Ralph's position.

"Dear me, this is easy," he said.

He started across the concrete, then paused and stared down at a jagged block of stone. It had clearly been recently displaced, and had occupied a delicately balanced position between a huge crack. It was overturned now. Chase, examining the spot, stooped and picked up a shred of strong twine.

"Flotsam," he murmured, and put the string in his pocket.

Peering into the narrow window, he poked his head into the musty, dank interior of the lighthouse. There was no wall on the opposite side, the bricks having crumbled and fallen away. Sighing, he walked carefully around the base of the breakwater and examined the jagged bulwark. Peter, closely following the round figure of the detective, noticed with growing excitement that he could look through the window in the opposite side and obtain a clear view of the ledge on which Jed Willard had stood.

"He was shot in the left side," he murmured to Chase.

The detective nodded.

"From this spot," Peter added. "But there was no one on the lighthouse!"

Chase dropped to his knees to examine the wet concrete. His glance passed over two holes in the stone about an inch in diameter, now filled with water, and fell upon a long, ragged scratch that gleamed whitely new in the wash of rain. He walked to the edge, following the scratch, and stared down. Deep green water, spurted by hard-driven raindrops, swirled about the base of the rocky island.

"It seems," he murmured, "that it wasn't necessary for the killer to be present in this unpleasant place. He was far too clever. He forgot to alibi the men who paused here, or else he failed to take into consideration the possibility of a swimming party. As a result, everyone is under suspicion, and that is most unfortunate—for the murderer."

"What are you talking about?" Whitney demanded, looking out of the rain.

"I mean I know how this particular murder was committed," was the calm reply. "For it's murder, and premeditated, at that. Because no one was alibied on their stay here on the island this morning, suspicion centered on this place and we were sufficiently puzzled to examine it, instead of assuming the shot was fired from land. Because of that, I can say—with pardonable pride—that I know the method by which Jed Willard was murdered…"

Chapter Thirteen
INTRODUCING—THE COWL

It was close to three o'clock in the afternoon. The rain had stopped, the clouds rolled aside, and the sun shone forth with increased brilliance. Hot sunlight beat down on the beach. Spears of light glinted off the smoothly galloping crests of waves as they rolled to a thundering climax on the white, glistening sands. Shoreward, over the stretch of lush green marsh, the sun hung low in a fiery, splendid court.

Peter sat in the shelter of a sand dune that was like a wave arrested in sudden flight. He bit moodily on his pipe stem, and his gray eyes scanned the limitless horizon to the east. A few yards to the rear was the ever-present Randall.

Over and over again Peter thought of only one name—the Cowl. The name was a synonym for murder, lust, robbery and dope peddling, for murder and petty racketeering. The sinister figure loomed over the stage, and from his nimble fingers dropped strings by which he moved his puppets, controlling the dark movements of the underworld. And for three years he, Peter Willard, had been one of those puppets.

Now he was searching for the Cowl, desperate retribution visible in the cold, clear eyes. Enemy of the Cowl and the police alike, he sat on the beach and pondered on the events that had occurred this day. The boat in Rapahawney and Phyllis—Phyllis with her soft, moist clinging lips. Then the death of Jed Willard, and the three men, Von Tolz, Dr. Whitney, and John Hark, any one of whom could be the Cowl. Arthur Chase seemed to know how the murder had been committed. Peter, turning over the evidence uncovered by the little bald man, also thought he knew.

There was also the matter of the radio transmitter. Someone had destroyed the two tubes, isolating the island from the rest of the world. What sinister purpose was behind this move, what fate was to befall the unknowing guests in Willard House? It made him uneasy, made him feel more acutely the loneliness of the island and the sinister force that enveloped it.

There was his own personal situation recalled to him as he glanced at Randall. Should Chase capture the Cowl, it would not affect Peter's immediate future. He was the Deuce, the nominal henchman of the Cowl, and Chase knew it. He thought of the waiting handcuffs in the detective's pocket and bit harder on the pipe stem.

Bare arms slipped around his shoulders and neck.

He turned and found Diana Woodward, clad in a dry bathing suit that did ample justice to her perfectly proportioned figure. She sat down beside him on the hot sand and slipped her arm through his, clinging tightly.

"Peter—I'm afraid," her voice drifted to him.

His eyes remained fixed on an imaginary spot far out on the heaving green sea.

"Of what?" he asked.

"The murderer, of course. Something dreadful is going to happen, something's going to happen to us all. Did you know the radio has been tampered with?"

"I knew. But how did you learn?"

"It doesn't matter how I learned. But it frightens me, Peter. What does it mean? I'm frightened, I tell you! Peter, please look at me."

He turned slowly and examined the girl's oval features. There could be no doubt about it. Diana's lips were pale, and in her clear, emerald eyes was a strange, clouded look. He thought of the bullet she had fired at him when he grappled with Arthur Chase in her apartment, and he touched his shoulder. Diana drew in her breath as though in sudden pain.

"I'm so terribly, terribly sorry, Peter. Nothing I can say will undo the wrong I've done you, I know. And you were right. I should have helped you when you came to me that night. You were alone against the world, and I turned you down. I can't excuse myself, except to say that all I knew was that you were the Deuce. But I do know you couldn't have done that awful thing this morning! It was someone else, and I'm afraid of what that person may do next."

"To you?" bluntly.

"To all of us. I can't help feeling that way. I look at Dr. Whitney—he has a police record, did you know that?—and at that lawyer Hark, and at Baron von Tolz, who was my very dear friend. And I shiver. I keep asking silently, when I look at each one, 'Are you the murderer?'"

"There's Ralph," Peter suggested slowly, "your fiancé. Why not talk to him about it? I'm worse than useless here. When the cutter returns, I shall be taken away with it."

Diana was silent for a moment.

"You're different, Peter. You're honest, and trustworthy, and really true. What you've done in the past was no fault of the real you. I don't pretend to understand what you've been or done, but I know the real Peter Willard. You're strong, darling—and Ralph is such a weakling. He's completely under—well, he has ideas that worry me. He's in danger, too."

"So you want me to play the guardian angel to him?" Peter asked bitterly, and his bitterness was not ill-founded, for once he had loved Diana, and once she had whispered she loved him. But that was long ago, before the days of the Deuce and the Cowl.

"You want me to protect him, is that it?" he repeated.

"And me, Peter."

"To whom have you been talking?" he demanded suspiciously. "You've changed your opinion of me in rather a short time."

"It's Mr. Chase. If anything should happen, can I depend on you? For the sake of all that's been between us? Because I'm really frightened, Peter."

He got slowly to his feet.

"Of course," he said.

Her arms were suddenly entwined about his neck. Her lips pressed tightly on his. He did not respond to the embrace. He felt he could not stir to the old mad longing that once would have possessed him. He felt only that he was being watched by reproving eyes....

Diana sank back, smiling slightly, a golden glow in her strange emerald eyes.

"Thank you, Peter," she said.

Peter turned on his heel in the soft yielding sand and walked over the dune. Randall immediately got to his feet and plodded after him. Two people were making their way through the tall, coarse reeds toward him. One was the slender Jane, her bright blonde head haloed with the setting rays of the ominous red sun. Beside her, short and solemnly clad, was Arras Gordon, his steel-rimmed spectacles reflecting the spears of sunlight as little, flashing splinters.

Together they walked toward Willard House.

Presently Peter wanted to know: "How did you find out that I was the Deuce?"

"Unks got a New York letter," Jane explained, "inclosing a photo of you in the papers—as the Deuce. We all recognized you, and oh, he was furious. Poor Unks adored you. He worried himself sick for three years wondering what had happened to you. When he finally became convinced that you were the Deuce, he intended to change his will— that's why Mr. Hark is here, to assist him. That's why, too, Miriam Whitney said those impossible, awful things, accusing you."

There was a moment's silence, and then Jane asked abruptly: "Peter, who do you think killed Unks?"

Her brother shrugged.

"Better refer that question to Chase—he knows all the answers. You see, the same person who killed old Jed is the one who made me the

Deuce. The murderer won't rest until he gets me, I suppose, because I may be able to identify him eventually—"

Young Jane was suddenly interested in the lines in her brother's face. Her fingers touched them lightly.

"Poor, poor Peter. You'll get out of it all in good shape. Arras here has been talking about a really good lawyer. He says you've got an excellent case, if the murderer of Unks is caught and can be made to talk—"

"If," Peter said bitterly. "But it all depends on a little man named Arthur Chase."

The short, stout little man named Arthur Chase was certainly doing his best. His pale blue eyes danced with interest as he looked at Phoebe Willard. He drew his chair up quite close to her, his white hands patting his bald scalp and then dropping to his rounded knees. He glanced at the remainder of the company grouped about him on the lawn and smiled benignly, his smooth, round face pink in the setting sun.

"You see, I make no effort to hide my knowledge from any of you. It makes no difference, as I see it, whether the murderer knows he's going to be caught or not. Dear me, he cannot very well get away from here, trapped as we all are. His very escape would fasten the guilt on him without question. So he must remain and watch me move steadily and relentlessly to point the finger of guilt at his black heart."

"Very poetic," Phoebe Willard sniffed with a twist of her dry, cracked lips. She had regained her poise in the hours that had passed and, save for the whiteness of her skin, she appeared normal. "And the very essence of conceit, too," she went on. "You think you know who killed my husband, and how he was killed"

"I only know how he was killed," Chase sighed. "The motive, alas, escapes me. That's why I'm questioning you."

"How can I help you?"

"Are you sure you know nothing, Mrs. Willard, that might throw light on this unfortunate affair?"

"If I did, don't you think I'd be only too glad to tell you?"

"But you were heard to cry out, on seeing your husband fall from the lighthouse, 'It's happened!'"

"Did I?"

"You did. Baron von Tolz, Miss Woodward, and the others confirmed it. I want to know why you said just those words. It strikes me that you expected the death of your husband."

Phoebe Willard stared vacantly into space.

"Expected? No—no! But I feared it."

"Ah!" Arthur Chase leaned back in the wicker chair with a satisfied sigh. "Now we're getting somewhere! Why did you fear it?"

Phoebe Willard pursed her cracked lips.

"I won't say."

"Why not?"

"It involves others who have suffered enough."

"Peter?"

"I won't say."

Chase looked speculatively at a soggy cigar, then glanced about at the silent, tense group. The baron offered him a cigar, which he accepted with evident preference to his own. He did not light it, however, but chewed moodily on the fragrant tobacco leaf.

"It does concern Peter," he said firmly. "Now I want you to listen to me, Mrs. Willard. I shouldn't say this, but I'm for this nephew of yours—outside my line of duty. My job, however, demands that I put him aboard the coast guard cutter when it comes back here—and it's overdue now. Peter's greatest defense would be the capture of the man who killed your husband. It doesn't sound as though it made much sense, but it does. Mrs. Willard, it does indeed. I ask you to trust me, to tell me why you said what you did when you saw your husband killed."

Phoebe Willard hesitated, then shrugged.

"I'll tell you. Jed feared a reprisal. He knew something about a man."

"What man?"

"I do not know. He would not tell me—or did not have the opportunity to do so privately. This man claimed he knew all about the activities my nephew Peter engaged in. Whether he threatened Jed with this knowledge or not, I do not know, but my husband in turn unearthed some damaging information about this man. Jed threatened to use this information, unless this man absolved Peter from all guilt—but that he evidently could not do. However, they decided to meet and come to terms."

"How do you know that?"

"While you men were away on Lighthouse Island, I went up to my husband's room. I found this note there, crumpled up in the wastebasket."

She brought to light a scrap of notepaper. Arthur Chase took it up eagerly.

He read aloud:

"'Meet me on the lighthouse after the rest have gone. Will come to terms over P. W. Also over your information concerning myself—the Cowl.'"

Chase smiled broadly and tucked the scrap of paper in his pocket.

"This," he said, "fits in very nicely!"

Chapter Fourteen
ARTHUR CHASE SUMMARIZES

Putting two and two together and making four is not at all a simple and easy thing to do. Arthur Chase, however, never gave the high command in Spring Street cause to scowl.

"The trail," he said, more to himself than to the group of people watching him with fearful eyes, "leads back once more to Lighthouse Island."

He glanced across the sun-smeared lawn and saw Dr. Whitney approaching across the newly sprouting grass. Chase got up and intercepted the medical man before he could join the party.

"I'd like to ask you some questions, in private, if you don't object," said Chase mildly, smiling up at the man, who stood a full head taller than himself.

"Are we going to exchange personal secrets?" the doctor demanded with irony. "Are you abandoning your laudable method of keeping everything open and aboveboard?"

"Yes, I think I must. You see, I'm so close to putting the bracelets on the guilty man that I would hate to convince him that I really know what I'm talking about. Once he gets that notion, I'm afraid my life won't be worth very much."

Whitney shrugged, strolled off to secure some drinks, and the two men seated themselves at a table on the shaded side of the veranda. The detective noticed that Whitney's features betrayed signs that the doctor was close to the point of exhaustion. An unhealthy, yellowish pallor was apparent under his skin.

"I'd like to prod your memory a bit," Chase began, putting aside the Scotch and lighting the baron's cigar. "I am dependent on you for the last link in my chain of evidence. The chances are fifty-fifty that you can answer my questions."

"You interest me strangely," Whitney replied with dry humor. "I had no idea I could further the cause of justice in any way."

Chase, in view of the other's past history, ignored what he suspected to be subtle irony. He leaned forward in the wicker chair.

"Suppose you recall the landing on Lighthouse Island. Not the first, mind you, when you were racing the women. I mean the second landing, the tragic one, when you all swam out to recover Jed Willard's body."

Whitney sighed.

"Recall it? I wish I could forget it."

"I want to know what each man present did."

"That's rather a tall order for me," the doctor returned, pursing his thin lips. "You see, I was busy attending to Jed all the time."

Chase nodded serenely.

"Precisely. That's why I question you, doctor, in preference to the others. Your movements are known and verified by everybody. But how about the others? Let's begin with Ralph Willard, the young man with the mustache. What did he do?"

Whitney frowned. "I believe the Woodward girl fainted. He took care of her."

Chase nodded again. "And Hark?"

"I know—he climbed up the lighthouse to see what Phoebe was doing. Said he was worried about her. Gordon had to go after him when we shoved off in the launch."

Chase sank back suddenly in the chair, pouting ludicrously. Then he leaned forward again.

"Now this is important," he said quietly. "What did Baron von Tolz do?"

"Von Tolz? Why, he was with me—almost all the time, helping me and soothing young Jane. He never left the beach for a single moment!"

"Double damnation—" Arthur Chase sighed.

Whitney laughed, a strange tone of exultant triumph in his voice.

"Did your carefully constructed theory go to smash, professor?" he chuckled.

Chase stared with abrupt suddenness at the doctor. In his blue eyes was the dawn of a light of understanding and reconstruction. His pink face opened into a complacent smile, and Whitney thought that, if Arthur Chase dared, he would have licked his chops.

"No, the theory isn't smashed," Chase said, smiling still more broadly. "It's just elaborated slightly, so to speak. You see, doctor, I was looking for one murderer. That was my mistake. I think it took two men to kill Jed Willard!"

"Two murderers?" Whitney asked.

Chase smiled indulgently, his features once again pink and smooth and clear of worry. He stared into the amber depths of his glass for a long moment before replying.

"Two men, Dr. Whitney. I think I'll tell you about it. Shut in as we are on this island, the murderer—or murderers—have free play, so to speak. If I'm the only person who knows they're guilty, they will not hesitate to—ah—bump me, as these people say. So I think I'll tell you all about it."

"It will be interesting, I'm sure," Whitney observed. He noticed two people approaching over the lawn. "But it seems as though we're going to have visitors. Young Peter Willard and the baron's niece—what's her name?"

"Phyllis Gale."

"If you don't mind, Chase, could you tip me off as to what lies behind that young man's brow? Who is he? What's he done?"

"He's the Deuce—although I don't know why. Sooner or later he's going to have a long talk with me, and then things will be a lot clearer than they are now. But it's the girl who interests me at present."

"What about her?"

"She's just the person I want to see," Arthur Chase murmured. "I may—ah—have to bully her a little. In that case, doctor, don't let your chivalrous instincts rise to the point of interfering."

Whitney's sallow cheeks flushed, as though he had been slapped. He should never have struck Miriam, he thought, in front of all these fools.

As Peter and Phyllis drew up chairs, Chase took a scrap of paper from his pocket and tapped his fingers on it.

"It's your turn to answer some questions, Phyllis, my dear," he smiled. "Then you can all listen to what I have to say. If four know the solution, then we'll all be safe."

"You know who did it?" Peter asked quickly. "You know who's the Cowl?"

"Phyllis is going to tell me."

"I?" asked, the girl.

"I refer to the note signed by that man. I want you to look at it."

The auburn-haired girl took it, after looking hesitantly at Peter. She glanced it over casually and returned it to the detective.

"It seems to supply a motive, doesn't it?"

"It certainly does. But is that all it suggests to you?"

"That's all. Why should it mean anything more?"

"Because you recognize the handwriting!" Chase snapped.

"What nonsense! I do not!"

"But you do! You've been familiar with this script ever since you came from the West Coast, haven't you?"

"No!"

Peter turned anxious eyes to Phyllis. "It would make things a lot easier if you'd talk."

She opened her red mouth, glanced at the three men in wonder mingled with fear, and shuddered.

"I don't know anything!" she said desperately.

"That message was written by your uncle," Peter hazarded. "Baron von Tolz, otherwise known as the Cowl!"

Another shudder wracked the girl.

"I—I don't know," she whispered. "He may be the Cowl, but I'm not sure. I'm not sure of anything any more! The whole world is upside down for me. Baron von Tolz may be the man you want, Mr. Chase, but you must understand this: he did not kill Jed Willard! He may be the Cowl, he may be guilty of any number of terrible things, but he didn't kill Jed Willard, I'm sure."

"Perhaps you'll change your mind about your uncle's implication in this tragic affair," Chase broke in. "Mind you, I did not say he is the murderer. I said 'implication.' Oh, I grant you his was not the finger that pulled the trigger of that missing rifle! No one present on the island pulled the trigger—but someone *caused* it to go off!"

"I don't understand—"

"I think you do. You could clear up many things—your relationship with the baron, for instance. We know he's a Prussian, a nobleman, a wealthy financier who came to America after the war. He is European through and through, while you, Miss Gale—if I may so compliment you—are a typical American girl."

"Nevertheless, he is my uncle. My mother was his sister, and she married a Californian—a tourist. My mother died when I was a very little girl, and my father rarely spoke of our aristocratic relations. He despised all attempts to separate people into castes and classes. I only knew of Baron von Tolz vaguely until he wrote to me to come to him. Since I had no living relation in the world, I wasted no time, I assure you, in coming east."

Dr. Whitney interrupted.

"All this is over my head. Just who is this Cowl person, and is he or is he not our baron in question?"

Chase replied earnestly; beneath his soft tones there was an undercurrent of restless pursuit.

"The Cowl is a man I'm going to get if it costs me my life. He is the biggest menace to law-abiding society we've known."

Arthur Chase turned to the auburn-haired girl. Her face was white, and when the stout little man indicated the note Phoebe Willard had discovered, her eyes were wide with newly discovered horrors.

"For the last time, Miss Gale: do you recognize this writing?"

The girl nodded. Her voice was a barely audible whisper above the distant song of the surf.

"Yes—it is the baron's...."

Arthur Chase nodded.

"Of course it is." He returned to Dr. Whitney. "We know a great deal about Baron von Tolz. We know, for instance, that the German government was milked of millions by this nobleman during the war. Von Tolz, as owner of a huge munitions and chemical works, had a death grip on his government, and commanded his own prices during the war. He came through that conflict with a fortune of millions, but, with the establishment of the Republic, he was formally charged with fraud and barely escaped the country. His is not a pretty record. What interests us in Spring Street is the fact that, according to all reports, the Prussian government confiscated all his vast fortune, and he fled his native land in a state of poverty. Yet today, here in the United States, he is a figure of commanding wealth, a well known financier and manipulator of the Stock Exchange, a figure of power in society and the banking world."

"And this man is the Cowl?" Whitney asked.

"He wrote that note," Chase shrugged. "And signed it with the Cowl's name."

Peter's face was suddenly not a pleasant sight. Arthur Chase, seeing him start up, checked him.

"And where are you going?"

"I'm going to see the baron."

"Not so soon. Sit here for a while," Chase suggested with a tone of authority.

"But I'll kill him, whether it happens sooner or later!"

"Let the state take care of the Cowl. Anyway, we know nothing for certain as yet."

"I can choke the truth out of him!"

"Not if I put handcuffs on you, Deuce!" Chase snapped, regretting the necessity for showing his teeth.

Whitney smoothed over the situation by putting a question to the detective.

"I still want to know how Jed Willard was killed, if it's not an official secret," he grinned sarcastically.

Chase nodded, sighing as a somewhat sullen Peter took his seat once again on the rail of the veranda.

"Let's reconstruct the crime by going back to the motives. We all know that Peter has been mixed up with the underworld for three years, during which time those who knew him came to believe that he was dead. That belief persisted until a note came by mail to Jed Willard enclosing a news clipping and a photo of Peter—labelled as the Deuce, the notorious gunman!

"Well, that wasn't pleasant. Naturally, Jed Willard was outraged. Suspecting some plot, he set about unearthing some facts in the life of the man who gave him this news of Peter. He found something vitally incriminating and made a proposition to this man. If he found Peter and cleared him of all guilt, restored him to his home, he would forget all he knew about the letter-writer.

"But the man in question knew he couldn't clear Peter of guilt, because he himself had led Peter into crime. Moreover, he was already suffering in the talons of one blackmailer at that very moment, and he was determined not to have the added burden of Jed Willard's knowledge on his mind. He decided, therefore, to kill Jed Willard. But the second unknown man, the blackmailer of the letter-writer, also entered into it. His safety was likewise endangered by Jed's knowledge. So the blackmailer joined forces with his previous victim and plotted the death of Jed Willard. All this, of course, is theory, based upon a few scraps of evidence I've had the fortune to pick up.

"We now come to the method of the crime, and that was very clever, indeed. Had I not been on hand, someone on shore would have been suspected, the shot would undoubtedly have been thought to have been fired from land, and there it would all go—into oblivion. Fortunately, I discovered, with Peter, some obviously new scratches on the opposite side of the lighthouse. I also found two shallow holes drilled in the concrete. I found a piece of twine and an overturned rock. Now as I see it, the murderers devised a mounting for a light calibre rifle, with a trigger attachment to the rock and twine. When Willard, on his way to meet the Cowl, stepped on that rock, as the murderers knew he must, it overturned, pulled on the twine and the rifle went off. The recoil was sufficient to throw the weapon through the guides and over the edge of the breakwater into the sea. All that was left to be disposed of was the mounting—and that was the work of a very few moments.

"Now this is the point where I'm stopped. Whereas the note luring Jed Willard to Lighthouse Island was written by Von Tolz, the baron at no time had an opportunity to remove that mounting! According to Dr. Whitney's testimony, he was with him at all times while removing the body!"

Chase paused, obviously enjoying the dramatic effect of his words on his listeners. Peter immediately grasped the situation.

"As I understand it, Chase, Baron von Tolz lured Jed to his death, but another man removed the mounting of the rifle. And the man who removed it is the Cowl's blackmailer. Is that correct?"

"That's what I think."

"Then what men had an opportunity to remove that mounting while everyone went to get Jed's body?"

"There were two men who were absent for a short time, according to the doctor. One was Arras Gordon; the other John Hark."

"Hark!"

"And Arras Gordon."

Peter said quickly: "Arras is out of it. I know. Hark is the man we want—and the baron, of course."

"You're rushing ahead too fast. We don't know which man it is. There are some questions I'd like to ask you about Gordon."

Phyllis put her hand to her brow and said wearily: "I think it's time I do some more talking, don't you? After all, my uncle is certainly mixed up in this, and I withheld information, so I'm legally an accessory to the crime."

Chase shrugged and spread his white hands helplessly.

"Too fast—all you young folks want to rush ahead too fast."

"But my uncle may be dangerous," Phyllis insisted. "I suspected a great deal, but the major link—this blackmailer—never suggested itself to me. I suspected my uncle was implicated in crime, but I warn you, if he thinks we know, if he thinks I've identified his handwriting, he won't hesitate to take steps—any steps—to save his neck."

"We can't be too sure that the baron is the Cowl," Chase reminded her. Then— "Speak of the devil and he comes in person."

He nodded toward the lawn. Approaching them was the military figure of the nobleman, walking from the sea to the house. At the same moment, while the four people stared at the monocled Baron von Tolz, several things happened in rapid succession.

In the late afternoon air, heavy with sultry heat and prophetic of yet more thunderstorms to come, there sounded a high, sharp crack, unmistakably a rifle shot!

The chilling sound was followed by a woman's high-pitched, shuddering scream....

A thousand thoughts raced through Peter's mind as he whirled in the direction of the shot. Everything was wrong; the baron was innocent, for no matter what had happened, he had been in sight of all them....

The seaman Randall came thudding around the corner of the veranda. He glanced quickly at Peter, and was obviously relieved to find him in the presence of his superior.

"Ah, there you are!"

Turning to Arthur Chase, the seaman said, without emotion:

"There's been another killin', sir."

Chapter Fifteen
DEATH WALKS AGAIN

Dusk came prematurely over Willard House. The western sky darkened with huge tiers of massed thunder clouds. It would rain again.

For one brief moment, a rent appeared in the veils that shrouded the dying day, and the lurid sun shone forth, baleful, ominous. Its scarlet fingers touched the huddled group of frightened people standing in the coarse marsh grass of the sand dunes.

Arthur Chase's round, pink face was suddenly drawn and white as he turned the body over. It sprawled face downward on the cooling sands, the arms outflung, the legs twisted awkwardly in a grotesque posture of death.

The dead man was Ralph Willard.

He was shot in the back.

Blood welled through his clothing and gleamed deep red in the sympathetic scarlet light of the sun. Then it turned a deep, dark maroon as the sun gave up its hopeless struggle and vanished behind the clouds. Thunder once again muttered, close overhead.

On the dead man's face, death had engraved a surprised look, one of astonishment mingled with a previous expression of excitement. His mouth, beneath the little black mustache, gashed open as though ready to shout.

Miriam Whitney broke the silence. For the second time that day, her carefully applied cosmetics oozed and gave way to a storm of hysterical tears.

"Another one!" she choked, and her voice was not pleasant. "The second dead one! Why, we're all going to be killed! What are we waiting around here for?"

"Ah, hush!" said Arras Gordon nervously.

"No! No! That's the second Willard dead. The whole family will be murdered, except that man over there, that—that—"

She glared wildly at Peter.

"Where were you? Where were you when your brother was killed? Can you tell us that?"

"He was with me," Arthur Chase said quietly, rising heavily from his knees. "And so was your husband."

"Was he?" Miriam Whitney collapsed, in bewildered fashion, and the doctor managed to put his wife in the background. He lounged up beside the detective, his hands plunged deep into the pockets of his slacks.

"Still cling to your two-man theory, Chase?"

"No—that is, this was a one-man job. One of our pretty partners went on a hell of a spree." The little man looked around. "Does anyone have any idea how it happened?"

Young Jane roused from her horror and managed to tear her wild eyes from the motionless body of her brother. "I do. So does Mr. Hark, and Miriam, and Diana—"

"You all saw it?" Chase almost shouted. "Again?"

"I saw him running toward the beach. I think he was calling to Von Tolz. Then someone shot him from behind that dune over there. I saw the smoke."

Chase turned to stare speculatively at the indicated slope. Then he plodded rapidly toward the spot. He found several vague impressions in the white sand.

"Here is where the murderer knelt. He probably had another rifle. Where in damnation are they coming from?"

The detective dusted the sand from his knees. In the gathering gloom could be heard the surf, murmuring in monotone an obituary for Ralph Willard.

"I suppose you all have alibis?" he demanded. "Peter, Phyllis, Dr. Whitney and myself were all together on the veranda at the moment of the tragedy. We also saw the baron walking to the house. What about the rest of you?"

Diana was strolling alone on the beach. John Hark had been in the house speaking to Phoebe Willard. Mrs. Willard, however, was not present to verify his statement.

"And where were you, Mrs. Whitney?"

"I? I—I don't know—exactly. Walking on the beach, too, like Diana, I think. I'm not sure—I'm so upset—"

"Of course you were walking on the beach, Miriam," Gordon cut in. "I was with you."

"Were you? Oh, yes—of course you were—yes, yes! I was on the beach with Arras, here."

Arthur Chase sighed with exhaustion and sat down on the slope of the dune.

"So everyone is nicely accounted for again. I'll have to see Henry and the little maid, Janet, but there isn't much hope in that direction. Someone take the body inside. Doctor, see what you can find."

John Hark and Gordon hastened to follow out Chase's suggestion, with Whitney striding alongside the burdened men. The baron, too, left the scene of the tragedy with the procession. Phyllis plucked at Peter's sleeve.

"My uncle is alibied in this, Peter," she said significantly. "He couldn't have committed this crime. We all saw him on the lawn before it happened."

"Much good it will do him," he returned crisply. "Von Tolz is the Cowl—you identified him yourself. That ought to be enough to hang him."

"But this killing—it proves what I've said, and what Chase suspects. There *is* another murderer on the island, someone we do not suspect."

"I suppose you're rather happy that your uncle is alibied?"

"No, no. I really regret it. If it were only he, we would have nothing more to worry about. We would know who the guilty party is. As it stands now, Peter, I'm afraid—just like the Woodward girl. Poor Diana! I— But, Peter, we're all in danger here now; you can see that. This murderer stops at nothing. Why do we all stay here where he can get at us?"

Peter shrugged.

"Probably Chase will do something. He's been waiting for the cutter up to now. Perhaps he'll authorize your leaving by the launch for Rapahawney."

But the little detective had no such plan in mind. For the first few moments after viewing Ralph Willard's body, his round face had taken on a sullen, angry expression, underlined by haggard care. He had failed. But not entirely, came his next thought. He still had several cards up his sleeve.

He sauntered over the lawn to the veranda and faced the little group. Baron von Tolz, Whitney, Hark and Arras Gordon were absent.

"Why?" Chase asked heavily. "Why should Ralph Willard have been killed? I think I should like to see a copy of Jed Willard's will. It might throw some light on the confusion I've been proud to call a brain."

"The will couldn't have anything to do with it," Jane objected. "It had no time to be changed, as John Hark will tell you. As matters stand, Unk's estate is divided equally between Phoebe, Peter, Ralph and myself. There are no other heirs or benefactors, save the usual bequests to the servants."

"Then we must look elsewhere for a motive. I don't for one moment believe that Ralph was killed because of his resemblance to Peter. The light was clear at that time, and Ralph, of course, had a mustache. Then why was he killed?"

Peter stepped forward, releasing Phyllis' hand, and spoke to Chase in an undertone. He told the little detective of the Cowl's boasting, when he had Peter a prisoner, that he had claimed Ralph Willard as one of his underlings.

"It might be a motive," he offered, "although, of course, if Von Tolz is the Cowl, he couldn't have committed this second murder."

"But you remember someone said he was running toward the beach—Jane, it was—had the impression he wanted to get to the baron, perhaps to tell him something. For there is no doubt that Ralph was under the Cowl's thumb."

"Isn't there?"

Diana stepped forward, momentarily losing the shudder that wracked her lovely body. She had thrown a gaudily colored beach robe over her bathing suit.

"What you say isn't true, Peter! It isn't! Probably the Cowl did really think that Ralph worked for him, but Ralph was deceiving him entirely! He spoke to me of it only this afternoon. I knew nothing about it before. It was he who unearthed the baron's real identity as the Cowl and turned the information over to Jed when Jed wanted to find out something about the letter-writer!"

"Ah—" Chase sighed.

Diana rushed on: "Oh, he did do some work for Von Tolz, and that's why he's dead! I told him, I warned him, I begged him not to interfere in this terrible business today—but he needed money, he said, and the baron had promised him ten thousand dollars if he could discover the identity of the man who had blackmailed *him!*"

"What's all this?" Peter demanded, unbelieving.

"Dear me, it's not necessary to repeat it," Chase smiled, feeling infinitely better. "The story is quite clear, even if it's somewhat startling. Evidently the baron does not know the identity of the man who blackmailed him into taking his orders! The whole case, it seems to me, is one of hidden identities. Von Tolz, anxious to be certain of the man who caused Jed's death—and who, incidentally, pinned it conveniently on the Cowl's shoulders—set Ralph on the trail. And Ralph evidently found out something of great importance—probably the identity of the second killer. It was important enough, anyway, to cause this second man, this super-criminal, I might say, to shoot Ralph, in spite of the great risk to himself."

In the thickening dusk, Miriam Whitney had edged closer to the little group. She had managed to catch the references to Von Tolz as the Cowl, and now she burst once more into uncontrolled excitement.

"So it's that greasy baron, is it? Von Tolz, is it? Well, then, what are you men standing around for? Why don't you put the handcuffs on him, before he kills us all? Why don't you? If the man's guilty, why don't you do something about it, instead of standing around idly?"

In the silence that followed her outburst, the sea murmured drowsily. The house was a blur in the gloom, suddenly illuminated by a jagged streak of lightning that plowed across the lowering sky. In the sudden brilliance could be seen the figures of Dr. Whitney and Baron von Tolz, striding over the dunes toward them.

Arthur Chase turned quickly to Miriam Whitney. "You must understand that what we do is for the best—"

"The best for the criminal, maybe! To give him a chance to kill another of us!"

"You forget, Mrs. Whitney, that Von Tolz is completely alibied in this second murder. That means there's another killer abroad on Little Swamp Island. It is our concern, our duty, to find him. For the safety of the women, however, I'm going to suggest—a little later—that we get a launch and send you all to Rapahawney, with Henry and Joe Lemons. All the men must remain here until the cutter comes back. In the meantime, it is vitally necessary that Von Tolz should not suspect our knowledge. I must ask you to make no sign, by word or hint, of our suspicions concerning the baron. Otherwise there is no telling what may happen. Do you understand?"

In the darkness, Miriam Whitney nodded her pale golden head, cowed by the serious undertone of the man's words. Her shoulders drooped as Jane and Diana accompanied her back to the house. Phyllis lingered near Peter and Arthur Chase.

"Are you really going to do that? Are you going to send all the women away?"

"We may have to. In the meantime, Peter, come with me. I want to ask the butler, Henry, for several little items he may have on hand—such as radio tubes. I'm afraid we've delayed this move entirely too long."

With the coming of darkness, a pall of deadly fear settled over the island. In the house, the party assembled in the great library, with every light blazing. In the mind of everyone present was the picture of two bodies lying in an upstairs room. Miriam Whitney, shivering constantly, clung to the side of her husband. Diana Woodward, considering that one of the dead men was her fiancé, had remained peculiarly unmoved since her first demonstration on the sand dunes. Phyllis sat in a corner, attended by John Hark and Arras Gordon. Jane conversed with Phoebe Willard in a low voice.

Over the silence of the house rose the monotone of the surf and the occasional wailing of a rising wind. Thunder muttered constantly, and lightning flickered like a dry tongue in the mouth of the sky, yet no rain fell.

Occasionally one of the party would rise and stare into the moonless darkness at the utter blackness, seeking to detect some sign of life or movement. Failing in this, he or she would turn and stare speculatively, some suspiciously, some with fear, at the other members of the company.

Had they been able to see to the dock at the end of the island, they might have observed something to form a concrete basis for their fears. The yacht *Junker,* though wrapped in darkness, teemed with activity. The figures of men slipped like shadows about her smooth, waxed decks, and dropped to the black dock like phantoms, to be swallowed up by the night. In their hands they held metal objects which glinted in the sudden dry glare of lightning.

A tall, darkly clad man commanded them.

"Dalton, Batty and Trigger will make for the radio shack. If anyone is standing guard or occupying the place, get rid of them—no, hold them prisoner until I come. I'll be there in a few moments."

The rest of the dozen or more shadows were ordered off on other duties. The debarking party split into small groups and filtered off into the darkness and solitude of the lonely sand dunes.

The seaman Randall was tired. He lounged in the blackness outside the radio cabin and envied his fellow coast guardsman, Steve. He had it easy, that chap. Didn't have to go tagging along everywhere after this restless young fellow the detective wanted to keep an eye on. Lucky fool.

Randall was also hungry. These two probably didn't even realize they had eaten nothing since landing. A lot of drinks, maybe, and a sandwich, but no square meal. Randall felt rightfully resentful.

Keep an eye on the young chap—Peter. Much good that was doing, with the detective with him all the time, anyway. Treated him more like another gumshoe than a gangster. Anyway, the young chap didn't look like a gunman. Hard, maybe—his eyes at times made Randall shiver—but no killer. If Smarty Arty didn't trust him, why go into this damned shack alone with him?

Randall yawned and glanced through the little window into the yellow interior of the radio cabin. Chase was carefully wiping his hands on a soiled handkerchief, and stepped back to admire his work in repairing the transmitter. Peter lounged by his side, talking. Randall could not hear what was being said, but things looked peaceful. He turned away as Chase seated himself in the swivel chair and began a tentative tapping on the key. Calling the cutter back, Randall guessed. Well, that was all right with him. Maybe he'd get a square meal soon.

Lightning wriggled across the black, turbulent sky, and in the split-second glare he caught sight of three men moving across the dunes toward the shack. More of these crazy people. Restless as the devil himself— always wandering about when they were told to stay put in the house.

The three men drew closer, and Randall stirred with a vague uneasiness. Two of the men were short and stocky, and the third was tall and thin. They did not look familiar. And they were holding something in their hands—something he couldn't quite make out, now that the lightning was gone.

Thunder crashed and more lightning streaked the black vault of the sky. The three newcomers were within a few paces of him when Randall recognized the objects they carried.

Rifles—

He opened his mouth to shout, but the shout never left his suddenly dry lips. Something cold and hard was jammed into his stomach.

"No peeps out of you, sailor boy," one of the men whispered hoarsely. "Not if you know what's good for you."

Since Randall valued his mid-section for the sake of the square meal he hoped to receive, he closed his jaws with an audible click of his teeth. The tall, thin man stepped quickly to the yellow rectangle of the window and looked in. His exclamation was fraught with both surprise and alarm.

"Deuce—and that copper!"

The man covering Randall hesitated and nodded to the third member of the party. The latter stepped quietly behind the seaman and raised his arm. A dull crack sounded in the night, and Randall slumped to the ground, a limp, inert figure.

Dalton grunted with satisfaction and brushed back his sparse sandy hair. His square features broke into a broad grin. "Somebody's gonna be surprised, boys."

He pushed open the door of the shack. It creaked, and Peter turned at the sound. The next moment pandemonium broke loose in the narrow, cramped quarters of the wooden cabin.

The sound of the radio key was abruptly stilled as Chase got to his feet, upsetting the chair with a crash.

Dalton shouted from the doorway: "Don't move, you two—"

His rifle exploded with a roar, and the bullet thudded into the ceiling as Peter hit him knee high with a flying tackle. Shifty crashed to the floor, and the weapon spun across the rough boards. Chase snatched it up, to find its use strictly limited in the crowded little room. He reversed it and held it by the barrel, intending to use the heavy stock as a club, but he was too late.

Batty, too, had his hands on the weapon, and gained the outside grip. He wrested it from the detective and swung viciously. It struck Chase on the shoulder, sending him to the floor with a crash. Trigger Malone, standing alone in the doorway, dived into his pocket and exhibited an ugly blue revolver.

"Now cut it, you mugs!"

Chase was beyond all movement for the moment. Peter glanced up and saw that Trigger had him covered. He released his crushing grip on Shifty's wrist and shrugged.

"And now what's the game?" he snapped to the flushed, heavily breathing Dalton. "Are you one of the eels that come up from the sea—or what?"

Batty hurled Chase aside and tore the headphones from him. Peter was treated with a little more respect by Trigger and Shifty, who had previously encountered him and learned to respect his physical abilities. He was allowed to gain his feet without the assistance of the cruel boot toe that spurred Arthur Chase up.

Shifty, clutching his wrist, cursed: "Damn you, you're both going to get it the right way, now!"

Peter looked at the gangster's distorted face and then at Shifty's red, swelling wrist. He hoped it was broken, but allowed none of his thoughts to appear on his face. Dalton was killing mad. Peter, without dropping his gaze from the gangster's glaring eyes, saw the knuckles of Dalton's trigger finger tighten.

They were saved from immediate death by the voice of Baron von Tolz.

"Drop it, Dalton!"

Shifty hesitated, glanced from the corner of his eye at the tall figure of the Cowl—minus his mask—and grudgingly relaxed, facing the baron with a sudden, almost defiant air.

"They ought to be bumped, I tell you!" Trigger protested in a high, thin voice choked with anger. "They sent out a message, chief. We're done for, I tell you. Bump them!"

"You're telling me what to do?" Von Tolz demanded, his voice faintly incredulous. His heavy black brows raised in an interrogative glance at Chase. "Did you succeed?"

Chase shrugged. Peter, listening eagerly, felt his hopes sink as the detective replied: "Frankly, I don't know. I hope so, however."

Von Tolz sighed with quick relief. Apparently he took Chase at his word. Whirling on the unfortunate, mutinous Trigger, he snapped harshly, in his autocratic manner: "When I seek advice from gorillas, I'll look to you. Until then, what I do with these people is my business.

Yours is to obey orders!"

"Members of your crew?" Chase asked mildly.

The baron grinned.

"From the *Junker*—yes, my dear sir. One place on Little Swamp Island that you neglected to examine."

"I'm sorry—I didn't have time. Suppose you tell me why we're having all this unpleasantness."

"In a few moments. I think it would be best if we all understood the situation and learned the facts at once. By all I refer to the remainder of the Willard guests, back in the house. We had better go there. But I want to make you understand I'm quite desperate, as you must well imagine. I will tolerate no nonsense on the way. In that event, I may yet take our impetuous Trigger's advice...."

Chapter Sixteen
THE COWL SPEAKS

The fear that hung over Willard House crystallized suddenly into terrified hatred as it passed from intangible apprehensions into something with a definite object—the Cowl. The ominous, pregnant thunder over the house provided a fitting background to Baron von Tolz' sonorous voice as he stood before the party in the darkly furnished library and explained to them in suave tones the situation with which they were confronted.

The Cowl, without his mask, seemed somehow to gain rather than lose in awe-inspiring, fearful stature. His dark eyes, with curiously overlapping eyelids, resembled nothing more than a bird's. He had discarded the affectation of the monocle. Add to his strange eyes his hooked, predatory nose, and in more than one mind there flashed a picture of a great, disgusting bird—a vulture. His thin lips curled back from his familiar white teeth in a twisted smile, and he stared slowly from one to the other of the pale or flushed faces before him—faces strained and lined with fear and anxiety.

As Peter and Arthur Chase were herded by Trigger and Shifty Dalton into the library, there arose an audible sigh of relief from several pairs of parted lips. Jane sobbed suddenly, Phoebe Willard made a satisfied sound, and Diana moved toward Peter with a sudden gesture, that came to a quick halt as Trigger brushed her roughly aside. Peter's eyes met Phyllis', and he felt warm at the thankful light that glowed there.

There was evidence of a struggle in the library of Jed Willard. A huge oaken table was overturned, and no one bothered to restore it to its original position. The rug was trampled and the curtains on the French windows were torn down.

Arras Gordon nursed a cut cheek—the one with the scar—but had somehow miraculously saved his steel-rimmed spectacles from destruction. He was calmly intent on straightening the frame as Peter came in. John Hark and Dr. Whitney, too, bore marks of physical encounter in the rumpled condition of their clothing. In the background, huddled against the wall, was the deflated person of the butler, Henry, and the frightened, tiny figure of the maid, Janet, with old Joe Lemons.

"I think our little group is now complete," Baron von Tolz said, smiling. "What I have to say to all of you concerning this sudden seizure of the island really should be said in private, I think, just among ourselves."

He nodded to the hesitant figures of Dalton and Trigger Malone. From the doorway, from the giant, red-haired person of one Reds Finnegan and the sleekly garbed Aces Spinelli, came a murmur of disapproval.

"It's quite all right. I want these people to know, however, that any hostile move toward me will be followed with unpleasantness at your hands. I think all these people will understand."

The gangsters departed. Silhouetted against the French windows appeared the ominous outline of a slouching man, a Thompson gun slung carelessly under his arm. The baron's men well knew the value of caution.

"You—you—" Miriam Whitney choked. Then: "Killer! Murderer! What are you going to do—massacre the rest of us, you butcher?"

Dr. Whitney hurried to his wife's side.

"Don't be a fool!" he snapped brittlely. "This man is mad, obviously insane. In his condition, it would not be wise to antagonize him!"

Von Tolz laughed mirthlessly.

"You're diagnosis is quite wrong, my good doctor. I am very sane. I think you will understand the situation and see my point of view before I am through. And you must all remember, you are under my authority for the time being. For the present, the island is in control of my men—my men who, as I have ample reason to know and believe—would not hesitate to—ah—massacre the lot of you."

He paused.

John Hark stood with his hand on the back of Phoebe Willard's chair. Arras Gordon polished his glasses and carefully put them on, to stare from behind their glinting lenses at the man who had the power of life and death over them all. Arthur Chase clucked his tongue in distress.

"And what do you expect to gain from all this lunacy, this hopeless display of your powers over the underworld?" the detective demanded.

His eyes snapped with a cold blue light as he spoke.

"I expect to achieve a great deal," Von Tolz replied. "You see, Mr. Chase, I respected you far too much not to realize how much you knew. You know I am the underworld figure called the Cowl."

"I know that."

"You know I wrote a note to Jed Willard asking for a meeting on Lighthouse Island." The baron glanced at his auburn-haired niece. She met his gaze unwaveringly, and it was the Cowl who turned aside, as Chase nodded: "I know that, too."

"You know I intended to kill Jed Willard?"

"Yes."

"But someone got there before me."

"Yes—very ingeniously, too."

"Too ingeniously, Mr. Chase! I have no doubt that you could name the man who killed Jed Willard."

Arthur Chase smiled and shook his head.

"That I do not know. I imagine you are going to learn that man's name?"

"More than that. I'm going to kill him."

Miriam Whitney sucked in her breath loudly and glanced fearfully at her husband. The doctor scowled. John Hark's hand tightened on the back of Phoebe Willard's chair. Chase sank lower in his chair and smiled.

"I believe you really understand my motives," the baron went on, addressing the detective. "I will explain them for the benefit of the rest of these people. You see, ladies and gentlemen—" he grinned maliciously and glanced at the silhouette on the French window—"I am the Cowl. I am accused of murdering Jed Willard. And if that can't be proved, I can still lose my life simply by the identification of Baron von Tolz with the man known as the Cowl. Therefore I am lost, one way or the other. There is no other way out for me but the course I have taken.

"I want just one man of the lot of you. I want the man who killed Jed Willard, the man who made me the Cowl by holding over my head the threat of losing everything I enjoyed—my position in the financial and social world. That man I want. Ralph Willard learned his identity for me, but, before he could reach me, he was killed by this mysterious person. For I do not know who he is, despite the fact that I have taken orders from him for several years. I owe that man a great deal. It would give me great delight and satisfaction to apply torture to him, but I would be content simply to have him stand before me, so that I could put a bullet through his brain."

"And that man is in this room?" John Hark queried with nervous excitement. His face was yellow as old parchment in the glow of the lights.

The baron turned to the lawyer and smiled pleasantly. "In this room, John Hark! For all I know, you may be that man."

"Not I," Hark said hastily. "I'm not. I—"

"That's for me to find out," Von Tolz returned quietly. "As for me, I make no excuses for my actions, nor do I intend to whitewash my character. I am a murderous criminal several times over. I know it. My niece suspected my underworld activities, but was never really sure. I make these disclosures so that you may the more readily understand the situation. I am a desperate man. I have no desire to lose my life in an electric chair. I was ready to kill one man today, and I intend to kill before I am through. After that, I have my yacht and my men, and you may be sure I am not fool enough not to have a route of escape prepared."

"What about the cutter?" Whitney sneered. "That will return long before you have tagged your man and pumped your bullets into him."

"Ah, no. Even at this moment, one of my men—the one with the ears, you may have noticed—is sending out a message on the transmitter that Mr. Chase was so good as to repair. I fear the commander of the cutter will find no reason to return here. And if necessary, we shall stay on for several days, until 1 decide which one of you men is the one I want."

"And how," came Arras Gordon's crisp, meticulous voice, "do you propose to find this object of your vengeance?"

"That will be turned by a little trick all my own," the Cowl replied. "Meanwhile, I would like to tell you that the freedom of the house is yours. You must not, however, make any attempt to leave the grounds, for they will be fully patrolled. I have more than fifteen men at my disposal, you see. The person who sets foot on the lawn will be judged the guilty party, and treated as such."

The baron suddenly turned to the portly butler and snapped: "Move, Henry. Get something for these people to eat, if they care to. And let me repeat, do not leave the house. I have no desire to harm anyone— except one man."

"How can we believe that?" Diana challenged him. "It isn't really credible that you will permit us to live and expose your identity."

The Cowl grinned.

"On that question, my dear Miss Woodward, I must leave you in suspense. I really haven't decided just what to do with you—not just yet."

Chase protested: "Why take justice into your own hands, baron? All this unpleasantness could be avoided if we could arrange—"

The Cowl paused in the doorway. He turned with a grin that revealed his even white teeth.

"Just so. I know, however, how impersonal Justice can be. It will give me ever so much more satisfaction to pull the trigger myself!"

Chapter Seventeen
ALLIES

Willard House was shrouded in darkness. The great clock in the hall struck nine. Phoebe Willard retired to her room for the night, alone with her silent grief. The remainder of the company huddled in the library, tense, strained, ill-at-ease. Every other moment some one would start up and wander restlessly about the house, only to meet silent, lounging men with snubby automatic rifles. At such times, the wanderer would receive a curt, growling warning not to attempt to leave the house.

In the music room, someone was playing Chopin's Fantasy. It was done with a light, deft tone, the touch of one who felt the weird rhythm and terrifying crash of the piece. The rippling notes floated through the rambling mansion, and the imprisoned guests shuddered when Dr. Whitney returned to the library to announce that the player was Baron von Tolz.

Peter closed his bedroom door with a sigh. He did not care for the baron's music.

A few moments later he was startled to see a man slip through the doorway of his room and quietly close the door after him.

It was Arthur Chase.

The detective quickly joined him, sitting down on the counterpane of the bed. Peter nodded a silent greeting and curled up in the window alcove, his long legs causing his knees almost to touch his chin.

Downstairs the music stopped abruptly.

"I thought you had gone to sleep, Peter."

Peter grunted, groped for a cigarette, and lighted one. Chase refused the packet.

"Not much chance of sleeping tonight, is there?" Peter countered.

"No. Not much."

"Chase, did that radio message get through?"

"I told Von Tolz the truth, and he knows it. I'm not sure whether it was picked up or not."

"Then we're in a fix, eh?"

"Dear me, it looks that way, Peter."

The detective glanced out at the lowering clouds and the gloom-shrouded night. He followed Peter's nod to the guard standing on the lawn below.

"Damn killers," Peter muttered. "They must be punished."

"They will be."

"Not much prospect of our getting a hand in it, the way things are shaping up. The Cowl has matters pretty much under his control."

"Expect a firing squad in the morning, Peter?" Chase chuckled.

"What else? If not that—" Peter's voice grew bitter—"there's always you, you know."

The detective was silent, watching the glow of Peter's cigarette. Again he followed Peter's glance to Trigger Malone on the lawn.

He asked: "You came up here to figure a way out?"

No answer was forthcoming. The detective went on: "Been considering the chances of making a break for it?"

"I might, at that. You know the old line—die fighting, all that. At least, I don't want a lot of machinegun slugs in my back tomorrow morning when I comedown for breakfast."

"It's better not to die at all," said Chase sensibly.

He went on: "You and I are not going to die—not so soon, at any rate. Dear me, but you are impetuous! Why on earth did you come here, if only to slip away before your job is done?"

"I came to save Jed Willard—and he's dead. I came to get the Cowl—and it seems he has me."

"So did I—I came here to get the baron. In our devious ways—approaching the same goal from different directions, so to speak—we seek the same end. Now why rush to escape?"

"All very well for you to talk. You've done something," Peter said slowly. "You're captured me—the Deuce."

A world of bitterness welled up in his voice as he pronounced his underworld title. Chase coughed.

"Er—you make it difficult for me, Peter. Don't you still wish to capture and bring the Cowl to justice? And more than that—the man behind the scenes, the Cowl's boss? Dalton has a leader, and that's Spinelli. Aces has a chief, and that's the Cowl. Now it seems as though we're reaching for the topmost rung in this ladder of criminals—the Cowl's director. He is either the good doctor, the good lawyer, or the young retired gentleman—Arras Gordon. Von Tolz is going to get one of them."

"The Cowl is mad," Peter offered in reply. "He doesn't hesitate to disclose to us his crimes, and now he even tells us of the next he intends to commit. Should he get it into his head to kill us all, to prevent our talking later, I do not doubt that he can carry it out. A convenient fire of Willard House, and all inside burned to death—"

"How gruesome!" Chase shuddered. "Von Tolz won't kill us, as you think, until he is—ah—ready. He wants to get his man first. I believe, if we can identify the fellow first, it will help us a great deal."

"We? Us?"

"Dear me, yes. You and I. I need help in this thing, Peter. The situation as it stands is not pleasant. It's full of potential danger to a number of innocent people. I would suggest your postponing any moves for escape—for the immediate present, at any rate."

"I intended to remain, in any event," Peter admitted. "There are the girls to be taken care of."

Chase nodded.

"Yes, I thought of that."

Peter leaned forward, the cigarette drooping carelessly between his fingers. The scent of tobacco filled the room.

"Then you're suggesting that we work together, Chase? If so, what happens to me if we win?"

"My dear Peter, I—ah—am suggesting a truce. I cannot, of course, promise to quit hounding you—as you might put it—if we get away from here successfully. But until our fates are decided, let's put our private hostilities aside and work together. Allies, you know. We would find each other extremely useful."

"If we're successful," Peter said earnestly, "will you give me twenty-four hours' start?"

Arthur Chase chuckled and looked at his white hands.

"Very well—yes."

Peter leaned back with a sigh. He felt infinitely better. Some of the gloom was gone from the dark night.

Chase pursued: "It's a bargain, then?"

"A bargain—even though I'm afraid it's all so much talk. Before the sun is up, Von Tolz will have his gangsters line us all up against a wall."

"On the contrary," Chase's voice came in the humid, hot blackness, "I think we will find our madman quarry quite harmless—until he decides which of the men downstairs is to be his victim."

A few minutes later Arthur Chase slipped noiselessly from the room, leaving Peter to finish his cigarette in thoughtful silence. He paced quietly down the corridor, rounded a corner, and paused before a bedroom door that was slightly ajar. He bounced thoughtfully on his toes, then stepped into the hot, still interior of the Whitney room.

Miriam Whitney sat by the window, staring out into the black murkiness of the ocean. She winced as lightning flickered across the scene, and shuddered at the momentary aspect of lowering, tumbling black clouds. She wished it would rain—rain, rain, and rain. Clean water to wash the blood from this place; clean water in which to stand and feel cleansed again, pure once more....

She heard the door open, and shivered inwardly as she thought of her giant, morose husband. She was agreeably surprised to make out in the gloom the short, stout little figure of that amazing person, Arthur Chase. She started up with a little cry of surprise, only to subside as the detective quickly put a warning finger to his lips.

"It would be best if no one knows I am speaking to you."

An old fear clutched at Miriam Whitney's heart.

"Dangerous?" she whispered. Her voice had the rasping quality of terror.

"It might be. Yet it is of the utmost importance that you answer my questions. If anyone later asks you if I've interrogated you, you must deny it. Do you understand?"

The woman nodded.

"What do you want to know? What can I tell you? I've been ill all day today."

Arthur Chase made a sympathetic clucking sound.

"I realize, Mrs. Whitney, that you are not in the best of health. And it is going to be difficult, for you were especially upset at the time of the event I am going to question you about."

"Ralph Willard's death?"

"Yes. You were hardly certain of your own whereabouts, you know."

"I didn't do it," she offered quickly. "Neither did my husband, as you know. But I do know what you're going to ask. I intended to go to you on my own accord—only I've been afraid. You see, I've been thinking it all over, over and over again, until my poor head—"

"Yes," Chase interrupted gently. "I do not suspect you or your husband, of course. I wanted to check up on your story. You say that is what you wanted to speak to me about?"

"Oh, yes! Yes! I've been afraid to talk to you before. But you see, I made a mistake when I gave you my—what do you people call it?—my alibi."

"You were not on the beach?"

"Oh, I was walking on the beach, myself. But—"

"The man you said was in your company?"

Miriam Whitney exhaled a shuddering breath. Chase waited patiently in the darkness, feeling as though he were performing a delicate surgical operation. A tiny trickle of perspiration ran down his forehead and into his eye, smarting and stinging.

"You see, Mr. Chase," Miriam said finally, "I was so upset at the time—I couldn't remember, I didn't realize what I was saying. But the man who said he was with me—lied. I was walking on the beach alone, quite alone. I have no idea where that man was at the time."

Arthur Chase breathed softly into the hot darkness.

"Thank you, Mrs. Whitney. Please do not repeat this conversation to anyone—for all our sakes."

Peter crushed the cigarette into an ash tray and stood up. Opening the door of his room, he stepped into the corridor and made his way down the staircase. Lolling on a chest that stood against the wall in the corridor was Shifty Dalton, a rifle across his knees.

"Hello, wallflower," Peter quipped.

To his surprise, the gangster did not flare up in anger. The sandy-haired man grinned and nodded.

" 'At's all right, Deuce. Take care of yourself."

The reply was infinitely more disquieting than if Dalton had replied with his usually vitriolic tongue. He wondered what the gangster meant by his solicitous words. He felt that something was in the air, something added to the tension that wound around and around the house like high-powered electric wires.

He had to find Phyllis.

He searched eagerly for her through the area of the house. He passed Dr. Whitney, in close conversation with John Hark. In the kitchen was the giant redheaded gangster, Reds Finnegan, in low conference with two other swarthy gunmen. They glanced up at his entrance and examined him with unexpected interest.

"That's the Deuce, eh?" Reds Finnegan asked his two companions.

Peter wondered at the expression in their eyes, and turned to look elsewhere for the girl. He wanted very much to tell her of the bargain he had made with Arthur Chase.

Arras Gordon was suddenly beside him, materializing out of the gloom from nowhere.

"Perhaps you've seen her," Peter suggested.

"Who?"

"Phyllis. Phyllis Gale."

Gordon took off his spectacles and rubbed his ears in weariness.

"I did—about ten minutes ago. She was with her madman uncle—Von Tolz."

"Where is she now?" Peter demanded impatiently.

"Probably on the *Junker*," Gordon replied.

"On the baron's yacht?"

DEATH IN A LIGHTHOUSE

"That's where the baron asked her to go. I didn't hear her object."

Peter felt his buoyant spirits suddenly go out of him like air from a deflated balloon. What did it mean? Had she thrown in her lot with the Cowl? He was her uncle, and perhaps he wanted to safeguard her, but more probably she had willingly joined his forces once again, just as she had been in the Cowl's ranks before.

Bitterness ate into his heart with the touch of acid. What had that kiss meant, that long kiss on the yawl, before the unpleasant events of this day began? What had the promise in her eyes meant, if she was to desert him like this?

Now he regretted the promise he had given Arthur Chase. He was suddenly no longer interested, no longer vitally concerned, in the future of the Willard household. For a brief moment, he longed to return to his room and utilize the method of escape that awaited him there.

The mood passed from him in the next moment, however. Down the corridor came the tall, graceful figure of Diana Woodward. There was a smile on her red lips and a warm light in her eyes as she recognized Peter Willard. He went toward her, and she linked her arm in his.

Having seen Diana to the door of her room, Peter walked quietly down the corridor through the murky darkness. He glanced in Arthur Chase's chamber, but the little detective was nowhere to be seen. Shrugging, he made his way to his own room, feeling impotent in the face of the circumstances that confronted him.

Two shadows lurked before the window. Shadows that carried ominous revolvers. At Peter's entrance, the muzzles pointed unwaveringly at his chest.

Automatically he raised his arms ceilingward.

Chapter Eighteen
PETER GETS A PROPOSITION

The night wore on, with its accompanying growls and threats from the storm-laden clouds hanging over Willard House. One by one, the members of the party succumbed to weariness and nervous exhaustion and retired to their rooms, hoping to snatch what rest they could until the next time the baron called them for questioning.

In an upstairs room, Peter Willard stared through the gloom at two muzzles aimed unwaveringly at his chest.

"And what now, narcissus?" he impatiently addressed Shifty Dalton. He recognized the second gunman by his amazing ears. It was Batty. "What new little game is this?"

Shifty grinned maliciously. His voice rasped in the darkness.

"If I follow out my orders, it will be the last game you ever play—and you'll be a lily!"

Peter judiciously remained silent.

"My orders," Shifty continued after a pause, "are to bump you."

"From the same cheerful cherub who killed Ralph?" Dalton scowled.

"We don't know anything about that. No, this is the Cowl's order."

"Von Tolz, eh?"

"He's the Cowl to us."

Peter reflected that he might have expected such a turn as this. He recalled Arthur Chase's warning early in the day to be on the lookout for the Cowl's sudden decision to take his life. In the event of the Cowl's capture by the police, Peter would certainly be the major witness against him. It was too bad, he reflected, that he might not remain to see the outcome of the situation in Willard House. He tensed himself for a struggle, and wondered why Shifty hesitated to pull the trigger.

"Well?" he asked.

Dalton lowered the gun and signalled to Batty to take up a position by the door, watching the corridor. Twirling the heavy automatic by the trigger guard, he crossed the room and sat down heavily on the bed.

"Listen, Deuce, what will you do if we don't bump you? This is between you and me and Batty, here? It's up to me, this thing is—"

"But what about the Cowl?"

"I'm in charge right now. The Cowl don't know it, but I am."

"Obviously he doesn't," Peter said with a humorless smile. "What do you suppose he'll do to you when he learns you disobey his orders?"

"I'm not worried about that. I'm supposed to bump you, see? I will or I won't. The question's up to you, Deuce."

Peter noticed the persistent, curious use of his former title, associated with his activities of long ago. Was the gangster going to accept him as one of the fraternity again? The answer was due to come in a moment.

Shifty adopted a confidential attitude.

"Listen, I don't want to bump you, Deuce. You're a good man, and in spite of the names you call me, I think you and me could get along all right together. I'd rather work under you than under the Cowl, any time. He's crazy."

"Work under me?" Peter asked, puzzled. "What's the idea?"

"Aw, you don't have to put on, Deuce. We know you didn't split with the boss for the fun of it. Whatever you're in this thing for, we're willing to work for you rather than the Cowl. I'm telling you—that baby's nuts!"

"Yes, he is," Peter agreed thoughtfully.

He sat down in the window alcove to consider this new turn of events. Shifty Dalton evidently did not understand that Peter had quit the underworld for good. Believing that Peter had some motive of his own in being embroiled in the events that were taking place in Willard House, the gunman turned to him. Why? From Dalton's words, Peter gathered that the sandy-haired gangster had lost faith in the Cowl.

"Who else feels the same way about this as you do?" he asked cautiously.

"Batty, of course. Then there's Trigger, Reds Finnegan, and some more of the boys. Not all of them. Spinelli and some of these lunkheads think the Cowl is a tin god. They swear by him. They're out of it."

Peter lit a cigarette, his face showing lean and alert in the glow of the yellow match flame. His gray eyes were suddenly narrowed.

"I must confess," he murmured, "I'm rather surprised. How do I know I can trust you? This is all pretty sudden, isn't it?"

"We've been thinking about this for a long time."

"What's your proposition?"

Shifty sighed and grunted.

"That's more like it, Deuce. You see, we ain't so dumb. We know when we're on the losing side. The Cowl can't put this stunt over, and we're smart enough to see the cards are stacked against us. It's too big, too nutty. Telling everybody he's gonna bump somebody off here before he goes! What the hell— Does he think we're on a desert island, or something? Between you and me, Deuce, I think that copper got off a message to the government boat, and it's only a matter of time until the police land here and lift the lid off this stinkin' pot. Then there'll be all hell to pay. We asked the boss to quit and leave, and he nearly chewed our ears off."

"So you want to call the whole thing off and leave, is that the idea?" Peter asked, betraying none of the hope that surged in him once again.

"That's the idea, Deuce. The plan we got worked out is this: Reds Finnegan was a lieutenant in the navy—that was durin' the war. That's a fact. He can sail the Cowl's tugboat from here to the gates of hell, if he wants to. We ain't itching to burn, and that's what happens to us if we're caught here. If you throw in with us, Deuce, we'll be glad to have you. We need every man. The Cowl might object, y'see."

Peter knew what form the Cowl's "objections" would take. Flaming muzzles and bullets singing a macabre song of death.

"And after that?" he asked, exhaling lengthily.

"The bunch of us are going to light out on the *Junker,* see? We sail out to sea—it's a big place, I'm told—and maybe hit around to the West Coast, or maybe land near here. There's plenty of good stuff aboard the *Junker*—cash, supplies, and fuel. We'd have a running start on the coppers. No telling what we could do with the Cowl's ship. Maybe we'll overhaul it and go into the smuggling racket. And you're the guy who can show us the way."

Batty interrupted from his post by the door.

"And don't forget about the dames!"

"We take them with us," Shifty explained with a grin. "For a while, anyway."

"No," Peter snapped, and thought of Phyllis' shudder at Dalton's attentions. He was revolted by unpleasant pictures of Jane and Diana with these gunmen. "Nothing doing," he said firmly.

Dalton was surprised.

"You won't throw in with us?"

"No, I don't want the women mixed up in this."

"We gotta. Half these gorillas won't come along with us unless we promise them we'll take the girls."

"Count me out."

"Then we follow the Cowl's orders, Deuce!"

Peter hesitated.

"Give me time to think it over?"

Shifty and his companion exchanged glances. Evidently they wanted very much to number Peter in their ranks. Dalton nodded.

"Okay. The Cowl gave us an hour to bump you. We'll be back in that time. And if your answer is still the same, we'll start our little campaign by giving you the works first. If you come in with us, then the Cowl gets bumped and we scram right away."

No sooner had the door clicked softly behind the departing gunmen than it opened noiselessly once more and Arthur Chase silently entered the room. He sighed heavily in the hot, tense darkness and seated himself on the spot where Shifty Dalton had been but a moment before.

"Had visitors, eh, Peter?"

He nodded.

"Things are going to break soon, Chase. All the hounds of hell are going to start yelping in a few minutes." Peter went on to tell of the gangster's proposition and speculated on the unpleasant possibilities arising therefrom. Chase listened seriously and clucked his tongue.

"Our friend the Cowl is going to have more than a peck of trouble on his hands shortly. But there is danger, Peter, if he gets in the first move."

Peter groaned.

"Shifty and his crowd won't make a move until an hour from now. If the Cowl acts first, it will blast all their plans and they'll have to keep in line with him. Then the rest of us will be completely at the Cowl's mercy."

Chase nodded again.

"It's up to us to put in the first move in this three-cornered game, Peter. That's the only way we can win."

"You have an idea?"

"Many of them. First, however, tell me how long it would take you to get to Rapahawney?"

"With the sloop, perhaps forty minutes, with this wind. I can go there and back in less than half that time in one of the launches."

"Good. Could you bring back a posse in a half hour?"

"Yes."

"Can you make your escape from here without raising an alarm? Can you get a launch far enough out to prevent the noise of the motor from being heard too distinctly?"

"Yes, to both questions. But what about the women, Chase? We must be on our toes for the next sixty minutes."

"I've been walking around," Chase said. "Freely, too. Half of this gang of thugs doesn't know what the other half is doing. I can get the women out of the house and to a safe place on the island. But it's up to you to bring help before either the Cowl or Dalton makes a move."

"I can do it," Peter said quietly. He laughed. "You trust me to come back?"

"I do, Peter."

They shook hands. Chase nodded his satisfaction and vanished from the room, bent on his own mysterious errands.

Chapter Nineteen
—AND ACTS ACCORDINGLY

Peter leaned out of the window. On the lawn below he could see the hot, tired shadow of Trigger Malone, still leaning against the tree.

He turned and rummaged in his closet, where he discovered a long-forgotten pair of tennis shoes and light cotton slacks. The latter he abandoned, after a moment's thought, and returned to his former choice of dark trousers. Pulling on a thin, black sweater over his white shirt and tucking the ends snugly under his leather belt, he crept cautiously to the window.

The night was hot and breathlessly still. Overhead, the clouds tumbled slowly over each other, seeming to drop lower with every passing moment. Lightning flickered and illuminated the heaving expanse of gray sea. A sudden spot of red flamed in the shadow below, indicating that Trigger Malone still kept his lonely vigil beneath Peter's window. Peter returned to his dresser, picked up a small military hairbrush, and then exchanged it in favor of an empty talcum can.

Tightening the laces of his tennis shoes, he stepped again to the window.

Cautiously and noiselessly he raised the sash. Then he stepped out upon the sill. A long limb from the tree under which Trigger Malone stood reached to within three feet of the window. Peter swung outward, gripping the limb, and allowed his feet to slip from the window-sill.

The branch dipped and creaked perilously. He hung motionless, holding his breath and staring anxiously down at the cigarette glow beneath him. It did not move. A moment later he swung carefully toward the tree trunk, and shortly after he was totally concealed from sight in the budding foliage.

When at last he stood, a silent, lean, black shadow on the branch directly above Trigger, he drew the empty tin can from his pocket and hurled it, in a slanting direction, against the stone wall of the house. It hit with a startling clang and clatter in the hot, still darkness.

The shadow of the gunman below him jumped, cursed, and flicked away the cigarette. With drawn gun, Trigger Malone left his post under the tree to investigate the noise.

Peter, a silently gliding phantom, dropped noiselessly to the ground and raced over the lawn into the security of the sand dunes.

Off in the gloom there glowed yellow rows of lights from the *Junket's* cabins. Moored close beside the yacht, Peter knew, were two motor launches. It would be a ticklish job to loose one and pole out into midstream and into the sea before starting the powerful engines.

He worked his way through the gloom of the sand dunes toward the docks, and paused in the high rushes just beyond the field of light that flooded the wooden pier. Two men were slowly pacing up and down the wharf, automatic rifles slung under their arms. On the deck of the *Junker* were other dimly moving figures. Peter thought of Phyllis, there on the Cowl's yacht. His face became grim in the darkness as he pictured the auburn-haired girl. He suddenly wanted to see her, to demand an explanation for her strange conduct, before embarking on his dangerous errand.

His wish was partly fulfilled as a rectangle of light suddenly shot across the yacht's deck and he saw two people step into sight—Baron von Tolz and Phyllis Gale. In the glow of the dim yellow bulbs, he made out her small clear-cut features. She was pale and wan beside the dark impressiveness of the Cowl.

The sound of thudding, running footsteps behind him sent him darting for the shelter of a sand dune once again. The newcomer was Trigger Malone. A dozen paces from where Peter hugged the sand, the gangster paused and was intercepted by Shifty Dalton. There was a hurried, muffled conversation, the sound of angry, annoyed tones mingling with savage curses. Peter grinned. Evidently Trigger had just discovered his little trick. The conspirators against Von Tolz, he reflected joyously, were in something of a predicament, now that the baron was returning to the house and he himself was wandering free over the island.

The two gunmen turned after a moment, and walked with disarming casualness toward the dock where Von Tolz and Phyllis stood, surrounded by several of his thugs. They proceeded quickly toward the lights of Willard House. Peter slipped through the darkness to a point where he could listen clearly. He derived a silent pleasure from hearing the baron ask Dalton:

"Did you follow out my orders?"

"About the Deuce?"

"Of course, fool!"

"Yes. He's bumped."

The Cowl murmured his satisfaction, then lifted his eyebrows in surprise as Phyllis gasped and turned white under the glare of the searchlights. She swayed unsteadily for a moment, then, under the watchful, interested eyes of the Cowl she regained her composure and walked quickly toward the rambling mansion.

Peter's heart ached. He yearned to let Phyllis know he was alive, but restrained himself with an effort. He had a new angle to consider: now that Phyllis was in the house, he did not care to leave the island. Von Tolz would return to grill the guests further and perhaps would want to view his, Peter's, dead body. If the baron obtained the information he sought, or if the Cowl discovered that Peter had escaped, then it would be a matter of moments before the open break occurred between Dalton's party and the Cowl's.

He watched with interest the way Shifty and Trigger hovered over Von Tolz—threateningly, like dogs longing but afraid to attack. The Cowl, too, noticed their attitude, and with a curt, guttural command, ordered them back to their posts. Shifty hesitated, then plucked Trigger by the sleeve and vanished over a dune.

Peter stood up—and regretted it a moment later.

One of the searchlights aboard the *Junker* swung aimlessly about over the shore. It darted inland for a brief moment, then focussed directly on his figure as he stood limned against the blazing light!

A shout arose in the hot, still darkness. Peter spun around and glanced quickly toward the house. The Cowl and Phyllis had already entered and were unaware of the alarm. He whipped about again and ran toward the dock.

"Hey, there!" came a second hail. "Who—where d'you think you're going?"

Peter did not reply. He crouched lower and ran as quickly as the yielding sand permitted toward the wooden wharf. The nearest of the two guards who patrolled the dock was gazing aimlessly about, apparently confused by the hail from the *Junker's* deck.

Peter dodged out of the radius of the pitiless searchlight and hurtled full tilt into the guard.

The man heard the soft swish of rapidly moving feet in the grass, but turned too late to save himself. He grunted as a black shadow crashed into him, then stumbled back under the impact, falling as Peter threw himself heavily on top of him.

There was no further resistance. The guard lay limp and motionless on the wooden pier. Peter breathed more easily. He noted the awkward, twisted position of the guard's head as it rested against a heavy piling. He was grateful for the chance that made the struggle so brief.

He picked up the guard's rifle, then abandoned it in favor of the pistol. Turning quickly toward the nearest gleaming launch, he recoiled as he saw two dim heads in the stern cockpit! A gleam of light splintered along rifle barrels pointed at him. Peter threw himself to the planks in time to avoid the stuttering blast of withering fire.

The next moment, the questing searchlight flashed over the dock and again picked up Peter as he stood silhouetted on the boards. An alarm siren wailed on the yacht and there were more shots. A rifle cracked, and a splinter of wood leaped from a piling.

Another probing beam spotted the dock, and yet a third, turning the night into day. Peter hesitated, darted forward, then saw gray shapes scrambling over the dunes toward him. He halted abruptly and fired at the nearest. Although the darkness prevented anything like accurate aim, the shot had the effect of scattering his foes and forcing them to jump for cover.

Peter, whirling in all directions, realized he was almost hopelessly trapped—that he had botched his mission as badly as he possibly could. The searchlights were fixed rigidly on him. More rifles cracked, and the shouts of men filled the air.

There was only one way out, and Peter seized it eagerly. He raced madly along the dock, one searchlight gliding easily along with him.

At the end he dived, cleanly and at full speed, into the icy waters of Litte Swamp Creek.

The searchlight swept on beyond the dock, then hesitated, its manipulator baffled at the sudden disappearance of the quarry. The beam swung back and rested on a series of ripples on the water.

A few random, experimental shots went cracking into the night, with no results. Above the excited shouts of the searchers could be heard the metallic bass of the Cowl, raging and angry, insistently calling for a vanished Shifty to explain Peter's liveliness.

Swimming under water as far as his straining lungs could carry him, Peter came up for air in the evil smelling rushes on the bank of the creek. A beam of light flickered dangerously close to his head, and a stray bullet kicked up a tiny spray two yards from where he swam. He looked up and saw with despair that the heavy clouds were breaking. In a moment the moon would be out. Glancing seaward, he saw men clambering into the two launches. By swimming cautiously inland, along the dark bank, he managed to avoid the thrashing search parties.

Then, at the same moment that the moon came out, he glanced up to see with dismay the alert head and shoulders of a man above him, clearly visible through the tall rushes.

The watcher heard the slight splash and turned his head.

"This way, Peter!"

Peter exhaled with relief in the shadows. The voice was unmistakable.

"Rorke?" he whispered, conquering his astonishment.

Somehow he had expected the reporter to arrive at the scene eventually.

"Right! Easy does it!" came Rorke's voice again.

A moment later he was seated in the reporter's canoe. He noticed with satisfaction the presence of two high-powered rifles in the bottom of the shallow craft.

"Having a little party, aren't you?" Rorke demanded, taking the night glasses from his eyes and gripping Peter's hand. "What's going on?"

"Two murders already," Peter gasped. "And another just avoided."

"Looks like martial law on Little Swamp Island."

"It is. The Cowl's."

"Baron von Tolz?"

"None other."

Peter took a deep breath and waited for his pulses to stop their strained, exhausted pounding.

Larry said: "The game's up for our little friend in the mask. Also for his company. Did you try to get to the opposite bank?"

"No. Why?"

"You'd have run into some more pals of yours—the police. There's a cordon of troopers surrounding the landward side of the island, and three coast guard cutters offshore. All watching and waiting for the Cowl to make a break. Look!"

Peter glanced landward over the narrow silver streak of water. Rushes stirred on the grassy meadows of the opposite bank. Once he caught the glint of moonlight reflected from a badged cap. He thought of the gray and blue and gold uniforms of the New Jersey State troopers.

"Who tipped them off?" he demanded.

"A radio message, that's all I know. But they're not sure what it all means. They're waiting for signals —rockets—from Smarty Arty Chase."

"Then Chase did get a message through?"

"It was pretty garbled. Rather incoherently received. It took some time before some smart young fellow made out what it all meant. They were especially confused by a second clear message completely contradicting the first. They—"

Peter suddenly turned his attention back to the island as a sudden rattle of rifle fire broke from the dunes about the house. Flashes of red-tongued flame came from the windows of Willard House. Shouts of excited men came faintly to them in the lapping, dismal darkness of the swamp.

"That must be Dalton's crew," Peter commented. He quickly explained to Rorke the proposed mutiny of the gunmen, and how he had been invited to join their rebellion against the Cowl. "They didn't stand for the Cowl's rebukes, I suppose, when he wanted to know why I was so much alive."

The rifle fire increased in intensity, then faded away to occasional random reports. Peter stirred uneasily. His mission to Rapahawney was unnecessary, now that police forces surrounded the island. Rorke sat in the prow of their frail craft, his night glasses glued to his eyes. Searchlights swept over the rambling stone house, and men could be seen scrambling for cover from the glare.

"Looks like Von Tolz is locked out," Rorke grinned.

"Why don't the troopers step in now?" Peter demanded impatiently.

Rorke glanced backward into the darkness.

"They're waiting for the rockets from Arthur Chase. They don't care how many gangsters kill themselves. It'll make it so much easier to clean them up. It may be dawn before they start sweeping out this rotten nest."

"But suppose Dalton's gang wins out. They can navigate the *Junker*—"

"They won't get away," said Rorke confidently.

"For all I know," Peter protested, "Chase might never show up again, and I can't wait—not until dawn! I've got to get back in that house!"

"You're crazy."

"But Phyllis—everyone's cooped up in there with those gunmen! The men are unarmed, but the women—Jane, Phyllis, Diana—why, Phyllis must be in the house with Dalton!"

Peter cursed himself for sitting there without thought for the safety of the girl, and lurched to his feet. He could not wait for the organized forces of the law to cope with the Cowl and Dalton, not when Phyllis was alone in the house with Dalton, Trigger and Batty.

He had lost his revolver in the creek. He picked up one of Rorke's rifles, then discarded it as the reporter shoved a heavy service pistol in his hand.

"Take this. I'll carry the rifle."

Knee deep in the cold waters of the creek, Peter turned and shook his head. "No, you're not coming this trip, Larry. Only one of us can get into the house, my way. I know how."

Peter hugged the damp sand until he reached the rear of Willard House and felt himself treading freshly mown lawn grass. Here, in the shelter of the hedge, he took stock of his surroundings. The rambling house before him was plunged into total darkness, save for a faint streak of light that shone through a second floor window. Three rooms in Willard House had no windows whatsoever, being located deep in the center of the rambling structure. Peter decided that the vague trace of light in the hall window came through the open door of one of those rooms.

From his right, the rattle of an automatic rifle interrupted the sultry stillness with its sudden tattoo of death. Willard House was very much in a state of siege, standing starkly silent under the leaden, ominous sky.

From Peter's left, across the lawn, came four running, stooping shadows. The clouds broke capriciously at that moment, flooding the grassy open space with momentary moonlight. An angry staccato of rifle and machine gun fire from the upper windows of the house told Peter that the mutineers were well on guard. The raiding party crumpled under the withering fire and broke into disorderly retreat, amid muffled curses and the scream of a wounded gunman.

Peter studied the clouds that once again drifted over the pitted face of the moon. The night plunged into absolute blackness, save for the weirdly flickering searchlights which played over the lawn.

Rising to his rubber-soled feet, Peter left the security of the hedge and raced across the lawn like a fleeting, disembodied shadow. In the nick of time, he saw a spot of light creeping over the lawn toward him.

He flung himself down, panting, by the broken-down porch leading to the kitchen. The beam flickered past him.

Once again he took careful stock of his surroundings. He heard voices from somewhere above him, and concluded that the kitchen was occupied by a mutineer machine gun crew. He shrugged and crawled into the dank dampness under the porch.

Many times, as a boy, he had done this very thing. It was a tight squeeze now for his muscular adult body. He gasped with pain as a rough joist ripped through his sweater and shirt and scraped the flesh of his shoulders. He reached forward in the darkness, and his fingers found what they sought. They groped for the latch to the tiny, dust-encrusted window under the porch, and a moment later it opened with a faint creak of rusty hinges. Peter squirmed through and dropped hands first on the cold stone cellar floor of the house.

An abandoned pile of gasoline cans toppled over with an echoing clatter.

Peter drew his revolver and froze into the darkness.

Minutes of utter stillness passed by, during which he could hear the faint ticking of his wrist watch. From above, he heard the shuffle of nervous, impatient feet. From ahead, from the cellar stairs, came no sound of alarm.

He breathed easier.

Weapon gripped tightly in a steady hand, he made his way up the cellar stairs, paying cautious attention to any further invisible obstacles in the darkness. At the top of the creaking wooden stairs, he opened the door and found himself in the familiar servants' hall, dimly illuminated by a wash of light coming down the circular stairs to the second floor.

There was no one in sight. From the library that faced out to sea, he heard the murmur of husky voices and the sudden crack of a rifle. An acrid smell of burnt powder hung in the air of the besieged house. A tinkle of glass sounded somewhere as a bullet struck a window pane. A searchlight focussed on a distant window; Peter flattened himself against the wall as a ray of light shot down the corridor for a brief moment.

The next moment he ascended the dark pit of the circular staircase.

At the top he paused, weighing his next move. It was impossible to search all of the twelve rooms for Phyllis. From behind almost every door came scraps of movement.

From one of the inner rooms came the sound of familiar voices. Trigger Malone's piping tones and Batty's throaty bass.

He stiffened as he heard: "I won't do it. I can't, you damned fools! I can't!"

The voice was Arras Gordon's. Dr. Whitney's acid, cynical tones came next. "Of course I'll help your wounded. But only on the condition that you keep the rest of us safely in this room, out of danger."

"There's nothing wrong with the idea, Gordon," Batty said. "We're scramming, see, even if you and the Cowl are against this. And the sooner you fellows decide to help us, the better! This whole game's up, see?"

Trigger grunted: "Yeah, the game's up, all right! Notice the boats hanging around out there? And who the hell knows what's out in that blasted marsh right now? And where's Deuce and the copper? They got the finger on us, all right."

"But I still can't do what you ask me," Gordon insisted.

"Then we take the girls, anyway."

"Has Dalton gone to get Phyllis?"

Batty laughed coarsely. "Yeah—they're upstairs."

There came the sound of a scuffle as Gordon apparently made a sudden attempt to escape. Then the thud of a falling body. Peter waited to hear no more. There were only three rooms on the third floor of Willard House. Probably they would not be occupied by any gunmen.

He grew cold at the thought of Shifty menacing Phyllis, and the knuckles about his revolver turned white. This time there would be a decision.

He turned, raced swiftly back through the darkness and padded softly up the stairs to the third floor.

Chapter Twenty
CONCLUSION

Peter suddenly halted in the gloom of the small corridor as the house trembled and shook beneath his feet. A smashing blast of lightning rippled swiftly across the sky, then darkness folded in again, accompanied by a lengthy, rumbling crash of thunder. Immediately following the reverberations came a low, frightened moan, and then a stifled scream. A girl's scream.

Peter wasted no time. His shoulder smashed quickly against the flimsy wooden door, which burst open to reveal the dusty attic room. In the glow of a searchlight sweeping the walls of the house, he made out Phyllis, shrinking from the squat, menacing gangster—Shifty Dalton.

The gunman whirled about at his entrance, an oath on his lips. There were no words exchanged between the two men. The intention of each was written all too clearly in his blazing eyes. Dalton whipped out his weapon and fired blindly at the lithe, avenging shadow in the doorway.

The bullet plopped harmlessly into the woodwork, and a moment later Peter returned the fire.

Shifty cursed, released his grip on the girl's arm, and staggered to the table, leaning heavily upon it. Peter held his fire, loath to shoot the wounded man. A moment later he deeply regretted it. Dalton whirled suddenly, and again a long tongue of flame spat in the darkness of the room. A fiery bullet slashed into Peter's left forearm, then, his gray eyes flashing bitter hatred, he took deliberate aim at the gangster's silhouette and fired the second time.

Shifty lurched forward, grappled with him, and then crashed suddenly to the floor. The weapon clattered to the rough wooden boards.

There came a hysterical sob in the darkness.

Phyllis was in Peter's arms, clinging tightly to him. He paused long enough to kiss her, then said quickly: "There's no time to waste, my girl. Got to get out of here fast. The devil himself has broken loose."

Another crash of pregnant thunder was followed by a rattle of gunfire from all around the house. For a moment, Peter debated whether he should remain in hiding in the attic room until the police arrived. Then, realizing their attack would not come until dawn, and that long before that a search would be made by Shifty's friends, he recognized that his only move was to get out of Willard House.

It was not so easy as entering. Fortunately, the shots fired in his struggle with Dalton were not noticed by the besieged mutineers amid the rattle of intermittent fire that was taking place. But he was handicapped now by Phyllis and his wounded arm. Evidently, too, another concerted attack was being made by the Cowl's men. With the place surrounded, it would be next to impossible to reach the safety of the north beach and Larry Rorke.

The shrill, piping voice of Trigger Malone came up the stair well, high and thin with excitement.

"Hey, Dalton! Come down here! Leave the girl alone!"

Peter strained his eyes to pierce the darkness below. A flashlight flickered upward, and heavy feet sounded on the stairs. Trigger Malone was swearing.

The footsteps halted as the house shook and crashing, rending sounds filled the air. Peter's first thought was that the flickering lightning had at last struck Willard House. Then, as the explosion was followed by a confusion of shots and the cries of struggling men, he changed his opinion.

Someone downstairs yelled: "Bombs! The Cowl's using bombs on us!" It was Reds Finnegan.

Trigger's footsteps paused, then hurriedly clattered down the stairs as the sound of battle grew louder. Peter whistled inaudibly in relief. He took Phyllis' hand and gripped it tightly. Then they descended into the darkness of the second floor. Here he paused long enough to learn that the inner rooms were deserted. There was no trace of the Willard guests.

From the sound of struggle, Peter concluded that Baron von Tolz' loyal forces had at last gained entry into the left wing of the house. Accordingly, he raced with Phyllis toward the music room and the French windows that opened out on the lawn.

His plan turned out to be trustworthy. The mutinous gangsters had swarmed toward the shattered, bombed wing of the mansion. The sound of struggle grew louder and nearer.

In the dark shadows of the music room, Peter halted and gently pushed Phyllis behind him.

Something warned him of danger, of another person lurking in the curtained vagueness of the room. He kept a tight grip on the revolver and stood motionless, back against the wall. He felt Phyllis shrinking beside him, her soft, slight body trembling violently. Her hand gripped his arm nervously.

Thunder rumbled again over the tumult in the opposite wing of the house. In the flash of lightning that preceded it, Peter made out the crouching figure of a man.

"Arras!"

The outline of the short, stockily built man appeared in silhouette against a window illuminated by a roving searchlight. In his hand he held a gun. It was pointed at Peter.

"Phyllis and Peter, is it?"

"Yes. Where in God's name are the girls, the men?"

"Safe on the north beach by now, I imagine. Chase got them all out by some magic of his own. What are you doing?"

"Trying to get out of this ourselves."

Gordon laughed shortly in the darkness.

"Not so soon! The place is surrounded by the Cowl's men. They're winning. We'll be all right in a moment."

"With Von Tolz gunning for me? We're running, and running fast!"

Gordon said stubbornly, keeping the pistol pointed at Peter: "Nevertheless, we're all staying right here."

Peter wondered if the man were mad. A curious tingle of apprehension swept up and down his spine.

He asked: "What do you mean?"

Whatever Gordon had to answer was postponed for all time. Through the curtained windows came a sudden blaze of white light, followed by red, then green. The lawn glowed weirdly under the drifting fireballs that floated beneath the lowering, tumbling clouds.

"What was that?" Gordon asked sharply.

"Rockets," Peter said, with a vast sigh of relief. He felt more sure of himself now. "From the north beach, probably. It's Chase's signal."

"Signal? To whom?"

"The police."

Gordon's voice had the vibration of taut wires.

"Where are they?"

"All around the island."

Lightning flickered savagely, and Peter noted the extraordinary wanness of the man's scarred face. Gordon licked his thin, curled lips, his eyes narrowed behind the glinting spectacles, his glance darting from side to side. Darkness settled down again.

Footsteps sounded nearby, and the cursing of men grew louder above the ringing shots.

Gordon said tensely: "Dalton's men will be forced in here in a moment! Are you absolutely sure about the police?"

"I saw them."

The other groaned.

"Then get out. Quickly! I'll hold them off if they come in here too soon."

"But why—?"

"Phyllis—"

Peter nodded as though he understood, but he did not. There was something strange here, something ominous underlying the rattle and shouts of struggling men.

Phyllis clutched at his arm. Losing no more time, they crossed the music room and opened the window. With Phyllis deposited on the lawn, Peter turned to glance back at Arras Gordon. The door was open and the man was no longer in sight.

Huge, warm raindrops started to fall. They raced hand in hand across the lawn through the rain until they reached the security of the surrounding hedge. They were not a moment too soon. A murderous burst of machine gun fire swept the lawn from one of the upper windows. Peter just had time to throw Phyllis to the ground and drop down beside her before the spray of bullets whined over the spot where they had been standing.

To add to their difficulties, the searchlights froze on the area they had to cross. There was nothing to do but wait for another opportunity to increase the distance between the embattled house and themselves.

Phyllis held Peter's hand tightly. She suddenly gasped and looked at her fingers. They were covered with blood.

"Shifty nicked me," Peter murmured. "It's nothing."

But the girl insisted on examining the wound, and afterward swiftly bandaged it with a handkerchief.

In the moments that passed, Peter eagerly watched the scene. Within the house, things were clearly going the Cowl's way. The music room was now the last stronghold of the mutineers.

Von Tolz himself suddenly appeared on the lawn, surrounded by several of his men. He drew back his arm, and a little black object went hurtling through the air, to smash through a window. There came a deafening roar.

As though the explosion of the bomb were a signal for the forces of nature to demonstrate their powers, the clouds opened and the slow rain developed into a torrential downpour. It came down with a suddenness that was paralyzing, obscuring the scene with driving, stinging curtains of cold wetness.

From the shelter of the hedge, Peter caught a glimpse of another man running across the lawn. It was Arras Gordon. In his hand he held his pistol, and he raced straight toward the Cowl.

Puzzled, Peter watched.

When within a few paces of Von Tolz' back, Gordon suddenly trained the weapon at the giant's body and fired. Through the driving rain the pistol shot was little more than a tiny crack. But its effects were devastating.

The Cowl screamed once, twisted halfway about to face his attacker, and then his great form crumpled like a paper dummy. He fell face downward in the sea of trampled mud that had been the lawn.

At the same moment, the searchlights suddenly went dead. The entire island was plunged into darkness.

Shaken, Peter lifted the pale, trembling girl to her feet, and stumbled off in the darkness and night toward the security of the north beach.

"The Cowl is dead," Peter announced a few minutes later to the huddled group of drenched people on the sand.

Arthur Chase stepped from behind Larry Rorke to announce:

"And here comes his killer."

Through the streaming curtains of rain they made out Arras Gordon, stumbling and groping his way toward them.

From the opposite end of the island came the murmur and movements of many men. A siren wailed somewhere out to sea, and regulation police pistols barked heavily as the troopers descended on Little Swamp Island.

With the Cowl lying dead on the muddy lawn of Willard House, the battle between the opposing factions of gunmen came to an abrupt, stunned halt. As the thugs huddled together, exhausted and thoroughly bewildered, the forces of the law launched their attack. The searchlights came on again, trained on the clustered, ominously silent gangsters.

There came a moment's dramatic silence as the two forces faced each other in the brilliant light. Then came a curt command from the police for the gunmen to drop their weapons.

Reds Finnegan glanced at the encircling cordon and shrugged in resignation. He threw down the automatic rifle he cradled under his arm. As if it were a signal for the remainder of the hesitant men, the weapons of the gunmen dropped to the muddy lawn.

Peter sighed: "That does it!"

"Dear me, not quite!" Arthur Chase replied. Turning abruptly on pale Arras Gordon, he placed his hand on the other's shoulder. "I think it would be wiser if you gave us no further trouble, Gordon."

The addressed man started violently. His face grew paler than before, his eyes flashed angrily. "What do you mean?"

"You're under arrest."

"What for?" Gordon asked. His voice was high-pitched, angry, demanding an explanation.

Chase said quietly: "For the murder of Jed Willard! For blackmailing and murdering Baron von Tolz! For complicity in the Cowl's criminal activities! For the murder of Ralph Willard! Enough?"

Peter protested, unwilling to believe.

"But, Chase, I told you that Gordon, Rorke and I—" The detective did not withdraw the pistol from Gordon. He sighed again, heavily.

"I know. He was very careful to make it appear that he was on your side. Throughout everything, he appeared innocent of all criminal connection with Von Tolz. He saw to that."

"If he's on the Cowl's side—or was—" Rorke drawled pointedly— "why did he pretend at all when Vol Tolz took over the reins?"

"Because," Chase said slowly, "Gordon is the man the Cowl wanted to kill!" The little detective shrugged and went on: "It's rather a long story. You see, Peter, when you knew Gordon, he was not by any means wealthy. He worked in John Hark's offices and misused various funds to make money in the stock market. He got away with that, managing to clear enough to give him a taste of wealth and an overwhelming craving for a great fortune. Von Tolz, too, was obsessed with the idea of regaining the wealth and power he once had in Prussia. It was Gordon, however, who first turned to crime. He unearthed certain financial misdeeds the baron had committed, and held them over his head. Gordon, you see, wanted an intermediary between himself and the actual thugs who were to steal, rob and kill for his money. He selected the baron, gave him the title of the Cowl, and induced him by threats and bribery to act as middleman between himself and the Spinelli gang. All plans for criminal acts came not from the Cowl—although he certainly must have embellished some of them—but from Arras Gordon. And Gordon was as unknown in identity to the Cowl as Von Tolz was to the members of the Spinelli gang!"

The accused man snorted angrily, his steel-rimmed spectacles shining in the searchlight's radiance. "You must be mad! You haven't a shred of proof behind all this!"

"I think," Chase returned quietly, "that an investigation of this legacy you claim to have inherited will clear that up. But you can distinctly be proved guilty of the murder of Jed Willard and Ralph—not to mention killing the Cowl. Only one man could have committed both of the first two crimes. Jed Willard's murder gave me the choice of John Hark or you. Ralph's death could have been brought about by only one, and that was you. Only one man had the time, the opportunity, and the *motive* to make the movements you did before and after the first crime. You had the chance to set up the rifle on the lighthouse. You had the opportunity to take it down. You were the only man not to have an alibi when Ralph Willard was killed. You tried to use Miriam Whitney's hysterics to cover up your mistake, but she recovered sufficiently to tell me you lied when you said you were walking with her at the time of Ralph's death. I think the Cowl managed to worm the truth out of her, and you knew it. That was why you killed the Cowl before the police could arrive. That was why—"

Chase broke off suddenly as Gordon, with a choked curse, twisted about and seized the weapon with lightning rapidity from the surprised detective. For a brief moment, the group was paralyzed into immobility, and in that fraction of time he broke clear of the circle and raced through the downpour over one of Jed Willard's breakwaters that curved out to sea.

Peter, with Chase and Rorke, leaped into pursuit, the other men trailing close behind. Gordon soon realized he was hopelessly trapped. The wall ended well out in the black, cold, heaving ocean, with the incoming tide swirling huge rollers about its crumbing base. He hesitated at the end and stared for a moment at the deep, inky waters, weighing his chances for escape.

Then, before Peter's warning cry reached him through the rain, he jumped.

The three men reached the end of the concrete wall in time to see the wash of waters recede, disclosing sharp, jagged rocks piled saw-tooth fashion in the slippery sand. Sprawled upon them, his body half-dragged out over the low seawall by the tug of the tide, was Arras Gordon.

Another roller came smashing in, and when it receded, it took with it the body of the would-be master criminal.

Peter found Phyllis once again standing beside him. The rain streamed down her small, oval features, made her seem like some live, wild thing out of the night.

"As long as we're getting a load off our chests," she murmured, "I'd better explain a few things you want to know, Peter. You wonder why I've been with the Cowl so long— Well, it really isn't a difficult thing to explain. The baron told me something of the man who was blackmailing him, but told it in such a light as to make him seem an innocent victim. He asked me to help him in his attempt to uncover Gordon's identity, and pretended that all his activities with the Spinelli gang were for that purpose. I joined him. It was not until you awoke that day, to remember that you were Peter Willard, that I realized my uncle was not nearly so averse to crime as he pretended. His mind, I discovered, ran in criminal channels. From that moment, Peter, I was against him, working for you. I wish you would believe that."

Peter looked at the auburn-haired girl who stood so straight in the lashing rain, and felt strangely miserable, strangely humble.

"I don't know what to say," he began.

From landward, the troopers were shouting for Chase. Searchlights flickered over the beach, and vague, shadowy forms of men moved phantom-like through the driving rain.

Phyllis plucked nervously at his sleeve.

"They'll put you with the rest of them. To the law you're the Deuce, Peter. You must do something!"

He smiled reassuringly, although he by no means felt so certain of his fate as he pretended to be. His eyes narrowed against the driving rain. Catching Arthur Chase's glance, he said:

"Mr. Chase, we made a bargain, you and I. I want to know now, before it's too late, whether you're going to keep your part of it."

He indicated the approaching troopers. Phyllis shuddered, clinging tightly to him, anxiously watching the detective's round face. Chase smiled and shrugged. His pale blue eyes twinkled.

"Dear me," he sighed. "I've never had a failure yet—not in my entire career."

He surveyed Peter and chuckled.

"This is going to be my first. I promised you, young fellow, a twenty-four hour start. That would eventually prove futile, you know. However, I find myself faced with a most peculiar situation."

"And that is?"

"I set out to find a man known as the Deuce, a gunman and underworld character. I never ran across the man. I don't suppose I ever shall. Something tells me he no longer exists. True, I met you, but you are—Peter Willard.

"There won't be any need, Peter, for you to flee these approaching men. The search for the Deuce is officially ended. He no longer exists. I'll swear to that, if it ever proves necessary."

There came a low, grateful sob from Phyllis. Peter reached out, found and gripped the hand of Arthur Chase. There was nothing more to be said.

Then he swung about and picked up the sobbing girl in his arms. They disappeared through the driving curtain of rain toward Willard House.

THE END

Murder Money
EDWARD S. AARONS

Writing as Edward Ronns

CHAPTER ONE
MONEY GROWS ON TREES

The Greek looked at the world and said. "Pretty night, isn't it?"

He spoke as though he, alone, were responsible for it; and only the land and the wind, the sparkling, impersonal sea and the secretly whispering forest replied to him, because his companion, Leo Storm, was too busy looking at them all to bother answering such an obvious question.

The road on which the two men stood was a ribbon carelessly tossed on the side of the ocean-washed cliff; it coiled in apparently aimless curves and dips until it vanished over the crest of the hill, beyond which peeped the windowed gables of an ugly, weather-beaten house. In the other direction, the road objected temporarily to its downward path and swept upward over an arm of the promontory, seemingly disappearing in the nodding crests of the trees. Up there, the wretched wooden railing was completely disintegrated, but in the spot where the two men stood, the owner of the nearby house had guarded well against the straight-dropping cliff.

Storm, the taller of the two men, leaned beside the Greek, with his elbows on a splintery post; he moved as a splinter tugged at the rough cloth of his shirt, and watched a potato bug wend its perilous way along the precipice. Then he lifted his eyes and examined the Maine coast.

Below him the waters of Kennicut Bay glittered cold under the summer sun. Five miles across, through sheer, wet-whipped air, was the wooded arm that hugged the bay and protected it from the furious assaults of the sea. On the clear point of the opposite promontory stood the Shady Grove, the resort club that catered to the wealthy summer colony of Kennicut. The town itself could be seen snuggling intimately in the green forest, well in the shelter of the inlet.

Craft of all sizes dotted the water, but outstanding was the white motor yacht belonging to the man Burton, who owned and operated the Shady Grove. Closer to the cliff where the two men stood, about two miles down the coast beyond the mountain, was the Kennicut Hotel, a pile of white stone in the mathematical center of flat green lawns.

The Greek, round and faintly ludicrous in khaki shirt and tight-fitting breeches, had his fill of the scene. His two hundred pounds shook as he shoved away from the railing.

"But it makes me seasick," he concluded, referring to the giddy drop to the rocks below. "Let's scram."

His tall companion remained motionless, answering the Greek's original comment. "Yes, it's quite beautiful Poppo. You go ahead. I'll be along later."

The Greek shrugged, irritably rubbed a red jowl, and trudged away over the brow of the road. The tall man remained looking pensively down at the saw tooth rocks; he listened to the never-ending roar as the sea battled to take a mouthful of the black, defiant cliff. The water was never quite successful, but it always persevered.

The sound of the ocean blended with the hum of insects and the rustle of the wind in the birches, and the man sucked in luxurious breaths of the tangy, wet air. It smelled of the sea and the pungency of the pines, and he pulled the crisp coldness deep into his lungs. For the first time in too long, he decided, he was happy.

It was rare that he got into the open like this. He was essentially a man of the city, knowing its topmost gilt and polish, that of the cloud-touched penthouses, and knowing equally well the yellow-lighted dens of the river people. His life was not one that called for much communion with nature. The effect of the salt air was revealed in the healthy red flush that pocketed his hollow cheeks and the return of luster to the slate-gray eyes that twinkled behind his rimless spectacles.

His broad, thin-lipped mouth marked him as belonging to the formidable school; and the slight stoop of his sloping shoulders, due to his excessively gaunt height, did not cancel that impression of hardness. He looked flat and thin, until his gaunt stature was considered, and then you realized that his body was hard muscle, compact under well-cared for skin. His hair was thick, deep auburn in color, and the wind looped it over his forehead. The rimless glasses he wore gave him a pedagogical look, belied by the quick alertness of his eyes, that jumped with interest from one object to another. Cultivating the pedagogical impression as much as he could, because its deceptiveness was useful to him, he lost much of it as soon as he was alone.

He pushed away from the rail and trudged along the road that slipped over the hill; his broad mouth puckered to form a little "O." As he went, he whistled a strange tune—the aria from *Aida*.

At the top of the rise, where the road left the cliff edge and descended through the forest to the bay, he paused as though struck by an afterthought, left the road and plodded with bent shoulders through the leafy shadows of the woods. He was perspiring from the warmth of the sun, and his checked shirt and khaki trousers stuck to his limbs. His whistle faded, welled, and went shrilling without any particular melody through the silent stand of white beech and pine.

Above him on the hill—the house was no longer visible—he sighted a lone mast-pine, a magnificent specimen of a type almost extinct, due to the voraciousness of the New Englander for straight spars in his dancing wooden ships. He walked toward the tree through a delicate pattern of shadows, his heavy cordovan shoes sinking deep into the till of the soil. A tall, gaunt man, he had to duck continually to avoid the low hanging branches.

The whistle welled louder, resumed its sonorous melody, and then abruptly stopped.

Light from a lost ray of sunshine was suddenly shattered into quivering splinters as Storm's head jerked up sharply, and he peered through his rimless glasses at the tree before him.

"Curious," he muttered.

The brief-case definitely did not belong there, Nothing belonged there, save, perhaps, the nest of one of the birds that betrayed their presence by excited calls.

The brief-case was stuck in a crotch of the tree, which stood in the center of the little clearing. It was not the majestic mast-pine, which stood on the crest of the ridge about twenty feet farther on; it was a birch tree, and the brief-case had no business sitting in it. some twelve feet from the ground.

"Funny," Storm said.

He walked around the tree, studying the turf; squatted at the base of the trunk and thoughtfully regarded the heel prints of a man's shoe. One set was deeply indented into the soft loam, as though the man who had put the brief-case into the tree—for it had scarcely flown there—had jumped from the crotch and landed heel-first.

Storm took off his spectacles and polished them absently, looking up again at the brief-case, shining black against the bark. He looked speculatively at the tree trunk, flattened his palm against it, shrugged and smiled. He hadn't ever climbed a tree, but crowding thirty was not too old to begin. Curious by nature, he had known from first sight that he was going to climb the tree and inspect the brief-case.

It was less difficult than he had imagined, for his gaunt stature helped him. Jumping up and catching at the lowest branch, he brought his heels up against the trunk and wriggled one leg over the bough. He sat there for a moment, almost exulting in his triumph; then he carefully considered his next move, for, besides being curious, he was also a methodical man.

He reached a foot-stand on the branch and found that his head was level with the shining leather case. He hugged the tree with one arm and swung the black bag from its nest. It was heavy, swelled to the bursting point with its contents. Carefully edging down, he resumed his seat on the branch.

He fully intended to return the case to its place, after a peek at its contents. He was certain that it was put there for a purpose; it could hardly be listed as a lost object, because articles are rarely misplaced in trees. He reasoned that someone intended to call for the bag and, because he had an unwelcome streak of inherent honesty, he fully intended to replace it. There he remained in the tree, for he did not relish returning to the ground and then repeating his Tarzan performances to return the case to its original position.

The leather straps offered no difficulty; the major obstacle to the satisfaction of his curiosity was the brass catch on the case. He frowned when he discovered that it was locked, but then reflected that, for his purpose, the straps allowed enough leeway to permit a glance at the contents.

Storm took his glance—and almost fell out of the tree.

"I'll be damned," he said slowly.

There was money in the brief-case. Cool, green packets of United States currency. Packet upon packet of it. By reaching his thumb and forefinger between the leather, he could ruffle the edges of the top packet.

He was pleased to see twenty-five one-thousand dollar bills riffle under his thumb. Thousand dollar bills. Funny. He stared, but the thousands remained.

Altogether, he reflected, there was quite a fortune sitting in his lap. And he was sitting in a tree, quite alone....

But the decision of honesty was quickly taken out of his hands.

A voice yelled, "Hi! Hi, you!"

After the voice came a crashing of underbrush, and finally a man broke into the clearing, out of breath, stumbling through the berry bushes and thorn-apple.

He was short and slight, dressed in a brown sack suit that marked him as coming from the wealthy resort colony down on the beach. His face was chubby and flushed, with a button of a nose that stuck out from his flat cheekbones. His ears were small and brick-red, perpendicular to the sides of his head. Storm recognized him. His name was Toogy, and he came from Burton's Shady Grove Club across the bay.

Toogy yelled again and came to a halt below Storm. "What are you doing up there, mister?"

"Just sitting," said the tall man, unperturbed.

The little man's ears went a shade darker in hue. "I mean, where did you get that case?"

"From the tree," said Storm, his calm deepening as he examined the little man.

"Well, hand it over," said Toogy. He added as an afterthought, "It's mine."

Storm laughed and smiled down at Toogy. He said airily, "Finders keepers."

"Yeah?"

"Certainly," said Storm, swinging his legs.

"It's mine!" Toogy rasped. "I want it."

"Prove that it's yours."

Toogy stepped back a little, suddenly apprehensive of Storm's swinging legs. The heavy cordovans, were coming perilously closer to his upraised jaw with each swing.

"Listen," Toogy said, backing away. "You listen. The money is mine."

Storm smiled broadly, and Toogy said defensively "Sure, I know what's in that case. Money! I guess that proves it's mine."

"How much?"

"None of your business, monkey. Don't try any funny stuff, or I'll get the law."

"Go right ahead," Storm invited. "I'll wait."

Toogy curled his lip at him. He drew back another three paces until he was well out of reach of Storm's swinging heels. His hand dropped to his hip pocket, and when it came in sight again, it was closed around an ugly looking black automatic. Sunlight spread a sheen along the barrel as it pointed up at Storm's middle.

Storm abruptly lost his smile. "Oh, my," he said.

"Yeah." Toogy breathed hard. "I guess I won't bother calling the law. I'm my own law."

Storm's lips twitched again. "Naughty boy."

"Nuts. Toss down the grip, monkey. I won't hesitate to use this gadget. I know how."

"Undoubtedly you do. My only regret is that I haven't one with me to prove I can use those gadgets better than you."

"That's too bad. Toss down the cash."

Storm shrugged, hesitated, then moved. He wobbled, as though he had momentarily lost his balance, and regained his equilibrium with a vast sigh of relief.

"Quick!" Toogy urged.

Storm looked away over his head. Beyond the clearing, with its surrounding wild raspberry and thornapple bushes, with their pink blossoms, he saw something stirring that had no part in nature.

He delayed, asking naively, "Is this money real?"

Toogy snarled. "Sure. Even queer-peddlers got more sense than to make such big bills, sap. Where'd you shove grand notes?"

"Yes, that's true," Storm nodded. "The money must be good."

The slight delay of his question gained his objective. From out of the bushes behind Toogy arose a strange figure. First a wide-brimmed Stetson sombrero poked over the brush, followed by an earth-colored face adorned by a broad, practically toothless grin. A body followed the head. A food-stained vest, ablaze with badges and medals of all grades and insignia, and a pair of tattered blue jumpers completed the main items of clothing.

What interested Storm was the business-like six-shooter in the man's grimy paw. It waggled at the unsuspecting Toogy's back.

"Stickum up. You just drop gun."

The command was flat, emotionless, coming out of that grinning, toothless mouth. Toogy started, whirled, and shivered involuntarily as he sighted the newcomer. He hesitated, the automatic in his hand pointing at the ground, and Storm took off from the tree in a flying leap.

He hit Toogy just below the shoulder-blades, and the little man went down like a tenpin struck by a sixteen-pounder. He squawked once; the air sizzled with his vitriolic curses.

Storm rolled over, freed himself of Toogy, picked up the man's automatic and calmly proceeded to empty the clip.

Toggy stared, transfixed, at the ragged looking man in the Stetson hat.

"Who—who the hell is he?"

Storm looked up, pocketing the shells. "The Sheriff. Everybody knows the Sheriff."

"Cops!"

Toogy's red ears seemed to stick out straighter from the side of his head. His bright little eyes were like a trapped animal's, slewing through the woods as though seeking a path of escape.

"Keep your gun on him, Sheriff," said Storm. He handed the empty automatic to Toogy, and indicated the black leather case that lay at the foot of the tree. "That money yours, Toogy?"

The little man was startled. "No—no. How come you know my name, mister?"

"I know a lot of people. You work for Wheels Burton. Tell him, if he wants this stuff, he'll have to come for it himself, with an explanation."

"Sure." Toogy swallowed and glanced at the Sheriff, who had seated himself on a log and was staring moodily at the big six-shooter.

"Scram," said Storm shortly.

Toogy looked dazed. "You mean I can go? This cop—"

"The Sheriff is a low-grade moron. A village character. He likes to parade around in badges, with a blank revolver. He never hurt a fly."

Toogy swallowed again and looked down at his empty automatic.

"Damn you," he muttered. He turned on his heel and trudged toward the trees. He called back over his shoulder, "I'll get you, monkey!"

Storm waved an airy hand at the gunman.

"I'll be waiting, Toogy."

CHAPTER TWO
EASY COME, EASY GO

Leo Storm stood for a moment watching Toogy's retreating form. Sunlight found his hollow cheeks, outlined the smile that quirked around his mouth and reflected the humor that twinkled in his gray eyes. He put on his glasses. The shadows of the forest softened his irregular features and made him attractive, in a reckless way.

Toogy disappeared, and Storm, with a little shrug, walked across the clearing and picked up the briefcase It was still locked, and he made no attempt to break the lock or cut the leather, but tucked it under his arm and looked at the "Sheriff."

The man was a breed Indian of indeterminate tribe, but probably both Passamaquoddy and Wawanock, with a goodly portion of French-Canadian. Mentally deficient, the Indian was a character of note around Kennicut, a sight to be pointed out to visitors, with his array of weird buttons and blank-cartridge revolver. He was seen only when he wanted liquor; when drunk, he vanished into the woods to some hidden shack of his own, and gave no trouble. As a guide to hunters he was invaluable, and save for the one mental quirk that convinced him he was the duly elected and sworn sheriff of the county, he had no further peculiarities. Since the legitimate Sheriff Corlwye did not object, no one else did.

The Indian pocketed his blank revolver and grinned toothlessly. "Shrimp had you treed, Mr. Storm."

Leo Storm nodded. "Thanks, Sheriff."

He dug in his pocket and gave the Indian a crumpled dollar bill. "Go into town and get drunk. Then go hide."

"Huh. You bet!"

Storm trudged off through the woods, brief-case under his arm. To his irritation, the earth-colored Indian slid alongside, moving silently and with a peculiar grace through the brush.

"My boss comes back today," the Indian offered. "Boss lives on hill."

"The Coulters? The people who own that big house on the cliff?"

"You bet. Come back today. Old Coulter rich as all hell. I work for him—for nephew, too. Gregory Dolman. Gimme plenty money, then I get drunk and hide like hell."

"Not a bad idea," Storm commented.

He said nothing more until they were close to the winding road that he had deserted some twenty minutes before. A tan Cadillac touring car was cautiously rolling around the escarpment, headed for the slight rise and then the dip into the valley and Kennicut.

There were three people in the car: the driver, a round-faced man whose hair was prematurely thin on top; a monkey-like, thin old man who looked straight ahead; and a girl who sat trim and straight, a neat white felt hat protecting her honey-colored hair.

"The Coulters," volunteered the Indian.

"The girl, too?"

The Indian shook his head. "Nope. She's the new secretary, Val'rie Feather. She lives at the hotel—room's not ready for her at the Roost."

"Roost?"

"Devil's Roost. Name of house, same name as mountain: Devil's Mount."

Storm watched the car go by. The young-oldish man who was driving would be Gregory Dolman. He nodded to the Indian when he saw him, and put on the brakes. The left rear tire exploded with a *pow!*

The Cadillac swerved, heading for the rail, then came to a halt in a cloud of rattling gravel and rolling dust. Dolman leaned over the door and looked back at the sagging chassis. He cursed, then apologized to the honey-haired girl.

"It's a flat," he said. "It will have to be changed."

The Indian left Storm and went up to the car eagerly. "I fix it, Mr. Dolman."

The Indian set to work. Storm leaned back against the tree, saying nothing, watching the car and the sky and always the girl. She looked once at him, a sidelong glance that settled with a little violet glitter on the brief-case tucked under his arm. For a moment he thought her eyes had gone slightly wider—they were quite beautiful eyes, he observed—and her red mouth puckered into a soundless "Oh."

She turned to the thin, shrunken old man. "I think I'll take a walk, Mr. Coulter. If you don't mind."

"No. But come back in time, however."

The old man had a nasal voice, high-pitched, that contrasted with the girl's quiet, "I will, sir."

She stepped out of the car, revealing herself as being rather tall and slender, and possessing good taste in clothing. She hesitated a moment on the gravel road, then struck off with a graceful, purposeful stride toward the top of the hill.

Storm gave her three minutes and then melted back into the shadowy woods. His cordovans made no sound as they crushed into the thick carpet of pine needles and soft till. For a few minutes his thin body achieved a silent grace of motion, of a different sort than the girl's. He reached the little clearing and the solitary birch tree that stood in a puddle of buttery sunshine and went down on his knees, pillowing them on the dryness of the black leather brief-case. He watched the clearing.

The girl arrived, as he had expected.

She came with a hurried step, walking awkwardly because of her high heels, which sank into the soft earth. Her face and her violet eyes were quick with alertness and puzzlement, her glance slewing around with quick stabs at the silently nodding, pungent woods,

She went straight to the white birch and looked up at the crotch in the branches where Storm had first discovered the brief-case. She looked puzzled, then half-angry, and finally frightened.

She knelt, as Storm had done, and examined the heel marks in the turf around the tree trunk.

Storm watched her from behind the brush and murmured, "So our honey-blonde knows about the cash, too, but not enough to be a convincing owner!"

The girl stood up with a little clucking sound of despair, searching the surrounding undergrowth with anxious eyes. He got up from his place of concealment, brushed his knees and tucked the brief-case under his arm once more.

He said politely, "Looking for something, Miss Feather?"

The girl started and made a little frightened gesture with her gloved hands at the sudden sight of the tall man. Her eyes ran away from him with quick panic: then they swiveled and fastened with unconcealed fascination on the black leather corner of the brief-case, which stuck out from between Storm's arm and his shirt.

She said, "I—why, no, I'm just—just walking."

She laughed and came toward him. Her eyes, drifting from the brief-case to his face, met his slate-gray eyes behind their rimless spectacles.

She asked with naive simplicity, "What have you got there?"

"This brief-case?"

"Yes. What's in it?"

"Leaves," said Storm soberly. "I'm making a leaf collection. I've got this brief-case just crammed with leaves. I specialize in green ones."

Perplexity lingered on her face for another moment, to be replaced with a flash of anger. A veil dropped over her violet eyes. "Oh," she smiled. "You're fooling me, aren't you?"

"Indeed, I wouldn't do any such thing."

"May I see your—leaves?"

She reached out an impulsive arm to take the briefcase, and Storm's smile was one of polite embarrassment. "I'm afraid not. The wind, you know—leaves like these are lost so easily."

He was mocking her, stinging her to anger, but she matched his calmness.

"May I—"

She paused, then said, "I suppose you often give exhibits of your famous collection—I'm sure it's famous. Your leaves must be well known."

Storm smiled and decided he liked the girl. He said with continued politeness, "Yes, you've no idea how popular my leaf collection is. And most rival collectors are so unscrupulous—they wouldn't hesitate to use any means by which they could steal the very choicest of my collection."

She bit her very red underlip. "Yes, I suppose they would."

"So," said Storm, still smiling, "don't try to get your gun out of your purse."

Her eyes darted quick hatred at him. "How did you know—"

"I'm psychic. Or perhaps it bulges." He shrugged and tucked the bag tighter under his arm. His voice was expectant as he said, "Of course, I'm not averse to private exhibitions with people I can trust. There are so many people who know more about my collection than I do myself. I'm really not much of an authority on the subject of leaves—green leaves."

She said, "Yes," in an abstracted tone, and then asked abruptly, "Aren't you Leo Storm? The man who took the cottage beyond Devil's Mount?"

He bowed slightly. "Yes, I am. But I'm staying at Kennicut Hotel temporarily, until the Greek gets the cottage in shape. The Greek is my aide-de-camp, you might call him. My hotel room is 715. And yours?"

"713."

"Next door neighbors," Storm murmured with mock delight. "I'm sure we'll get together soon."

"It will have to be soon," Valerie Feather smiled. "I'll be living at the Roost in a short time—Mr. Coulter's secretary, you know, and I—"

The sound of a starting motor recalled the girl to her position. She turned hurriedly, glanced with reluctance at the brief-case, and then ran toward the road and the waiting touring car. Storm watched her trim, lithe figure until it was out of sight. His gray eyes became thoughtful.

"Let come what may—" he murmured, and poked his spectacles higher up on the little bump below the bridge of his nose.

He waited until the sound of the car was gone, and then circled the little clearing until he found a log that would make a comfortable seat in the underbrush. He fully expected someone new to visit the clearing. It was obvious to him that the real owner of the money had yet to put in an appearance.

The sound of the sea tearing savagely at the cliffs and the twitter of birds and unseen little animals were all he had for company. He seated himself on the log and watched the solitary birch tree.

He did not have long to wait.

Presently a voice said, "I'm sorry to have kept you waiting."

The voice was a man's, cultured and resonant, and it was accompanied by the shocking-cold feel of the muzzle of a gun that was pressed tightly to the back of Storm's neck.

"No, don't turn," said the man.

There was a faint odor of bath salts in the air. Lavender. Storm sniffed and sat motionless. He did not turn his head.

The man with the gun spoke, with the faintest of lisps "I could have shot you down like a rabbit, Mr. Storm, but for the fact that I do not believe in injuring innocent bystanders. And I know you are innocent of any preconceived connection with my business affairs."

Storm sniffed again.

"I saw you discover the money quite innocently," the man with the gun went on. "I was watching you. Let me assure you that the brief-case and its contents are mine. I'd describe the money to you and give you the exact count—it's close to a quarter of a million dollars to satisfy your curiosity—but I haven't the time to prove my ownership."

"Your gun does that," Storm said easily.

"True. You are sensible, I see. And let me again assure you that the money is mine."

The man reached around Storm and lifted the brief-case from his knees. Storm saw a smooth, plump white hand, the fingers ornamented with a single green scarab ring, and a shirt cuff of London-tailored fabric. Then the hand disappeared and the gun muzzle was withdrawn from Storm's neck.

"Please sit right where you are for ten minutes. I may have other men covering you, you know."

Storm nodded and pulled a pipe from his pocket, loading it slowly with rough-cut tobacco. He struck a match to the bowl as the stranger's footsteps faded toward the road at his back.

He sat there, patiently, for double the time, for twenty minutes, peacefully smoking his pipe.

He was not in the least anxious to be killed.

CHAPTER THREE
GIRL WITH FRIGHTENED EYES

It takes a peculiar type of courage to occupy the table in Lucci's that is placed by the window, and the girl who slid into a chair and ordered chicken salad on toast did not look particularly courageous. She gave her order to Lucci himself when the maestro of gastronomics approached her with his famous toothy smile.

"Miss feather, you're not occupying your regular seat."

Valerie made no answer, only scanned the menu. Her voice had a strained quality when she said, "I feel like watching the beach."

With her honey-colored hair and deep, murky violet eyes, reminiscent of a summer twilight, the girl was a delight to Lucci, who worshipped beauty not alone for beauty's sake, but because it attracted more male customers to his Kennicut restaurant. He merely observed that her eyes were beautiful, and did not stop to consider that the smoky haze in their wide depths veiled a blazing, bright flame of terror in her mind.

Despite her inward agitation, her oval face, with its red, red mouth, remained perfectly calm as she awaited her order. She smoothed her white linen suit, inspected the tips of her brown-and-white sport shoes, and adjusted the smart little hat that sheltered the honeyed coronet she fashioned of her hair.

Then she turned to the newspaper she held in her hand. She opened it to the features page and read the article in the upper left-hand corner. The column was unsigned; its writer was a mysterious figure even to the editor of the mighty *Post-Tribune*. There were many men who skulked in the big cities' canyons who would gladly have sat in the chair up the river for the opportunity of greeting the writer in the next world. Everyone read the column; and that included the police. It was a crime column from which even the dapper Lieutenant Tilliman of the Maine state troopers had gained an occasional clue—and whose writer Tilliman had cursed many, many times in his mildly weary tones.

Valerie read only the opening paragraph:

SKELETONS IN YOUR CLOSET
What retired jewelry merchant has gone haywire over the Spiritualist Foundation, believing so much in the powers of the Celestial Sphere that he sells this week the major part of his jewel collection for a quarter of a million dollars, and plans to make a public donation of the cash to the earthly guiders of Spirit-Land? ... We say: watch this affair. That kind of money floating around in public generally winds up floating in a pool of blood.

No signature; no further explanation. Valerie pushed aside the paper with a little shudder and looked up again at the window. Her features grew a little more pale, and her fingers went to her lips to suppress a tiny, choking gasp.

The object of her fear looked harmless enough. He was a little man with brick-red ears that stuck out perpendicularly from the sides of his head; his eyes were bright, set deep in his flat, puggish face. He pressed one little red ear against the window and stared at Valerie with intent interest.

"Toogy," she said, and crushed the paper in her grip.

Lucci came back with a waiter and set her sandwich before her. There was none of the lambent fear only mild annoyance—in Valerie's eyes as she looked up and said, "Lucci—that man. Can't you make him move?"

Lucci pulled in his fat bulk and stared through the window at Toogy, who stared right back with unblinking brown eyes. Lucci flushed, embarrassed. He raised his eyebrows.

"I'm so sorry, Miss Feather. These people, they have no manners. We cannot stop them. If you care to change your table?"

"That won't make any difference. He'll still watch me. He's been watching me for three days."

Lucci said, inflecting his syllables to make it a question, "I don't understand?"

"Neither do I."

She scarcely touched the chicken salad; whenever she looked up, there was the little man, pressing first his brick-red ears to the window, then his nose. He looked at her with bored impatience shining quick in his bright animal eyes.

In five minutes Valerie got up, her red mouth compressed into a tight little line. She walked through the revolving doors into the blasting heat of the sidewalk. Toogy turned slowly and watched her unblinkingly and, after a moment's pause, followed her as she walked quickly through the crowds of vacationers toward the Kennicut Hotel.

Her heart was a thudding triphammer in her breast. She told herself that she was being a fool, that no one had reason to suspect her of anything, that she was a nobody. The little man with the ears could not possibly want anything from her.

She paused and glanced deliberately into a shop window, then turned around. Toogy was strolling after her, hands in his pockets, his lips puckered into a soundless whistle.

There couldn't be any doubt about it. She *was* being followed!

Here eyes cruised over the hot, murky street, her under-lip caught tightly between small white teeth. She examined the green slopes of the land above her, then the curving coast of the bay and the distant hotel, whose white walls reflected the glare of sunlight. She began walking along the shore, her high heel twinkling with her frantic urge for speed; then she suddenly slowed as she considered the plan she had just evolved in her mind. Her full red lips curled into a smile.

"I'll just see neighbor Storm about Mr. Toogy," she told herself.

Every morning for the past three days, since meeting Storm near the birch tree, Valerie had come down the hotel corridor to the accompanying click-click of smartly moving high heels; and every morning, on passing down the hall from her small suite to the elevator, she had seen the tall, thin man with the rimless glasses, lounging against door 715 and watching her.

She learned nothing about Leo Storm. She did not speak to him again, nor even glance at him—at least, not so that he could observe that she was looking at him. She had not approached him about the affair of the brief-case, since she had suddenly found no value in his insolent banter. But she could use him now. And if he were as good as he looked, the problem of Toogy would soon be settled.

She paused before 715 and pressed her forefinger to the ivory bell with a determined little jab. She waited, listening to the tinkle of a bell somewhere, and heard some scuffing sounds, a muffled exclamation of annoyance, and then heavy, slow footsteps approaching the door.

A short, squat man, with the homeliest face Valerie had ever seen, bulked large in the doorway. He was partly bald; had a wide mouth, deep-set raisin eyes, and lifted eyebrows. She concluded that this was the Greek.

"Yeah?" he asked.

Valerie hesitated, then said, "I want to see Mr. Storm."

The man in the doorway shrugged. "He's gone, lady."

"That's right, Poppo—tell her I'm out," said a voice.

Valerie pushed her way determinedly past the chunky man and stepped through the foyer. The tall man, in a white gabardine suit, squatted on the floor, legs folded under him, Buddha-fashion. But he was not contemplating prayer. He was watching the tantalizing gyrations of a pair of dice that spun on the hardwood floor against the wall.

He did not look up at Valerie.

The dice came down six and three.

"My win," said Leo Storm. "One more cast and you owe me a five-spot dinner at Lucci's, Poppo."

"Let's see," asked the Greek, leaving Valerie.

Both men examined the dice. Poppo agreed regretfully that Storm had won. Storm twisted his neck and looked up at the girl in the white suit.

"Good afternoon," he smiled. "Come to pay a neighborly call, Miss Feather?"

She detected sarcasm in his voice, and said, irritated, "It's business."

"If it's about my leaf collection," Storm said wearily, "I haven't got it any longer. And I don't want it."

She said briskly, "I know that. But I *am* being followed, and I want you to help me."

"And what makes you think *I* can help you?" he answered.

She said doubtfully, "You just look like—like the sort of man who would."

He looked shocked. "Poppo, get me a mirror—I want to see what kind of a face I'm wearing today!"

"I thought—I mean, you look like a detective," she said desperately. "Aren't you?"

He considered for a moment. "Yes—and no. In my spare time, I would say."

"And what do you do as your regular business?"

Storm straightened his legs, but kept sitting on the floor, palms flat behind him. He laughed up at her.

"You know, I don't really mind answering your questions. I'll tell you what I do: nothing. Just nothing. Unless you count fishing and swimming and digging mummies as a vocation."

"Mummies?"

"Egyptians. Dead ones. I'm first a man who loves to do nothing: a parasite; secondly, I'm an archeologist—at least, I kidded myself into believing I was one last summer; thirdly, I'm a detective, of sorts. I dabble," he smiled, "in crime."

She raised her eyebrows. "Versatile, aren't you?"

"Oh, yes. Very."

"And modest."

"No."

He grew tired of keeping his neck twisted. He flexed his long legs and got to his feet with a groan. He looked very tall and slender, with his slightly stooped shoulders and spectacles giving his eyes the opaque expression of a student dazed by the vast compass of this world's knowledge. He smiled self-defensively and waved a hand at the Greek.

"Now that you know all about me, meet my assistant: Xerxes Byron Nikopopolis," he said expansively. "Poppo, for short."

Valerie glanced briefly at the squat, broad-shouldered Greek, whose homely face cracked momentarily into a mechanical smile.

"I don't believe it," she said.

Storm nodded seriously. "It took me a long time to convince myself, too—No, don't touch, Poppo!"

The Greek was reaching for the dice that lay on the floor. Storm scooped them up with a long arm and stood rattling them in his hand.

The Greek muttered, "I think they're loaded."

"One more toss, Poppo," Storm said briskly. "Then you pay for dinner at Lucci's." He turned with a little bow and a smile to Valerie. "Care to join us, Miss Feather?"

She stared unhappily at the tall, thin Storm. His smile was pleasant. Eyes twinkling. She decided with inward humor that, if he were insane, it would be best to humor him. She might as well play.

The Greek lost his cast immediately and, for some reason, Storm failed to make his point of eight. Valerie knelt, rattled the ivory cubes awkwardly, and cast a trey and an ace.

"What do I do now?" she asked.

"Roll until you get seven or four. Four you win, seven you lose."

Valerie's eyes became determined. She wriggled to a firm position and asked, "How do ducks go to water?" And answered herself, "In pairs."

She cast, and a pair of two's showed up.

The Greek exploded into a stifled exclamation. "What an amateur!"

Storm smiled. "So we treat *you* to dinner at Lucci's."

"No, thanks," Valerie answered. "If you will just condescend to act sane for a few moments, and listen to me, I'll call the debt off. As a matter of fact, I'm in terrible trouble, Mr. Storm."

"You said you were being followed."

"For three days," she nodded. "A man has been watching me for all that time. It's the same man. Just now, I almost had to run to get rid of him. But he knows I live here at the hotel; he'll pick me up again."

"Has he ever spoken to you? Annoyed you?"

"No."

"Do you know who he is?"

"He goes under the name of Toogy. He is one of Wheels Burton's men."

Storm opened his mouth, shut it, poked his spectacles up higher with his middle finger.

He said, "You know that Wheels Burton is New York's number one gambler?"

Valerie nodded. "I know."

"Why should Toogy, who is one of Burton's many stooges, be following you? What could Wheels be wanting that you've got?" Storm looked suddenly at the Greek. "That—that leaf collection?"

"No. I don't have it—I know you don't, either. I don't know why Toogy should be following me. I only want you to—"

"Perhaps it's because you know something about it."

"I don't!" she said passionately. "I don't know anything about it. I only—"

Her voice trailed off, and she sat down in a leather armchair, flexing her fingers around the oak knobs.

Storm expelled a little puff of air and walked to the window. He felt annoyed, primarily because he had expected a few more moments alone with the Greek and the dice. His eyes were irritated as he looked beyond the window into the shimmering July heat that crushed the bay and its resort settlement. Most of the streets of the small town of Kennicut were deserted, blasted empty by the temperature and the breathless, sticky air.

Finally he said to the girl, "What do you want me to do?"

"I want you to get rid of this man who is shadowing me, I'll—I'll pay you well. I want you to get rid of Toggy."

"We charge five hundred dollars for murder," said the Greek sourly. "You could get it done cheaper by hiring big-city talent."

"I—I didn't mean that. I just want to be free of this man."

Storm said, "But if you won't tell us why he is following you—"

"I can't tell you, because—because I don't know."

"Nuts." That from the Greek. "Why not call in the cops?"

Valerie's eyes jerked around, settled on a spot on her brown-and-white sport shoes. "No," she whispered. "No. I don't want any publicity. You see, I work as secretary to Myron Coulter—the wealthy man who lives on Devil's Mount. He's not exactly good-natured, and I—I need the job."

"Coulter's the one with the jewel collection?" the Greek asked ponderously.

"Yes. He's rather ill. I'll be going to the house tomorrow, and I can't have Toogy or any other gangster following me. The reason, you see, is Mr. Coulter's jewels. I'm afraid there is some plot afoot to steal them."

She took the newspaper she carried and showed Storm the crime gossip-column she had read in the restaurant. "You see, this writer believes—"

"He's full of beans, whoever he is."

Valerie looked indignant. "But this column has often predicted events that actually happened. I'm afraid Toogy's following me has something to do with this prediction about money floating in—in blood."

Storm exchanged glances with the Greek and shrugged his sloping shoulders. "How does your problem fit in with this crack in the column about a sale of jewels for cash?"

"Myron Coulter is the man who is selling his jewels," she explained, suddenly breathless. "He's receiving cash, a quarter of a million dollars, and he insists on making a public donation to this Spiritualist Foundation." She clasped her hands nervously and anticipated Storm. "No, what you found in the woods wasn't it. The sale hasn't been made yet."

"Then suppose you tell the police all about it," he suggested again. "I'm here only to loaf—besides, the problem belongs in the hands of the legitimate police, not in mine."

Valerie looked down at her sport shoes once more, then lifted scornful eyes at Storm. "You won't help me?"

"No. Any other time you find someone trailing you—well, put it down to your looks, Miss Feather."

The girl's eyes snapped anger at him, and he thought she looked quite beautiful when she was angry. He started to say so, but the girl bounced out of her chair, exclaiming, "I think you're quite hateful!"

She high-heeled out of the room, the slam of the door echoing in the silence that accompanied Storm's worried glance.

The Greek said, "It's a simple case, Leo. The girl is in the second stage of developing paranoiac tendencies. She has what the book calls delusions of reference. She believes everybody watches her. It's simple, Leo. She lives a dull life as a secretary to an old and grouchy millionaire, and has no social opportunities, She probably *wishes* someone would follow her. And so she picked out someone she thinks adventurous. Toogy, the little rat. She's just repressed."

"Shut up," said Storm briefly.

He walked to the window and watched the girl's trim figure cross the lawn about seven stories down. He was doing a little thinking. Not too much. Enough to make him observe the two little bugs that crawled along after her on the sidewalk. The two insects got into a car and rolled slowly in the girl's wake.

Storm reached for his felt hat and sloped his shoulders into his coat.

The Greek looked at him with puzzled eyes. "I thought we were going up to the cottage."

"You go. I'll meet you there, Poppo. Maybe tonight, or tomorrow. Pay me the dinner you owe me some other time."

"And where are you going?"

"After the girl. She's in trouble. She's really being followed."

CHAPTER FOUR
THE CORPSE—

Dikran Nakesian's apartment was in the Wawanock, a poor second to the Kennicut Hotel, as hotels went in the resort colony. His apartment was designed in a U-shape. The third-floor corridor of the Wawanock did not go completely through to the back of the building, but ended in a dark-paneled doorway that simply had the spiritualist's name on it in tiny letters. The doorway opened into a reception chamber, with rooms on either side that flanked the common corridor. One arm of the *U* consisted of Dikran Nakesian's living quarters; the other constituted his business chambers, in which the Nakesian told gullible old women and fluttery young girls the secret of what would come to pass in their lives.

The business quarters were further divided into a seance room and a smaller room where the spiritualist retired when exhausted from his efforts to contact the departed spirits—who sometimes were very shy of appearing, and often mischievous in giving out misleading information.

Dikran Nakesian was, ordinarily, an exclusive creature. Rarely did he have more than one client in his place at a time. His appointments were made by the Hindu, Ali: an efficient man with yellow eyeballs who saw to it that none of the receptions ever conflicted. It was all the more remarkable, therefore, that, on that summer afternoon in Kennicut, Nakesian was playing host to three men simultaneously in his seance chamber.

The room was circular, its walls completely hidden by maroon drapes that reached from ceiling to floor. A little Buddha held a bowl of incense in his lap and squatted on the floor, just as the three men were obliged to do, there being no chairs in evidence. A deep-piled rug covered the floor; along the walls were cushions. The place had a definite feminine touch. The only solid object of furniture was a knee-high table on which were placed a milk-white globe—the only source of illumination—and a gleaming, chalky skull.

Nakesian sat behind the table, his long, tapering fingers stroking the white globe. His eyes were closed. His immaculately tailored London clothing remained miraculously uncreased by his squatting position.

He intoned in a vibrant voice. "It was a revelation, gentlemen. A revelation of evil thoughts which the spirits were pleased to show me in the minds of some unscrupulous men."

The three visitors stirred uneasily. One was a broad-shouldered man with iron-grey hair, a lantern jaw and hard, agate eyes; he had a beak-like nose, under which was a carefully tended military moustache. He snapped, "I can do without all this bunkum, Nakesian. It does not affect me. Let's come to the point."

"Shortly, Mr. Taite." Nakesian's closed eyelids fluttered, then opened to reveal deep pools of mysticism. Hurt was reflected in their fathomless depths. "It does concern you, sir. It concerns us all. Especially Mr. Coulter —and his nephew."

The leathery old man who leaned forward with such rapt attention sighed his approval.

"True. Tell us, Nakesian, what the spirits have said."

His nephew, Gregory Dolman, a man of thirty, was partly bald, with a round, moon-like face that matched Nakesian's in lack of expression. He said wearily, "Come to the point, mister."

"We all know," said Nakesian, "that Mr. Myron Coulter is a firm believer. We know of his generous offer to the Spiritualist Foundation—"

"Nothing but a racketeer labor organization of all you fakes," grunted Romwell Taite.

"You may think as you please! Mr. Coulter is selling his jewels to you for a quarter of a million dollars. That money he intends to donate to our fund. It should be needless to point out or remind you that there are criminal elements everywhere who would not hesitate a moment to steal that money."

"Including yourself," sighed Dolman.

Old Myron Coulter chuckled. "That's Mr. Taite's look-out. When he delivers the cash to me, it will be safe. I've made arrangements with Sheriff Corlwye to guard my house well. Once Mr. Taite gets his cash there, there's nothing more to fear."

Nakesian nodded, looking at the three men with heavy-lidded, somnolent eyes. He was a handsome man, of indeterminate age. He might have been thirty, or fifty. His features stood out in ghostly fashion above the glow of the milk-white globe. The shadows of his tapering fingers slid sinuously along the draperies and the ceiling.

"It is before the money is paid to you, Mr. Coulter, that danger enters. Last night, I received a message from the other world—"

"You mean the underworld," Dolman gibed.

Taite guffawed; Dolman's round face remained impassive.

Nakesian smiled slowly with his lips. Not his eyes. "Very well. Let's make it brass tacks. Three nights ago I learned of a conspiracy. I obtained proof of it. Proof from a criminal whose name you would all recognize if I mentioned it. I gained that proof, I say, and now I will show it to you."

He got to his feet with a quick, pantherish grace. He stood tall before the three seated men. He clapped his hands, and the light in the milk-white globe dimmed and faded. His voice came to his listeners.

"Wait, and I will show you."

Darkness choked the perfumed room, settling in sinuous folds around the three men. Taite's growled curse came through the blackness, then Gregory Dolman's weary, tortured sigh. Only from old Myron Coulter came no sound.

There was a rustling of the draperies, and a soft click as a door opened and closed. Another click as the movement was repeated.

A scream resounded.

It was a woman's scream. High-pitched, shrill, it hung in the choking black air in eerie cadences. Then it bubbled and died away.

Storm was on the street in front of the Wawanock when he heard the scream; it came to him faintly, but unmistakably.

He started, and looked down at his shadow, corrugated on the steps of the apartment-hotel where he had trailed Valerie Feather. His white gabardine coat was beginning to feel damp. He was carrying a gun in a shoulder-holster.

Storm looked down the street, his eyes bright and alert behind his glinting spectacles. Two men stood on the corner, their lips tight with silence. A black coupe, like a big beetle, squatted by the curb and breathed blue exhaust into the sultry air.

The desk in the Wawanock lobby looked deserted, until a sleekly black scalp poked itself slowly over the edge. A chalky face with a long pink nose stared out at Storm.

"I thought I heard a scream."

"You heard correctly," Storm agreed uneasily.

The elevator was in use. He hesitated between watching to see who came out of the cage or going up the steps; he chose the latter. Trouble hung in the air like too much strong perfume.

A man threaded past him on the steps, clattering on leather heels. He was big and beefy, dressed in a green suit and pink plaid shirt that hurt Storm's eyes. The man's face was wild; his mouth was open as if about to burst into a sun-maddened yell. Storm did not stop him. He went on up the steps, three at a time.

Lucius, otherwise known as Lucky Lamonte, he thought. Wheels Burton's stooge, like Toogy. Now what—

His thoughts were chopped off by a concerted hammering, as of fists on a door. A muffled voice yelled, "Let us out of here, curse you!"

The voice was husky, harsh with anger and fear. Storm's scalp tingled. He covered the last flight of steps and looked down the shadowy third-floor corridor to the door that stood half ajar, light streaming from it to emphasize the duskiness of the hall.

He padded quietly along the heavy, muffling carpet, stood silhouetted in the rectangle of sunlight. Looked in the apartment.

He said, "What's up, Hunk?"

A man with yellow eyeballs, looking like a Hindu, turned around with a wild gasp and leaned with his back against a door. Heavy fists pounded on the panel, and again Storm heard a man's voice:

"Let us out, you fool! What happened?"

The man who looked like a Hindu turned a perspiring, anxious face toward Storm. "You! Hell, Leo—something's broke loose."

Storm's look of astonishment gave way to a mirthless grin. "Hunk, I thought you were in New York. Where did you get that get-up? And who's behind that door? And who screamed?"

"So help me, Leo, I don't know. I'm goin' straight now, see? This Hindu outfit is part of the racket. I'm workin' for Mr. Nakesian now. He's a fortune-teller. He had three lugs in there, and then I heard this scream. Sounds like murder to me, Leo, but I didn't have—"

Storm cut off the rapid flow of words with a chopping gesture of his hand. "Give me the key to that door."

Hunk thrust a key at him with a shaking hand. Storm thrust it into the lock, then took his gun from its holster and held it ready. He opened the door suddenly.

"Come on out, gentlemen."

Three men tumbled out of the dark room. Romwell Taite was in the lead. His heavy-jowled face was flooded with angry red, and his hair was disheveled by his efforts to force the door.

"What's going on in this clip joint?" he bellowed.

He caught sight of the gun in Storm's hand. It pointed directly at his middle and, as though he had been prodded by the muzzle, Taite folded backward, bumping hard against the old man and stout Gregory Dolman.

"Take it easy," Storm suggested. "Hunk, get some light in that room."

The pseudo-Hindu snapped a switch, and the milk-white globe sprang into existence once more, shining on the gleaming skull that grinned beside it.

The room was empty.

"Who screamed?" Storm asked next, his voice a sharp rap.

Taite began cursing with sizzling virility. "I don't know, and I don't give a hoot! Let me out of this den."

"No." Storm shook his head. "No, I can't."

"Who are you? And why the gun, mister?"

He shrugged. "Leo Storm is the name. Somebody screamed; a girl screamed. It came from this apartment somewhere. Now, who was it?"

Hunk, the Hindu, suddenly blurted in a scared voice, "Gee, where's the boss? Nakesian!"

Gregory Dolman spoke for the first time. His rolypoly lace was blankly expressionless. "I got the impression that Nakesian left the room."

"I didn't see him. He didn't come out here," said Hunk. Then his frightened face brightened with an idea. "He's gone to his private room, where he relaxes. That's where the scream came from."

The Hindu-assistant-from-Brooklyn crossed the audience chamber, yanked at the drapes and revealed a door in the convex wall. He rattled the knob, pushing and straining; then he looked helplessly at Storm.

"It's locked."

"Any other way of getting in there?"

"Sure. Through the hall. That room's got a door opposite the elevator. I got a key to it, too."

"Let me have it."

Storm took the key, and stared for a moment at the four men. To Hunk he said, "Watch these three." To Romwell Taite and the Coulters he snapped, "You'd better stick around. All of you. There's no telling what may have happened."

He left Taite to entertain them with his explosive Anglo-Saxon and went out into the hall again. Opposite the elevator was a door, and the key fitted easily into the lock.

He look a good look at the room, then at the body on the floor. The sun spread white light over a twisted, handsome face; glinted with hot slivers off the shining chromium handle of a knife that stuck incongruously out of the sprawled man's back.

The dead man was Dikran Nakesian.

CHAPTER FIVE
—AND THE CASH

Storm's mouth jerked spasmodically. He poked up his glasses and wrinkled his nose at the lavish scent of perfume in the apartment. He stood for another moment in the doorway, sweeping the room with hard, bright eyes. The floor was a checkerboard of black and white squares. Geometrical chairs, two squat lounges of maroon mohair and a wall of books completed the major furnishings. His eyes swept back to the corpse, which lay in almost the exact center of the checkerboard floor, for all the world like a chess piece knocked over in a game.

He knew the dead man was Dikran Nakesian. He knelt beside the dead spiritualist, avoiding the thin trickles of reddish-brown that puddled the floor near the man's body. Nakesian lay on his face, one knee flexed, his head resting on a pillowing arm as though in sleep. But the fixed expression of the heavy-lidded eyes told amply well that the sleep was permanent. They looked excited, with a hot and wild glare deep behind their black, shining surfaces.

The knife's chromium handle was imbedded deep between Nakesian's shoulder blades. Three thin trickles of crimson separated from the wound and ran down the various folds of the spiritualist's clothing, to drip on the waxed floor. Storm squinted interestedly at the knife handle. He noticed little bits of lint caught on the cross-guard. There were no fingerprints on the knife. They had been wiped off by the murderer, who had used a silk handkerchief, but had left the lint on the handle to betray his work.

Storm got to his feet with a tired sigh. On a low-squatting table stood a pinch-bottle of Scotch, a siphon and two tumblers. He poured the Scotch, ignored the siphon and drank. He felt better. It helped him think.

He glanced around the room, seeking the source of the feminine scream, and a sad little smile curled around his mouth. Crumpled in a doorway was a huddle of white: Valerie Feather. She was still dressed in her white summer suit, a skirt and short jacket. Her coroneted hair had become undone, framing her oval face and melting, honey-like, into a ray of hot sunlight that buttered the checkerboard floor. She was not dead; not injured. She had fainted.

He murmured softly to her, "Maybe now you'll consent to have dinner with me, darling."

He knelt, lifted the girl off the floor and carried her across the room, depositing her on a lounge. He stared thoughtfully, with puckered lips, at her clear features, relaxed in unconsciousness. His attention centered on red-tinted fingernails. They were done in a deep, wine-colored tint, with clear white half-moons showing—except on the little finger of her right hand.

A red stain spread over the first joint of her little finger. Storm touched it carefully, and it wiped away. It was blood.

"Nice girl," he muttered.

He began to feel sickish. He took a handkerchief from his pocket and carefully cleaned the damning evidence from Valerie Feather's little finger.

Then he folded and replaced the handkerchief in his pocket. Straightening, he flicked another glance at the body. From this new position, he caught sight of Dikran Nakesian's right hand, pinned under his head. A scrap of paper was crumpled tight in the dead man's fist.

Storm knelt and painstakingly removed the paper from the thin, delicate hand. He expelled an explosive breath through his nose as he glimpsed the printed heading:

SKELETONS IN YOUR CLOSET

Murder walks the rock-bound coast of Maine today. To Sheriff Corlwye we say: stop the proposed sale of jewels that the richest man in your county intends to make. The stipulation of cash will bring death. As we predicted before, that money will wind up floating in a pool of blood ... and the first of the sacrificial offerings will be made today....

Incredible. The prediction in the *Post-Tribune* had come true; Dikran Nakesian clenched in his dead hand the prediction of his end.

Nakesian, Storm reflected, was one of the head men of the Spiritualist Foundation. The Foundation, he knew, was a racket organization, mulcting foolish women and girls of millions every year. Myron Coulter, who was donating the quarter of a million dollars in cash to Dikran Nakesian, was doing so for two purposes: to gain publicity for spiritualism, and to invest money in a profitable business.

He recalled the price of the jewel sale as reported in the column Valerie Feather had shown him. A quarter of a million dollars. Funny. He sucked in his cheeks and licked his suddenly dry lips. Walking around the room, he paused before the lounge on which the girl lay. Behind it, in a half-open door of a closet, he found what he had been seeking.

It was a black Gladstone bag, and it was partly open. Electric currents of excitement shook his gaunt body. It had to be true, and if it were, then there was the money—too much money, too much motive for this killing—

He opened the bag with trembling fingers.

It was the money again. A quarter of a million dollars. The neat packets of thousand-dollar bills, fastened with gummed strips of blue paper, were the same he had found in the woods of Devil's Mount. Two hundred and fifty thousand dollars. Had the sale gone through, and this money been stolen from Romwell Taite? It didn't make much sense.

"This much money," he mused aloud, "is worth almost any amount of trouble. Few Jack Horners could resist sticking their thumbs in this particular currency pie!"

The telephone rang, buzzing like an annoyed gnat. He glanced around the room and found the ivory hand-set beside the lounge at Valerie Feather's head. He used his handkerchief to pick it up and clipped into the receiver: "Yeah?"

A woman's voice answered, husky with quick impatience "Hunk," she said, "Hunk, I've got to talk to Dick. It's important. Get him, will you?"

Storm pushed his tongue into his cheek and listened to the husky, frightened voice; he said, "This isn't Hunk . Who is calling?"

"I—who are you?"

Storm sighed. "Okay, I know your voice. You're Dawn Detras. You sing at the Shady Grove."

The voice in the receiver went sharp with haughty resentment. "I wish to speak to the Nakesian."

"Dikran Nakesian is out," Storm said, looking at the window. "He'll be out for a long time—until the Day of Judgment, I think. What do you want, Miss Detras?"

Dawn Detras was a singer at Wheels Burton's Shady Grove. A small, dark, vitally alive girl, with sloe eyes that could knock any man off his pins. He rather liked her, and deplored the company she kept. He asked again, "What do you want?"

Her voice was disturbed.

"Nakesian."

Storm glanced at the body on the floor.

"Look, this is Leo Storm. Sometime private snoop. Remember me?"

Dawn Detras remembered. Her voice was a frightened gasp that hissed in the receiver.

He went on, "You can't have Nakesian. No one can have him now, except God or the devil. He's dead."

There was a long silence. Too long. He felt his stomach curl with tension before her voice came through the receiver again. He had difficulty understanding her words. They sounded very far away.

"Who did it?"

A smile parted his thin lips. "Did what?"

"Murder. It's got to be murder! I *know* Dick was murdered. Who did it, Leo? Please, who did it?"

"I'm not sure," he said gently. "I'd like to talk it over with you, if that is possible."

Her voice took on a high, tinny quality. "Are the police there?"

"No. You don't object if I call on you tonight? I'm private, you know. The cops are not my bosom chums, Dawn."

"Yes, I know. Meet me at the Grove tonight, after my songs. Will you do that? *Please!*"

She didn't have to say please to Storm, and he told her so. She laughed weakly and hung up.

Storm looked at the money again, then bit off a fingernail with a savage suddenness. He was a fool. Whoever had killed Nakesian would come back for the money. The murderer had been frightened by Valerie Feather's presence and had gone away temporarily. But with the money there, the temptation was sure to prove too great. The murderer would come back.

He thought of Lucky Lamonte, the man in the green suit and pink plaid shirt who had come clattering down the steps after Valerie's scream; he thought of the elevator that had been descending when he first entered the Wawanock.

He went to the window and looked down. The black coupé that looked like a beetle should not have been at the curb any longer. But he was wrong, for there it was: the beetle still breathed in the same place.

He took his .38 from his holster and dropped it in his side pocket. It made a bulge in the suit, spoiling the cut completely. It might be too late, but he had to try.

He picked up the Gladstone and went to the hall doorway, swinging the bag. Opening the door with his left hand, he stepped out into the corridor, opposite the elevator.

It was not a complete surprise when he walked between the two men who flanked the doorway.

They stood flat against the wall, their hands in their pockets. They were ugly men. One was Lucky Lamonte, scintillating in his green suit and pink shirt. Lucky was a tall man, almost as tall as Storm, and heavier. He was cursed by having been born with one blue eye and one

MURDER MONEY 167

green eye: a matter of great convenience to the men of Center Street, who had kept an interested eye on Lucky Lamonte since he put on his first pair of long pants and packed a gun in his back pocket. Lucky never got into the upper brackets of criminal society, but he was not to be ignored, by any means. Like most hoods, Lucky thought he was tough, and he could act tough. But, deep inside, he really wasn't.

Storm looked at the other man. Toogy. Uglier than Lucky, Toogy's face looked as though it had been made of rubber at birth, and as if the good doctor had squeezed it out of shape, pushing his scalp too close to his chin. His face was all bunched together, with his button-like nose sticking out from the rest of the features. Flanking the mess were his two little red ears.

Storm said, "Good afternoon, rats."

They ignored the murmur of conversation that came angrily from behind the main doorway to Nakesian's apartment, where the pseudo-Hindu, Hunk, was holding Dikran's three visitors at bay until the police arrived.

Lucky smiled, twisting his lips into a zigzag grin. It was cold and mirthless. Contemptuous. It held death in it.

His voice was throaty with reluctant admiration.

"You work fast, snooper. How'd you get in on this?"

"You came back for the money," Storm remarked. He looked carefully through his spectacles and weighed the Gladstone in his hand. "But why bump Nakesian? Or didn't you?"

"How did you know about this?" Lucky persisted. His face was close to Storm's, and Storm pushed him back roughly.

"A little bird told me. A vulture. Did you stab Nakesian?"

"It don't make any difference to you, and I don't have to tell you, mister. Maybe I did. But I didn't."

Toogy was watching the Gladstone with bright, hungry eyes. Lucky's multi-colored glance stuck to Storm's hand as it drifted casually into his side pocket. Storm deplored the gabardine suit. It was cool and thin and comfortable. But a gun in the pocket showed up a hundred yards away.

Lucky murmured, "Don't," and Storm didn't.

Instead, he took off his spectacles and flipped them expertly into a case. He said softly, "This is a terrible tragedy. It's fortunate that there was a witness on the scene—meaning me."

"Yeah," said Toogy thoughtfully.

His button-like eyes sized up Storm speculatively, coldly, with clinical interest.

"Yeah, fortunate for us, monkey, that we caught you."

Storm put his spectacle-case into his pocket. He bounced lightly on his toes and dropped the Gladstone on Toogy's foot. The little gunman yelped and hopped aside, holding his injured toes with both hands.

"I didn't know you had corns, Toogy," Storm murmured.

Then he addressed, stamped and delivered a quick elbow jab to the little hood's midriff. Toogy forgot both the weapon in his pocket and his bruised toes and doubled up with a moaning, agonized yelp.

Lucky swung viciously, not daring to fire the gun in the apartment house. Storm's left flicked upward, caressing Lucky's jaw, and continued its swing toward Toogy. Lucky spread over the corridor floor. Toogy slewed out of the way and yanked out an ugly black automatic that looked to Storm as though it had the bore of a field cannon. He grabbed it and twisted Toogy's wrist. He heard little bones cracking in the flesh, and then the gun thudded to the hall carpet.

The door at the end of the corridor opened and Hunk's scared face poked into the hall.

He yelped, "Hey, what—"

He caught sight of the gun in Storm's hand and slammed the door quickly, ducking out of sight. Startled voices came up the stair-well, and Storm knew that Lucky Lamonte and Toogy had more friends hanging around. A white flash blinked in the glass elevator door, and he gave up that idea, too. He snatched up the Gladstone and loped down the hall to a window with a fire-escape, feeling more than a little irritated.

He yelled, "Hunk, guard that room!"

Tossing one leg over the sill, he looked down the hall. Three men were stumbling up the steps after him, guns in their white hands. Behind them, Lucky Lamonte yelled, egging them on.

Storm fired, with his hand resting on the window sill. The shot cracked the sultry heat, and one of the gunmen tripped over himself and hit the floor with his nose. The others shouted their fear and dived for cover down the staircase.

Storm looked over the window-sill at the hard, white dust of the areaway that led to the street. He swung the Gladstone over the sill and dropped it. It hit the dry ground with a thwack, sending out a circular wave of dust, and burst open. He followed the money, floating quickly down the fire-escape. He picked up the bag and ran down the areaway to the gravel street.

A bullet slammed into a wooden fence; splinters showered his white suit. Across the dusty, deserted street was a rambling frame boarding house. He pounded over to it. A gun barked again, this time from a side window, and more lead spurted into the gravel. He thanked the fates that Lucky's men were poor shots.

He looked back and saw that no one was watching him: the heads had retreated from the windows. He hopped over the veranda rail of the boarding house and ducked into a shadow-darkened parlor.

The room was cool, and so was the blonde who lay on the sofa, dividing her attention between a box of chocolates and a book. She watched Storm with disapproving eyes as he skidded through the doorway and dropped behind the window-sill at her feet.

"Call the police, baby," he gasped. "It's murder."

The blonde had not heard the shots, or, if she had, had thought they were back-fires.

He kicked the Gladstone bag under the sofa where she lay.

She raised thinly traced eyebrows. "You crazy?"

Three men shadowed the pavement. He said hoarsely, "Listen, baby, and learn. There's a murder across the street in the Wawanock. They've got me on the list, too. They're after this bag. Keep it under the sofa 'Way under."

The blonde's sleepy eyes, suddenly frightened, looked out from under their load of sticky mascara.

She whimpered, "You're a gangster!"

Storm watched the street and answered over his shoulder, "Call the sheriff and hang on to this bag. And how do I get out of here, except by using the front door?"

The blonde stared at the black .38 in his hand and stammered, "Back of me, mister. There's a door at the end of the hall. Cross the alley at the back of the grocery store. Please, don't get me killed!"

Storm jerked his head toward the wall telephone, but there was no time to enlarge on instructions. The three men were coming in.

He slid out of the parlor and went down a dark hall to a kitchen that smelled of the last meal cooked there.

"Hon, did a bozo come in here?" someone rapped. "In a white suit?"

The blonde chattered, "No. But somebody ran past the door."

Storm knew the three men did not believe her. They hesitated, shifting their weight on uneasy feet. Storm drifted through the kitchen and found himself in sunlight once again, in a stone-walled enclosure.

The fence was not too difficult to scale. The other side was a grocer's back yard, littered with barrels and wooden egg-boxes. The screen door was propped open, and at the end of a black hallway he saw a public telephone, hanging on the wall at what would be the rear shelves of the grocery store.

He ducked into the house, fumbling for a nickel. The receiver buzzed, clattered. Shadows moved in front of the dirty store-window, and he cursed. The neighborhood was well in hand. The murder of Dikran Nakesian for a quarter of a million dollars was no individual affair. The locality was covered by men of Lucky's gang—and they belonged to Wheels Burton's organization.

"Listen," Storm yelled into the telephone, when he heard the Greek's thick voice. "Listen, Poppo—Pop, there's been a blasting. Nakesian—"

Shadows filled the grocery store entrance. He had only one chance. He rapped loudly, "That's the dope! That's right! Throw out a net for Lucky Lamonte—I saw him. No, he's not alone. That's right."

He did not care what kind of headache that sort of talk gave the Greek. He hit the floor behind two barrels of kippers and poked his gun between them. The shadows in the store jumped when he yelled:

"Okay! Up with them! Reach!"

He knew it was not his words that made them scatter for safety, nor was it his gun. As far as they knew, he had succeeded in spreading his information, and they could not chop off an alarm by adding a second killing to their day's pleasure.

The shadows melted, faded into the sunlight outside. He heard a car start up, then another, and two sedans flashed past the fly-blown window, whining around the corner in a billowing cloud of rolling dust.

He got to his feet, trembling slightly, his eyes glinting with anger. The grocer came up from behind the counter and stared at Storm with round, open-mouthed suspicion.

"What was the trouble, mister?"

Storm looked at the wreckage of the white gabardine coat.

"They wanted to collect on the tailor's bill for this ice-cream suit. I didn't want to pay."

"Why not?" asked the grocer....

CHAPTER SIX
TOO MUCH MONEY

Storm bought a pack of cigarettes from the grocer and lit one. The smoke trickled down to his lungs, feeling like cool silver. A siren on a car started wailing in the distance, but he was in no hurry to get back to the apartment and the dead man. The dirt street was deserted now. He left the grocery store and walked around the block toward the bay. He circled the frame houses and went into the vacationers' boarding house that faced the side of the Wawanock Hotel.

The blonde was sitting up now, nursing a black eye.

She looked up as Storm stepped into the parlor through the screen door and screeched, "Darn you, look what you made them do to me!"

He paused before her, feeling a sensation of constriction about the spot where his heart should have been.

"Have you got the suitcase?" he asked.

She shook her platinum, close-cropped hair. Her whole voluptuous body, in its sheath of tight green silk. was quivering with anger. Her green eyes snapped with two malevolent spots of hatred.

She said between tight carmine lips, "Your hoodlums came in after you, mister."

"The suitcase," Storm repeated. "Have you still got it?"

She indicated her rapidly swelling eye.

"Does it look like I do? The girl came after it."

He was startled.

"Girl?"

"Honey-colored hair. Sweet thing, I'll say not! She came in after the grip."

"Did she give you the—um—black eye?"

"No. I'd scratch her to shreds if she tried. Her boy friend was the one. A little lug with red ears and a nose. She called him Toogy."

Storm was silent as the blonde paused. Then she asked in a curious voice, "Was there really a murder across the street? The sheriff's car is there—and troopers, too. Has there really been a killing?"

He nodded, feeling sick. Valerie Feather had recovered and reclaimed the cash with Toogy. She had told him that Toogy was following her, and had indicated that she was afraid of the little gunman. It was all senseless, lacking very much in point. He shook his head, and the blonde looked at him.

"They smacked you around, too, didn't they? Say, will I be a witness? I can use publicity, mister. Get my legs on the front pages and maybe I'll land a job in the movies! Who knows?"

"I don't," said Storm wearily.

He crushed the cigarette under his heel and left the boarding house, crossed the street and went around the corner to the front of the Wawanock. The black beetle-car was no longer at the corner. A red touring car, a state trooper's 'chaser and two motorcycles stood before the lobby entrance.

A trooper and a sheriff's deputy barred his way to the elevator, then drew back as the deputy recognized him and grinned.

"You mixed up in this, Mr. Storm?"

"Yes, and I wish I weren't."

Every branch of the law was on hand, crowding Dikran Nakesian's apartment. There was Sheriff Corlwye, with his straggling moustache and horsy farmer's face. He looked outraged and irritated, only outmatched by Kennicut's Constable Cafferty's wide-eyed, fluttery helplessness. The real business was being done by the uniformed crew of the state car.

All the men looked up when Storm entered, eyeing him with clinical detachment. One trooper had a camera, but was busy sampling the Scotch in the pinch-bottle in between languid efforts to snap a picture of the dead spiritualist. Another, who was numbered among Storm's innumerable acquaintances, hummed a blues song while dusting the telephone cradle for fingerprints. Beside him, staring curiously at an indentation on a pillow of the lounge, was a thin, dapper little man: Lieutenant Tilliman.

Corlwye raised irritable eyes at Storm's entry.

"Hugh! You look like you been in a dog-fight, Leo."

"You boys got here fast," he retorted evasively.

"We were havin' a meetin' down the block a ways. Coincidence, I guess."

The slender Lieutenant Tilliman suddenly rasped, "Unger, check on this pillow. Somebody was asleep on it. There are some blonde hairs scattered about."

Kluger, the fingerprint man, said, "Wait a minute, Tilly; there's a smear of blood on the telephone."

The delicate-looking lieutenant nodded and swiveled round to stare at Storm.

"And what's your last name, Mr. Leo?"

"Storm," said Kluger. "He's a New Yorker. Come here on vacation."

Tilman kept looking at Storm. "And what's your share in this business? How do you come into it?"

Storm plucked the bottle of Scotch from the photographer's fingers and poured himself a glass; he sank into a chair, snuggling the bottle in his lap.

"I walked right into it, lieutenant. Have you got the three men who were here?"

"You know about them, eh? They're in the next room."

Sheriff Corlwye jerked his thumb at the closed door.

"I don't like that Hindu."

"Hindu from the Bronx," said Storm. "Or maybe Brooklyn. His name is Hunk Hubert, and he did five years on various charges. His job with Nakesian required a Hindu get-up. The color of his face is due to stain. Wash him and see."

Lieutenant Tilliman coughed delicately. Storm looked sleepy, blinking his gray eyes behind his spectacles. He could not remember when he had put his glasses on again, but they rested, as usual, below the bump on his nose. He pushed them up with the tip of his middle finger and watched as Constable Cafferty herded Hunk and Nakesian's last three visitors into the death-room.

It was their first view of the body that sprawled in the center of the black and white checkerboard floor. Sheriff Corlwye had pulled up the Venetian blinds for more light, and the body lay in a brilliant pool of hot white sunshine.

Hunk turned pale and gasped, "The boss!" His eyes darted around the room, settling on Storm. "Tell these guys I'm goin' straight, Leo! Cripes, tell 'em I didn't do this."

"Okay, you didn't do it," said Storm.

Kluger, the fingerprint man, chuckled. "A real bull-session, that's what we're going to have." He was a wiry man, with gold-rimmed glasses and an olive face. His eyes were keen and bright. "No cherchez la femme, lieutenant? What the hell, there's no interest in this case without a flossie."

"There was a girl here," said Storm, and immediately he bit his tongue.

Lieutenant Tilliman swung around to him.

"Damm right there was! These hairs on the pillow—they're female, or I'll eat them. A honey-haired girl. Who was she, Mr. Storm? No, tell me what you know and how you happened to come into this in the beginning."

"Suppose I talk later," Storm suggested quietly. "You better question these three gentlemen first. Then we'll have something to go on. I came in after the murder; they were here when it happened."

Romwell Taite's heavy face flushed with throttled red, and he advanced toward Storm, fist clenched. "If you're insinuating that we know anything at all about this—"

Storm snuggled lower in his chair and extended the bottle of Scotch.

"Console yourself, sir, and tell the lieutenant your name."

Taite looked undecided, smoothed the little military moustache on his upper lip, grunted and accepted the bottle.

"Listen," he said, "let me tell you fools what I know and let's end this. I got a letter this morning from Nakesian telling me to come here at one o'clock sharp. I got another from Mr. Coulter, here, confirming it. The first letter stated that it was most important for me to be here, that it concerned the jewel sale that Coulter is going to make to me."

Storm interrupted: "You're the man who is buying the jewels? And Coulter is the one selling them?"

Tilliman asked sharply, "What's this all about?"

"If you read the papers, lieutenant, and especially the *Skeleton Closet*—"

"That rat's column. If I ever get my hands on the writer, he won't write another word, except perhaps a few more verses to the Prisoner's Song."

Storm persisted gently, "If you read it, you would know that Taite is buying jewels from Mr. Myron Coulter, for the sum of a quarter of a million dollars in cash. That money is to be publicly donated to the Spiritualist Foundation, of which Dikran Nakesian was quite a big-shot. Mr. Taite is the buyer; Coulter is the seller. And Nakesian was to be the ultimate person benefited."

"I'm just buying the jewels," Taite said, "and I'm not interested in what Mr. Coulter chooses to do with the money after I pay him for his gems. If he wants the money in cash, that's his business. I'm concerned only with buying the jewels for my firm in Chicago. Mr. Coulter can throw the money into the ocean afterwards, for all I care."

Tilliman swiveled around on his polished black heels to the little dried-up old man. "You're selling your jewels to Mr. Taite?"

Myron Coulter bobbed his skinny head.

"I am, for a quarter of a million in cash."

"And then you're making a donation to the—um—Spiritualist Foundation?"

Again, the old man nodded, his eyes bright and keen, his birdlike face cool and interested as he stared down at the body of Dikran Nakesian.

Kluger, the fingerprint man, chuckled again. "What a sucker!"

Tillman scowled; his eyes were narrowed.

"No, he isn't. The Spiritualist Foundation is a racket feeding on a racket. Mr. Coulter is simply making an investment."

"Please," said the old man, with a patient smile.

"Oh, you can act the martyr, but some day I'd like to split that crooked ring wide open and put you fakers where you belong," snapped the lieutenant. He paused, bouncing his small, fragile height on his shiny patent-leather shoe-tips. "So I gather you three—Nakesian, Coulter and Taite—were interested in the same thing."

The lieutenant swiveled to Gregory Dolman, who stood with his hands folded over his little paunch.

"Where do you come in?"

"I am Mr. Coulter's nephew."

"Alright, so you all received letters from Nakesian which concerned this proposed jewel sale," Tilliman summarized. "Now what did

Nakesian say about it?"

"Nakesian claimed he had knowledge of a criminal plot," snapped Taite, irritated. He waved his hand, found the bottle of Scotch in it, and put it down with an embarrassed flush. Storm leaned over and took it in his lap again.

"Nakesian claimed he knew of an attempt on the cash," Taite began again. "You see, I'm to transport the money to Mr. Coulter's estate, where the sale of the jewels is to take place."

"Well, what kind of a plot did Nakesian say it was?"

"He never got a chance to speak! He left the room, presumably to get some evidence that he wished to show us, and the next thing we knew the girl screamed. And when we tried to get out, this fake Hindu locked the door on us. When he did open it, Storm covered us with a gun and made Nakesian's helper keep us here until you men arrived. We had no chance to view the body, didn't even know what had happened until you brought us in here just now."

Tilliman puckered his lips.

"Don't any of you three have an idea as to what Nakesian had in mind?"

They shook their heads. Tilliman sighed and sent all of them out of the room, with the exception of Hunk Hubert. While the lieutenant questioned Hubert, Storm got up out of the chair and walked to the window, his brow wrinkled with thought.

"Hubert, when did you hear a girl scream?"

"About one:fifteen. The four of them—includin' the boss—were in the audience room about fifteen minutes. I didn't know what had happened when the dame let out her yip, but I wasn't takin' any chances, see? I locked the door on those men and kept it locked until Leo Storm showed up. That was about five minutes after the scream."

"Did you know there was a girl in the apartment?"

"No, *indeed!*"

Tillman made a clucking sound and said to Kluger, "Get Taite back in here again."

The jewel buyer came back, his broad, heavy face still revealing his frank irritation.

"When is this foolery going to stop?"

"Murder isn't foolery, Mr. Taite. You said you heard a girl scream. None of you saw the girl?"

"No, she must have come in through the corridor door. There are two doorways, as you see."

Tillman snapped pettishly, "Yes, I've got eyes. While you three were sitting in the dark, did any of you move?"

"I can't say. I didn't. I heard no movements, except Dolman; his legs were stiff. I couldn't see anything, and I had no physical contact either with Dolman or Coulter. But there was no reason for any of us killing Nakesian. We were all anxious to discover what Nakesian knew."

"Yes, sure," sighed Tilliman. He waved his hand. "You can go. Leave your address so I'll know where to find you, just in case."

Taite looked relieved. "Tomorrow I'll be going to the Coulter place to buy his jewels. You could find me there."

Storm raised his eyebrows and asked curiously, "But your cash—you don't have it."

Taite was puzzled.

"What do you mean? I haven't withdrawn it from my bank yet."

Excitement suddenly sent Storm's blood pounding. "You mean you didn't bring two hundred and fifty thousand dollars to this place today?"

Taite laughed with genuine amusement.

"I'm not that crazy," he said briefly.

Lieutenant Tilliman's eyes crinkled. "What are you talking about, Storm?"

"I mean I found a quarter of a million dollars in cash beside the body when I first investigated!"

Taite said quickly, in a curiously high-pitched voice, "It wasn't mine!"

"Then there is too much money around—a quarter of a million too much!" Storm snapped.

CHAPTER SEVEN
STORMY WEATHER

Sheriff Corlwye pulled his nose. "Hugh! What fool would carry that much money around loose?"

Lieutenant Tilliman stared at Leo Storm with bright, hard eyes. Fingerprint man Kluger chuckled again, his sharp olive face limned by the sunlight streaming in the window at his back. A medical examiner arrived, out of breath, and set down his little black bag with a thump and a sigh, then stiffened as he felt the coiled, tense silence in the room.

Tilliman said, "Start talking, Storm. There's no money in this apartment—explain your statement about that business. And explain the crack you made about the girl."

Storm shrugged.

"I can't explain the money. When I got here, I found Hunk holding back the door and keeping those three men inside. I ran through the corridor and came in this room and found Dikran Nakesian dead. There was a girl here. She had fainted. There was a suitcase full of money—I had no time to count it, but it must have approximated a quarter of a million dollars."

"Lot of cabbage," observed Kluger.

Storm ignored him.

"I've been figuring, going on the idea that Taite already had the cash in his possession. Under that assumption, there was some rhyme and reason to Nakesian's murder. I thought Nakesian may already have received his—um—donation from Coulter, or that he had stolen it from Taite. I figured Nakesian was killed for the money. But if that cash wasn't Taite's, or Coulter's, then—" he shrugged helplessly—"then I don't understand any of it."

"Sounds fantastic to me," Sheriff Corlwye muttered.

Storm sighed. "I'm sorry I mentioned it."

"I'll bet you are!" Tilliman snapped. "What happened to this money you say you saw?"

"I stepped back into the hall with it, and two rats tried to cop it. They did get the money, after a chase. I had to dive down the fire-escape, and I tossed the stuff into the boarding house across the street. They caught up with me and got the money. It was in a black Gladstone bag. You can check with the blonde across the way. They gave her a black eye."

Tilliman cleared his throat again. "Who are 'they'?"

Storm leaned back in his chair and poked up his glasses.

"You won't like to know, lieutenant. It was Lucky Lamonte and Toogy—Burton's guns."

The delicate-looking Tilliman stiffened as though he had been slapped; his face went gray, and then a red sheen spread under the fine texture of his tightly-drawn skin. Wheels Burton had made a monkey out of Lieutenant Tilliman too many times; Burton had political influence. When Tilliman had once tried to rid the state of Burton and send the gambler back to New York, he had suddenly discovered that his captaincy was gone and that he was demoted to a lieutenant. There was nothing Tilliman could do about it.

For a moment, the lieutenant looked eager, his thin face sharpened and pinched. "Are you sure you could identify Burton's men? If you'll appear as a witness—"

Storm shook his head.

"What good will that do? You can't prove them guilty of anything. Any one of the three men who were here might have committed the murder, for reasons we know nothing about as yet. The girl—no, she wouldn't. And then there was someone coming down the elevator—unknown quantity X."

"What a baby to cradle," Kluger sighed.

But Tilliman's eyes were keen on Storm. "Who was the girl?" he asked, his voice soft.

Storm slowly straightened, finally got out of the chair, and reached for a glass. He had another Scotch, his eyes fixed on the bright window. He was thinking of the three mornings he had stood outside the door of his apartment in the Kennicut Hotel and watched Valerie Feather's trim figure come swinging down the corridor. He could see every contour of her fresh, oval face, see again the clear brilliance of her violet eyes.

And he heard once more the blonde across the street saying, "She came in after the grip. Her boyfriend with the ears—"

And he saw again the drop of scarlet on Valerie's fingernail.

It appeared that she was mixed up with Toogy, and Storm did not believe it.

"Who was the girl who lay on that pillow?" Tilliman repeated.

And Storm said quietly, "I don't know. I never saw her before."

Tilliman snapped at his words, for all the world like a barking Pekinese. "You're a liar! What brought you here in the first place? The girl! What's the cause for the cock-and-bull story about a quarter of a million in cash? To make us forget the girl! You heard Taite say the money wasn't his. Don't tell me there are two fortunes drifting around loose!"

Kluger's uniformed figure suddenly spanned the room, his dark face smiling. He reached Storm and whipped the silk handkerchief from his breast-pocket. Unfolding it carefully, Kluger exhibited the rusty red stain on it, holding it up by the corner for Tilliman to see.

"Oh, my," mocked the fingerprint man.

Storm said nothing. He felt a wall of animosity spring up between himself, an outsider, and these men on a rural police force. Their faces were hard and cold as they swiveled their glances from the damning evidence held high in Kluger's fingers to Storm's impassive lace. He understood their resentment of his reputation in New York, and it did not make him feel any easier.

"Explain *that*," Tilliman suggested.

But Storm could not explain it. He couldn't say that he had wiped blood from Valerie's fingernail; and he suddenly decided to remain equally silent on the matter of the telephone call from Dawn Detras, when he had been careless enough to smear the blood from his handkerchief to the hand-set—where Kluger's sharp, ferrety eyes had spotted it.

And looking at Nakesian's body, he likewise determined to remain silent about the fact that he had found the same amount of money in the woods of Devil's Mount. The money of which Dikran Nakesian had relieved him—and for which Nakesian had died.

Tilliman sensed the hard set of Storm's face to signify stubborn silence. He snapped, "Search him."

Rough hands took Storm's gun, his wallet and his permit to carry the weapon. Tilliman broke open the .38 and sniffed. "Who did you shoot at?"

"Lucky Lamonte. In self-defense."

The lieutenant's eyes glinted with frustrated anger.

"You can't prove it. I wish to God you could, but you can't. You can't say what brought you here. You can't explain that slip about the money. You know who the girl is, but you won't talk. You're in a bad way, Storm," the lieutenant concluded.

Storm waved a lazy hand at Dikran Nakesian's body.

"Maybe you think I did it."

"Maybe you did. You're going to be held on suspicion. You can't prove you didn't, anyway. You can't alibi yourself— You could have knifed Nakesian, then run around to the main door of his apartment and come on Hunk Hubert as though you had just come up the steps. The fingerprints on the knife are gone, wiped clean by a white silk handkerchief. Like yours."

Storm sat down with a sigh. "Okay, so you think I did it. You're too yellow to buck Wheels Burton."

One of the crew of the state car walked slowly across the room and smacked his gloved hand across Storm's face. The leather seam made a little cut on his cheek.

"Don't say that again, guy," the trooper warned.

Storm sucked in his hollow cheeks and took off his glasses. He stood up and repeated, "Tilliman, you're too yellow to buck Burton."

He was deliberately baiting them, with their blind loyalty to the dapper little lieutenant, raising them to anger.

The trooper sighed and looked at his superior. Tilliman said, "Oh, hell, Storm. Get him down to headquarters. Bill. We'll talk to him there."

From beyond the door, in the corridor, came a sudden thumping sound and a squeal of terror. The company in the sunny room whirled as one man. There followed a scuffing noise, and then a slam on the door.

The Greek stood there, holding a thin, trembling man with a partly bald head and an exaggerated pink nose. It was the desk clerk from the lobby downstairs. The Greek shoved his ponderous two-hundred pound bulk into the room behind the man.

"Hello, boys. Look what I found."

"The Greek!" said Kluger delightedly. "Storm gets his reinforcements. Achilles and his Grecian heel!"

"Nuts," said Poppo impassively.

His little eyes in his round face remained tired, as they always were. Exertion was distasteful to the Greek, He did not even seem surprised at the sight of Nakesian's body being examined by the medical man.

"This weasel was snooping in the hall," he said.

Tilliman faced the terrified desk clerk. The Greek looked across the room to Storm, who brushed his finger across his lips, and the Greek understood. There was to be no mention of the garbled telephone call Storm had made from the grocery store.

Tilliman said impatiently, "Well, man, what were you doing in the hall?"

"I was curious—curious, that's all," said the clerk. He rubbed his long nose, staring with morbid fascination at the body on the floor. "Murders don't happen every day."

"You'd be surprised," said the irrepressible Kluger. "Statistics show—"

"Shut up," said Tilliman, examining the clerk. "And what do you know about this business, eh?"

"Me? Oh, I don't know anything—nothing at all."

Storm interrupted, his slate eyes dancing with vibrant sparks. "He knows enough to clear me, lieutenant! Ask him where I was when he heard the girl's scream—which, you can't deny, fixes the time of the murder."

The clerk stared myopically at Storm. "Oh, you. I remember you. They accusing you of this, buddy?"

Storm crossed the room.

"Tell these dumb coppers when you saw me," he ordered the clerk.

The long-nosed man looked malevolently at the troopers and the sheriff's deputies. "Sure. I saw you right after I heard the scream. I saw you come in off the street, and you went up the steps three at a time. If the scream marks the time of the murder, you couldn't have done it, pal."

"Thanks," said Storm. He turned to Tilliman, his lips quirking. "May I have my gun, license, and my handkerchief?"

The lieutenant looked out the window.

"Are you going to talk, Storm? If you're in on this case for a fee—we can co-operate as well as New York."

"I'm not on this case. I'm in it this far completely by accident. I don't know what happened. I've told you the truth about the money and the girl being here. I can't do any more. And I'll be obliged if you don't object to my checking out of the Kennicut Hotel tomorrow."

"Not on your life!"

"I've got a bungalow up past Devil's Mount. It's staked out for two weeks. I'm done with detective work for that time. Through. I need a rest."

"How about our new W.P.A.-built jail?" Kluger cracked.

"Some day I'll take you apart," Storm promised. "And I won't forget to wipe my hands on a hanky when I do."

Tilliman came back from the window with a sigh. He waved a curt hand at Kluger, who looked dissatisfied,

"You can go."

Storm got up, looked at the bottle of Scotch to make sure it was empty, then stalked out through the doorway. The fat Greek, waddling after him, paused only long enough to waggle his fingers from the end of his pudgy nose at the squelched fingerprint man.

CHAPTER EIGHT
GIRL IN THE CASE

It was after three in the hot afternoon when Leo Storm and the Greek stood once more on the pavement before the Wawanock. The two men said nothing. A morgue wagon was parked before the hotel, and the number of police cars had been augmented by two: the medical examiner's Ford and another touring car from the sheriff's office.

The desk clerk had done his work well in spreading the news of the murder. A crowd of morbidly curious vacationers was being held back with difficulty by sweating constables. The blasting heat of the late afternoon sun did nothing to allay the interest of the thrill-seeking crowd.

Storm and the Greek moved off the sidewalk, skirted the knots of people and found their convertible coupé parked behind two state trooper motorcycles. A taxi rolled up behind the coupé as they got inside.

The fat Greek drove in silence.

"Slowly." said Storm. "Six blocks north, then around the station, then six blocks south."

The taxi that had pulled up behind them started up almost immediately. It went six blocks north with them, was lost for a moment, and then bumped over the railroad crossing to proceed the next six blocks south. Storm watched the taxi's progress with interested eyes.

"Lieutenant Tilliman put a tail on us," he told the Greek. "I didn't think he would let me go just like that. He knows that I know something, and he thinks I'll lead him to it. Give him another think. He has almost as many facts about Nakesian's killing as I have, but he doesn't believe them. And the whole business doesn't make sense to either of us."

The fat Greek looked sideways at Storm, as though expecting him to pull a rabbit from his hat.

"It doesn't make sense to me, Poppo," Storm repeated "So let's go home. To hell with the tail."

Storm took a shower, changed into a fresh linen suit, cleaned his gun and had another drink of Scotch—this time from his own bottle. The Greek was busy in another room of their flat, opening bureau drawers, carefully packing clothing. The Greek was invaluable to Storm. Lacking the rapier thrusts in mental capacity that Storm possessed, the Greek was father and mother to the tall, gaunt man, cooking for him, guarding him, lending his huge, round weight to the battle whenever the occasion demanded.

Poppo came into the oak-furnished living room, rattling something in his hand.

"These dice, Leo," said the Greek petulantly. "I found them in your suit. What say we finish the roll for dinner tonight?"

They rolled; Poppo lost.

The Greek muttered, "I should have known. I don't like them."

"Just pay for the dinner you owe me tonight."

The Greek nodded sadly and went to the window.

"Those dicks outside, front and back—they can't afford Lucci's. Isn't that a shame?"

Storm changed his mind as he made a sudden decision. "Better give me the five bucks now."

He got to his feet and looked out the window. "You're going to the cottage tonight. You're not eating at Lucci's. You're taking the car and you're going to drive. Something that looks like me is going to be seated beside you, but it won't be me. It will be a dummy, and Lieutenant Tilliman's fair-haired boys can drive along after you and leave me free to work."

The Greek looked disappointed. "Aw, lissen, Leo—forget this crazy case! There's no money in it for us."

"A fee might appear at any minute," Storm said benignly. "The case reeks of money, and surely there may be a few thousand for us in it somewhere. Besides, there's the girl."

"What about her?"

"She's in it—and I can't forget her—and that settles it."

"But maybe she killed the fortune-teller! She got away with the money—she and Toogy. She's a gangster's moll."

Storm laughed. "Don't be crazy. She's just mixed up in this quarter-million dollar jewel sale, and she's in trouble. Otherwise, why did she come and ask me for help earlier this afternoon?"

Poppo's eyes slowly widened.

"Maybe Toogy and Lucky Lamonte ain't her boy friends?"

"There are two answers to that, Poppo. Either she's a scheming adventuress working out a detailed plan—in which case, I'll slap her in jail and forget her. She *may* have killed Nakesian for the money—there was a fortune in cash there, Poppo, in spite of that Taite man's denial. Maybe it wasn't Taite's money; maybe it belonged to some one we don't know about yet. But, in any case, the money was the motive for Nikesian's murder. And the girl may have killed him."

Poppo shook his head. "Aw, I don't like to believe that, really, Leo," he said uneasily.

"No more than I. The second alternative is that the girl was caught by Toogy. She may be meddling in this affair for other motives than we know yet. If Toogy came back, after chasing me around the corner, and found the girl in Nakesian's apartment, just coming to, he may have forced her along with him. In which case, she's in a pretty bad spot."

"That's got to be it, Leo," the Greek said. "She's in bad hands; she's in danger."

"We'll see," Storm answered. "Then again, she may be at home. She may be sitting in her apartment across the hall, laughing at me and everyone else."

"Easy way to find that out; just look in her apartment."

"Have you got a key?"

"No."

"Then call Sammy, the bellboy."

Sammy had the keys. He wouldn't have given them up willingly, because that was against the rules, so he gave them up unknowingly. The Greek urged a drink on Sammy from the bottle of Vat that the busboy had brought up in reply to a telephone order, and while the bellboy tasted the liquor, Storm's slender fingers investigated Sammy's uniform pocket and transferred a master house-key from the bellboy's pocket to his own. After that, Sammy was politely but firmly shunted out of the room.

The corridor was deserted when Storm stepped out, and so was Valerie Feather's apartment. It was tastefully furnished. It was not too feminine—the major clue to the sex of its inhabitant was the subtle scent of perfume that hung in the air. Ordinarily Storm disliked scents. This one he wrinkled his nose at, considered for a moment, and decided was nice. It was expensive, difficult to place. It was an incongruous factor, that argued against Valerie Feather's story that she was a simple secretary to old Myron Coulter.

A picture attracted Storm's attention. It was of old Myron Coulter himself, and it occupied a prominent place on the table. Curious, that was. Secretaries are rarely that fond of their employers—at least, when the latter are old, withered men of grating temperament. To keep a picture of Coulter's sharp, birdlike face was inexplicable to Storm.

He pushed away these thoughts and examined the room in detail, to the extent of emptying the bureau drawers of their frothy, lacy contents. A grin appeared on his features and remained there. The bedroom and bath revealed nothing. The grin faded into an expression of perplexity when, in the swiftly gathering gloom of evening, he turned his attention to a little secretary desk.

It had a typewriter on it, which Storm examined carefully. The ribbon was well used. In a drawer were two fresh bands. Valerie Feather evidently did much typing. Well, that was to be expected, since she was secretary to a millionaire like old Myron Coulter.

He found something in the last drawer that made him expel his breath with a long sigh of piqued interest. It was a scrap book, like a photograph album, and inside it was a collection of newspaper clippings. Column after column. Unsigned. Headed *Skeletons In Your Closet.*

"Pretty Valerie is interested in crime," he said uneasily to himself. "Perhaps she *is* an adventuress—a heartless gold-digger—a murderess."

His eyes were hard and gray when he closed the door of Valerie Feather's apartment and crossed the hall to his own rooms.

The Greek looked up anxiously at his entrance.

"Well?"

"You go to the bungalow tonight. If I don't join you in two days, Poppo, come back and look for me."

"Where shall I look, Leo?"

"I'll either be in the ocean or in jail," said Storm.

The Greek's round, full face puckered distastefully.

"Aw, I ain't gonna leave you, Leo. I can't."

"You've got to drive that car and that dummy to the cottage. And you've got to take Tilliman's leaches off my trial when you do it. I can't have them following me. If the lieutenant finds the girl, and she is involved, no matter how innocently, she stands to take a rap on circumstantial evidence for the murder of Dikran Nakesian."

Storm held out his hand. "Well, pay me the fin you owe me."

CHAPTER NINE
DATE WITH DEATH

The Shady Grove was four miles around Kennicut Bay, on the opposite tongue of heavily wooded land that lapped out into the ocean. Before Storm went there, he got out of his white suit and donned a plain dark coat that efficiently hid the two guns he packed under his armpits.

The Greek's eyes were disturbed as he watched him get ready.

"Expect trouble, huh, Leo?"

"Burton always means trouble," said Storm. "And he may not like to have his little singer talking to me. Dawn Detras went pretty regularly with Lucky Lamonte, and the big rat beat her for going to Nakesian, who was quite a lady-killer. Lucky thought of Dawn as private property, but I guess she liked our dead spiritualist more than she liked her gun-toting boy friend with the rainbow eyes. Lucky was jealous as hell, and I think Dawn will want to talk."

"You've got something there," observed the Greek.

Wheels Burton owned the Shady Grove, just as he owned a string of such places along the resort coasts from Maine to Florida, of which the Shady Grove was the biggest and most ambitious. The name he gave the nightclub was appropriate, Storm thought. It was plenty shady. What Wheels got out of the foolish public was a crying shame. Upstairs he had a floor devoted to roulette wheels, from which the gambler derived his title. Downstairs was a gaudy bar, with orchestra and handkerchief-sized dance floor. The waiters were Burton's thugs, imported from Avenue A. The gambling machines upstairs were not bothered very often by the state racket and gambling squads. Sheriff Corlwye's salary was rather low, but during the summer vacation season his funds increased considerably. That was Burton's way. Wheels had more men on his graft-roll than a dozen state congressmen, and he readily obliged his friendly enemies in return for accepted favors.

Storm gave his hat to the redhead in the checkroom booth, who said, with bright innocence in her blue eyes, "Hello, mister amateur-copper. Is Lightning Leo going to strike?"

Her smile said it was all in fun, and he answered in a mock whisper.

"I'm pretending tonight that I'm an amateur nothing," he grinned. "I have a date. Twenty bucks says you'll keep it under your wig."

The redhead promptly put out her hand. "Show me," she said, and the twenty changed owners. Storm decided to charge it to expenses.

He crossed the room and took a booth table on the far side of the floor. His eyes were alert behind his rimless glasses. The lights dimmed, and a pink spotlight shone on a trim little figure in a silver evening gown. It was Dawn Detras. Her frock was completely unadorned, save for a red rose fastened to one white shoulder.

She was singing something about love being dead, and her eyes, behind their long lashes, melted with the sentimental pathos of her lyrics, cruising leisurely over the smoke-obscured audience until they settled on Storm's spectacles. When the song was over, she smiled, bowed slightly with infinite grace, and made her way through the spattering applause to Storm's booth. She slid into the seat across from him.

Despite her make-up, Storm knew she had been crying.

She began with false casualness, "So Dick—Nakesian is really dead?"

"Yes, that's true," Storm admitted. He added, "Where's the boy friend?"

"You mean Lucky?"

"That's the one."

Dawn lifted her dark eyes, and Storm saw she was really frightened. Her white teeth clamped down on her pouting lower lip to prevent it from trembling. She waved a vague hand.

"I don't know where Lucky is, and I don't care. Lucky's no friend of mine, Leo."

"Split up again?"

"For good. He beat me twice."

Storm told her he would cheerfully break Lucky Lamonte's neck when he got hold of it, and he meant what he said.

She asked in a tight voice, "Why do you ask about Lucky?"

He leaned back in his chair. "Because he stuck a knife in Dikran Nakesian's back. He was jealous of your visits to Dikran. He went up there and got rid of competition the only way he knew how."

Storm did not mean to be funny, but the little brunette started to laugh. He didn't like it; the shrill quality in her voice gave him chills. He told her to stop. She didn't, not until a minute later. Then she leaned across the table toward him and took his hand in a tight, nervous grip. Her fingernails pierced deep into his knuckles.

"You're wrong," she said. "So awfully wrong, and yet so nearly right! I'll tell you about it. Lucky did want to kill Nakesian. He hated Dick, and me because I was going with Dick. But why shouldn't I have done that? Dick was a gentleman, wasn't he?"

"Sure," said Storm. He did not wish to disillusion her. "Now—how am I wrong? Didn't Lucky do it?"

"Nakesian was knifed, and that's why you're wrong, and you know it, Storm. Lucky would never use a knife, not when he's so used to carrying a gun regularly. Lucky is more familiar with bullets than steel."

"That's true. But he did have jealousy as a motive for killing Nakesian. And he was there. You better tell me why Lucky was on the scene, if it was not for the purpose of killing Nakesian."

She looked at the white tablecloth. "There was another reason, but only one was important to me," she whispered. "I mean, it's important to me that he went to warn Dick away from me."

"Then what was the other reason why Lucky was on the scene? If Lucky didn't kill Dikran, who did?"

"I don't know."

Dawn shrugged, and her shoulders gleamed smooth and rosy in the light of the little pink lamp. The rose on her silver evening gown stood out blood red against the milkiness of her skin.

"I don't know who killed Dick, but Lucky didn't do it. Someone beat him to it."

"Can't you guess who?"

"No, I don't know."

"What was Lucky's purpose, then, in visiting Nakesian—besides discussing you?"

Dawn Detras' eyes became frightened again.

"If I tell you, Leo, my skin won't be worth more than a cat's."

"I'll take care of you," he promised.

She laughed at him. "You can't beat Wheels Burton. You can't help me at all. Listen, Storm, Lucky had a quarter of a million reasons why he should visit—"

"Say it again," said Storm tensely. "Slowly."

She was startled by the change in his voice, then laughed with a little tinkling laugh. "That's all I know about it. Nakesian had two hundred and fifty grand that Lucky was sent to get."

"Who sent him?"

"Wheels Burton."

"Whose money was it?"

"Wheels said it was his. He said that Nakesian had stolen it from him."

"And who has it now?"

"I don't know." She gestured helplessly. "I suppose Wheels got it back."

Storm puffed air through his nostrils and settled back in his seat to stare in perplexity at Dawn Detras.

He asked, "It's mixed up with old Myron Coulter selling his jewels to Romwell Taite for a quarter of a million, isn't it?"

Dawn nodded her sleek, dark head.

"This Romwell Taite," she said, "doesn't know the score, even if he is tough. He comes from Chicago. He doesn't have anything to do with the business except to buy old man Coulter's jewels and pay him spot cash for them. Nobody intends to take over Taite. It's after old Coulter gets the cash, and before he makes that publicity play by donating it to the Spiritualist Foundation, that Wheels plans a grab. I don't know what the details are."

Storm let the front legs of his chair touch the floor and leaned forward over the table.

"It looks to me as though Nakesian would have ultimately benefited by this deal, providing nothing went wrong. I suppose Nakesian and you were keeping a close eye on the business, to prevent Coulter from losing his cash. Looks to me like you and Nakesian were in a soft spot to collect a lot of money."

Dawn looked up impatiently. "Dick and I didn't stand to gain much. The Foundation is just another racket. The publicity angle that old Coulter worked out is just to strengthen the organization through its clients. The old ladies, you know. I hated them, the way they fawned over Dick. But that doesn't matter. The Foundation was a union, collecting dues from the spiritualists on the threat of exposing them as fakes. Old Coulter was due to get his money back, with plenty of interest—and you can't break up the Foundation, Storm, not yet. They've got it organized so that it's really legal, so far."

Storm said nothing, interested in the fact that this little black-haired singer knew more about the coming transaction than the police.

Dawn Detras continued, "Listen, Leo, I'm going to tell you about Wheels Burton. He has a lot of rackets, Wheels has, but only his roulette wheels are known to the police. First of all, he's a shake-down artist—first class. He has a lot of people staying awake nights, wondering what he'll do. People you wouldn't dream of associating with Wheels Burton. He's a louse, a crum, and I hate him until I could kill him, because he ordered Lucky to kill Dick."

"But you said Lucky didn't do it."

"The intention was there. That's enough for me."

Dawn Detras' eyes were bright and hard now, like black china, with a glinting luster that sparkled of red revenge. Her tiny, pert little face had hardened into a cruel mould.

Storm muttered, "If Burton's a blackmailer, perhaps that's the reason why Lieutenant Tilliman never could get an okay to ax this joint. But where does Wheels figure in on the quarter million?"

She shrugged.

"Wheels is out to get it," she said simply. "That's all I know."

"It doesn't make sense," Storm said. And then, suddenly, "What sort of people does Wheels shake?"

Dawn bit her red lip, and her fright came back to her. Storm asked, stabbing in the dark, "Does he have a chap by the name of Gregory Dolman under his thumb?"

The girl was startled. Her pouting mouth opened, and she made a funny little waving motion with her hand, winding up by covering her mouth with it.

A shadow fell across the table, and Storm saw it was a waiter: a chunky man with ears that somebody had long ago pinned back. The waiter put down two glasses of liquor and went away without a word.

Storm looked across at Dawn Detras.

"I didn't order any drinks."

"Neither did I."

He picked up his glass, sniffed at it and grunted. It had a fruity smell, and the stuff was not brandy. He told the girl not to touch her drink and looked around. Across the floor, over the heads of the patrons, he saw the redheaded hat-check girl and Wheels Burton. Burton and the redhead were watching him and Dawn. A captain of the waiters had his eyes open, too. They all looked as though they were waiting for something to happen, and were none too patient about it.

Storm got up and glanced into the next booth. Not too conspicuously. Just for a glimpse. There was no one in it, but he still did not feel quite right. He went back to his table and looked around. The little pink lamp, close against the ply-board wall, attracted his attention. He picked it up. looked under the base, and put it back again.

The lamp had a microphone under it.

Wheels Burton saw him make his discovery. The big man started across the floor as Storm picked up his liquor glass and stood beside the table. When Burton got about three steps from Storm, the latter picked up the girl's glass, also. Then he deliberately poured the liquor on the floor. After that, he dropped the tumblers and ground them to powdered splinters under his hard heel.

Burton looked annoyed. He asked, "What's the matter, Mr. Storm?"

Storm took his time examining this man, who did as he wished and laughed at the law when he did it; who paid his hired killers with money mulcted from people too foolish to realize that Wheels Burton had crooked roulette machines; who paid politicians with votes and contributions, and cracked the whip with his dirty knowledge, gleaned from snooping maids and spying butlers.

Wheels Burton looked like a lawyer, a banker, a broker—anything but a gambler. He was a big man, not so tall as Storm, but bulkier, with a figure carefully tailored by a medically prescribed course in athletics. He wore a little black moustache that crawled around under his blunt nose, and his tuxedo had a distinctly sporty cut, thereby proving that nothing was impossible. In his early thirties, the general contour of his face was that of roughly hacked stone; his jaw was strong, muscular, set with will and physical strength. Exuding masculine virility, Storm would have grudgingly summed him up as handsome, had it not been for Burton's eyes. There was scarcely any color in them. They were such a pale blue-gray that they looked almost all white, giving anyone who looked at him a creepy, uncomfortable sensation, and giving Burton a look of complete indifference and callous disregard for the world and its occupants.

Storm, looking at the redhead who had followed Wheels Burton, did not care for the way her lips smiled.

He said to her, "Hello, double-crosser. You owe me twenty bucks for services not rendered."

The redhead threw back her head slightly and looked at him with level blue eyes.

Wheels repeated, "What's the matter, Mr. Storm?"

He was talking to Leo, but he kept looking at Dawn Detras.

Storm breathed through his nose and said to Wheels, "Chloral hydrate has a distinct fruity smell."

"Chloral hydrate?"

"Yes. Ordinary thieves' knock-out drops. Be more subtle next time, Burton. You might land your fish."

Burton's face grew rockier. "I don't know what you're talking about."

Storm thought that he had better take off his spectacles, and he did. He could see just as well without them, if not better. He used them for reading, generally, and because he knew very well that his appearance with them was that of an underfed jellyfish. Which came in very useful sometimes.

He pinched the bridge of his nose and yawned. Pressure was slowly creeping along all his muscles.

Wheels spoke to Dawn Detras. "You better go up to my office, Dawn. I'll want to talk to you."

"No," she whispered. "No."

She looked at Storm, and he felt empty inside. Her eyes reminded him of those of a puppy he had once accidentally hurt. She half got up, but he pushed her back with one finger.

"Pretend you didn't hear him, Dawn."

Burton's angular features grew ugly with slowly rising anger. Storm's thin, hollow face remained a mask that hid his own growing irritation. He did not intend to stand for anything, not one single little thing. He felt pretty ugly himself. He had gotten Dawn Detras into a difficult and dangerous spot, and he had promised to cover her. He intended to cover her.

He had expected the hat-check girl to cross him and tip off Burton that he was in the club, but he never counted on the microphone. He knew, as surely as he knew that Wheels wanted trouble, that there were wires leading to Burton's office, and that Wheels had heard everything Dawn had told him. That spelled trouble for the raven-haired girl.

Wheels was smiling.

"Now, Mr. Storm, you're forgetting yourself. After all, the little lady works for me."

"Not any longer."

It was a simple statement of fact.

"Leo—" Dawn plucked at his sleeve with nervous little tugs.

"I'll land you another job in no time, Dawn."

He knew he could find her another spot, whenever he wished to, through his innumerable contacts, but there was more to the affair than just that. Wheels had heard her talk, and Wheels was not letting her go.

Storm got what he thought was a bright idea. He look one of his two guns and shoved it into the girl's hand. It looked ridiculously big and black in her tiny, crimson-tipped fingers.

He said, "Dawn, walk straight out of here and go down to the sheriff's office. Say I sent you. Stay there until you see me—not *hear* from me. If anybody tries to stop you on the way, let them have it. The whole clip. Do you understand?"

She bobbed her head in a jerky nod, slid around Wheels Burton and started walking.

Before the girl was halfway across the floor, Storm knew he had made a mistake.

She did not know how to use the gun, for one thing. She simply let it hang from her fingers, and walked as though in a trance.

He took a quick look at Burton, and saw that the gambler's face had gone chalky; and then he knew that the girl was a walking death warrant for Wheels Burton. Dawn Detras knew too much, a lot more than she had told him.

He moved after her, surging forward, pushing Burton ahead of him. The captain of the waiters followed. The waiter looked at Wheels, and Wheels looked back with his colorless eyes, and the man ran forward after Dawn Detras.

Storm yanked his gun.

"Hold it!" he yelled.

They didn't.

A blare of noise came from the shadows of the sobbing orchestra. Trumpets howled and saxophones wailed; a drum beat a mad dervish tattoo. The sound was deafening, spiraling like a tornado through the room, and the noise was perfectly timed. The men in the orchestra played like the fiends of hell, but their mad music failed to cover completely the stutter of an automatic rifle.

The thing rattled and gibbered for a second; then everything was quiet, save for the orchestra music that sank down to a soft moan.

Storm had his gun ready, but there was nothing to shoot at.

The nightclub patrons were unsuspicious, unwarned. They did not know anything was wrong. The lights were half dimmed. Storm ran ahead to Dawn Detras.

She was slumped in a deserted corner among some empty tables. Curled up like a sleek kitten, her little body lay tight in its sheath of silver. The red rose on her shoulder strap had fallen off, but there was another crimson blossom to take its place—glistening red that stained the silver-whiteness of her gown and skin.

Storm's body trembled with a racking shiver. He felt hot and cold prickles go up and down his spine, and then he spun on his heels to face Wheels Burton.

"You'll sit in the chair for this, Wheels," he said, and his voice shook in spite of himself. "You'll squat, and so will your hired killers. I'm a witness. You can't chop me down like you can a defenseless girl. I'll swear you ordered her death."

His voice was a vibrating blade that cut through the smoky atmosphere with deadly intensity. Wheels knew that he was in earnest. And Wheels' face betrayed his fear.

He rattled quickly, "I didn't do this, Storm! I don't know who did this! I'm not responsible for it!"

CHAPTER TEN
SHOWDOWN

Storm waved his gun at Burton and said hoarsely, "Let's go to the orchestra pit, Wheels."

The nightclub operator nodded, and walked among the tables, with his waiter beside him. The musicians, playing a new swing tune, watched their ominous approach. Saxophones wailed in alarm. Pocketing his gun, Storm cat-footed after Burton.

The orchestra was seated on a little raised dais. White-faced musicians watched Storm as he went from one man to the other, searching for the rifle. Wheels stood by, helpless, his strange, colorless eyes sending unspoken commands to his employees.

"I had nothing to do with this, Storm," Burton repeated. He cleared his throat. "Someone could have shot her from there, from outside."

The gambler indicated the stained-glass window behind the orchestra. It was slightly ajar. Behind it was the gloomy mystery of the pine-scented woods.

A ferret-faced drummer with a scrubby moustache muttered, "That's where it came from, all right. Chow-chow! I felt the slugs comb my hair, practically!"

"That's nice co-operation," Storm murmured.

He stared in distaste at the drummer, and the musician swiveled and hammered savagely on the taut kettledrum. The orchestra had not paused in its mad syncopation. The leader waved his baton automatically, his frightened eyes fixed on Storm's figure, his glance pinned to the hand that Storm kept thrust in his sagging pocket.

At last Storm said, "You'll still be under arrest, Wheels."

Burton walked quietly back with him to the corner table. A waiter was just getting up from his stooping position. He held a wet rag gingerly by one end, a rag which was strained crimson. The waiter looked sick. Dawn Detras' body was gone.

Burton chuckled.

"Arrested for what?"

Futile anger churned upward in Storm's chest.

"I practically insulted your boys when I said they co-operated with you. They know their parts to perfection! But just because you've already removed the poor girl's body doesn't mean I didn't see murder done."

"You can't prove it," said Burton coldly. "Not without a body. And you're the only one who claims he saw a killing. Come, be reasonable, Storm. I didn't do it, and I didn't order it done. It's a coincidence, see? The girl had a lot of enemies, and somebody took advantage of the orchestra to chop her down. It won't do any good to raise a stink. And I'm not responsible. Murder isn't in my line, and that's the truth."

Storm felt uglier. He sucked in air, chewed on his lip, and did some thinking.

The more he thought, the more he wanted to take Wheels Burton down to the sheriff's office.

He wanted to, but he knew he couldn't.

Wheels Burton divined Storm's thoughts. "You can't prove anything,

Storm. If you act fresh, I'll pull every political string I've got—and if you know Lieutenant Tilliman, you'll also know it's a healthy handful of strings I've got in my fist. Now, listen: the girl's body will be found, but not around my place of business. I can't afford the damage to my reputation. If you try to buck the story I'll have planted and act foolishly, you'll find yourself tied up in the worst jam you ever dreamed of. Now be reasonable, and listen to me."

"Murder isn't reasonable! The girl was killed because she talked about you. I could kill you right now, to even things up—and get away with it, too."

Wheels' angular face was the color of a badly-peeled potato.

"That murder-gun doesn't belong to me, Storm, but it can still talk!" he rapped. He waved a ringed finger around the murky nightclub. "It might still be somewhere around. Pointed at your back."

"That doesn't frighten me."

Burton looked narrowly at Storm and shrugged, with a ghost of an admiring smile. "I guess it doesn't."

Storm chewed on his lip some more. His hands were tied: if he jugged Wheels, the man would wriggle and bribe his way to freedom. And discounting the possibility of the murderer still lurking in the vicinity, there was the problem of the missing Valerie Feather. If she were in Burton's hands, then her release was more important than jailing Burton. With Wheels held on charges, there was no way of finding out what had happened to the girl. It was a callous thought, perhaps, but it was a choice of avenging the dead or saving the living.

He grunted, and Wheels looked relieved—until Storm said, "Okay, march."

"Where? Now, listen, Storm, you didn't hear what I said—"

"I heard. We're going upstairs to your office. We have a lot of—ah—gum-beating to do, you and I."

Wheels appeared to hesitate, then shrugged his shoulders.

"Let's go."

Burton's offices were up on the third and topmost floor of the rambling building. A private elevator took them up in tense silence. The waiter remained below, at. a sign from Wheels, and the two men emerged from the cage directly into Burton's living quarters.

Burton flicked a wall-switch. Lights, concealed behind a silver moulding, reflected an indirect glow over the mahogany-paneled ceiling.

In contrast to the gaudiness of the Shady Grove, down below, the man's living quarters were done in hushed and conservative tones. The furniture was masculine, square and chunky, in gray mohair and silver banding. Over against the curtained window stood a solid desk, with chromium paraphernalia arranged on the glass top. Two walls were lined with books from floor to ceiling. They were good books, and looked as though they had been often read.

All this Storm saw with a quick, sweeping glance, even as he became aware of the man who sprawled in one of the deep chairs. He would not have seen the man nor been aware of his presence had it not been for the betraying clink of ice in a glass.

He tightened his grip on the gun, motioned Burton over against a wall, and then stepped around the chair to look into the man's face.

It was Gregory Dolman, short and squat, with his rolypoly face flushed and his heavy-lidded eyes shot through with a network of swollen little veins. One eye was blackened, and an ugly bruise stood out on his chin, purple against the powder-white of the man's face.

Dolman spoke, and Storm knew he was drunk. Dolman waved a glass of amber liquor, splashing some of it over his shirt cuff, and grinned vacuously.

"Welcome! Welcome to our little love-nest! So Wheels got you, too, eh?"

Storm looked up at Burton. The man was sitting on a corner of his big desk, the ends of his mouth drawn into annoyed little puckers under his moustache.

"He's drunk," said Burton, as though that ended the matter.

Storm remained in front of the chair. The paunchy Dolman looked up at the very tall man, his bleary gaze drifting from Storm's hollow face to the automatic that bulked black in his hand.

"Oooh," said Dolman. "Bad mans!"

"Yeah," Storm breathed. His throat ached with dry tension. He turned to Wheels Burton, who was examining his fingernails. "Often have drunks popping in on you like this?"

"No, not often. In fact, almost never."

Dolman stirred in his chair, twisting around and looking sideways at Wheels. "You're a liar, my good host. I'm always here. I've been here for ages. You wouldn't let me leave if I wanted to. And I don't, not as long as this nectar retains its flavor."

Storm lifted murky eyes back to the gambler, who looked totally unconcerned, save to repeat, "Dolman, you're drunk."

"Now here are some more things I don't understand," Storm said, his lips compressed to a paper-thin line.

"A pity," Burton sneered. "There's no difficulty in understanding that what Mr. Dolman needs is to be dunked suddenly into an ice-cold bath."

"You're poor at avoiding the issue," Storm pointed out. "Dolman is your prisoner. You've been beating him. First murder, now kidnapping—or was it vice versa?"

Wheels, laughing, waved his hand at the rolypoly man.

"Does it look as though I have a ball and chain on him?"

Storm returned to Gregory Dolman.

"Who beat you up? Who blackened your eye and jaw?"

"Are they black?" Dolman asked. His pudgy fingers touched his puffed left eye, and he winced, then pointed accusingly at Burton. "He did it."

"Why?"

But Dolman wobbled his head and returned to his glass. His lips made little sucking noises as he drank the liquor. He had no more interest in Storm or the gun or Wheels Burton.

Storm shrugged. Burton was smiling, still leaning against the desk, and the fact that he was not worried made Storm feel uneasy. Burton stared down at Storm's gun, which pointed directly to a spot between his whitish eyes, and merely smiled.

Finally Burton turned to his desk, his hand reaching for a drawer. He looked over his shoulder and saw Storm rigid, the gun twisting to cover him before his lingers could touch the bright handle.

"Don't be jittery, Storm."

"I'm not. I can put six bullets into you before you can get your gun."

"I told you I don't believe in murder. Not when it's unnecessary. There is quite a bushel of facts *I* don't understand, Mr. Storm. Between the two of us, we could sort the chaff from the wheat, so to speak."

Burton paused, and rolled his tongue over his thin lips. "Perhaps ten grand may help pave the way to a clearer state of understanding between us. Although I insist I'm innocent of Dawn's death, I had to have her body removed. It will turn up in a day or two and go down on the books as unsolved. I had to get it away from the Shady Grove. Murders are bad for my business."

The gambler's hand came out of the desk with a thick sheaf of banknotes. Storm kept his face expressionless as Burton glanced inquiringly at him.

Then Gregory Dolman intruded again, speaking from the depths of his lounge chair.

"Don't touch it, Storm. Don't bother with it. It's chicken—chicken feed. We got a much better racket, we have."

Wheels said for a third time, without taking his queer, colorless eyes off Storm, "He's drunk."

Dolman surged out of his chair, clutching his glass. "And why shouldn't I be? Answer that simple question. You've kept shovin'—shoving wonderful liquor at me, and who am I to say no?" He hiccoughed. "The truth is, Wheels, you're a very, very generous host. But irksome."

Dolman giggled. "Irksome, Wheels. You irk me." Then, abruptly, "I wanna go home."

He got up and weaved across the room, reaching wearily for the elevator button as though expecting it to disappear before his eyes. With a quick mutter of annoyance, Wheels crossed the room in front of Storm's gun and grabbed the paunchy man by the slack of his coat. Dolman was whirled around and thrown back in his chair with force enough to make him bounce.

"Now stay there until you're sober and can tell me what happened."

Storm said nothing, watching the business with half-closed eyes. Burton turned back to him.

"Now about this ten thousand—it's yours. You know what to do, or rather, what not to do. I don't have to tell you."

"It will take more than that just to cover up a dead body," said Storm tonelessly.

Wheels said, "If you want more—" with a contemptuous gesture.

"It would take more than you can afford to pay," Storm went on. "Suppose you answer questions. Why arc you keeping Dolman here?"

"I've been questioning him about this Nakesian rub-out," Burton shrugged. He eyed Storm's gun. "I want to know what happened over there. This fat little fool doesn't know."

"Well, I do," said Storm curtly. "Nakesian stole a quarter of a million from you, and you murdered him, through Lucky Lamonte, and got it back."

"So you know about the money?"

"I saw it," Storm stated flatly. "And you know well enough that I laid hands on it. I'd have kept it, too, but your boys were too many for me. They got it back."

Burton shook his head and announced, suddenly angry, "But they didn't get it back! The girl got it, damn her!"

"Girl?" Storm asked cautiously.

"Whoever she is. I don't know."

"Don't lie," said Storm wearily. "You know where she is. She turned the money over to you."

"No, she's got the money."

"Then who's got the girl?" Storm snapped.

Gregory Dolman piped up from his deep-cushioned seat, "What young lady are you gentlemen talking about?"

"The girl I saw in Nakesian's apartment," Storm replied, looking at Wheels. "The one who disappeared."

He did not mention Valerie's name. He was treading dangerous and treacherous ground, working down an unwelcome path.

Burton smoothed his moustache, turned and stared out of the curtained window with folded arms. His voice drifted over his shoulder to the man with the gun.

"Look, Storm, it was my money that Nakesian stole. It was a matter between ourselves. I admit I sent the boys over to Nakesian's apartment to get that money back—sure. But I gave no orders to kill, and my boys didn't kill Nakesian. Just like Dawn—the thing was framed on me. Lucky and the boys didn't get the money or snatch the girl, as you seem to think. I don't have her."

Storm's lip curled.

"I suppose your little rat Toogy didn't turn the money over to you? He picked it up; he was with the girl. I cached the money in a house across from the hotel while your rats were chasing me all over Kennicut. Toogy picked it up, and Toogy had the girl with him."

"Toogy?" Burton spoke as though surprised. "Toogy with her? The little punk—I haven't seen him all day. So Toogy got the money with the girl!"

"That's one possible explanation."

"Have you got any others?" Burton asked, swinging around from the window to face Storm.

"I'm doing the questioning," Storm reminded him.

He lifted the muzzle of his automatic to follow Burton's nervous pacing. "Tell me how the money Nakesian stole from you fits in with the Coulter jewel sale for two hundred and fifty grand!"

Burton lifted shaggy eyebrows and crossed the loom, sinking into a chair that nestled deep in a corner.

"So you know about that, too, eh?"

Storm nodded. "You're playing a deep game, Burton."

"So are you. I don't see why you're butting in at all. You're not a cop, and you don't need money. I know about you, Storm. You are one of these guys who haven't any business of their own, and relieve their boredom sticking their noses into other people's business."

"And sometimes it's profitable," Storm said, "but not through taking bribes. Your game has only begun. Nakesian was killed, and now Dawn Detras—"

Gregory Dolman interrupted once again, getting to his feet with a lurch, swinging a bottle in one hand and an empty glass in another. His eye was puffed now until it was almost closed, and the blue-black bruise on his fat jaw stood out like an ugly smudge against the slack whiteness of his features. His eyes were wide, and perspiration made his round face look glittery.

"Dawn Detras?" he croaked. "She's dead?"

"Sit down," Storm suggested.

"She's dead! I know it! Maybe Lucky bumped her, eh? He was jealous as hell."

"It's an idea," Storm admitted. He repeated, "Sit down."

Dolman jelled into the chair again.

Storm returned to Burton, who had slumped far down in his corner chair, gloomily surveying the shiny tips of his patent-leather shoes.

"Two murders, Burton, and the sale hasn't even been made yet! Taite hasn't withdrawn his cash from the bank yet. That means there is an extra two hundred and fifty grand around. You're not bidding for Coulter's jewels yourself, are you, Wheels? You're not competing with Taite, are you?"

Burton looked up, stared thoughtfully, and then spoke as though he had just reached a decision that was troubling him.

"No," he said. "No, I'm bidding for nothing. But I'm sorry you figured out there's extra cash around. You and the blonde girl both know it. I'm sorry, but I'm afraid I'll have to kill you both."

Storm laughed, a curt, ringing sound that echoed through the room. He looked down at the gun in his hand.

"You're in a fine way to make threats, Burton."

"I didn't want any killings," Burton went on tonelessly. "I haven't done any yet. But you're smart, Storm. You'll hit on the right answer soon. So I'll have to kill you before that unfortunate thing happens."

Burton leaned back in his chair with a smile that was pleasant and certain. He said nothing, did not shift his queer glance away from Storm's gun. Yet Storm knew, as surely as he knew that the gun butt in his grip had suddenly grown slippery, that danger hummed vibrant in the air around him. It reached out for him with hot, tingling tentacles from the rear; it rocked under his feet. Danger lurked in the elevator door at his back, although he heard not the slightest sound to indicate that the cage was operating. And danger lurked in the windowed curtains—

He understood too late why Burton had gone to the window, why he had later shifted his position to a seat in a deep, protected corner.

There was something moving behind the big windows, reaching almost down to the floor. But they were on the third level—

Flame spat viciously, glass tinkled, and the sharp, spiteful hiss of a bullet was heard as it buzzed past Storm's ear.

"Take him!" came Burton's shout.

Storm flung himself aside; snapped a shot at Burton that went wide because of his own movement; slipped with his right foot on the shiny waxed floor; and went down as bodies tumbled through the window from the *terrace* beyond!

There were two men, in addition to Wheels Burton. Burton, lunging out of his chair with startling speed, ducked aside as Storm's gun spouted flame and lead at him. Then their bodies crashed and locked together, and they went down to the floor as the two gunmen leaped in from the terrace and tore at Storm's body.

His knuckles spattered across one man's mouth and came away with a streak of red. With his other fist, he smashed at the second man's groin, and the fellow rolled on the floor, groaning.

But Wheels Burton had his hand on the gun, and Storm's attention was concentrated on retaining it. They rolled, heaved, twisted and squirmed over the floor. A standing lamp went over with a crash and tinkle of smashed bulbs, and the light in the room grew two shades darker. They came up against the corner of the lounge, smashed an end table to kindling wood, and then Storm got to his feet.

His breath was coming in long, shuddering gasps; his face was a mask of desperate power. Burton lurched up after him, equally silent, equally intent, his arm streaking for Storm's gun hand. The man with the split lips cursed and groped for the revolver he had dropped. Then they wrestled for the automatic that Storm held high above his head.

Burton twisted with savage force, and Storm bent far over sideways. He pounded his free fist into Burton's body, surprised at the muscular compactness of the big man's physique. And then, with a final twist, Storm regained complete possession of the black gun.

It meant his defeat.

The wrench he gave sent him spinning off balance across the room, tearing away from Burton. He staggered against the hood with the dented middle. The gunman was quick to seize his opportunity. The revolver in the gunman's hand came down in a swishing, blurred arc on Storm's face. It smashed on his forehead, sending blinding pain searing through his brain.

He slipped, staggered, and went down on one knee. His automatic dropped from nerveless fingers. Through a reddening haze he caught a glimpse of Gregory Dolman, still seated in the deep lounge chair, with a bottle in one hand and a glass in the other, staring owlishly, with unblinking eyes, at the tangle of struggling men.

Then the gunman, grinning viciously, smashed the gun once more on Storm's head.

Leo went dropping into a spiraling tunnel of roaring wind, a tornado that sucked downward into dizzying, bottomless depths....

CHAPTER ELEVEN
ESCAPE

At first Storm thought it was beetles. Thousands of beetles, buzzing, rattling, swarming around inside his head.

He did not open his eyes immediately. He lay still, trying to find his body. But, when he did discover his limbs, he regretted it. Every muscle was a leaping flame of agony; his head felt as wobbly as a run-down top.

Voices drifted to him, punctuating the rattling and buzzing that he heard. He opened one eye and winced as a shadow fell over his face; he saw the round outline and partly bald head of Gregory Dolman. The man was leaning over him intently.

Storm opened both eyes, and Dolman swayed back, grinning and blinking rapidly with his sleepy eyes.

"Oh," he said. "Oh, you woke up."

Storm watched a gold tooth that glinted far back in Dolman's mouth. The buzzing sound still persisted. He tried to sit up; he couldn't move. He found himself tied hand and foot to a couch.

He was in a bedroom of mahogany paneling, with deeply alcoved windows. Rain beat with a thousand silvery hammers at the glass panes. The hissing downpour was the source of the rattling beetles.

"Hail, comrade," Dolman said. "Have a drink?"

Storm accepted the invitation. Dolman held a glass to his lips. The liquor was strong, slaking its way down his throat to land with a resounding splash in his interior. He looked up at Dolman incredulously.

"That what you've been drinking all night?"

"Yep. Wonderful stuff, huh?"

"The wonder is that you're still on your feet."

He started to get off the bed again, but the sharp jolt of his bonds sent his head spinning. He sank back with a groan.

"Can't take it," Dolman observed owlishly. "Go on, ask me."

"Ask what?"

"Say, 'Where am I?' Everybody asks that. It's the thing to do."

"Okay, where am I?" Storm asked, humoring him.

"You're still in the apartment in the Shady Grove," Coulter answered, with a smirk of satisfaction. "In Wheels Burton's private apartment. In fact, you're in his own bed."

"Well, I don't appreciate it."

Dolman pondered that for a moment. Then, "No, neither would I."

"What time is it?"

Dolman consulted his wrist-watch, peering for a long time at the dial. "You've been out twenty minutes. It started to rain just when you got slammed. Thunderstorm. It's stopping now."

So it was close to midnight. Storm lay back and listened. There were still voices in the air, coming from behind the closed door.

He asked, "Why don't you leave, Dolman? Burton's keeping you here for questioning, isn't he? He beat you, didn't he? If you're free to walk around, why don't you escape?"

"Because I'm drunk," said Dolman flatly. "I'm fine, so far. Let me hit the air and—*whoosh!* Blotto. Besides, they have guns. That's a reasonable argument, isn't it?"

The man's speech was perfect, unimpeded. It was a miracle. Dolman went on, "I can't leave because my amiable host has fifty thousand dollars' worth of IOU's signed by me. That's bad—bad for me. If my precious old uncle hears of it, what will he do?"

Storm blinked at him.

"I'll tell you what old Myron'll do," Dolman insisted, wagging his hand. "He'll disinherit me, that's what. And that would be a tragedy. So I'm here to answer Wheels' questions, only I don't know anything and he doesn't believe me. So I think I'll tell him some lies and then he'll let me go free. Wonderful idea!"

"How about cutting me loose?" Storm suggested.

Gregory considered for a long moment, then shook his round head. "Nope. Wouldn't do any good. They got guns outside the door. Besides, little Val'rie will have us out in no time."

Storm lay still suddenly. "Valerie?"

"Shh!" Dolman spread his plump fingers flat over his mouth. "Listen!"

From beyond the door that led to Burton's living room came the sound of voices rising in determination and anger. Storm felt a chill run through his blood as he recognized the tones of Valerie Feather. Interrupting and overruling her speech came the husky, suave accents of Wheels Burton.

They were arguing. Burton was saying, "You have my money, young lady, and that's the only payment I'll accept in return for Storm's release."

"I haven't your money," Valerie returned. "Your rat Toogy took it away from me."

"I don't believe that, and don't ask me to. You probably tricked Toogy and got away."

"No, that's not true! I'm giving you straight facts, Wheels. Besides, the money's not the point. You've seen these papers. They're duplicate copies of what I know about your affairs—and a little of what I know about your plot on Coulter's jewels and Romwell Taite's cash. I could stomach some of your plans, Wheels, but not this."

Storm frowned and bit his lip in anxious thought as he recognized Valerie's tone as indicating a familiarity with Wheels Burton. She sounded as though she had been in league with the gambler on previous occasions, and was now rebellious! Somehow, the thought turned his hopes gray.

Burton queried softly, "You wouldn't cross me, would you, Valerie?"

"No, I wouldn't. But those papers are safe—the originals are where you can't get your hands on them. I expected you'd take in Storm sometime tonight. Unless you release him—and Greg Dolman, too—the papers go in the mails. It won't do you any good to search for the person who is holding them for me. You won't find him. Unless you release Storm, the expose will be mailed to Lieutenant Tilliman. He'll get them tomorrow morning. You can imagine the rest."

Burton's sneer was sharp. "You're pulling an old gag, my girl."

"But it's still effective; I'm not a fool."

"Tomorrow morning is a long way off," Burton considered. "Plenty of time for you to die before that."

"I'm not afraid. You'll die, too, if those papers are mailed. You'll die in the electric chair. Either you set Storm free—or the other thing, in which case we'll both go under together. You're not a fool, Burton. You'll agree to my terms. I've already told you that Storm knows nothing of value to tell you."

"No, but he's dangerous."

In the room beyond the door, Dolman nodded his head in solemn agreement. Then he suddenly stiffened as Burton murmured something in reply to Valerie Feather. His moon-like face turned whiter, pastier. He got up, crossed the room, and returned to the bed with a gleaming knife. He stood over the bound Storm and blinked at him.

Cold chills rippled in delicate feathers along Storm's spine. The man was drunk, with a dangerous weapon, and Dolman's eyes were set with groggy determination. The knife glistened above Storm's head, little splinters of light leaping from the blade.

Dolman giggled.

"I'll cut you free," he said.

Storm exhaled in relief. "Do that, quickly."

It was the work of a few moments for Gregory to manipulate the blade and saw through the cords that kept Storm flat on the bed. When the job was done, Dolman stepped back with a grunt of satisfaction.

"Now, when Burton comes in, you grab him," he said. He balanced the sharp weapon in his pudgy hands. "I'll kill him," he concluded with satisfaction.

Storm watched the drunken man with narrowed eyes. Dolman was set in his purpose, chuckling with satisfaction at the thought.

"I'll kill him, and he won't bother me any more. He won't bother anyone with his dirty blackmail racket. The world will be a cleaner place without him. I'll tickle his heart with this nice, shiny point."

"No," said Storm.

Dolman's round, bloodshot eyes opened wider, and he held the knife with the point toward Storm.

"Yes. Maybe I'll finish you, too. Burton said you were dangerous."

The man was criminally insane. Kill-crazy, overflowing with raw liquor. From beyond the door came slow footsteps on the lush carpet: the heavy, reluctant tread of Wheels Burton, and the staccato clicking of Valerie Feather's high heels.

There was quick brittleness in Storm's manner as he sat up, slid his feet off the counterpane and stood before Dolman. He held out his hand.

"Give me that knife," he said.

Dolman backed away toward the door, shaking his round face, a broad, vacuous grin on his battered features. His black eye was completely closed, the bruise on his jaw lividly purple. He would have looked ridiculous but for the knife that gleamed wickedly sharp in his white paw.

"I'm going to kill Burton, so don't act silly, Storm."

There was no time for further argument. The door handle suddenly went down, and Dolman moved with amazing alacrity toward the entrance. Storm leaped at the same instant. The door swung inward, and Storm's heart froze as he saw Valerie Feather framed in the entrance, slightly preceding the bulky, athletic figure of Wheels Burton.

And Dolman was launching himself toward the doorway, knife raised to strike with drunken strength.

Storm dived headlong across the room. He heard Valerie's frightened gasp, then smashed hip-high into Dolman as the fat man drove forward. Gregory went staggering to one side, but, by a miracle, maintained his balance. Storm was down on his knees for an instant, and Wheels Burton, pushing through the door around Valerie Feather, tripped and staggered over his legs.

Dolman snarled, "You fool!" and moved with a lurching sway toward Burton. Storm got up, his fist driving forward and upward from the floor. It smacked crisply on Dolman's chin, and Dolman grunted and slid down to sit on the floor with a thump. The knife dropped from his hand and stuck point-first in the hardwood floor.

Burton lunged for the weapon at the same time as Storm, and the two men crashed together.

"Taste some of this, Burton," Storm breathed.

His fist hammered with deadly accuracy at Burton's middle, drummed on the gambler's heavily handsome features. Burton went sideways with a muffled yell, and Storm followed him up. He was a deadly machine, intent on revenge for the previous attack. He was meeting Burton man-to-man now, without the balance of guns in the gambler's favor.

But Burton was tough. He stepped back quickly, covering up, and Storm's swift, slashing blows were blocked. In a moment the gambler had regained his balance, and drove forward. Storm checked him with a left to the stomach, sliced upward with his right, and again his knuckles spattered crisply on Burton's jaw.

Still the man did not go down. But he was suddenly haggard, and his breath came in shuddering, sucking gasps.

A voice said, "Stop it, Leo."

It came clearly and with no uncertainty in it, as sharp as the knife that vibrated in the floor. It was Valerie Feather's voice, and it had the effect on Storm's red anger of a douse of ice-cold water.

He checked himself, remained motionless for a moment, staring at Burton, and then swung around to face the girl.

She was wearing a light box-coat over a blue skirt and jacket. A light felt hat sloped sharply over one eyebrow. Her red, red mouth was a gash of brilliance in the paleness of her oval face. He stood and examined the girl's tall figure, noted the straightness of her stance and the easy familiarity with which she handled the little .32 revolver in her gloved hand.

"Stop it, Storm. It's not necessary," she said again.

Her voice was husky and compelling. He dropped his hands to his sides and stepped back.

"We're getting out of here," the girl said crisply, brittleness in her tone, ice in her violet eyes.

Burton said, "I've changed my mind."

Valerie waggled her gun.

"You can't."

Woman-like, she held a purse in her left hand. Now she tossed it over to Storm, who caught it and opened it.

"You'll find another pea-shooter in there," she said.

Storm took out another .32. Burton opened his mouth to protest, but

Storm merely laughed softly, poking the gun at him.

"You heard what the fair lady said, Wheels. We're leaving. And we're taking Dolman with us. He's going to answer *my* questions, and you won't chop him down like you did Dawn."

Dolman sat up from the floor. He should have remained completely out, but the man had amazing resiliency. He bounced back like rubber, completely losing his murderous air.

"Bravo!" he crowed. "I wanna go home."

Burton watched him as he slowly climbed to his feet, with infinite difficulty. The little lines around the gambler's sharply chiseled nostrils tightened. Then he waved a limp hand.

"Go ahead, beat it."

Storm said, "With you, Wheels. Come along. Escort us to the door, at any rate. I'd hate to find your rats waiting for us when we get downstairs."

Burton had regained his composure. He smoothed back his thick hair, straightened his tie and opened the door. Storm nodded to Dolman.

"Come along, toad."

The little procession went down the elevator in silence. Storm and Valerie hid their guns. In the blare of noise from the Shady Grove, two hard-bitten, lean-jawed gunmen started to approach Wheels, but lie waved them away, after a quick look at the unpleasantness of Storm's face.

Valerie had a little blue roadster parked in the gravel road outside. She slid behind the wheel. Storm nudged Dolman along, keeping Burton close by his side. In the yellow doorway of the Shady Grove were the two gunmen and the saturnine captain of the waiters, and Storm had no intention of offering himself as a separate target.

Valerie prodded the starter. Storm put one foot on the running board, kept a firm grip on Dolman's sleeve, and said to her:

"When I say go, honey, slam the juice down to the floorboards, and don't worry about speed limits."

She nodded.

Storm suddenly planted a foot behind Burton's heels and stepped into the car, dragging Dolman in after him. His maneuver jerked Burton off balance, and the man hit the pavement with a thud. His three hoods yelled and came running out under the marquee.

Before they could get their guns up, the roadster was skidding and churning down the gravel highway toward the village.

CHAPTER TWELVE
JUST TALK

There was nothing said for a while, as the girl expertly circled the bay through the forest. Storm felt a chill wall of silent animosity spring up between him and this graceful, soft girl, who could be so hard and familiar with a deadly game like this.

Dolman finally spoke up. He kept his eyes closed.

"We won't be bothered by Wheels any more. He won't try to get us back. Li'l Valerie did a good job, whatever it was. Wheels will let us alone—you and me, Storm. But he's got it in for Valerie."

Storm said, "You just keep still."

"No. Look, Storm, I'm very much attached to Valerie. We're old friends—even more than that, Storm. I want her to be safe."

Storm made no reply. Every new thing he learned was unwelcome. Valerie an old friend—even more— to this man: That was a distasteful thought.

Dolman sat forward, fumbling in his pocket, and brought his hand out with something crackling in his fingers.

"You're a detective, aren't you, Storm? You're a bodyguard?"

"Not as a usual pastime."

"Well, this is an unusual thing," Dolman said. His voice blurred for a moment. "Guard Val'rie. She deserves it. And I'll pay you well."

The girl did not seem to be listening to the conversation.

Storm said quietly, "Valerie seems more capable of taking care of herself than we do, Dolman. But you wouldn't have to pay me to take care of her. It's the least I can do."

"But I insist—I really do. You take this—it's a hundred. Take it."

Dolman leaned forward and shoved a paper bill into Storm's hands. Something fluttered to Valerie's lap, dropped off and whirled to the floor in slow gyrations. It was a scrap of blue paper.

Storm checked his exclamation and, before he could move, Dolman spoke again.

" 'Bye, now. I'm leaving you."

And the man opened the door of the roadster and jumped.

Storm tried to clutch at Dolman's coat, but missed. The fat man hit the road, went down, and rolled over twice. Valerie jammed on the brakes with a shuddering gasp, and then Dolman stood up in the center of the gravel highway and waved a white paw at them. He started to run, ducking into the woods.

Valerie gasped, "Get him! Stop him!"

Storm shook his head.

"Let him go. He'll pass out any minute and sleep it off. Drunks never get hurt. He'll be safer in the woods than we'll be in the village. Besides, we're not far from town, and he'll be all right."

While he spoke, he leaned forward, his lingers groping for the long, thin scrap of blue paper he had seen Dolman drop. It had swirled under the clutch pedal, and Valerie had her foot on it.

She said in a tight voice, "I saw it, too, Mr. Smarty."

"Oh. Then you know what it is?"

"Of course."

She guided the car into the bayside road to the hotel, and removed her heel from the scrap of blue paper.

"I was hoping you hadn't seen it. It's one of those gummed strips of paper that are used to hold packets of money together."

"Yes?" he prompted.

"The money in Nakesian's apartment was fastened with gummed strips of paper. They were blue, like this one."

"So Dolman has the money," Storm said pensively.

He settled back on the leather seat with a muttered sigh.

They left the roadster in a garage near the Kennicut Hotel and walked the remaining two blocks in silence. The wall of mystery was crystallizing between them with every additional second, and neither liked it.

Coming through the revolving door of the Kennicut was a familiar figure. Small, stooped, pimply-faced, morose: Sammy, the bellboy. He was dressed in street-clothes, an unusual and unfamiliar sight without his smart red uniform.

He muttered, " 'Lo, Mr. Storm—Miss Feather," and then he noticed the tall man's appearance. "Gee, Mr. Storm, what happened to you?"

"I ran into an accident and it hit back. What's the trouble, Sammy? You look like your pet cow died."

The boy's face was disgusted.

"Aw, I lost a key."

Compunction struck at Storm's heart. "And you lost your job?"

"Yeah, that's right. Caldwell—he's the manager— he tied the can to my tail. I don't know what I did with the damned thing."

"The house-key?"

"Yeah. I know I had it before I went to your rooms to deliver that '69, Mr. Storm. I missed it about thirty minutes afterward. I can't find it anywhere."

Storm delved in his pocket and brought to light the little metal object that he had used to explore Valerie's rooms.

"Is this it?" he asked with a smile.

Sammy snatched at it with glee. "Yeah, that's it! I musta dropped it in your room. Lots of thanks, Mr. Storm."

"It's quite all right."

He took Valerie's arm and piloted her up to the elevator. The girl's red mouth was compressed into a light little line of contempt.

"So you've been snooping in my rooms, Mr. Storm?"

"That's right," he said easily. "You think fast. I thought I'd find out what part of the jig-saw puzzle you represent."

"Very ethical," she sniffed.

"Killers aren't ethical," Storm observed with emphasis. "So I can't afford to be, either."

"I'm not a killer. Why did you search my rooms? Really?"

He sighed, fitting the key to his door-lock.

"For various reasons," he said. "I wanted to find out more about you. Don't you think it's high time you behaved sensibly and stopped acting so mysterious? You—"

He paused, suddenly, for the girl had gone several shades whiter, the color draining from her cheeks. Her eyes clouded, went murky and dazed. A shudder racked her slim body; then she laughed shakily and put her hand to her forehead.

"This is a fine time to be afraid," she whispered.

She conquered her reaction with a stiffening of her shoulders, and Storm swung the door open, gently guiding her into his rooms.

"I've been an ungrateful cur," he said. "You saved my life, after all, and while it may not mean anything to you, it does count up to some pile of beans in my estimation. Maybe in yours, too. You risked your life for mine."

"Don't flatter yourself," she said flatly.

"The least I can do," he went on, "is get you something to eat and drink."

The girl followed him into the kitchen. His head throbbed with a giant, hammering pulse when he stooped to get a bottle and glasses from the shining porcelain icebox. When he straightened, he noted the girl watching him with fearful wonder.

"Anything wrong?"

She laughed, with a tremor in her voice.

"I don't think you know it, but somebody split your head open."

His fingers wandered to the cut on his scalp, and he winced as his clumsiness sent aching flames of pain through his head.

"I hadn't noticed," he grunted.

"It looks quite nasty," she said briskly. "If you've got a medicine closet handy, I'll fix it up for you."

"Nasty men did it," he mocked.

When she vanished to get the iodine, he went into the Greek's room. It was empty, for the Greek had followed out his orders and gone to the cottage beyond Devil's Mount. Storm wished now that he had the Greek's ponderous, stable presence to steady him.

The Greek had prided himself on his collection of guns, and it occurred to Storm that he had lost two of his best automatics in the Shady Grove. He opened a closet door and examined a rack of two automatic rifles, three revolvers and an equal number of automatic pistols, including a long-barreled Luger with a bulbous silencer fitted over the nose. He selected a flat .38-40 and was sliding it into his pocket when the girl came swinging back into the room, carrying white gauze bandages and iodine and a basin of hot water.

She paused abruptly as she saw the array of deadly weapons.

"Quite an arsenal," she murmured.

She put the medicinal articles down with lowered eyes. "You don't need a gun in your pocket because I'm here," she said.

"Maybe it's—"

He checked himself, and waved an abruptly disgusted hand at the bandages. "I don't need all this. It's silly. I'll just wash it with peroxide."

"Maybe it's what?" she persisted, her eyes boring into his.

It was his turn to look away. "I'll mix some drinks."

"You just don't trust me, is that it?" she demanded.

Her voice had the vibrancy of a taut wire and the lash of a whip. "Listen, Lee—"

She used his first name. Lee. Nobody called him Lee—he was Leo. Leave it to a girl to make it sound better, he thought grimly.

"As a matter of fact," he said, "you could do well by explaining your part in Nakesian's murder."

Her eyes became pools of hurt.

"Sit down," she said, "and I'll wash this cut." She splashed in the basin of hot water, and added irrelevantly, "I ought to hate you for thinking what you do of me."

"Well, do you?"

Her voice was tired. "I just said I ought to."

The atmosphere was charged with misunderstanding. Storm said bruskly:

"You'd better get out of here. Don't bother with the cut. It's nothing I can't fix myself."

She said, "You're afraid of me."

"No, I—I—"

Stammering like a love-sick fool. He damned himself. The girl looked at him helplessly, then said in a meek voice:

"All right, I'll tell you everything I can. Just let me fix this cut. It's really bad."

She went on in a small, crushed voice, "First, I'd better tell you what I *don't* know. I don't know who killed Nakesian, and I can't explain the money he had. It's all part of a plot to loot old Myron Coulter of his jewels and get the cash that Romwell Taite will give him."

"How did you find out about this vague plot?" he asked.

Her eyes were distressed. "Please, I don't think I should tell you. Not—not yet."

She dabbed at the cut, squeezed water from a soaked wad of cotton, took a dry bit and patted the wound.

"I used the corridor to Nakesian's apartment. I came to you first to get rid of Toogy, you remember. I didn't want Toogy following me to Nakesian's. I knew Nakesian was in terrible danger."

"Are you permitted," he asked bitterly, "to tell me how you knew that?"

"I can't tell you that, either." She shrugged. "Listen, Lee, please. Trust me. I reached Nakesian's too late. I came in that side door and found the money and saw him—dead. I—I fainted, like a fool. When I came to, I heard shots in the corridor. I slipped away in the excitement, went to the front window, and saw you run into the boarding house across the street. I had an idea that you would get rid of the grip you were carrying. For a moment I thought you were—"

"Stealing it?"

"Just a little black thought about you on my part. It makes us a little more even." She smiled anxiously. "We haven't trusted each other much."

He was brutally curt. "You're not giving any evidence of improvement. But you ran across the street and—"

"Toogy was waiting for me. He followed me into the boarding house while Lucky Lamonte went chasing after you. He guessed what you had done, just as I had. He used a gun on the blonde girl in there, struck her down and picked up the money. He tried to force me to go along with him, but I—I got away."

"And Toogy has the money?" Storm asked sharply.

She looked at him unhappily. "You don't believe me."

"It's hard to swallow. It's hard to make sense out of the whole business. Nakesian learns of a plot against the sale of the jewels. He doesn't want anything to go awry, because he is the one to profit by the sale, since old Coulter is donating the cash received to the Spiritualist Foundation. Nakesian steals a quarter of a million—which curiously enough is the same amount as the value of the jewels—and cops the money from Wheels Burton. Burton tries to get the money back and claims he did *not* kill Nakesian. He further claims he did not regain possession of his money. Burton thinks that Toogy must have double-crossed him. Or that you and Toogy crossed him, working together."

She said queerly, "What makes you think I'm an ally of Burton?"

"You came along and talked to Wheels as though he were an old acquaintance. You threatened him with exposure of facts, the nature of which you won't tell me. Whose side are you on, anyway?"

"My own," she said, with sharp independence. "You—oh, I can't tell you, because I don't know it all myself! I threatened Wheels with an exposure of his blackmailing racket—it has nothing to do with Nakesian's murder. It was a good whip to crack over him to set you free."

Because Storm was by nature a methodical and careful man, he choked down the impulse to accept her words without challenge.

"I can build up a good case against almost all of the persons involved," he said. "Including you. But we'll start with Taite. Isn't there a possibility that Taite is playing a game of his own, for his company's money—and, possibly, the jewels? Taite could have murdered Nakesian, and if the money is not Burton's but Taite's, then—"

"No, it's Burton's," Valerie said simply.

"Okay. Then take Gregory Dolman. Like Taite, he could have killed Nakesian easily enough, by slipping out of the darkened room and returning unnoticed, He certainly handled the money Nakesian had—you saw that blue wrapper that dropped from his pocket in the car. That wrapper was identical with the ones on Nakesian's money. But no," Storm said sarcastically, "Toogy has the money."

Valerie sighed, "Then why should Dolman wish to kill Nakesian?"

"Perhaps Burton ordered him to. Burton has fifty thousand dollars' worth of IOU's signed by Dolman. And Gregory can't pay. Then again, Gregory Dolman stands to gain if his old uncle does not donate the money to the so-called spiritualists. Dolman wouldn't want to lose a quarter of a million out of his inheritance."

Valerie looked shocked, pausing as she uncorked a bottle of iodine. Her honey-colored hair gleamed as she lowered her head.

"Hold still," she said clinically.

The antiseptic burned a livid scar across Storm's scalp. He bit his lip and went on:

"Then there's you. You have no motives, beyond personal gain of the money Nakesian had. But you could have come into Nakesian's apartment, seen him with the money, killed him—"

"And then fainted. Very likely," she scoffed. Her eyes were hurt.

"Your nerve may have given out at the last moment. And then Toogy beat you to it by getting to the house and getting the money when I cached it," Storm concluded. He sat up suddenly. "And you can't possibly explain by your story how you got some of Nakesian's blood on your fingernail!"

She paled, and looked at her hands with a little shudder.

"On my fingernail? I—I didn't know. It must have gotten there when I stooped by Nakesian's body to examine him."

"So you can examine a corpse, like one of Tilliman's men, and then faint?"

She waved her hand in a little gesture, then said abruptly: "Who took the blood off my finger?"

"I did. I don't know why."

He was the one who raised the wall of animosity now, until it became akin to active dislike in the girl's eyes. She walked away, clasping her hands.

"So that," said Storm, "is what I insist on having explained."

She came back and stood before him.

"Thank you for concealing my identity from the police. But I can't explain or tell you more. If I told you the truth, you would jump to even worse conclusions about me."

"Let me be the judge of what I'll think about you."

"No. If you think me guilty now, it proves you're a very poor judge. After all," she said, "I hardly know you."

Her words were quick, jammed between her small white teeth. She sank into a chair, and Storm muttered:

"We're getting nowhere fast."

She shrugged, then said passionately, "Why torture ourselves? Listen, Lee, please. You can't deny that I saved your life—that's not very sporting of me, io remind you—but you thanked me for it."

"I can't deny it, but I must feel pretty small about it. I always deluded myself into believing I was old enough to take care of myself."

She persisted anxiously, "You owe me something, then, don't you?"

Now it was coming, Storm thought. He waited grimly, and the girl went on with a quick rush of words.

"Then give me your trust. I can't say any more beyond what I've told you. You must believe in me. Romwell Taite is going to the Roost tomorrow evening, and he'll have the money to buy Coulter's jewels. He's already gotten Tilliman's permission to leave town and withdraw the money from a Boston bank; Tilliman didn't deny him, because he's up against a blank wall, just hoping for further developments. He knows that nothing new will break if he pins Coulter and Taite in Kennicut."

"You interest me strangely," Storm murmured mockingly.

"Taite won't accept a bodyguard. He's a pig-headed fool; he claims he can take care of himself."

"Well?"

"That sale must be made without further bloodshed," she pleaded. "They won't call it off, neither Coulter nor Taite. But there need be no more killings! And there won't be if—if you guard Romwell Taite."

Storm threw back his head and laughed.

"Taite won't accept a bodyguard. You said so, yourself. Besides, I'm in this business, frankly, for money not for the sake of letting someone sieve holes in me."

She snapped, "You're a coward."

He spread his hands. "Okay, I'm a coward." But she knew he wasn't.

He dug his hands deep into his pockets. "I'll take your job on one condition—and the money doesn't count."

She sighed helplessly. "I know. You want me to explain my interest in the whole business."

"I want to know three things: how you enter the murder of Nakesian, the meaning of the money in Nakesian's apartment, and how well you know Wheels Burton and Gregory Dolman."

She asked in a small, desperate voice, "So I can't get you to trust me?"

"No," he said. "I can't trust you. Not if you won't explain."

She expelled air in a little sigh, as though the effort she had made had left her limp with exhaustion. Her body lost some of its straightness for a moment. Then she slowly stiffened, in proportion to the blaze that slanted in her eyes. It was a little spark, at first, that spread and spread until her wide eyes seemed to flame with contemptuous anger.

She bounced up from the lounge and stood motionless before him, staring at him for a quick moment. Storm almost waited for her to stamp her pretty foot, but she didn't. Instead, she said quite calmly: "I hate you."

And she walked to the door with quick, hurrying steps, her high heels shattering the silence with their rapid tattoo.

CHAPTER THIRTEEN
SKELETONS IN YOUR CLOSET

The Boston *Post-Tribune* had its offices quite a lengthy distance from secluded Kennicut Bay.

The editor of the *Tribune* was a sober, conservative man who wore nothing but pearl-gray cravats, except when he felt extraordinarily dashing and donned a blue polka-dot. Like a few others in the old city of beans and crooked streets, the editor felt that journalism should be confined to a strictly objective dissemination of news.

But there were radicals, even in Boston. People demanded a features page. And to tell the truth, Mr. Daly—such was the curiously appropriate name of the head man of the mighty *Post-Tribune*—had a streak of daring deep down in his iron-clad soul, and sometimes the feeble thing stirred for a free breath of air.

That was why, when one day Mr. Daly received the anonymous manuscript of a column entitled *Skeletons In Your Closet,* he had succumbed to a momentary spasm of abnormality, probably due to his being surfeited with events on the Charles River. He put the box, two sticks wide, in the upper left hand corner of the Inner Section, the first page of which was commonly called Features.

The crime column was a sensation overnight. For two years it appeared at irregular intervals, and always just prior to some crime. So even the gray-haired police chiefs read the column—when no one was looking, of course. On the other hand, the column occasionally learned of a planned coup of the police, in which event the criminal had a better than even chance of escaping, if he read the features page of the *Tribune*.

For the last reason, the police—including Lieutenant Tilliman in nearby Maine—would gladly have parted with half their prospective pensions to lay violent hands on the anonymous writer.

On the evening after the death of Dikran Nakesian—an event the *Tribune* had printed as a half-stick on the second page—a familiar blue envelope was tossed irreverently in the wire basket marked *IN* on Mr. Daly's desk.

Mr. Daly wore his polka-dot tie and felt the little devil of Smash-Convention scampering around inside the hard shell of his conservative soul.

He looked carefully around his cubby to make sure he was alone.

Then he said, "Gosh!"

And the latest *Closet* was on its way to see the light of day in the pages of the mighty *Tribune*.

It read:

The money that Myron Coulter, jewel collector, was to receive from Romwell Taite, buyer, has already received its baptism of blood.... In exclusive Kennicut Bay colony, Dikran Nakesian, one of the leading spiritualists of the Foundation—if that's an honor, but let's speak well of the dead!—joined those with whom he had so much converse while on this earth. Namely, the spirits.

He was found this morning with a knife planted deep in his back; and no amount of aid by his fellow-spiritualists can contact Nakesian's ghost to find out what happened....

What puzzles this Skeleton In The Closet is the quarter of a million dollars in cash that was found beside the dead man's body.... And equally puzzling is the disappearance of that same $250,000....

Who has it?

And is it just a coincidence that this money totals the same amount as that which is to be paid for Myron Coulter's jewels? And is it also a coincidence that Mr. Coulter, his nephew, and Romwell Taite, jewel buyer from Chicago, were present in Dikran's apartment at the time of the murder?

We don't think it was coincidence.... But let the high-geared mentalities of our police department crack that one....

Mr. Daly dashed off a juicy check and kept his bargain with the anonymous writer by sending it to a specified general delivery box and promptly forgetting the number.

The oil-sweating presses of the *Tribune* rolled and thundered all night, and in the early hours of dark morning the train carried its bale of news up the Maine coast to Kennicut Bay, where it was scattered and deposited on various doorsteps.

Wheels Burton received the paper, folded with the column face-outward by a worried Lucky Lamonte, and cursed long and violently. He shrugged out of his dressing gown, left his coffee untouched, got into a dark blue serge and prepared for a day of strenuous business....

Sheriff Corlwye was also shown the newspaper, by Lieutenant Tilliman of the state police. The sheriff merely grunted into his moustache and said that he would wait and see, that people in the cities couldn't know as much as he did—he, who had been on the spot during practically every minute of the investigation of the murder of that danged fortune-telling feller.

But Lieutenant Tilliman, whose authority extended beyond the sheriff's, thought it his business to call on Mr. Myron Coulter and Mr. Romwell Taite.

He accordingly left the sheriff and climbed into his police car, ordering the chauffeur to proceed to the Devil's Roost and not spare the horses.

The two men he sought were seated on the veranda that stuck like a pouting lip over the edge of the cliff. The air was wet with spray, dashed high by the tumult of the waves on the rocks far below. The world was shot through with the monotonous crash of the sea and the murmur of the wind soughing through the pine and spruce.

They were having breakfast. Coffee at the Roost was excellent, as Lieutenant Tilliman well knew, and he readily accepted the invitation to join the two men.

His eyes were bright as the two others hedged for a few moments, then eventually brought the topic down to the points of interest that were uppermost in all their minds.

Tilliman looked over the rim of his coffee cup and asked with peculiar surprise, "You gentlemen aren't going through with this sale, are you?"

"Of course we are, lieutenant." Myron Coulter nodded his head, which looked like a shriveled, dried-up apple. "Dikran Nakesian's death can not affect my purpose to donate the cash to the Spiritualist Fund."

"I didn't mean that—"

The little old man cut him off with a wave of his blue-veined hand.

"I fully intend to sell a part of my jewel collection to Mr. Taite. We've already gone over the selections and are decided. And as long as Mr. Taite is willing—"

"Of course I'm willing!"

Tilliman's bright eyes darted from Coulter to Taite. There was only scorn for danger in the Chicagoan's bluff red features. His white moustache was smoothed, however, by fingers that betrayed their unsteadiness to Tilliman's quick black eyes.

"But aren't you—um—nervous? Gentlemen, it's dangerous! One death in this case is one too many—"

"Fine way for a cop to talk!" Taite snorted. "Bluffed by a cowardly murderer. If you ask me, the killer is that Storm man. Besides, there is nothing to prove that Nakesian's death is really tied up with this sale. I'd argue that assumption."

Tilliman said quietly, "Nakesian was killed because he learned of a plot against you two men. There can be no doubt about it. And the matter of money found beside Nakesian's body is too much of a coincidence to be lightly dismissed."

"*That* money! We have no proof there was any, except for the statement of a man who could not explain his own presence in Nakesian's apartment."

Tilliman smiled a tight little smile.

"Leo Storm's word may be taken as truth, gentlemen. I happen to have heard of him before. He's quite a wealthy man, the type of adventurer who is born squalling for excitement. He has had his nose in most of New York's criminal affairs—and has helped the metropolitan police on more than one occasion.

"Besides—" Tilliman smiled, and showed his folded newspaper across the table—"someone else besides Storm was present and saw the money. We've told no one about it—nor would the gunmen who were present be likely to contact a paper like the *Tribune* and give them such information. Yet the writer of the column knows about it—and that baby hasn't missed once in two years—damn him!"

Coulter coughed and looked at Taite. The man from Chicago considered his coffee cup for a moment, then looked up with defiance in his pale blue eyes.

"The sale is going through, regardless," Taite muttered. "I stand to make a good commission from my company, and Mr. Coulter here wants a cash stipulation. I'm going to Boston in an hour to get the money. I'll be back this evening. And tonight the sale goes through."

Tilliman looked incredulous.

"You mean you're going to ride back from Boston with a quarter of a million in cash?"

"Tcha! Nobody will bother me. An overnight grip looks innocent enough."

"Nakesian didn't think anyone would bother him for a quarter of a million, either," Tilliman pointed out sharply.

"I can't help that."

"Well, then, I suppose you have arranged for a bodyguard?"

Taite looked surprised.

"No, I can take care of myself, lieutenant."

"By the way," Tilliman mused, his eyes narrowed shrewdly, "is your money insured?"

"No, confound you, and how do you like that?" Taite exploded. "Insinuating that I would deliberately frame a robbery—"

Tilliman spread his white palms in self-defense. "Please, I'm only an officer of the law. Such action as yours is extraordinary, to say the least."

"Mr. Taite is rather an extraordinary man," Coulter put in with a placating wheeze. "But surely, Mr. Taite, you will admit the necessity of a guard."

"No," stubbornly.

Tilliman tried again.

"Isn't the man Storm retained by you, Mr. Taite? If not, I'd advise—"

"No, your Leo Storm has nothing to do with me."

"Then I'll go along with you to see that the Nakesian affair doesn't repeat itself," Tilliman said decisively.

"I don't need you," Taite snapped curtly.

Valerie Feather was busy before her dresser, trying to repair the damage done by a sleepless night, when Sammy the bellboy slid a copy of the *Post-Tribune* under her door. She turned on the little bench and looked thoughtfully for a moment at the newspaper, then got up, with a weary little smile, and picked it up to read it.

She turned first to the feature page and read the crime column. The smile on her lips lost some of its weariness, and the veil over her eyes lifted for a moment to reveal a sparkle of mischievousness. She read the column through twice, eagerly, and then turned to her dresser and used a scissors to snip it from its surrounding text.

Then she made haste to get dressed. Her bags were packed, her room was in order. She searched it carefully to be sure that she had left nothing she needed. Satisfied, she returned to the now empty dresser, rang lor Sammy to take her bags down, and stepped across the hall.

The time was only ten minutes before seven. Storm was still asleep. He did not hear the slight rustle of paper as Valerie Feather shoved the clipping under his door. She hurried downstairs, with Sammy laboring in her path with her grips and portable typewriter.

Storm slept until nine.

He took a cold shower, walked through the living room twice without seeing the paper under his door, and prepared his own breakfast in the little white kitchen, silently annoyed at the Greek for remaining in the cottage and not being on hand to prepare the meal.

Grapefruit, bacon and eggs, two cups of coffee and rolls found their ultimate destination. Satisfied, he walked to the door; and then, for the first time, the scrap of paper caught his eye.

He picked it up and read it through three times.

His expression changed from one of puzzlement to a broad grin. Folding the clipping carefully, he tucked it in a pocket and crossed the hall to Valerie Feather's door.

He knocked lightly at first, tentatively, then louder, with more insistence. He got no answer.

"Val!"

Bang.

"Valerie, listen!"

Bang.

"I'll take that job, Valerie! Wake up!"

Bang.

Sammy stuck his carrot-top over the head of the stairs and surveyed Storm with outraged dignity.

"Hey, Mr. Storm, you'll wake up the residents. Not so much noise, please, sir."

Storm's face was lined with anxiety.

"There's no answer, Sammy. Something's wrong. Get your key."

Sammy's lip curled. "Maybe you want I should have a *duplicate* made for you, sir?"

"Never mind the chit-chat," Storm snapped. "Get this door open. She doesn't answer."

"Sure there's no answer," Sammy replied. "She isn't there, Mr. Storm. She left almost two hours ago."

"Left? Where?"

"The Roost. She told me to tell you—"

Sammy's face wrinkled with perplexity. Storm said, "Well, what did she say?"

Sammy scratched his head and considered.

"It was darn funny, and it didn't make any sense to me. She said to tell you, 'Romwell Taite is coming in on the evening train with the leaves. He's your job. Take care of him.' What's the leaves part of it mean, Mr. Storm?"

Storm smiled, chuckled, and finally laughed aloud. Sammy looked at him sideways, the corners of his eyes crinkling with disgust. There were too many crazy people in the world to suit Sammy.

"Scoot, Sam, I'm leaving, too."

"You, too? Aw—yes, *sir!* I'll call for your bags whenever you're ready, Mr. Storm. I'm sorry you're going."

CHAPTER FOURTEEN
TRAIN TRAP

The train had to be an Anglers' Special. There couldn't be such luck as to find an empty or nearly empty train of a couple of cars hitched to a rattling locomotive. This train was sleek and new, but it swayed, bounced and bucked like the best of its historical predecessors. Its wheels thrummed along with a devilish rumbling; then, as the train hit a curve, the jangle increased and the momentum sent the laughing and screaming holiday-seekers into confused piles of arms, legs, and torsos.

MURDER MONEY

They seemed to enjoy it.

Behind the club-car and the two Pullmans it was comparatively peaceful. There was one drawing-room car, in which Romwell Taite occupied compartment B. Storm lounged in the corridor, walking back and forth.

He was irritated. Whatever it was that Valerie had recognized in the newspaper clipping, she had betrayed a knowledge of the way his mind worked, and no man likes to discover that someone can anticipate his thoughts. She had known that a reading of the crime column would make him change his mind and accept her plea that he guard Romwell Taite.

He was mildly irritated both by the girl and by the recognition of his own weakness. For the trip, as he perceived it, was valueless and a waste of time. Although he had seen Lieutenant Tilliman tripped up in Boston by the special train's schedule, and left behind to await the regularly listed train, Storm's examination of the Anglers' Special revealed nothing suspicious. His trip through the cars enabled him to allay the tedium of the ride by occasionally resorting to the crowded bar up forward and soothing his inwards with Scotch.

It was on his third trip back to the drawing room that he gained the first intimation that something was wrong. As he stepped into the vestibule, the rattle of the wheels on the tracks suddenly swelled to a deafening crescendo, mixed with a whistling wind that swept out of the gloom-gathered Maine forests. They were reaching their destination, Kennicut Bay, where it had been arranged with the conductor to drop Taite and him off.

Storm balanced himself on the steel plates, glancing at his watch. It was five-thirty. In fifteen minutes they would disembark and he would escort Romwell Taite up to the Devil's Roost. After that, his part of the job would be finished, except to see Valerie Feather. He had many things to say to Valerie.

Then the little man was there, suddenly catapulting into him. One swift glance and Storm, recovering his balance, clutched for the man.

It was Toogy, white-faced, except for his little brick-red ears. Toogy, who would know about the money found in Nakesian's apartment! How or when Toogy had boarded the train Storm did not know, but his hand flashed out to collar the gunman.

The little hood yelped and dived into the coach, struggling through the crowd of alcoholic anglers. Storm drove after him. The roar of the wheels on the tracks was suddenly drowned out by the chatter and noise of the holiday-seekers. A fat man crossed Storm's path, obliterating the sight of Toogy's wriggling little form. He tripped over a girl's leg, stumbled, caught his balance, and went on.

Toogy, white-faced, reached the end of the coach and disappeared into the vestibule. Storm reached the door half a minute later and passed into the next car, after briefly examining the men's cubicle. He saw Toogy halfway down to the end of the train. The little man reached the last door, tried it, rattled the locked panel, and cowered, the very picture of fear, his palms pressed flat against the steel behind him.

As Storm came up to Toogy, the little man tried to duck under his arm. Storm caught him by the slack of his collar, slammed him back against the door and held him there, breathing hard through his nose.

A tanned, burly young man detached himself from a group of giggling girls and said, "Hey, stop hitting the little fellow."

"Take care of your lady friends," Storm snapped, and shoved the man's fish-pole back at him. "This little guy's a killer."

One of the girls screamed, and Storm bit out, "Keep quiet." To Toogy, he rapped, "Come along, rat; you and I have some cheese we'll nibble at together."

Toogy tried desperately to free himself, attempting to wriggle free of his coat and leave it in Storm's hand. The attempt failed. Storm clipped his right fist up hard under the little man's chin, and Toogy promptly lost all thought of resistance. Slinging Toogy's body under his arm, as though the hood were just so many potatoes, Storm made his way back through the crowded coaches, ignoring the curious glances and comments directed his way.

At the Pullman car he paused, abruptly dumped Toogy to the floor, and ran toward the door of drawing-room B. It was open, and it shouldn't have been. Romwell Taite had no business going out of his compartment; and no one had any legitimate business going in. But doors are only opened for one of two purposes—

Ice flowed in Storm's veins before he reached the door. Toogy—the little man's appearance had been to serve as a decoy, to lure him away for a while—

He was right.

Romwell Taite was in the compartment, but Romwell Taite did not know it. The big man's head rested a foot away from the compartment door, face turned sideways on the floor. The limbs were sprawled, the right arm thrown forward as though the big man had collapsed in the act of reaching for the door. His face wore a look of stark terror, and his iron-gray hair was disheveled.

Storm breathed loudly through his nose.

"Hell."

He turned and dragged Toogy's body in out of the corridor, then went

MURDER MONEY

back to the door and rapped to a startled onlooker, "Get the conductor!"

Closing the compartment door, he dropped down beside Taite's body, turning the jewel buyer's head in his hands. He breathed easier.

Taite was not dead.

He pulled back the man's eyelids and carefully examined the sightless, staring pupils.

"Drugged," he muttered. "What—"

His attention fastened on a zipper case. It hung on a little hook between two black windows. The glass reflected the yellow electric bulb and the gauntness of his own face. Beyond the windows there was nothing to be seen.

Storm hefted the case, transferred it from one hand to the other and frowned. It was heavy.

He lifted back one flap, after an effort that bent the thin metal lock, and caught sight of green currency. But it wasn't the money Romwell Taite had withdrawn from the Boston bank. These packets had the familiar blue bands around them. And one of the topmost bundles had been torn open and several bills withdrawn!

Storm suddenly produced the scrap of blue paper he had picked up on the floor of the roadster the night before, while riding with Valerie Feather and Gregory Dolman. He compared it with those in the zipper case. His scrap of blue paper was identical with those on the packets in the brief-case.

The money didn't make sense. A thought buzzed around inside Storm's mind like a trapped beetle. That money wasn't the money Romwell Taite had obtained from the Boston bank. The person who had drugged Taite had substituted this money. Perhaps the attacker had not been aware that Storm was on the train, and had hoped the deception and substitution would not be discovered for some time. But then, what was the purpose of drugging the man to obtain one fortune in cash, if only to leave another? Or had Romwell Taite never withdrawn his cash from the bank? Had there ever been more than one of the quarter-millions floating around loose at one time?

He turned with a puzzled frown, sighed, and searched absently in his pockets for a cigarette, looking thoughtfully at Romwell Taite's unconscious body. His glance picked up the empty liquor glass that had rolled under the seat, and he pulled it into sight with the toe of his shoe. He lifted it, wrapping it in a handkerchief, and smelled it.

"Mickey Finn—Wheels Burton's favorite. What the hell!"

The conductor was coming down the aisle, talking loudly, demanding to be shown the location of the trouble. Storm went to the door of the drawing-room and crooked a finger at the fat man.

There was a little crowd of curious people collected around the doorway by now. The conductor forged through them with pompous importance, his face perturbed. His perturbation became worse when he saw the bodies of Toogy and Romwell Taite on the floor of drawing-room B.

"Well, well, what—*oh!*"

"One of them is drugged," said Storm crisply. "The other I knocked out."

"You knocked out? Why? Drugged, eh? How do you know?"

"I've had experience," Storm said bluntly, and the conductor's round face quivered.

"Well, well, I'm glad it's nothing more serious. Very glad. Robbery motive, I expect? And you caught the criminal? Very commendable, young man. Very commendable."

Storm said, "The robbery was successful. This little rat wasn't the criminal. There was an overnight bag stolen, full of rather valuable papers."

"Papers, eh? Well, well! Well."

"I want to know how this man—" indicating Romwell Taite—"was drugged." Storm indicated the handkerchief-wrapped glass he had discovered under the chair. "If it's not too much trouble."

"Trouble? No trouble. But how? You reach Kennicut in ten minutes, young man. Ten minutes. What can you do in such a short time?"

"Get me the steward, or whoever totes the liquor to patrons who ring for it."

"Oh, yes. Yes, that's a good idea."

It took three minutes to find the steward. He was frightened: a white-faced, long-legged, thin man, with a bald pate that shone under the yellow train lights.

His story was brief.

"I brought a tray with two ryes in here by accident. I apologized and started to back out when that gentleman—the big one on the floor, sir—reached out and grabbed one. He was shaky. His hands were trembling. I thought he was ill, or frightened, and I gave him the drink, of course. What else could I do, sir?"

Storm poked his spectacles up higher on his nose, put his head back and stared thoughtfully at the frightened man. "What sort of accident could it be that made you step into the drawing-room?"

"Why, a gentleman ordered these drinks. Told me to bring them to this compartment. He must have been mistaken, of course."

"What did he look like?"

The steward rolled his eyes and looked at the two men who sprawled unconscious in the crowded little compartment. He licked his lips and started to speak twice before he finally said anything coherent.

"I—I could not say what he looked like. I didn't pay much attention."

"Tall?"

"Er—yes, sir."

"Bushy hair?"

"Possibly, sir."

"Hooked nose?"

"I—I think so, sir."

"Fat?"

"Uh—yes, sir."

Storm clucked with disgust. "You'll answer yes to any question I ask you, won't you, steward?"

"Uh—no, sir."

Storm cursed softly and turned to the conductor. "We'll have to search this train from one end to the other. And hurry! I'll recognize whoever did this!"

The fat conductor protested, "But we're almost at Kennicut! The train can't be delayed. There's been no real trouble; I can't see—"

But Storm had already pushed through the door and through the crowd of curious passengers. The conductor waddled after him, muttering to himself. He locked the drawing-room door on his way out.

The two Pullmans and their human contents yielded nothing in the form of a familiar face. Storm went on until he came to the vestibule that led to the mail car. The door swung on its hinges with each buck of the rattling train.

Storm yelled to the conductor, "That the mail car?"

"There's only Tony in there. Nobody could hide in I here, mister."

The raucous, shrill wail of the locomotive whistle drowned out Storm's reply. The train lurched as the engineer applied the brakes, and steam hissed up around the vestibule in which they stood. Storm rubbed at the fogged window and looked out. The lights of Kennicut were drifting past.

The conductor was jittery. "You'll have to get off. You and your friend. If, indeed, he isn't just drunk. I wouldn't be surprised if he was just drunk, young man."

Storm looked into the mail car and turned around with a taut smile.

"Your mail clerk ever get drunk?" he asked curiously.

"Tony? No. Tony never drinks."

"Take a look at him, conductor."

"I— See here, you'll have to get off. You must— Oh, *my!*"

The young mail clerk, in vest and rolled-up sleeves, was sprawled on the floor before the letter sacks. His hair was disheveled and, even from where Storm stood, he could see that the young man had been struck down from behind.

The conductor waddled into the mail car. "Government property," he muttered. "Robbery."

But there was nothing missing, as the conductor hurriedly checked the bags of mail. The clerk was moved to a comfortable position until he should regain consciousness. The train slowed, rumbled over the Kennicut river bridge and hissed to a standstill beside the wooden station platform of Kennicut. Steam exploded in sizzling, deafening jets from the boxes.

"The mail for Kennicut—I'll have to get it off. Goodness, what a trip! Here, help me."

The conductor quickly lifted two bags marked Kennicut and dropped them into a chute. They tumbled out of the mail car onto the station platform.

Storm, starting for the door, turned a politely curious face to the stout conductor. "Does Kennicut always get that much mail? Two bags?"

"Sometimes. Not often. Getting off?"

Storm turned and ran through the Pullmans to the drawing-room. A sizzling exclamation left his lips as he forged through the reluctant crowds of curious passengers to compartment B.

Toogy was gone.

CHAPTER FIFTEEN
A GAME WITH DICE

Storm stood on the station platform and held Romwell Taite erect with one arm, carrying the brief-case in his free hand.

A flat rectangle of light suddenly fell along the warped platform boards, and the shadow of a man plodded alongside.

"Hey."

Storm turned carefully, Romwell Taite's legs wrapping around his own. The station-master of Kennicut stood peering at him: a frizzled, gray, stooping man, with ruddy cheeks that bulged with chewing tobacco.

"Your partner looks drunk— Oh, hello, Leo. And it's—"

"Mr. Taite. Joshua, did anybody else get off that train?"

"Nope. Nothin' and nobody, not that I seen. But can't say's I'm sure; I was nappin' inside."

A stream of tobacco juice spattered the coals on the roadbed. "What's-a-matter with him?" jerking a thumb at Taite.

Storm shifted his arm again, bringing his burden up higher. "Sick, or asleep, or drunk. I don't know. It must have been something he swallowed."

"That city hooch. Bath-tub gin."

"Prohibition is long over," Storm informed him. He made slow progress toward the shack, his eyes trying to pierce the gloom on either end of the curving platform. The forest pressed in on the little pool of light he stood in, dark and whispering of many secrets. His flesh crawled as he realized that he was a perfect target for anyone hiding in that fringe of mystery.

He dragged Romwell Taite's body inside the shack and dropped him into a chair with a sigh of relief. Joshua ambled in after him, his jaws working methodically.

"Old Coulter's niece been calling here for you, Leo."

"Who?"

"Valerie Feather."

Storm tried to keep from appearing too astonished.

He said, dropping the brief-case into Taite's lap, "I mean, who did you say she was?"

Joshua grinned and squirted tobacco into a brass cuspidor. "Nobody knows, except me. She's a poor relation. Niece of old Myron Coulter. Poor as a sand-sniper, she is. He tuk pity on her, the old skinflint—gave her a job workin' for him. And him with millions. Old miser!"

"So she's old Myron's niece—that's news! No wonder she wouldn't say—she knew I'd think—"

"Eh?" asked Joshua.

"Nothing." Storm was suddenly brisk. "Who took care of the mailbags?"

"Bags? There was only one."

"Two," said Storm.

"Only one due. Might be two, at that. See the Sheriff, up t'other end of the platform."

"The Indian?" Storm rapped, his query like an explosion.

"Sure, he does odd jobs. Good at mail work. Always catches bags off evenin' train, when he's not too blind drunk to see what he's doin'."

Storm waved a brusk hand at Romwell Taite and the brief-case.

"Take care of him, and that bag. Call for a taxi and wait. Don't let either Taite or that case out of your sight until the taxi comes."

"Ain't more'n one taxi in Kennicut. Ab's got it. Ab's my brother. He's eatin' supper now."

"Call him. Ship Taite up to the Roost and be sure the brief-case goes with him. That is, unless I fail to come back right away."

"You goin' somewhere?"

"I want to see that Sheriff. You call that taxi."

The breeze came in from the ocean, raw and damp, and brought with it a wet chill. Storm moved his gun from his shoulder-holster to his side pocket and stepped quickly out of the pool of light in the doorway toward the second shack at the end of the platform.

Light streamed from the windows, coming from a solitary lamp that hung from a cord in the ceiling. The room was deserted. A table, polished by long wear, had a single bag resting on it, marked: U. S. Mail. Beyond that, the room was empty. The Indian was not in sight, but someone had taken in the bags.

One bag. There had been two. The other, filled with the money stolen from Taite—that was gone.

Across the tracks, the tree-line pressed in close, edging surreptitiously toward the encroaching railroad right-of-way. Storm thought he saw a vague movement there, and suddenly dropped to his knees before he could recognize or define it. Flame winked with a gush of red and orange from the dark mass beyond the roadbed. Something whanged overhead, and the glass in the shack window vanished with a merry tinkle. A shard dropped beside his right foot, broke into a dozen fragments.

He swore in a tense whisper and ran off the platform, his gun in hand. There was nothing to be seen in the dense undergrowth ahead of him.

He picked his way across the first set of rails, and his foot dislodged a microscopic avalanche of gravel. It fled down the incline with a little rattling noise; then bright flame once more licked at him from the blackness ahead.

A bullet plucked suggestively at his sleeve.

This time Storm caught a glimpse of movement, of faint starlight on a blued barrel. He lifted his own gun, fired once, and then walked rapidly to the left, crouching low, and gained the opposite embankment.

He had missed with his shot.

He reached the fringe of undergrowth and listened, breathing through tight lips.

A twig snapped.

He ducked, squeezing the trigger of his big automatic. The report crashed with resounding echoes through the ghostly pines and white birch. Lead bit spitefully into the hole beside him. The shot almost coincided with his own reply; and this time he heard a startled exclamation and a word of command.

His enemy was only twenty feet away from him.

He heard a hoarse voice and leveled his gun. Then he heard another voice, coming from the opposite direction.

So there were two of them.

For a moment panic tore with clawing fingers at his brain. He crushed it down, stepped cautiously toward the last voice.

Its owner was gone, vanished in the shades toward the mountain. Behind him, over the route he had taken, came the sound of cautious feet and cloth brushing on the bushes.

He whirled, again caught the blue gleam of a gun barrel, and fired. His feet slipped in the soft till and shot out from under him. His bullet buried itself in the ground. So did the muzzle of his gun. There was soft mud under him, and his automatic was shoved deep in the muck by his involuntary attempt to save himself.

Now his gun was useless.

The skulker in the woods behind him was coming closer, with cautious footsteps that slid over the fallen leaves. The man was holding his fire, drawing nearer until he could be sure of the kill.

Storm got to his feet and scrambled up a slope, tearing through the brush with long legs.

Whang!

Thank God, the man could not see to shoot straight.

He clambered on, sucking in his breath, and in five more harrowing minutes came to a little clearing. A tumble-down shack loomed crazily in the dark pattern of the trees.

He heard water chuckling over rocks, and he could see the sky. Mist was coming in from the ocean, obscuring with the ghostly sweep of a vague hand what little starlight there was.

His opponent at last grew impatient.

"You stop! Let's talk!"

Talk? Was it a trap? Storm was helpless, in any event. He paused and stood under a tall pine near the cabin. He was only a faint shadow in a fantastic pattern of deeper shadows.

"Your gun no good!" called the stalker.

And Storm knew who the man was.

It was the Indian. The "Sheriff."

The starlight brightened momentarily as the Indian stepped into the clearing. Storm could see the man's food-stained vest, his ragged trousers, his fantastic Stetson hat.

A grin was on the Indian's earthy face. A gun was in his gnarled fist. It was no blank revolver now. It was a heavy .45, and smoke still trickled from the muzzle from the last shot that had been fired.

Storm rasped, "What's the idea? Why have you been shooting at me?"

"Told to."

"Who told you?"

The Indian grinned again, prodding him with the big gun. "That not your business. You come along to cabin. You sleep there. Sit there. Don't care what you do. You just stay."

"But why?"

"You make trouble, that why. March."

The Indian was carrying, incongruously enough, a new overnight grip of black pigskin. Storm eyed it, eyed the gun, and "marched."

The cabin ahead of them was their destination. The Indian prodded him in before him, closed the door, bolted it, and scratched a match. An oil lamp flickered, illuminating a filthy interior. There was a broken-down iron bedstead, a table scarred with many knife marks, and a chair; these completed the furnishings.

The Indian pulled down tattered green blinds and turned to Storm. "Maybe you want to sleep?"

Storm shook his head impatiently. "How long am I going to stay here?"

"Tonight. Maybe all day tomorrow." The Indian looked indifferent. "Maybe I have to kill you. I'm not sure. I'll see what boss says."

"Who's your boss?" Storm asked.

The Indian grinned and made no reply. He put the overnight bag under the bed and sat down on the ragged mattress. He pulled a knife from a hunting sheath and began to whittle at a peg of wood. He whistled a lugubrious tune.

Storm got up out of the chair and walked to the window. The Indian picked up his revolver again and waved it at him.

"No, sit down. Stay down. Otherwise, kill you now. No funny business."

It would be foolish to antagonize the Indian moron. Had it been another person, a normal man—if a killer could be called normal—Storm would have taken his chances in a rush to gain possession of the revolver. But with the Indian, force was useless. The Indian was a mountain of brute, animal strength and, despite his ragged appearance and shuffling gait, he could move like a streak of light.

No, there had to be some other way to get free.

Precious minutes dragged by.

Storm delved with his fingers in his pockets, finding nothing of value save a few crumpled bills. He tried his vest pockets, and discovered the dice he had been carrying for the past three days. He leaned back in his chair thoughtfully, his eyes fixed on the black overnight bag.

He asked, "You were the only one who shot at me?"

MURDER MONEY

"Me," said the Indian, unblinking.

"Who got you to pick up the mailbags?"

"Mr. Joshua."

"I mean the second bag—the one that had the overnight bag in it?"

"Huh," grinned the Indian.

Storm shrugged hopeless and resigned shoulders.

"Okay, have it your way, Sheriff. But if I have to stay here, let's lighten the tedium. Let's have a drink."

"Haven't got any liquor. No money."

It was the answer Storm sought. He laughed and pointed with his toe at the bag under the Indian's feet.

"Don't you know what's in there?"

"Sure, I know."

"What?"

"Money, lots of it."

"Well, then, why not use some of it? You can tie me up, go into town, buy some good stuff, and come back. We'll drink together."

"Nope. Won't touch. Money no good."

A little shiver curled the bones of Storm's spine. He looked down at the little pile of shavings around the Indian's feet.

"That money is all right, Sheriff. You're going to be paid for tonight's work, aren't you? You may as well take it in advance. You're important to your boss."

"You bet. That what he say."

"Then take your pay."

"Nope. I tie you up, though, and take your money, not his."

"No, that would be stealing," Storm said calmly.

Muscles twitched about his mouth as he spoke, but he dared not smile. The Indian nodded soberly, and looked puzzled.

"I'll tell you what we can do," Storm offered, taking the dice from his vest pocket. "I'll roll you to see who pays for the drinks."

"Have no money."

"Use some of that in the grip. Whoever wins buys some of Lucci's best."

The Indian wet his lips and considered. Storm held his breath. Then the Indian sheathed his knife, tossed the whittled peg into a corner and pulled the grip out from under the bed. He opened it and looked for a long time at the piles of crisp, green currency that Romwell Taite had withdrawn from the Boston bank.

"Lot of money," the Indian muttered.

"Sure. Nobody will miss a couple of bills. I've got thirty dollars on me— Let's roll."

He let the Indian win the first cast, and had difficulty convincing him that there should be another roll. Finally the Indian agreed. They rolled on the table, which the Indian had shoved against the cabin wall. The gun in the Indian's hand was always held on the alert.

Storm rolled and won. They were even.

He rolled again, and won thirty dollars. The smallest the Indian had was a hundred-dollar bill.

"I'll roll you for the century," Storm said. "My sixty against your hundred."

The Indian licked his lips and nodded. Storm cast a six and a trey. His next cast totaled eight. His third point was nine. He took the hundred dollars.

The Indian was perspiring.

"That too much money. Boss wasn't gonna give me so much. You give it back."

"That's not fair," Storm protested easily. He rattled the cubes in his hand. "I'll roll you this against another."

He got a seven on the first cast, and took a second bill from the Indian. The "Sheriff" licked his lips and rubbed his earth-colored face. His sloe eyes crinkled around the corners as the muscles of his face lifted to express worriment. He was beginning to look petulant.

"Roll again," the Indian commanded.

Storm won once again.

He was playing a desperate game. He made no effort to conceal his manipulations of the dice. It was a matter of time until it dawned on the Indian that he was being cheated. The sooner it came, the better.

The Indian muttered, "Lemme rollum."

The Indian lost. Storm had five hundred dollars.

He stepped back and said, "I quit, Sheriff. I've had enough."

The Indian, scowling, wiped perspiration from his slanting brow. "You can't quit. Boss kill me, I lose so much money. Gimmie it back. Rollum!"

Storm rolled. He wagered the whole five hundred dollars, and won. He had a thousand dollars. He had won on the first cast, with the third straight seven.

The Indian suddenly blurted, "Lemme see dice. Think you cheat me! Dice crooked!"

Storm's face sagged and went gray.

"Cheat you. Sheriff? I— No, what do you want to see the dice for? Why should I do anything like that?"

The Indian was convinced. He snarled suddenly, put the gun down on the table, and reached out a lean brown hand for the dice.

"Gimme!"

"Sure. Right on the button!"

Storm exploded into action. His hand shot out and gripped the Indian's extended wrist. He yanked savagely, and the Indian went off balance, pulled sharply away from the table and the gun. The man cursed and dug a claw-like hand at Storm's face. He took it on the cheek-bone, rolling his head, and the Indian crashed against him.

The smell of earth and sour clothing reached Storm's nostrils. He released his grip on the Indian's arm and lunged toward the gun. The Indian bellowed angrily and yanked at the knife in his sheath. Storm gave up reaching for the revolver. He caught the Indian's arm again and yanked suddenly, bracing his feet.

The Indian's middle came forward, his knees bent, his head shot back by the force of the savage pull. His chin was exposed, a perfect mark.

Storm's left came up almost from the floor in a drive that knocked the Indian off his feet and sent him flying into the corner. He crashed into the log wall, his head making a queer thumping sound. He sank slowly to his knees and pitched forward on his face, his crazy sombrero rolling in loops over the floor.

The back of the Indian's head was bloody.

"Poor fool," Storm gasped.

He turned to the table and scooped up the money. The gun was gone, hidden under the Indian's body. The Indian was dead, and Storm felt a cold distaste to touching the gun.

He shoved the loose currency into the grip and walked unsteadily to the door, sucking in great gulps of air. He unfastened the lock and turned to look at the "Sheriff."

"You didn't have to tell me who put you up to this," he muttered. "I know."

CHAPTER SIXTEEN
AND MORE MURDER

Fog came in over the ocean: deep, thick, tasting of the sea.

Storm walked with long, jolting strides down the side of the slope toward the station. His legs trembled with the urge for speed. He had been gone about an hour. Down below, the station lights came nearer, until he scrambled across the railroad embankments and up on the creaking wooden platform.

He kicked open the door of the shack and put down the bag of money.

A head came up over the round, pot-bellied stove. It was the ruddy face of Joshua, the station-master.

"Hi, Leo. Mr. Taite is— Hey, what happened to you, young fellow?" Joshua's eyes took in Storm's battered appearance.

"I slipped," Storm grunted.

His glance swept the bare shack. It was empty, except for Joshua and himself. Romwell Taite and his brief-case full of alien money was gone.

"What happened here?" he rasped.

Joshua rolled his head. "Mr. Taite, he came to, and picked up his 'folio mad as hell and went out of here. My brother Ab tuk him to the Roost in his taxicab. I tried to get Mr. Taite to wait for you, but he wouldn't even listen. He was in one big hurry."

Storm muttered something between tight lips. Then, "Any other cars around?"

Joshua shook his ruddy head.

"Nope. No other taxis in Kennicut. Don't need them. Folks that come here have their own cars." He paused, struck by an afterthought. "Miss Feather was here again, 'bout ten minutes ago. She was looking for you. She didn't stay."

A gnawing deep in the pit of Storm's stomach urged him to haste. He was losing time, talking to Joshua. There wasn't another car he could take to Devil's Mount. He would have to walk—a good four miles. It would take almost ninety minutes, climbing uphill. He had no time to waste. Something was brewing, indicated by his encounter with the Indian, that boded no good for the occupants of the house on the cliff.

He picked up his bag and swung away into the night, heading through the thickening fog to the mountain. He was thinking only of the fact that Death lurked above him, and that he was going to be too late to prevent it....

He had walked for what seemed like ages when a hail washed out of the darkness.

"Halt, you!"

Storm paused, with a sigh of relief. His legs ached, and he put the grip down and sat on it. The relaxation was heavenly.

He waited.

Presently a lanky shape materialized out of the darkness of the lawn around the Devil's Roost: a tall man with a wispy beard and deep-set eyes in a hatchet-face. He carried a shotgun under the crook of his arm, cradling it so that it could be dropped at an instant's notice into his hard, calloused palms.

"What're you doing here, hey? You crazy?"

"Just tired," Storm sighed. His eyes took in the deputy's badge on the man's suede windbreaker. "Has anybody been murdered yet, do you know?"

"What's that funny business, hey? Answer me!"

"I must see Myron Coulter and Romwell Taite. That is, if they are still alive."

"And why shouldn't they be alive? What reason should they be dead—"

"Half a million green reasons," Storm replied. He got to his feet as another shape came out of the gloom from the direction of the big, rambling house.

"What's up, Jeff?"

"I caught a prowler. A bug, Sheriff Corlwye. He talks crazy-like."

"I'm just tired, that's all," said Storm easily. "Hello, sheriff."

The lean and grizzled sheriff peered at Storm with his cheated-looking eyes. His horsy face grew longer, then relaxed.

"Oh, it's you, Storm. What do you want?"

"First, I want to rest. Then I've got to see Myron Coulter and Romwell Taite. It's important, sheriff."

Corlwye considered, then said to Jeff, "Search him. Take his guns. He carries them."

"Not this time. I haven't any guns," Storm said.

They searched him, anyway. Satisfied, the three men walked to the veranda, where the deputy left the others to return to his post on the lawn.

Sheriff Corlwye walked around Coulter's Cadillac touring car, which was parked in the driveway, and clumped up the steps.

"It's all right, lieutenant. My men are wide awake. It's only this Storm fellow."

"Only me," Storm agreed meekly.

The thin and dapper lieutenant stood in the doorway, his sharp, delicately chiseled face looking disagreeable.

"Storm, how did you manage to follow Taite?" Tilliman demanded. "I got on the regular train and missed him. He wasn't on it. I had to fly part of the way and come the rest by a state border-patrol car. I'm lucky to be alive."

"Taite took an Anglers' Special," Storm explained. "I trailed him around in Boston every minute while he was there. I took no chances. He learned about this special vacation train and took it. I just managed to hop the last car."

Lieutenant Tilliman snapped, "And what happened? Taite looked like the last rose of summer when he came in here."

"He was drugged on the train; I slipped up. Someone stole the money he had."

Tilliman looked at him with suspicion. "See here, Taite had his money with him—"

"Not the money he took from the Boston bank," Storm said wearily. He said, "Look, I'll explain later. Just let me sit down."

Lieutenant Tilliman looked puzzled. He led the way down the main hall, and then through a darkly paneled corridor into a library, furnished in equally somber colors. A log fire crackled in a large hearth; and, showing over the back of a lounge before the fire, was a head of honey-colored hair.

Valerie Feather sat up, looked around, and smiled shortly at Storm. "Hello, Mr. Storm. You didn't take on my job."

"Yes, I did. I fell down at the very end. But if Taite is here, that's okay."

She looked at him more closely. "You're all scratched up, and—"

He remembered that she was the niece of Myron Coulter. "I climbed the mountain," he said shortly.

"There is only one taxi in Kennicut, and Taite grabbed that. And this time I can dispense with your expert services as a nurse."

She sniffed and went out of the room. He heard her footsteps going up the big staircase to the second floor.

Lieutenant Tilliman walked around the lounge to the fireplace. He came to Storm and prodded the traveling bag with his toe.

"What have you got there?"

Storm was still looking down the hallway. His eyes were puzzled, uncertain. He said, "It looks like an overnight grip to me. I go on a trip prepared for anything—with an extra shirt and socks."

Fortunately, the little lieutenant did not ask what was in the grip. And the sight of Valerie Feather did not prompt him to take Tilliman into his confidence. If the girl were Myron Coulter's niece, then she had the best motive of all to kill Dikran Nakesian. Of the impoverished branch of the Coulter family-tree, she would scarcely view old Myron's donating two hundred and fifty thousand dollars to Nakesian with an easy eye.

He was suddenly aware that Lieutenant Tilliman was also staring down the hall after the girl; it occurred to Storm that Tilliman might connect the blonde hairs found on Nakesian's lounge with the honey-colored hair of Valerie Feather.

He said rapidly, "Where are Taite and Coulter?"

Tilliman took his glance from the corridor and jerked a slender thumb toward dark-paneled double doors at the opposite end of the library.

"They're in there, making their deal in privacy. Taite's looking over the gems. He took the money in with him. I've got two troopers here—" He pointed toward the shadowy wall of the library, and Storm was startled to observe two heretofore unnoticed troopers in their state uniforms. "And Corlwye's got a half dozen deputies with shotguns and rifles patroling the grounds. I imagine the deal's safe enough."

Storm said, "The deal isn't as safe as you think it is, lieutenant. I haven't time to explain, but—"

He started for the double door, but one of the two troopers stepped forward and barred his path.

Tilliman snapped, "Stay away from there, Storm!"

"But you're a fool, lieutenant. There's been a mistake, I know! Those two men in there—"

"Tell me what's wrong, Storm."

Storm looked into the lieutenant's eyes; they were cold and hard and intent. He would hate to have Valerie Feather at the mercy of those eyes.

He shrugged. "I've got something to say to Taite."

"Sit down. They'll soon be out."

Storm seemed to hesitate. "On your responsibility, Tilliman. Perhaps nothing has gone wrong, and in that case you shouldn't have to hear what I have to say to Taite."

"Sit down."

Storm picked up the bag without another word and walked over to a chair in the corner. He put the bag under his feet and began tucking it in under the chair. With every movement Storm made, he managed to push the grip deeper into the shadows, using his heels at every opportunity.

Sheriff Corlwye entered the library and asked Tilliman a question concerning the bluff and the necessity for a guard. Tilliman went out with him, jerking his head at the two troopers and then at Storm. They nodded understanding.

Storm did not have long to wait.

The low murmur of voices from beyond the double doors suddenly burst into angry, staccato speech. He distinguished old Coulter's high-pitched, nasal tones, and Romwell Taite's growling rumble.

The two troopers looked uneasily at each other.

One of the two doors popped open, then, and Storm gained a glimpse of a cozy, well-lit study. He could see French windows that showed only the black night beyond them, and a table with a shaded lamp spilling yellow light on jewels that rested on black velvet. The jewels were on one side of the table. The other end held the brief-case, open to show its contents of paper currency scattered about. The little old figure of Myron Coulter stood before one of the windows, hands elapsed behind him, his back to the library.

Romwell Taite came out of the study and glared angrily at the two troopers. He did not see Storm, who sat well back in the shadowy corner.

Taite's heavy jowls shook with rage. His face, paled by the effects of his drugged drink, had two high spots of color on his prominent cheekbones.

He snapped to the nearer of the two silent troopers, "Where's the lieutenant, man? I've been robbed!"

"Robbed?"

The two troopers glanced at each other with white dismay. One of them licked his lips and stepped forward, hand outstretched.

"How could you be—"

"Don't pose there like a fool! Where's Tilliman?"

The trooper bolted for the door, and Romwell Taite went after him.

The shot came like the sudden snapping of a taut, thrumming wire. It whanged through the walls of the house, seemingly echoing from everywhere with a thunderous bark.

Someone yelled a question in the back of the house, and heavy feet clattered on the hall floor. The remaining trooper, standing before the door, literally jumped a foot sideways at the sound. Yet the shot really was no more than a quick *pop!* that echoed away, and it was not repeated.

Storm got to his feet, ignoring the trooper's gun. He moved toward the door with long strides. The trooper looked at him with indecision, then muttered: "Come on, we'll see what goes on."

The big double doors were not locked. The room beyond was empty. There were the jewels on the table, and the cash. Storm now saw a little Corot that had been taken down from the wall to reveal the gleaming interior of a chrome-steel safe. The jewels and the money lay under the glow of the table-lamp—a half million dollars in cash and gems.

The trooper looked at the table and swallowed loudly.

"Gee!"

Storm cast only one swift glance at the assembled array of wealth. He got down and looked on the floor under the table. It was clear and empty. The whole room was empty—empty of little old Myron Coulter. He was simply not in it.

A stray gust of wind blew fog into the room. The French windows were open, the windows through which Storm had glimpsed the old man peering while Romwell Taite had gone in angry search of

Lieutenant Tilliman.

The trooper spoke up. All he said was, "The old man is gone."

"But not far," Storm suggested.

He stepped through the window. He went three paces and drew back with a quick, rasping intake of breath. The trooper crowded close behind him, bumping against his shoulder.

"Hell."

From the wall of the house to the iron grill fence that protected stray feet from the edge of the cliff was a distance of perhaps twenty feet. A flower-bed was plotted in the center of this ground. In the light that streamed from the study window, it was a gaudy riot of plants, a mad conglomeration of nature's lavish color schemes, neatly arranged in symmetrical designs.

There was only one odd note in the symphony of flowers, and that was the incongruous, darker mass of deep maroon that could not have been one of the gardener's arrangements.

It was the body of old Myron Coulter, clad in a maroon dressing-gown.

He lay on his side, almost on his back—which in itself was an added incongruity. One arm was outflung over his head, the other was at right angles to the body. A dark stain appeared close to the old man's silvery hairline and wriggled down one side of his wrinkled, seamed face. The stain welled up in a dark spot far up on the old man's scalp.

A nasturtium waved over his head.

The trooper choked. "I guess he's—"

"Dead as they make them," Storm blurted irreverently.

CHAPTER SEVENTEEN
ENTER THE "SHERIFF"

One by one, the people on Devil's Mount came to the scene, drawn by the shot like iron filings to a magnet. Footsteps thudded on the lawn. Shapes hallooed anxiously to each other.

The trooper took a step toward the body, only to be reminded by Storm's tug at his arm.

"The ground is soft—don't make any prints."

The trooper nodded and swallowed noisily. Storm moved cautiously around the flower-bed, the wind pushing and tugging at his clothing, the ocean murmuring like a giant voice, in a monotone. Shreds of fog occasionally fled through the scene like frightened wraiths.

The light that streamed from the open study window glinted on blue steel and a snubby barrel, close by the mesh iron fence that guarded against the cliff. It was the murder gun. Storm did not touch it, but swept the surrounding ground with a thoughtful glance.

Near the wall of the house, almost under the trooper's boots, was a pebble. Not an ordinary pebble. It had a thin piece of white string tied around it. It was knotted twice, and one end of the twine trailed in loose coils over the ground. Storm looked up at the wall of the ugly, rambling house and clucked his tongue.

Lieutenant Tilliman came running out of the night, his thin face sharp and anxious. His little eyes puckered as he saw the body of old Myron Coulter.

"Ah.... Hell."

"The gun is over there," said Storm, indicating the fence. "And I found this."

He pointed with the toe of his shoe to the pebble.

Sheriff Corlwye, with two deputies, came up and said, "Aaah."

He was in time to see Tilliman examining the pebble.

"Trash," the sheriff commented briefly. His lean face was sallow in the yellow light.

"That gun—" said Tilliman.

The lieutenant knelt and lined up the man's out-flung arm with the weapon.

"Suicide, maybe," Tilliman muttered.

"My guess is murder," said Storm.

"Eh? How?"

"That remains to be seen."

He turned and walked into the study, where the table-lamp shone down on the exhibition of jewels and scattered packets of money.

"Half a million dollars," he sighed.

"Half a *million!*" repeated one of the deputies, following him inside.

Sheriff Corlwye bellowed from the flower-bed, "Get back to your post, Jeff! Now is the time we've got to be on guard! Somethin' mighty funny is goin' on."

"Funny isn't the word for it," Storm murmured. He walked around the table and picked up a jeweler's loupe that had fallen on the floor.

Tilliman plucked at his sleeve.

"Why not suicide, Storm?"

"No. Why should old Coulter kill himself?"

Only the muttering voice of the ocean answered him.

Romwell Taite came through the partly open French window. His heavy-jowled face was saggy and yellow. His military moustache looked as though it were pasted on his upper lip, and worriment etched deep creases in the lines from his nose to the corners of his mouth.

He said shakily, "Oh, there you are. How did this thing happen, with all you men—"

"What did you want of me, Taite?"

That from Tilliman. Taite shrugged and looked frightened; he glanced at the window and back again with a quick shudder.

"I was robbed, but that hardly matters, now. Death is much more important, isn't it, than money? And yet—"

Taite shoved his fingers through the piles of money. His gesture was disdainful, as though his hands held contempt for the fortune he held in his grasp.

"This money," he said, "is not worth the paper it's printed on. Old Coulter examined it, although I told him it had come from the bank. Coulter said it was counterfeit!"

"Counterfeit!"

Tilliman gasped, and Sheriff Corlwye went "Hugh!" The word was like an explosion; only one man seemed totally unmoved by the announcement, almost as though he hadn't heard it or grasped its significance. That was Storm. His thin smile broadened for a fleet instant, and then he took a quiet, inconspicuous place in the background. He was not to remain there long, however.

Tilliman's eyes widened, narrowed, and he snatched up one of the thousand-dollar bills in his well manicured white hand.

After a moment's hushed silence, he sighed. "Yes, it's queer. But *why?* Damn it all, Taite, you got this money from the bank, you said."

"I—"

Taite suddenly spotted Storm, and pointed an accusing finger at the tall man who looked so unconcerned.

"He did it—Storm! You switched on me! This isn't the money I got from Boston! You drugged me on the train and switched money on me! I understand that whole business now!"

Storm shook his head; mockery danced in his deep gray eyes.

"Why can't I come back at you and say that it was you who plotted this business all the time?" His voice was harshly metallic. "Taite, you had this counterfeit money printed in the first place. Nakesian stole it from you, and you murdered Nakesian to prevent your switch-plot from leaking out. Your plan was to buy the jewels with the good money and later substitute the counterfeit quarter million, thus getting Coulter's jewels at the simple expense of finding a good engraver and having the cash printed."

With each lashing word Storm said, Taite had taken a step backward. Now, at the end, the jewel buyer's heavy face flooded with angry purple.

"You're a damned liar! That's a good one—me getting this fake money! Why, you were on the train—don't try to deny it! That—that stationmaster told me you got me off! You bribed the steward to bring drugged liquor to my compartment and, while I was unconscious, you substituted the queer money."

"And then I came up here to join in the fun, I suppose?" Storm rapped, his retort blasting Taite's sudden confidence to shreds. "No, my theory is better, Taite. You could have planned this robbery all along. You had the queer money printed and intended to substitute it for the good. And you were in Nakesian's apartments when he was murdered—just as Nakesian was about to explain the plot to Mr. Coulter! You had to shut Nakesian's mouth to save yourself, but you didn't have time to conceal the counterfeit money that Nakesian had stolen from you! But your helper, Toogy, got it back."

Taite sneered.

"Then I suppose I drugged myself on the train?"

Storm shrugged and pushed up his glasses. He said with a little smile, "Now we're even."

Tilliman whirled to Storm with a tight-lipped denial. "No, you're not," the lieutenant rapped. "You've got a lot to explain about this train business, and why you're up here. The money was substituted on Taite aboard the train, and you were present when it happened. You left Taite in the station and disappeared, leaving Taite to recover and bring the fake currency up to the Roost. Joshua called and said you had the grip that Taite owned, Storm. I've checked on that. You brought that grip into this house! You have a lot of explaining to do—"

Storm sat down and crossed his legs.

"Yes, I have the real money. But I didn't substitute this valueless pile of paper on the train. Somebody else did that neat little trick. Moreover, I owe Taite an apology, because I know he didn't plan this thing, although the murderer's counterfeit plot is essentially the same as I've described it to be."

Storm thrust his hands deep in his pockets and went on: "The counterfeit money was that which I found in a tree—you don't know anything about that little episode, lieutenant—and the same queer money was in Nakesian's apartment. Nakesian learned that someone was working a switch scheme, and he copped the counterfeit coin from whoever had made it. He was going to tell old Myron about the switch plot, and intended to show Coulter the queer money as proof of his exposure. But Nakesian was murdered, and—well, *somebody* got into the flat and escaped with the money, the same that I had cached in the house across the street. That somebody decided to go through with his—or her—plans, although not exactly as originally scheduled. Originally, the queer money was to be substituted *after* the sale of the jewels, and Taite, here, would have taken the rap. The switch would not have been discovered until it was too late to determine the exact time of the substitution. The murderer now decided to substitute before the jewel sale, and went through with his plan by drugging Taite on the train."

Sheriff Corlwye looked with frank admiration at Storm's lithe and lazy figure.

"It begins to make sense," he muttered.

But Tilliman's black eyes snapped with impatient suspicion. "The money," he said. "You don't deny, Storm, that you have the real money. Yet you can't explain how you got it!"

"But I can," Storm said easily. He seemingly went off on a tangent, speaking dreamily. "I should have known the money I found in the tree, and later at Nakesian's, was queer. It seems so simple, now. But you know, Tilliman, I never had a chance to take a really good look at it. And then again, what fool would manufacture thousand-dollar bills? They would be impossible to pass. The only purpose was that of substitution, and that didn't occur to me until a short time ago."

Tilliman persisted, "You have the real money?"

"Yes. And I didn't substitute this pile of pretty paper while on the train, either. The real money was stuffed into Taite's brief-case while I was chasing Toogy. The cash was taken to the mail car, where the postal clerk was slugged, and then dropped out on the station platform."

Sheriff Corlwye leaned over the table, his long and craggy face twisted with disbelief.

"Fine thing for the murderer to do! Rob Mr. Taite here and then toss his loot off the train. Why shouldn't he have just kept right on traveling? Why should he throw it off and stick around here, where he'll certainly be caught?"

"Certainly? Well, I hope so. But listen to the facts: I began a search of the train immediately. The man who drugged Taite is one of us, one of the people involved in this case. I'd have been sure to recognize him. He had to get off the train before I saw him, and, naturally, he'd take his money with him."

"Hugh!"

"But the Mr. Somebody planned to get off the train, in any event," Storm continued. "He shoveled the money into a mailbag and tossed it on the platform, where the Sheriff, who worked with him, grabbed it and lammed."

Corlwye's jaw dropped in astonishment. He turned red with anger and took a quick step toward Storm, doubling his fist.

"Why, you—you can't say that I had anything to do—"

"I mean the Indian. Our village character," Storm said quietly. Lambent flame danced in his slate-gray eyes. "The Indian worked for Joshua and the robber, as well. Simple-minded as he was, he knew how to carry out orders. And his orders were to grab the money that he knew was coming off the train."

Tilliman asked, "And where is the Indian now?"

"I think he's dead," Storm said soberly. "He tried to kill me when I trailed him into the woods. Then he tried to keep me prisoner. I had to hit him. The Indian was holding the real money, you see."

Tilliman said acutely, "Then that would indicate that the robber had laid plans to return to the Devil's Roost!"

"Exactly," Storm nodded. "He came back here to kill Myron Coulter. I wanted to tell you, but I wasn't sure myself, and you wouldn't listen. I didn't figure out this counterfeit scheme until just now. The murderer had to kill old Myron because the old man would be sure to recognize the money as counterfeit—as he did—and would immediately figure out the whole plot and know who was behind it."

"Very pretty," Taite growled. "But I don't believe it. The fact remains that you have the money—my money—and I want it. You can't deny possession of it."

"It's in this house," said Storm, nodding. "In the other room. I brought it."

"Good," someone said....

The voice did not come from any of the men in the room. It came from the half open French windows, and it was brought into the study with a gust of wind and the sudden increased swell of the ocean's monotonous rumble.

"Don't move. Drop all guns, or I'll kill."

It was the Indian.

He stepped lightly over the sill and stood close to the wall, his shapeless sombrero low over his muddy yellow eyes, his brown face a mask of twisted pain and set purpose. His hands were raw and bleeding, but the right, which held the revolver, was steady.

Tilliman let his positive slip to the floor. His troopers followed suit. The light in the Indian's narrowed, crazed eyes did not allow for any other course of action.

The Indian swiveled back to Storm.

"You think I'm dead. But I got hard head."

"So I see," Storm said. "What do you want, Sheriff?"

"Gimme back th' money you stole from me."

"I don't have it any longer. I gave it back to its rightful owner," Storm said calmly.

"No, you didn't. Give it back to me or I'll kill you. Right now. Not afraid, Leo."

Storm looked at the revolver in the Indian's torn hands. "How did you get up here, Sheriff? The place is surrounded and guarded—"

"Climbed up cliff, from ocean side."

Sheriff Corlwye gasped. "That's impossible. There ain't a man alive could climb that precipice."

The Indian did not smile. He simply said, "Me, Sheriff can. I climbed up. No guard on this side." To Storm he snapped gutturally, "Gimme money."

Storm looked at the troopers, at Sheriff Corlwye, and lastly at the shining-clean face of Lieutenant Tilliman. His thin lips twisted into a wry smile.

"All right, Sheriff, I'll give you the money."

Taite rasped harshly, "You can't! You can't give away my money to this madman—this moron."

"Do you want to argue with him?" Storm invited.

Taite looked at the silent, earthen figure of the Indian. "I—I—" He swallowed and rushed on. "There must be something! See here, my man, you can't just—"

"Shut up," said the Indian.

Storm spread his hands. "That's that. Come along. Sheriff; I'll give you the money back."

He moved through the knot of men toward the door, and the Indian followed him on silent feet. Pulling open the doorway, Storm started into the library. The Indian paused.

"Everybody walk ahead—" he commanded.

But he was too late. Tilliman had slipped around to the Indian's back. He scooped up his positive that he had dropped on the floor, at the Indian's order, and held it by the long barrel.

The lieutenant took no chances. He stood on tiptoe and brought the butt down in a swishing, murderous arc that ended on the crown of the Indian's head.

There was just a dull crack, and that was all. The Indian's gun bellowed once, spitting lead into the floor, fired by reflex action, and then he sagged forward to pitch flat on his face.

Storm expelled air between his lips in a sigh of relief. "Thanks, lieutenant."

He walked to the library and came back with the grip; he waved a hand at the safe.

"Better stow it in there. It will be safe, then."

Tilliman worked for a few minutes in a queer silence that settled over the men like a muffling cloak.

Tilliman finally twirled the knob and turned around, his small eyes bitter.

"So the Indian did it. The Indian shot old Coulter. He came up over the cliff and killed him there."

"No," said Storm thoughtfully. He started toward the library, then came back to the study, his hands thrust deep into his side pockets, his thumbs extending. "No, the Indian didn't shoot him. Old Coulter was shot from upstairs."

"Upstairs?" Tilliman stepped over the Indian's body and poked a stiff forefinger at Storm's chest. "How do you know old Coulter was shot from above?"

Storm's face was gray and bleak. "Take a look at the wound. The bullet entered Coulter's hairline and came out through the base of his neck. It killed him instantly, of course, but that's a most peculiar path for a bullet to take."

"He may have been bending forward, looking down at the ground."

"In that case he would have fallen flat on his face, not on his side and almost on his back."

Storm moved across the room and picked up the pebble, holding it by its length of string.

"The last I saw of old Myron, he was standing looking out of the window—probably already realizing the plot against him and the significance of the counterfeit money. He heard a tapping at the window that aroused his curiosity, and he stepped outside to see what it was. He feared no danger, knowing the deputies were keeping guard."

Corlwye flushed and rubbed his big jaw. Storm paid no attention to the sheriff's embarrassment.

"Coulter stepped out and looked up. The murderer had the pebble attached to a string, and lured the old man outside by tapping it on the window pane. The murderer was standing on the little balcony of the second floor, letting the stone hit the window. When he saw old Coulter's face looking up at him, the murderer shot the old man, dropped the pebble—probably accidentally—and tossed the gun away in an attempt to clear the cliff and let it fall into the sea. It hit the grill fence and bounced back to the ground. And Myron Coulter, looking up, fell over backward, hurled down by the impact of the bullet."

Tilliman whispered, "But who's upstairs? The only person up there than I know of is—good Lord. Valerie Feather went upstairs."

Storm's face was a weary mask. "That remains to be seen."

Corlwye said hoarsely, "Whoever it is, the murderer is on the second floor!"

Storm nodded, feeling drained suddenly of all vitality.

"Yes. Let's go."

CHAPTER EIGHTEEN
RAID

The body of men surged forward, squeezing between the big double doors and flowing in silent knots through the library. The red, dancing firelight from the hearth was not particularly kind to their savagely twisted, drawn faces. There was nothing to be said.

Storm moved on his long legs ahead of Lieutenant Tilliman, breasted the lanky, horse-faced sheriff, and reached the foot of the dark, oaken stairway that led to the floor above. He got one foot on the first step and paused, his hand on the round knob of the banister post.

The knuckles of his hand suddenly stood out white.

Tripping down the steps was the graceful figure of Valerie Feather. With her, her arm in his, was a tall, handsome man with thick hair and smiling lips. There was no mistaking the straight, ramrod bearing, the lean jaw and hard, rocky outlines of the man's face, nor the queer, pale color of his eyes, noticeable even at this distance. It was Wheels Burton.

He was smiling, showing his white, even teeth, and covering the girl's hand with his own as it rested on his arm. He was looking with fond interest into the girl's laughing eyes.

It was incredible, shot through with the vagaries of a nightmare, Storm thought. They paused and stood motionless for a brief instant at sight of the suddenly silent group of men at the foot of the steps. Then they came on.

There was puzzlement on Burton's features; but the girl's oval face retained its faint smile, rather like a Mona Lisa smiling over her newest fool-proof plan to get rid of her most recent husband. The smile told Storm nothing, yet told him everything.

Burton came to the bottom of the steps and said airily, "Well, well, well! What's all this?"

Sheriff Corlwye cleared his throat and stepped forward, brushing little Tilliman aside.

"I suppose you don't know?" he asked huskily.

Perplexity clouded Burton's pale eyes, and he puckered his mouth thoughtfully. "Know? Know what? Here, what's the trouble?"

"Murder," said Corlwye impressively, and Storm felt a strong urge to throttle the man. "Murder, and I'm arresting you two for doing it."

The girl's fingertips fluttered up and brushed her red lips. Her eyes slid sideways, met Storm's quickly, and returned to Sheriff Corlwye's weather-beaten face.

"Murder?"

Her voice was little more than a whisper that went scampering through the silent hall.

Burton laughed uneasily. "Come, now, you're frightening the girl."

Storm moved forward, adjusting his glasses.

"On the contrary," he said, and the smooth timbre of his voice was in sharp contrast to the raw tension visible on his companions' features, "I think you two know all about it. Myron Coulter has been shot and killed. The murderer is—or was, until now—upstairs. We've proved that. And you can't really claim not to have heard the shot."

The girl only said, "Uncle Myron...." in a frightened little voice.

But murder was nothing new to Wheels Burton. He shrugged his broad shoulders callously. "We heard no shot. It's too bad, but we didn't. And to say that we—"

The girl found her voice. Her chin came up and she looked straight at Storm. "Wheels and I were outside on the western veranda. It's impossible to hear anything there above the wind. We've been there for the past half hour, Mr. Storm, watching the lights of Mr. Burton's yacht down in the bay. We've been there ever since you came in."

"And how does Wheels Burton happen to be in this house in the first place?" he demanded.

"He's a guest here. Gregory—Mr. Dolman—invited him up this morning."

Burton nodded, his rocky face serious. "Yes, we've been together on the veranda. It may be awkward, our alibi-ing each other, but I really don't see—"

He shrugged his muscular shoulders and smiled. Corlwye cleared his throat again.

"I see it all now, Miss Feather. You needn't try to conceal from us that you were Myron Coulter's niece—"

"Let's get back to the library," Tilliman suggested abruptly.

Corlwye was insistent. "You were poor relations to Myron Coulter. But you stood to gain a sizeable chunk of his money if he died before making any more financial deals. You and this—this gunman, here—"

"Oh, say, now," Wheels protested easily. "I never carry a gun."

"You keep quiet. I know your kind. Slick city gangsters, that's all you are." Corlwye pushed into the library, his long, horsy face working with excitement. "Burton, you and this girl engineered these killin's together. The girl didn't want to see old Myron giving away most of the inheritance she was bound to get, and she determined to stop it. You gangsters know how to make counterfeit money, and the two of you planned this whole thing, planned to substitute the counterfeit cash, just like Mr. Storm here explained."

The girl's fingers fled to her lips again. Burton moved behind her.

Valerie said, "Counterfeit? Counter— Oh, I understand now." She parted her lips to say more, her violet eyes suddenly alight with excitement, when Wheels Burton put his hand on her shoulder.

"If you're accusing Miss Feather and me of this murder, sheriff, say so, and I'll call my lawyer. Until then, we'd better not talk, eh, Valerie?"

Storm leaned back against the wall, a lithe and lazy figure; then he sank into the corner seat. His heels doubled under the chair, hooking on the rungs. His eyes were carelessly watching Wheels Burton and the girl, and they were clouded with something that he didn't understand.

He said quietly, "It adds up, of course. Burton's men were on the scene when Nakesian was murdered. And if Burton planned to substitute the money, Taite would have been framed. Burton claimed that this queer money was his!"

"I said nothing of the sort," Burton snapped. "You can't prove I made any such ridiculous claim."

"No, but I know you did. You made it to me. The money Nakesian stole from you to show Myron Coulter had blue paper bands around it. The money that Taite brought here—not the money he got from the bank, but that which was substituted on the train—also had blue bands around it, and your hophead Toogy was on the scene when Taite was drugged. That money is inside there, on the table. The same lot of currency. Worthless. You claimed once it was yours."

"I deny it."

Tilliman coughed. "The motive is certainly established. You must admit, Miss Feather, that if Myron Coulter went through with this sale and got the cash with which to make his public donation, you would have lost a great portion of your inheritance."

"But I—I didn't kill him," she said in a small, crushed voice. "I wouldn't do such a thing."

Romwell Taite suddenly stepped forward, excited by a discovery. He pointed to Valerie's honey-colored hair.

"She must be the girl who was in Nakesian's room when he was murdered! I didn't believe Storm when he spoke about her being there, but—don't you see, lieutenant?"

Tilliman nodded wearily. "Of course. I've been thinking of that for some time."

The girl turned pale, stepped toward Storm, and then leaned back against Wheels Burton. The puzzled light in Storm's gray eyes became more intense. There was something wrong in the room—something in the girl's wide eyes, in the manner in which she kept close to Wheels Burton. There was no necessity for it, unless—unless, he concluded to himself, Wheels Burton had a gun in his pocket and was keeping it pointed at Valerie Feather....

He got out of his chair with a groan. The assembly turned to stare at him. Hands deep in his pockets, he walked to the fireplace, turned his back to it and faced the group of white-faced people.

"We're forgetting something," he said. "Several things. First, Miss Feather is not the only one who would benefit by Myron Coulter's will—" Corlwye opened his mouth to speak, but Storm waved him to silence. "Secondly, it might be a good idea to search this house thoroughly. Miss Feather and Burton may or may not be telling the truth about killing old Coulter. The murderer may still be in the house."

Wheels Burton laughed. "I told you you were smart, Storm."

Corlwye snapped his bony fingers. "Right!"

He rasped orders to his deputies, and two of them started for the steps at the end of the hall, their shotguns ready in their rough, calloused hands. The sheriff watched them go, and the company listened to their heavy-shod feet on the staircase.

Two minutes dragged by.

Then came the hail, "Nobody up here, sheriff, but somebody *was!*" And one of the deputies came running back, to be followed shortly by his fellows. "Somebody was upstairs and got down by a rope left out of a window!"

Taite sneered. "It's only a blind, by these two—"

He was interrupted by a sudden howl of throttled fear that came from the adjacent study. There followed the sudden thump of struggling bodies, a curse, and a muttered guttural.

Tilliman gasped, "The Indian! He has got a hard head—"

Storm was already halfway across the room toward the big double doors. The Indian was necessary for his case, necessary to prove the theory that had been revolving in his mind since the sheriff had made his first accusations against Valerie. The Indian was necessary to identify the man who had given him his orders to get the money off the train.

Lieutenant Tilliman was possibly thinking the same thing, thinking of the necessity of keeping the Indian safe—and harmless. In their urge for speed, both men crashed together at the door, and lost a valuable moment while they fumbled for the handle.

Storm got it open and banged it back. He saw the Indian lunging for the table, a trooper trying dazedly to get to his feet. The Indian whirled as Storm shot through the doorway, then darted toward the French windows.

Storm dove for him and missed as the Indian ducked into the open. He cursed the fact that he had no gun. Tilliman came up to him, shrilling, "Where'd he go? We need him!"

Storm thought he caught sight of the Indian's blurred figure, vague in the foggy, milky night. He started running without answering Tilliman's question.

Someone fired behind him, and the Indian zig-zagged, running close to the iron grill fence. He came to the end of the rail with Storm a dozen paces behind.

Beyond this point the fence ended, and the cliff sloped downward in a disintegrated cleft of rubble.

Storm dug his heels in sharply and skidded to a halt as he caught a glimpse of blue light to his left. The Indian ran on ahead, a fleeting gray shape in the black, sea-tasting fog. Occasionally wind would eddy over the lip of the mountain, and then the fog would be torn into clawed shreds for a brief moment.

Storm suddenly gasped and dropped forward, trying to bury his body in the rocky, gritty soil.

The blue streak of light to his left had suddenly blossomed into a stuttering, ghastly tongue of red and orange flames; an automatic rifle rattled and gibbered, and lead whistled low over Storm's flat body. The rattle-gun kept firing, in quick, staccato bursts, at the Indian.

First the "Sheriff's" sombrero was snatched off his head as though by an angrily sweeping hand. Then the man's body jerked, his legs tangled and he went down, skidding on his stomach.

The Indian screamed.

His body rolled; and kept rolling down the rubble of the cleft until it bounced over the overhanging lip of rock and dropped out of sight.

Only the Indian's continued scream marked his plummet-like fall to the jagged rocks many feet below. When the scream ended, the Indian was dead....

Fog swept over the lip of the cliff in whirling eddies, adding to the moisture that already dewed Storm's face. He swallowed, licked his lips and cautiously raised his head to look around.

Blurred shapes moved swiftly across the flat top of Devil's Mount; moved toward the house with guns in their hands. Storm felt a sensation of sudden stricture around his heart as a shotgun went off with an explosive blast. A man yelled in frantic fear and warning; then the shout was drowned out in the sudden rattle of automatic rifles.

Storm wet his lips again, running his tongue around the inside of his suddenly dry mouth. It was a raid.

Over a sudden tumult of sound he heard the thud of footsteps coming toward him: heavy, ponderous, yet moving with speed over the gritty soil. Storm drew his legs up under him, getting his toes firmly imbedded in the ground, and waited. When he heard the man's gasping breath, coming in long, shuddering puffs of agony, and when he suddenly saw a large bulk loom up directly ahead of him out of the fog, he thrust forward and upward.

He hit the man in the stomach, and the runner went down, exclaiming, "Storm, you damn fool!"

Storm gasped, "Poppo."

The Greek did full justice to the mercilessness of certain Anglo-Saxon words. He ended with, "You're pretty tough, Leo."

"Save it." Storm's words came in staccato syllables. "Hell is breaking loose. Where'd you come from?"

"The cottage—mile back along the coast. Burton has the Roost surrounded with coked-up gunmen. He's promised them a share of the loot; he's gone crazy-mad, I think, because somebody double-crossed him, and he's out for blood. How many men does the sheriff have?"

"Not enough."

Storm got to his feet and squinted at the house. Tongues of angry flame winked all around it. There came a roar, as though from a hand grenade, and in the bright blossom of red he saw that the struggle was centered about the study and the shining chrome-steel safe. Men were ducking through the French windows, rifles in hand.

"My," said the Greek. "Just look at that."

The man who loomed out of the fog coincidentally with the Greek's speech was quick, but not quite quick enough. A Tommy-gun chopped off his words, and jittery bullets spurted up the ground in a crazy pattern. Somebody yelled, and then Storm hit the Greek and dragged him down with him. Bullets poured over their heads in a hot blanket of lead.

"Guess that'll keep you two!"

The voice belonged to Lucky Lamonte. Storm could see the gunman's big body and square shoulders looming through the fog. He groped for the Greek's gun, couldn't find it, and the Tommy-gun went jittery again. Something burned across his forehead, and he thought his head was going to spin off his neck. He sank down, and the ground heaved under him. He couldn't see; blood was trickling into his eyes.

Lucky Lamonte pounded away toward the house.

The Greek asked anxiously, "You all right, Leo?"

Storm wiped the blood away. His scalp had a new furrow about two inches long in it. He helped the Greek to his feet and rasped, "Give me a gun."

The Greek shoved a long-barrelled Luger into his slippery palm. "Keep it. I got another, Leo."

"Then come on."

From the house came a hollow boom that echoed along the mountain top. The rifle and pistol fire abruptly choked away. Men groaned and cursed in the sudden silence.

Curiously enough, it began to rain, and the sudden, intense hiss of water was all that was to be heard for a moment. Then there came the sound of feet and bodies crashing through the undergrowth, heading down the mountain-side toward the bay.

Storm staggered over the lawn, weaving crazily. He spotted two wounded deputies and one gunman, lying in the mud. The gangster was dead. He had no face.

Storm whispered, "Valerie...." and went into the house through the crazily hanging French windows.

CHAPTER NINETEEN
A SOCIABLE EVENING

The study was a shambles. The windows were half off their hinges, and all the furniture in the room was tossed as though by a giant hand against one wall. A hole gaped in the other wall. There was nothing left of the Corot; the hole was behind the spot where the painting had been, where the chrome-steel safe had been located. The mohair on the chairs and settee was gray-singed by the blast that had blown open the safe and enabled the raiders to clean out the loot.

A gun barked and Storm hit the floor, yelling his name. The croaking voice of the lieutenant answered him, so hoarse that he scarcely recognized it.

"Hell, it's you, Storm. I thought you were dead."

He shook his head wearily. One of the deputies swayed into the room with a bottle. Storm plucked it from his hand and split it evenly among the straggling members of the police force.

He took a long swallow and spat it out, like a fighter recuperating between rounds; then expelled air luxuriously from his nostrils.

"By the way," he asked the exhausted men, "has anyone seen Gregory Dolman?"

"Dolman? He hasn't been around all night," said one of the deputies.

"That's what you think." Storm paused. "I see Wheels Burton is gone."

Lieutenant Tilliman gestured wearily with his right hand; his left arm hung limp and useless.

"It was Wheels Burton's gang, although we'll never prove it unless we catch up with them—and they've got too big a start. They're down the mountain by now. There must have been twenty coked-up gunmen. Automatic rifles, and everything. Even a grenade. We didn't have a chance."

Corlwye spoke from the door, his long face splotched with mud. "Well, I'm not taking the blame for this! This will cover the front pages of every newspaper in the state!"

"In the country," Storm corrected him.

Tilliman shook his head and sank hopelessly into a chair. "The money's gone, the jewels are gone. A half-million dollar raid. I'm licked. Through."

"Damned killers," muttered the sheriff in a blurred voice. "Got Bert and Jeff." Corlwye passed a dazed hand over his eyes. "Jeff, he just got married. To Julie Patterson."

Storm asked sharply, "Where's Burton? And the girl?"

Tilliman laughed in a high-pitched voice that bordered on hysteria. "They're gone! Burton grabbed the girl. He had a gun on her all the time he was talking to us, and she didn't dare make a break! As soon as the Indian went over the cliff, he showed us the gun and backed out, pulling the girl with him."

Poppo, the Greek, shoved his bulk through the French windows. "I know where they went," he whispered hoarsely. "The *Joy Boat*. Wheels Burton's yacht. It was anchored down in the bay. I've been watching the lights. It's moving north."

Tilliman got to his feet. "Let's go."

"We haven't a ship that could catch them," Corlwye said.

Storm put aside the bottle and rapped, "They won't be going far. They'll land soon, before we get a chance to send out an alarm on the teletype and block off the coast from them."

"They could sail clear to Canada in that boat," Corlwye objected.

"Then we'll follow them there. Wheels won't go far. He has to have this thing planned."

Light suddenly bubbled up in Storm's brain. He wasn't thinking of the murderer, but suddenly he knew the answer to many questions; he knew why Valerie had been kidnapped and taken along on the *Joy*

Boat with Wheels Burton. And he knew suddenly why Gregory Dolman had not been seen that evening.

He spun on his heel and took the Greek's arm. "Get a car," he said. "Any car."

The motor whined and growled, racing through the alternate rain and fog that swept around it like gray cotton wadding. It was Valerie Feather's car, the little blue roadster that had seen many better days; but since it was the only other auto at Devil's Roost besides the big tan Cadillac of Myron Coulter, Storm and the Greek had accepted it.

Behind them, visible only occasionally because of the innumerable rises and drops in the road, they could glimpse the lights of the touring car, crammed with the sheriff's deputies, Tilliman and his two troopers. There had been no time to call for reinforcements, nor was there any means of doing so, the telephone lines having been brought down by the one bomb that had been thrown.

Storm was driving. He could see little beyond the eagle on the car's radiator, and he was depending more on instinct than on sight. Occasionally, through the patches of rain, the visibility lifted and he could glimpse the sea, sometimes far below them as they skirted a cliff, sometimes off to their right along some flat, rock-strewn tidal beach.

They had long since passed the cottage where Storm had planned to spend a few idle weeks.

"This last cove—" Storm said suddenly, wiping his palm over the fogged windshield. "If Wheels doesn't put in there, we're licked. The road is impassable farther on."

"If it is a road," the Greek commented, peering forward. "I can't see anything."

Storm twisted the wheel again and they rounded a curve. There was nothing but deep, billowing fog to their right.

The Greek sucked in air nervously. "There *wasn't* anything there."

"No," Storm agreed. He went on abruptly, "Wheels is the kind of man who can hole up for a year, until the stink blows over. He'll land his gunmen and send them scattering. This fog must cover the whole Maine coast, and they have a good chance of getting away in it. With a half a million in cash and jewels, Wheels figures the game is worth it. Unless we stop him now, he's got an excellent chance of escaping with the money and the jewels, not to mention causing a number of unadulterated deaths."

At the top of the next rise, Storm cut the motor and switched off the lights. The Greek clutched at the door handle as the car bounced down the slope in almost utter darkness. Trees floated past them and sometimes before them, always avoided somehow. They coasted across a heavily wooded spit of land, and then water glittered ahead. A cove. Storm applied the brakes and the roadster ground to a halt on the gravel road.

There was nothing but silence, that was only accented by the muttering rumble of the surf, choked and swathed in the white, wet fog.

But riding at anchor offshore was the yacht, sheltered from sight from the ocean by the wooded tongues of land that licked into the sea. From the shore road, it would have been invisible to anyone who was not particularly looking for it.

"You were right, Leo," the Greek sighed. "But now we'll have to wait for Corlwye."

Storm shook his head.

"No. I'm swimming out there. I've got to get the girl. Wheels would hold her for hostage and keep the sheriff under control by threatening to kill her. And he would kill her, too. I've got to get her off, first."

"But those gunmen, Leo. They—"

"Most of them will be off, if they're not all gone already."

"No, there's a light, see?"

Storm nodded, slid carefully from the seat of the roadster and walked down to the shore. He paused under the shadows of a spruce tree and took off his shoes, coat and tie, depositing the articles on the sandy beach. The Luger he jammed in his waistband. It would be useless, once wet, but it could serve as a threat.

As slowly as possible, to avoid a splash, he waded into the blood-freezing iciness of the water and eventually took off for the yacht, which lay about twenty-five yards offshore.

In ten grueling minutes he floated around to the stern, which was extremely low, and reached up to hang with his fingers curled over the edge of the afterdeck.

The fragrant aroma of cigarette smoke came to his nostrils; then he heard a quick, impatient sigh, and he knew that someone was lounging against the rail directly above him.

Storm began to lift himself out of the water.

It required infinite patience and infinite strength. If he were discovered as he was, his situation was helpless. He could not have raised a finger to protect himself.

The first hint the guard had that a visitor had come aboard was the feel of two wet, strong, deadly hands that encircled his neck and squeezed....

There was not a sound to disturb the fog-wrapped quiet until, in the

MURDER MONEY

faintest of whispers that drifted on the wet, salty air, Storm said, "Don't answer me, rat. Let me talk for a minute."

His whisper was fainter than the ripple of water below. "If I release you, you might howl and wake up the dead, and if I'm to visit the young lady you're keeping aboard as a guest, it might not be discreet to carry you along with me. So what shall I do with you, eh?"

The gunman clawed and wriggled spasmodically.

Then he shook his head to signify his perfect willingness to remain quiet.

Again came the whisper. "Fine. Good. But a word of advice, cherub. All good-mannered people speak softly, and for your own health, let me advise you to practice the custom. Otherwise I may unfortunately break your neck. I'd like to, you know."

One hand was released suddenly from the gunman's throat and searched swiftly through his clothing until it took possession of a heavy automatic.

"Or I might decide to let cool night into your carcass," Storm concluded. "So answer quietly: How many cabins on this boat?"

The gunman gurgled: "Four. The fluff—the girl is up forward. Burton's in the middle cabin…. Who the hell are you, anyway? Cops?"

"Hundreds of them," Storm said quietly, and regretted the dull crack the automatic made when he slapped it down on the thug's head.

Catching the limp body, he carried it silently into the deep shadow of the cabin wall, and then padded forward on his bare feet. The feel of the heavy automatic in his hand made his steps almost buoyant—until he heard heavy-shod feet coming along the deck toward him. With one bound he caught hold of the top of the cabin; with a second quick convulsion of his muscles he drew himself up on the cabin roof; and then he peered down at the big man walking toward the stern.

It was Lucky Lamonte, wearing a trench coat, his felt hat pulled low and rakishly over one eye.

The hood walked slowly to the stern, turned around with a mutter of annoyance, and returned to the bow. Storm pulled his head back over the edge of the cabin roof and fingered the automatic; he decided to postpone the pleasure of shooting Lucky until he had located the girl and the loot. Lucky would realize that his name was all wrong when Storm met and smiled at him, for it wasn't going to be a pleasant smile.

Something wedged uncomfortably in his ribs and, when he turned to examine the sharp point, he found it to be a skylight. It creaked slightly when he lifted it and laid it back carefully on the cabin roof. Below was complete blackness, like the interior of an ink well. The next moment

Storm dropped feet first into the dark hole.

A startled, shuddering gasp came out of the gloom.

Storm recovered his balance and stood on his bare right foot to rub the sting out of his naked left.

He whispered: "It's all right, Valerie. This is Leo—come to take you from this floating den of vice."

"L-Lee! I—I'm glad you found me! Who is with you?"

He strained to pierce the darkness, and finally saw the girl, a faint outline of her, on a bunk. He answered, "No one is with me except my shadow, my good humor, and my very wet feet. They all are very anxious about you—I suspect they love you. But I wasn't cut out to be the barefoot boy. Speak softly, darling."

He felt around in the darkness, then struck a match, cupping the flame. He held it over his head. The girl was tied to the bunk with three big leather straps, fastened with buckles that were out of her reach. There was a bruise on one of her cheeks. It looked like Lucky Lamonte's signature—and Storm mentally added one more count against Lucky.

The buckles were easy to undo. She could not stand alone, and he slid his arm around her to support her slender body. Her arms went around his shoulders, and she clung weakly for a moment. Her lips brushed his, and the flavor of her lipstick tasted very good to Leo Storm.

"Now we're even," she murmured.

Storm sat down on the bunk in the darkness, took the girl's hand and made her sit beside him. "Listen carefully, because I won't have time to repeat myself. There are only a few men aboard the boat. Most of Burton's hoods are ashore, paving the way for a grand lam. I think I can round up those who are left. I've got two guns. I'm going after the cash first—I think it's going to be yours, you know. If you hear any rumpus, stick close in here until I call for you. The air is likely to be filled with drops of lead instead of rain."

She was silent for a moment, her hand tight on his arm. "I'd like to have a gun, Lee," she said. "I don't want to be left—"

Storm shoved the Luger in her hand.

CHAPTER TWENTY
THE MONEY

She pecked a little kiss at him, and her hand tightened momentarily on his shoulder, as though she were reluctant to have him go.

A little corridor ran between the ship's housing, ending in a doorway at one end and a companionway at the other, leading up to the deck. Storm padded along on the cold floor, choosing the doorway. From what he had seen of the yacht, he could guess that it led to Burton's cabin. He slid along the wall when he got close to the door, then put his hand on the doorknob. He pushed it open quickly, his gun ready to talk business in a split second.

Nothing happened. The cabin was as dark as the corridor.

Something stuck out from the wall and prodded him between the shoulder blades. It was a light switch. He suddenly flicked up the button and threw himself flat with the same movement.

Wheels Burton was sitting on the bunk. A revolver dangled from his limp hand. Yellow light washed his face, spreading from the little bulb in the ceiling to limn the granite outlines of the gambler's features.

Storm took another look at Burton and planted his feet more firmly on the cabin floor. His glanced wandered from the big automatic in Burton's hand to the puddle of red on his shirt front, and then hopped up to the knife that stuck low in the gambler's throat. It stuck in there up to the hilt.

He made an involuntary sound, and Wheels opened his eyes. They had been closed before, and now Storm knew that Burton had not even heard him come in. He looked at Storm with his whitish eyes and smiled, reminding him of a sick cat. Burton did not get off the bunk. He made a gurgling sound and waved an arm in short, jerky circles. The gun in his hand wagged up.

Storm said, "Don't."

He stared with a sense of dizzy unreality at the knife hilt that stuck like a little cross in the man's throat. It was a miracle that Burton was not dead. But he would be, soon enough, in fifteen minutes at the outside.

Burton's breath bubbled. "Storm, I—I'm done for."

There was neither fear nor complaint in the gambler's voice. It was just a plain statement of fact.

Storm said, "Yes." He was very thoughtful.

"I can shoot you, Storm," said Burton suddenly. "I can kill you. And if you get me in return—that won't make any difference to me. I'm going, anyway."

Storm murmured, "That's reasonable."

Wheels muttered, "But I won't shoot you."

"Thanks," Storm said drily. "Who stuck the hardware in your throat?"

"Who do you think?" he grinned. "The master mind!"

Storm told him he was in no condition to be humorous. Wheels coughed, his breath bubbling deep in his throat. "I'm not. Listen, Storm, you think I planned this whole game. But I didn't. I've been a sucker. The rat had every detail worked out from the start. He even knew I was going to shake him down, knew what I'd ask for when I did. And he led me on like that—me, Wheels Burton. And I always kidded myself by believing I had the best brain in New York."

While Burton spoke, Storm looked around the cabin, the palm of his hand slippery against the gun. He noted the desk, the bunk, and the heavy leather curtains that covered the two portholes. There was a door, painted ivory, that he figured opened into a closet. His stomach suddenly crawled.

Burton coughed, and blood flowed over his under lip in a gush of crimson. He wiped his mouth, moving laboriously, and began to talk again.

"He came to me first just to play my wheels, Storm. He was like all the rest of the society playboys, and I figured on taking him for a lot, like he deserved. I did, too. He dropped plenty to me. But he welshed on his debt, claimed he had no money of his own, and just asked me what I was going to do about it. He was plenty slick. He edged in with his talk about Myron Coulter's jewel sale, just casually at first, then in detail. I became interested. Anything that deals in figures of half a million interests me. But he was not the one to suggest anything to me. Not him. He let me do that. He knew I would get an idea on it; he knew I'd figure he owed me plenty jack, and that I could scare him into working with me. So we figured out a plan, and all the time he acted as though he were reluctant to do it, as though I were blackmailing him into playing along with me."

Storm said, "Save your breath; I know the rest. You figured out a plan based on the fact that the jewel sale was to be made in cash. You didn't want an outright raid; you didn't want murder.

"You had some swell counterfeit money made up—you had access to forgers and engravers—and you printed a quarter of a million, the price of the jewels that were for sale. Your friend knew the combination of the safe in the Devil's Roost. After the sale, he was to open it, substitute the queer money and get away with the good cash. The substitution wouldn't have been discovered for some time, maybe not until Myron Coulter made his donation to the Spiritualist Foundation. And by that time no one would know when the substitution was made. And the rap would fall on Romwell Taite."

Burton grinned. "You got it figured exactly. But I was double-crossed."

Storm nodded his head slowly. "First Nakesian got wind of your plot, probably through Dawn Detras. I believe you know about her death, Wheels. Lucky killed her because he was jealous of her affair with Nakesian. The girl loved Nakesian, and she helped him steal the counterfeit money from you. Nakesian planned to expose you and your pal to Myron Coulter, because he wanted to see the jewel sale go through without any hitch. He stood to gain by the donation to his racket organization. He cached the money in a tree, and I butted in for a while, but he got it back.

"Nakesian was murdered by your pal. He was in Nakesian's apartments at the time. He slid through from the reception room and knifed Nakesian—just like he knifed you. But he didn't have time to hide the money; he had to go back and insure his alibi. But he was thinking. And having seen the queer money, he realized that, if he could get hold of it himself, he wouldn't need you any longer. He ran the whole works like that, like a puppet-master pulling strings. You thought you were the one who directed the works, but you were always merely following out his plans. He kept one jump ahead of you, Wheels, as far as thinking went. He wanted to hook his fingers into old Myron's cash box, and he needed your guns and your counterfeiters. Once he got the queer money, he crossed you. He had a rat named Toogy—who was supposed to work for you—cop the money after I got hold of it a second time."

Storm expelled air through his nose and wet his lips. In the momentary silence he heard careful footsteps in the hall beyond the door.

He went on, "Your double-crossing friend still had you fooled, until tonight. He drugged Romwell Taite on the train and substituted the queer money to make the sale go through its preliminary stages. He got the Indian to grab the good money and he came up to the Roost himself to kill Myron Coulter. He had the good money, Taite had the bad. And he knew Myron Coulter would recognize Taite's money at once as being counterfeit, and from there on Coulter would figure out the whole game. So he had to kill Myron Coulter—and he did. He hid upstairs, unknown to you and the girl, and shot the old man. Then he slid down a rope and—that's all. Where is he now, Wheels?"

Wheels Burton said, "He's trapped, as long as I sit tight here. He's hiding—"

Storm knew very well where Burton's attacker was hiding, but he had no chance to act. In between Burton's bubbling, gasping words, he had listened to the footsteps that came creeping down the companionway at the other end of the hall, coming slowly toward the door to which he had his back.

He was ready for it when it happened, and at the first sound he threw himself aside, before the door had opened two inches. A Tommy-gun gibbered and chattered and spewed lead across the cabin, dotting the opposite wall with big holes where the slugs tore into it.

Behind the gun was the face of Lucky Lamonte, and behind him was a little frightened man with brick-red ears—Toogy. Lucky had the machine-gun cradled in his arm, spouting flame through the doorway. He was a picture of death gone amuck. His hair was done over his low forehead, his lips twisted by the most vindictive grin Leo Storm ever hoped to see.

Lucky rasped: "I know you're in here, Storm! I found Nickels conked; and I know you're here, damn you! I'll blast your insides all over this ship."

Storm dived for the floor, ducking under the blanket of slugs, and hit Lucky just above the knees. At the same time he triggered one shot at Toogy. He wasn't quick enough to prevent Toogy from snapping off the light, but his aim nailed the little man's hand to the wall—and Toogy's violent reaction snapped the light on again.

Hitting Lucky Lamonte just below the hips, he sent the gunman caroming back, the gun jerking up into the air. It kept spewing its lead, chunking away at the ceiling, and then Storm got his hands on it.

Lucky drove a pile-driving fist into his face, and for a moment Storm could see nothing. His grip on Lucky loosened, and the gunman started to bring the rifle down on his head. And that was the last thing that Lucky Lamonte ever did.

Storm heard Valerie running down the corridor. Before she got in the line of fire, he pointed his automatic a half inch to the right of Lucky's green eye, and a half inch to the left of his blue eye, and shot him, right there, adding a little black hole to the rainbow.

Storm looked around for Wheels Burton and felt a cold shock. Burton was still sitting on the bunk, in the same place. He hadn't stirred once during the play. The knife still stuck in his throat, and he just sat there, leaning back, yet without touching the wall, appraising Storm with his whitish eyes.

Storm rasped to Toogy, "Line up over against the wall; Valerie, get out. It's not over yet."

She held the Luger he had given her and looked at him, puzzled. Storm repeated his order, but she failed to understand. She said, "But you've rounded up everybody, haven't you?"

Wheels Burton chuckled, and the sound was ghastly.

"No, Miss Feather. Not everybody. We're waiting for Gregory Dolman—"

Storm wasted no more words on the girl. He shoved her in the general direction of the corridor, but she resisted and bumped against the wall, inside the cabin.

Storm pointed his gun at the closet door. "Come on out, Gregory; we're waiting for you."

Storm had known that Gregory Dolman was in the tiny compartment ever since Wheels had started talking and wouldn't move from the bunk. From where Wheels sat he had a clear view of the bulkhead, yet had a split-second advantage on the person inside when it opened, because Dolman would have to push the door open about ten inches before he could see Wheels.

That was the sort of game the two men had been playing when he had come on the scene, a few minutes back. Good, clean fun. Wheels sitting there with the knife in his throat, hoping he wouldn't die before Gregory Dolman came out for air. It had to be air, Storm thought crazily. That closet door was a tight fit. Sooner or later the man inside had his choice of opening that door or suffocating to death inside....

Dolman came out of the closet fast, a gun blazing. He moved faster than Storm. His heavy-lidded eyes were not bleared with sleep or liquor now. He took one look at Valerie Feather and leveled the gun at her.

"Don't shoot, Storm, or I'll kill this girl."

But Storm knew that Wheels Burton was not going to stop. Burton cared for nothing now, just so long as he got Dolman before he died himself. Storm saw Burton's movement out of the corner of his eye, and he snapped one shot at Wheels. Not to kill him. The big gun in Burton's hand went spinning to the floor, and now he had a broken wrist to add to his wounds. Not that he cared.

Dolman was going to shoot the girl, in any event.

His heavy-lidded eyes were wide open, crazed with desperate fear. He leaned forward and dragged Valerie to her feet, holding one arm around her to protect his own chunky body. And Storm dared not fire.

That was when Wheels Burton put on his act. It happened in a split second. Burton did not get off his bunk. He just pulled his hand up to his throat, waved it around a little, and twisted the knife that was jammed in his neck; twisted it out of his own body and tossed it quick as light across the room in a straight, flashing line at Gregory Dolman.

The knife had no sooner left Burton's hand than Storm was across the room, slamming into the man and the girl. Valerie went sideways, out of the way, and Storm hit Gregory almost at the same time that the knife bit deep into the murderer's back.

Wheels Burton's face suddenly went gray. He had finished himself by throwing the knife at Dolman, but he had finished Dolman, as well....

That was when Sheriff Corlwye and his deputies came in.

They bunched up in the cabin door, letting their jaws hang and looking as though they suddenly wished they weren't there. Storm tried to grin, couldn't make it, and dropped his gun to the floor.

He whispered hoarsely, "Come on in, boys. But the party's over."

He walked unsteadily across the room and reached around Wheels Burton's body. He had seen Burton lean back, apparently resting, yet not touching the cabin wall; and he knew that the man was not leaning on air. He was right. It was the black grip. The jewels stolen from the house took up little room. They were scattered like so many multi-colored gleaming eyes among the green packets of currency. Crisp green banknotes, belonging to Romwell Taite. And the jewels—

Storm picked up a few of the gems and trickled them into Valerie Feather's hands. "Take them—they're yours."

Her red lips twisted in a pitiful way, and she looked down at the floor. "It's terrible," she whispered. "It's got blood all over it."

"All money has blood on it. It will wash off. It always has."

He took Valerie's arm and went on deck. He needed air, lots of it; and he needed more than that.

Valerie Feather said quietly, "I've been such a fool, Lee."

"No, you haven't. I wouldn't have believed you if you had told me the truth about yourself. I figured on Gregory Dolman a long time ago, knowing he was Coulter's nephew. His relationship gave him plenty of motive to prevent the jewel sale, and adding that to his frequent appearances at suspicious moments, I knew it was Dolman, working with Wheels Burton. If I had known that you were old Coulter's niece—and getting around the way you did—I'd have thought the same about you. I was that kind of a sap. It's I who ought to ask—"

Her fingers brushed his lips, and he was silent. She said, "I should have told you long ago that I was Myron Coulter's niece. I come from the other branch of the family—the one that hasn't any money or jewels or anything. The one that has to work for a living."

"And what a job you picked," he sighed.

Her eyes were startled, luminous through the fog that slipped silently around them.

"You know?" she asked.

"Gregory Dolman in the closet—that's a scoop for you. For once you've got a story that fits the head of your column: *Skeletons In Your Closet*. I knew you wrote it when I read the copy you slipped under the door. It mentioned the money found by Nakesian's body. The only persons who saw and knew about it were you and I and Burton's thugs. They wouldn't talk about it, and I didn't, so I knew that you were the writer of the crime column."

She shuddered. "Don't joke. I—I don't feel humorous. It's true, I write that awful thing. Through my activities I first picked up a lead on Dolman and Burton's plot, but I wasn't sure of anything then. I—I couldn't tell you. I didn't want you to laugh at me, at the idea of a woman being a police reporter. I—I couldn't have you laughing at me, Lee."

Somehow she came into his arms, with a little sigh and a little sob, like a trim craft sailing into port. She seemed to belong there.

And then a hoarse voice interrupted him, and a paw-like hand prodded Storm's shoulder. It was the Greek.

"Leo," the Greek said. "If it's not too much trouble, Leo. You owe me five bucks."

"Eh?"

"Five bucks. Dollars. I heard about the way you chiseled the Indian. Those dice you used on me were crooked. One of the deputies went to the Indian's shack and got them. I got them now."

"Let's see them," Storm offered.

He took the cubes from the Greek's fingers and examined them carefully. Somehow, he wasn't quite sure how, they slipped from his hand and dropped over the rail.

Storm listened to the two tinkling plunks as the dice hit the water below.

"You can't prove it, Poppo," he said gently.

The Greek looked crestfallen. Then he took another look at Storm and the girl, and it finally dawned on him that Leo Storm was not thinking about dice.

THE END

Edward S. Aarons Bibliography
(1916-1975)

Assignment series: Sam Durell
Assignment to Disaster (June 1955)
Assignment—Treason (April 1956)
Assignment—Suicide (November 1956)
Assignment—Stella Marni (April 1957)
Assignment—Budapest (October 1957)
Assignment—Angelina (March 1958)
Assignment—Madeleine (August 1958)
Assignment—Carlotta Cortez (January 1959)
Assignment—Helene (March 1959)
Assignment—Lili Lamaris (August 1959)
Assignment—Zoraya (March 1960)
Assignment—Mara Tirana (September 1960)
Assignment—Lowlands (January 1961)
Assignment—Burma Girl (January 1961)
Assignment—Ankara (September 1961)
Assignment—Karachi (September 1962)
Assignment—Manchurian Doll (1963)
Assignment—Sorrento Siren (January 1963)
Assignment—The Girl in the Gondola (March 1964)
Assignment—Sulu Sea (1964)
Assignment—The Cairo Dancers (1965)
Assignment—School for Spies (1966)
Assignment—Cong Hai Kill (1966)
Assignment—Palermo (1966)
Assignment—Black Viking (1967)
Assignment—Moon Girl (1968)
Assignment—Nuclear Nude (1968)
Assignment—Peking (1969)
Assignment—White Rajah (1970)
Assignment—Star Stealers (August 1970)
Assignment—Tokyo (February 1971)
Assignment—Golden Girl (September 1971)
Assignment—Bangkok (May 1972)
Assignment—Maltese Maiden (November 1972)
Assignment—Silver Scorpion (June 1973)
Assignment—Ceylon (November 1973)
Assignment—Amazon Queen (April 1974)
Assignment—Sumatra (October 1974)
Assignment—Quayle Question (May 1975)
Assignment—Black Gold (November 1975)
Assignment—Afghan Dragon (June 1976)
Assignment—Unicorn (1976)
[series continued as by Will B. Aarons, ghosted by Lawrence Hall]

Non-series:
Nightmare (1948)
Escape to Love (1952)
Come Back, My Love (1953)
The Sinners (1953)
Girl on the Run (1954)
Hell to Eternity (1960)
The Defenders (1961)
Deadly Curves (2017)

As by Edward Ronns

Death in a Lighthouse (1938; reprinted as *The Cowl of Doom*, 1946)
Murder Money (1938; reprinted as *$1,000,000 in Corpses*, 1942)
The Corpse Hangs High (1939)
No Place to Live (1947; reprinted as *Lady, the Guy is Dead*, 1950; reprinted under original title as by Aarons)
Terror in the Town (1947; reprinted as by Aarons, 1964)
Gift of Death (1948; reprinted as by Aarons, 1970)
The Art Studio Murders (1950; reprinted as by Aarons, 1964)
Catspaw Ordeal (1950; reprinted as by Aarons, 1970)
Dark Memory (1950)
Million Dollar Murder (1950; reprinted as by Aarons, 1973)
State Department Murders (1950; reprinted as by Aarons, 1965)
The Decoy (1951; reprinted as by Aarons, 1969)
I Can't Stop Running (1951; reprinted as by Aarons, 1971)
Don't Cry, Beloved (1952; reprinted as by Aarons, 1967)
Passage to Terror (1952; reprinted as by Aarons, 1963)
Dark Destiny (1953; reprinted as by Aarons, 1973)
The Net (1953; reprinted as by Aarons, 1972)
Say It With Murder (1954; reprinted as by Aarons, 1968)
They All Ran Away (1955; reprinted as by Aarons, 1970)
Point of Peril (1956; reprinted as by Aarons, 1965)
Death is My Shadow (1957; reprinted as by Aarons, 1965)
Pickup Alley (1957; movie tie-in)
Gang Rumble (1958)
The Lady Takes a Flyer (1958; movie tie-in)
The Big Bedroom (1959)
The Black Orchid (1959; movie tie-in)
But Not for Me (1959; movie tie-in)
The Glass Cage (1962)

As by Paul Ayres

Dead Heat (1950; based on radio series)

Rediscover the hard-hitting, character-driven fiction of

Lorenz Heller

The Savage Chase
(as Frederick Lorenz) $19.95
"...a sexually frank, violence packed thriller with vividly crisp dialogue."
—*GoodReads.*

**A Rage at Sea /
A Party Every Night** $19.95
"Lorenz's characters are what keep the pages turning."—Alan Cranis, *Bookgasm.*

Dead Wrong $9.99
Black Gat Books #26.
"These interesting, well-developed characters propel this rather standard crime-noir plot into something special and unusual."—*Paperback Warrior.*

**Hide-Out /
I Get What I Want** $15.95
"... his writing is electric and alive with unpredictability."—Paul Burke, *CrimeTime.*

**Crime Cop /
Body of the Crime** $15.95
"One of the better entries, outside of 87th Precinct, in the paperback police school." —Anthony Boucher, *New York Times*

Woman Hunter / Kiss of Fire $15.95
"What makes this one ding is not necessarily the plot, but the great characterizations which serve to humanize all the players."—Dave Wilde

Hot / Ruby $17.95
"[Heller] writes in a hard, fast, crisp style and he has a feel for colorful language and characters that makes the story sing." — *Mammoth Mystery*

Pulp Champagne: The Short Fiction of Lorenz Heller $15.95
"... a complete delight and showcased Heller's superior characterizations.... terrific collection by an author worth remembering."—*Paperback Warrior*

**Wild is the Woman /
Lovers Don't Sleep** $15.95
"This one is very different: wacky & bizarre with some nasty menace at the core, but with enough humor and pathos to put the story and characters over."—Bill Kelly

**Desperate Blonde /
Dungaree Sin** $15.95
"...a pure suspense yarn... Heller was really good with setting, character, and pace, and he keeps the reader flipping the pages to find out what's going to happen."—James Reasoner

Stark House Press
1315 H Street, Eureka, CA 95501
griffinskye3@sbcglobal.net /
www.StarkHousePress.com
Available from your local bookstore, or order direct via our website.